End

Book Two

Aaron Oster

For my wonderful wife.

Contents

Prologue

Tomas Sal, leader of the Tom-Tom Guild, leaned back in his chair. He stared up through the skylight of his guild's meeting hall in their conquered city of Eastforge Seventeen. The various captains within the organization were making their way in.

The sky above looked nothing like the view he'd had from his high-rise apartment in Houston back on Earth. Then again, there was nowhere on Earth where one could have gotten a view like this.

Entire galaxies spanned the star-strewn sky above, painting the world in shades of brilliant color. He found that the lanterns within the small house were hardly needed, despite it being nighttime.

Fae, his vice-commander, was the last one to enter, closing the door behind her with a gentle *click*, the black number *31* standing out on the back of her right hand as she turned to face him, clutching a rolled-up scroll of some sort.

Tomas began to speak then.

"So, care to tell me why you called us all here in the middle of the night?"

He hadn't been sleeping anyway.

"Yeah," Quentin said, rubbing his eyes. "I'd just gotten the baby down too."

"Sorry, Quent," Fae said, giving him an apologetic smile. "But I didn't think this could wait."

She strode to the head of the table and stood by her seat, placing the large scroll on the table before Tomas.

"I just got this, as well as news from Centrifuge, the floating city at the center of the continent."

"Really?" Tomas asked, leaning forward to unroll the parchment.

He hadn't seen the city personally, as it was too far out of the way and he had people to protect, but he *had* wanted to go see the marvel at some point.

"The city fell from the sky," Fae said.

Tomas looked up sharply at that, not having gotten the chance to really look at what she'd brought him.

"What do you mean by *fell*?" he asked.

"Exactly what I said," Fae replied grimly. "Apparently, something must have gone wrong because the entire city fell out of the sky. Hundreds of people were already living there, and from what I understand, there were barely any survivors."

Tomas's mouth flattened to a hard line as he pictured the mass of stone plummeting to the ground. If there was one bright spot in all of this, it was that more people hadn't been killed. He'd heard of more than one group heading that way to live in the massive city. If this had happened just a few months from now, who knew how many more would have lost their lives?

"If that city fell from the sky, are we safe here, Sheriff?" Ray asked, looking nervous.

Tomas had been a sheriff back on Earth and knew most of the people here personally, as they'd all lived in the same building, been friends, or worked together in some capacity. He hoped they would start calling him by his name soon, as he didn't feel like much of a law-enforcement agent at the moment. He felt like he was barely holding things together.

"Well, seeing as our city is on the ground, I'd say we're fine," Fae said, thankfully stepping in and quelling the panic. "That being said," she continued, looking at the parchment. "I think you should open that and take a look."

Tomas had already been itching to read it, so he was glad Fae had given him the go-ahead. Grabbing one of the edges, Tomas peeled it back, unrolling the surprisingly large sheaf of paper across the table.

He stared at it for several moments, noting the markings. His eyes swiveled to the bottom of the parchment, where text had been neatly scrawled. He followed the line, his brows coming down further the longer he read. Finally, after a few moments of silence where the others started to fidget, he looked up.

"Is this real?" he asked.

"As far as I can tell, it is," Fae said grimly. "Everything on there is spot on. I even made sure to check before calling the meeting together just in case it was a hoax."

Tomas became even more grim at that, looking around the table and noting the ranks on the backs of each of his commanders' hands. While he and Fae were above 30, none of the others were, let

7

alone their family members. They'd all followed him here because they'd believed they would be safe. Thus far, they'd managed to keep it that way, especially after finding the mechanic that allowed him to take the city for them.

If what the parchment said was true, they wouldn't be safe here for much longer.

"Well?" Quentin asked. "Don't keep us in suspense."

"It's a map of the entire planet," Fae said. "There's more than that. There are specific areas for hunting monsters, the best strategies for fighting them, and so on. There are also portal locations, leading to a second planet called Laybor…" Fae trailed off as Tomas motioned for her to stop.

"I'll give you the basic details because this will be a *lot* to process. According to the map, we're all going to have to leave in the next six months. This planet's gonna blow and kill everyone who stays. On top of that, the minimum rank for anyone crossing over is thirty or more. Any weaker than that, and the monsters on the other side will tear through us like week-old cheese."

"Cheese, Sheriff?" asked Roberta, one of his deputies from back on Earth.

"It's a metaphor, Bert," Tomas said.

"Do you have to keep calling me that, sheriff? You make me sound like a middle-aged man."

"My mother had a nanny by the name of Bert," Tomas said. "Bert's a girl's name."

"Are we really going to have to leave after just managing to settle down?" Quentin asked, looking worried. "It was dangerous enough out there before, but if we have to go to an even *more* dangerous world, how will we all make it?"

"We'll have to stop being sissies and hiding behind the walls," Tomas said, looking back to the map. "Looks like whoever's passing these out also gave us some pointers. If we follow 'em, we should be safe."

A low muttering went through the room as Tomas looked back to the map, his mind churning. He didn't like this one bit. If Fae hadn't already told him this was real, he would have burned it without a second thought, as the information in the bottom left corner sent chills running down his spine.

It was the depiction of a monster, one with gleaming teeth and glowing red eyes. The drawing was crude, but the warning about staying away from it was clear enough. If anyone came across this monster, they were to run as fast as they possibly could. It would be ready and waiting for them on Laybor.

***

Air steamed from the woman's mouth as she looked over the landscape, feeling a small chill from the breeze that tickled her cheeks and fluttered the corners of her fur cape. The breeze had smelled fresh just a few minutes ago but now brought with it the scent of iron and soiled clothes.

She wrinkled her nose as she turned away from the glowing triangular portal, looking at the corpses littering the ground around her. The bodies were all twisted and mangled, blood and innards staining the ground around them. Her followers moved about, collecting items and picking the corpses clean.

This was the fourth such group they'd accosted on the way to a portal, but she knew that they couldn't keep operating this way, as people would begin to catch on. The trick would be to attack people as they were coming through from the other side, but according to the map her sister had found, they hadn't been strong enough to leave this world quite yet.

At least, not until this last raid.

"Does that make everyone?" she asked as Genevieve approached her, scanning over the map.

"Yes," her sister said, rolling the parchment and storing it in her ring. "Everyone is now over level thirty."

The woman looked down at her own hands, which were now covered by delicate silk gloves. She didn't need to see the black *36* to know how strong she was. Killing people had its advantages.

"Good," she said, giving her sister a smile. "Then once they're done cleaning up, we head through the portal. I'm sure the rush will continue. I want to make sure we're all there waiting for them."

Genevieve nodded, turning back to the group of corpses their comrades were picking through.

"Are you sure this is okay?" she asked, looking a bit disturbed. "These are people…"

"They are *not*," the woman said, steel entering her voice. "They are phonies. Their bodies are made of nothing more than zeroes and ones. Whoever made this sick game will pay, but we will not play by their rules while we're here."

The woman, of course, didn't believe a word of it. She knew this was their new reality and what needed to be done for her and her students to thrive. So what if they had to kill a few people? They would have been eaten by monsters at some point, so they may as well get the kanta from their corpses.

Genevieve relaxed a bit, her youthful features looking less worried.

She was just a girl. When she was a bit older, she would understand that her sister was doing this for her own good.

"Does the map have any information on Laybor?" the woman asked, looking back to the portal.

"Yes," Genevieve said, removing the map once again and scanning the bottom. "It has a warning about a monster we shouldn't try and fight."

The woman looked as her sister held up the map, showing a hastily scribbled creature straight out of a nightmare. A light shiver ran down her spine at the sight, though she didn't allow her fear to show on her face.

It was a good thing their group only went after people, as she didn't want anything to do with that thing.

"Come," she addressed her students, who'd begun to gather around her. "Now that you're all strong enough, we can move on. Your teacher has found a cheat code in this game that will allow us to grow quickly in rank. We won't let this world beat us."

A low cheer echoed from the throats of her forty-odd students, though only about half of them looked enthusiastic. The rest appeared worried, like Genevieve. The woman wasn't worried though. When they'd first come to this world, only a couple of them had accepted the path she'd decided to follow. Now, that number had grown.

The longer she prevented casualties and continued growing their strength, the more they would come to trust her. In just another couple of weeks, she would have them all. The young were always so impressionable, and despite the group consisting of older teenagers between fifteen and nineteen, she'd always had a way with words.

She'd never told her students what her true abilities were, no matter how many times they'd asked. All they knew was that she was never hurt, nor had a speck of blood touch her.

The woman smirked to herself as she began striding to the portal, her group of soon-to-be brainwashed killers following her.

She had always said that the pen was mightier than the sword.

1

Sunlight streamed in through the slotted doorway of the small inn, painting the wooden floors in stripes of light and shadow. Thankfully, the strange lightning didn't reach all the way back to the bar, as its sole occupant was enjoying the dimness of the lantern light.

Nate let out a long breath, eyeing the glass sitting before him. It was the same thing he'd ordered every day after returning from his hunting, and just like every day, the glass was left untouched.

As much as he wanted to drink himself into a stupor, he knew it would be pointless and ultimately, self-harming, getting in the way of his ultimate goal to save his family and humanity as a whole.

"Are you going to drink that?" asked the bartender, a short winge with long hair, eyeing his glass.

"Have at it," Nate said, wondering how on earth this bartender was allowed to keep working here when he got blackout drunk pretty much every day.

The winge swiped the glass and downed the clear liquid in two quick swallows, letting out an unattractive belch when he was finished.

"Care for another?" the winge asked, extending the glass.

"I'm good for today, thanks," Nate said flatly.

Points were a precious enough commodity as it was, and he wasn't going to waste them all to help this winge fuel his addiction. The man shrugged, then walked away to start his late-afternoon tradition of sneaking drinks.

Nate leaned his elbows on the counter and closed his eyes, trying to blank out the sounds of the falling city. The crunching of bones as innocents died by the hundreds echoed in his ears. Though his eyes were closed, he could see the bloodstained, corpse-strewn field of bloody rubble that he'd forced himself to walk through in the aftermath.

It had been two weeks since he'd brought Centrifuge plummeting from the sky and killed Xavier Kent. The memory haunted him every waking moment.

Nate hadn't thought it would bother him this much. He had done it for the good of humanity. If things had been allowed to continue, hundreds of thousands would have died in Warine's explosion in several years.

He was already seeing the fruits of his labor. People were scared and on edge, and the talk of leaving Warine was becoming commonplace, especially with all the copies he'd made of his original map. It hadn't been nearly as detailed as the ones he'd made to trick Freya and Noam but had all the information he believed to be critical in getting people off this world.

Thanks to him, they now had less than six months to leave as the stars slowly vanished from the sky, so it was only right that he do everything in his power to assure that humanity was strong enough to leave within the needed time.

Spreading the maps had been difficult for the first couple of days, but once Freya and Noam took a bunch of them and headed in opposite directions, it had become easier. He hadn't seen either of them in nearly two weeks. They should be returning later that day, which was why he remained at the bar after giving his drink away.

He knew they were going to want a proper explanation once they arrived and the maps would no longer cut it. He still couldn't tell them the truth, that he had seen humanity's end and had come back to prevent it, so he'd invented another lie, though this one should be far more believable. He'd be able to prove it *and* keep them from asking any further questions.

To distract himself, Nate turned his hand, seeing the dark *26* standing out against his skin. He hadn't been idle in his time here, having gone out to hunt and kill monsters, pushing himself to the 26th rank just that morning. Of course, he'd need a few more before he felt comfortable going over to Laybor, but they weren't leaving Warine just yet.

Once Freya and Noam returned, they would be going together to finish spreading the word. Although it would be impossible to personally get their maps to all the corners of Warine, he was confident that they'd spread them enough that more copies would be made and passed further along.

By the end of the month, the entire planet should know. The information contained within was accurate enough that everyone should believe it. He knew that some of the less savory types were going to be getting their hands on it as well, but there was nothing he could do about it. Either everyone had access, or no one did.

Nate did a quick internal check of his available points, finding a measly total of 21,700. Unfortunately, not all monsters awarded massive point totals like the Froster Drake had. Then again, none of them were starred monsters, which was probably a good thing. The monsters he'd fought and killed had netted him around 1,200 on the high end and 550 on the lower end. After blowing a huge chunk of his points on the Whitefire Injection scroll, he didn't have much left.

21,000 wasn't *bad*, per se, but he had skills and items he wanted to upgrade and couldn't right now, due to the lack of points. Then again, Whitefire Injection had been more than worth it. It was just a shame it would cost so much to bump it up to the next tier.

Sighing, Nate pulled his Cultivation Manual, the book containing his Path of Gilded Steel, from his storage ring and examined it. The manual was already at the 2nd tier, but he'd need a whopping 150,000 to bump it to number 3 and unlock new techniques and strengthen himself.

The book was heavy in his grip, though not nearly as heavy as it had once been. The manual vanished back into his ring, and he pulled his kanta orb from within. The orb was full to his current capacity, but he knew that once he hit the 30th rank, there would start being a disparity between how much he could store in his own core versus how much was in the orb – unless he paid the 50,000 points needed to upgrade it to the next tier.

The orb vanished and two scrolls appeared. His Cycle of Regeneration scroll was currently his most powerful at the 3rd tier. His kanta would passively regenerate as he fought, though, at this point, it wouldn't regenerate nearly fast enough to constantly keep him topped up. Additionally, he could heal from any injury so long as he could cultivate. The healing wouldn't be fast – that would come at the 4th tier – but it had saved his life many times over. The cost for the next tier was 75,000 points.

Finally, there was the scroll of Whitefire Injection. He remembered its description quite well, as it had appeared in the shop.

Technique scroll Whitefire Injection tier 1 (266,000 points to 2)(Maximum of 3 tiers)

14

Whitefire Injection: Inject your muscles with white flames, resulting in explosive power and speed. Heat generated by the technique will extend out into any others used in tandem.

Warning*: Power has a price. Using this technique for more than 30 seconds in a 12-hour period will result in your body beginning to break down.*

That warning was no joke. The pain he'd been in after pushing the technique too far had been excruciating, but despite the cost, he knew he'd chosen wisely. It was currently his most powerful technique, and his Cycle of Regeneration would be able to counteract those negative effects to an extent at the 4th tier and mitigate them completely when it was maxed out.

Nate stashed the scrolls, looking around to see if Freya or Noam had shown up yet.

Still nothing.

He was beginning to feel antsy, and with the distraction of his items gone, the ugly memories were starting to return. Gritting his teeth, Nate rose and strode from the bar, exiting into the light of the setting sun. He shouldn't be feeling this way. He'd gone into the mission knowing what needed to be done.

He had executed it perfectly, kept the losses to a minimum when considering the future, and even gone as far as spreading vital information in the aftermath. His brain didn't seem to care.

Grumbling to himself, Nate walked around the inn, heading to a small, deserted area in the back, walled off and invisible from the main street of Eastcut Two. The city was just a few days from Centrifuge's wreckage, but closer to the south, where they were going to be heading once his two friends returned.

Nate strode into the back and took a few moments to calm his racing mind. He needed to focus, to clear the death and destruction from his consciousness. He was here for a reason, and he couldn't afford to allow himself to fall into a pit of despair. Nate suspected that his time away from most people was what was doing this to him. He hadn't had a conversation with anyone other than the bartender and a few muttered words with people as he passed on his maps.

He had made sure no one saw his face as he passed them out and had told Freya and Noam to do the same. The last thing he needed was to draw *more* attention to himself.

Nate's breathing calmed his racing thoughts as he took up a stance, then began to move in a familiar martial arts form. In his previous life, he'd mastered several forms of unarmed combat, and while his mind remembered it all, his younger body did not. It was why he'd been unable to fight to his true potential, but he was slowly working his way back to his previous skills.

It was still going to take a lot of time, as muscle memory didn't develop overnight, but he was already seeing some marked improvements since he'd begun training again.

Nate wasn't sure how long he worked through his forms. All he knew was his breath, the precision of his movements and how his muscles stretched and contracted with each individual set. Eventually, he moved on to the sword, summoning a blade of gilded steel and starting to work his sword forms.

He trained like he fought, summoning the blades for the instant of the strike and dismissing them immediately after. In this way, he would preserve kanta and his enemies would never know where and how the blade would come. He could summon any type of blade he wanted, so he made sure to mix it up, switching between his backsword, rapier, and broadsword. Right now, he didn't want to concentrate on anything else, as it would slow his progress.

As he trained, he allowed his Gilded Skin to flow over his body, a golden sheen of metal coating his skin. These were his first two techniques, the ones he'd gotten with his 1st tier manual. They were now stronger, thanks to the upgrade, and cost less.

His Goldshield hovered before him and he could immediately feel the strain on his core. The newer techniques were significantly more costly to use, though much more powerful. Gilded Skin cloaked him in armor, while Goldshield not only protected him but also reflected attacks back at the enemy.

The offensive attack, Steelshod, cloaked his hands and feet as he threw himself forward in a lunge. He exploded forward, as the technique acted like a piston, giving him explosive power and speed for just an instant. It leant extra strength to attacks, though nowhere *near* what the Whitefire Injection could do.

He turned into a slash, then stopped, finding the blade just inches from Freya's face.

"Nice to see you too," she said, giving him a smirk.

"Warn me next time," Nate said, dismissing his techniques and allowing himself to relax.

His heart was still racing, his body full of adrenaline as sweat coated his brow.

"Figured you'd be back here when I didn't see you inside," Freya said. "I spotted Noam entering the city, though I think he made another stop, so he might be a little late."

"That's fine," Nate said, feeling his heart lighten just a bit.

"So, are we going to keep standing here, or are we going inside?" Freya asked, raising an eyebrow. "Because I've been scootering all day and could use something good to eat."

"As long as you're paying, I don't mind," Nate said.

"And here I thought you were going to offer to buy me dinner," the woman shot back, flashing him a smile.

Nate returned it, feeling a bit more tension leave his body. He had missed her.

2

Just five minutes later, the pair of them were seated at a table. Nate had taken a moment to go change into something not drenched in sweat and Freya had gotten herself a room. They were relatively inexpensive here – only 6 points for a night with two meals included – so she was happy to get her own instead of sharing.

"So, what kinds of depravity have you gotten yourself into since I left?" Freya asked, propping her elbows on the table, interlacing her fingers and resting her chin on her hands.

She waggled her eyebrows up and down a few times suggestively.

"Glad to see you haven't changed," Nate said, feeling oddly glad to see she was acting like herself around him after what they'd done back in Centrifuge.

"Me? Change?" Freya asked with mock surprise. "Never. But you still haven't answered my original question."

"Oh, you know, the usual," Nate said, finding himself relaxing further. "Peeping into windows, following people home at night, sneaking into the girls' changing rooms."

"Ah, the classics," Freya said. "You know, I expected more from you. I'm disappointed."

Nate snorted out a laugh at that. It was the first time he'd laughed since Centrifuge, and with that, the last of the stress he'd been harboring bled away. He knew they were still going to have to talk once Noam arrived, but he could deal with that, so long as he could have this time with Freya to unwind the knot of tension that had been twisting tighter and tighter since they'd parted ways.

"Tell me, how was your trip?" Nate asked.

Freya paused for a moment as a winge approached the table, setting two plates of steaming chicken and mashed tubers before them.

"Romantic, actually," Freya said when the waiter left.

Nate quirked an eyebrow.

"I met this man named Eduardo in one of the cities I was passing through," she said. "You know, a real swarthy type with loads of muscles and long hair that always billows in the wind. He treats me well, unlike you."

"Oh?" Nate asked, deciding to go along with it.

"Yup," Freya said. "He *always* walks around without a shirt. He answers the door without one. He trains without one. He cooks without…Well, you get the point."

"What you're saying is that he can't afford a shirt," Nate replied.

"No, not at all," Freya said, taking another bite of her chicken. "He's actually loaded."

"I bet he looks terrible without that shirt on," Nate said.

"Nope. He's jacked. Plus, all that oil he rubs into his muscles really makes them stand out."

"So then he's just a slab of meat for you to ogle."

"Oh no, he's so sensitive and caring, at least around me. But he has a dark and mysterious past he doesn't want to talk about. I'm in the process of getting him to open up to me. So yeah, I've got that going on."

"You literally just described the plot of every trashy romance novel out there," Nate said.

"Admit it, you're just jealous of Eduardo. Now, just take your shirt off, confess your undying love, and we can complete the triangle."

"I hope you and Eduardo are happy," Nate said, taking a big bite of his chicken and chewing with his mouth open.

"That's disgusting," Freya said, though the wide grin on her face told him otherwise.

"She's not lying. Didn't your mother ever teach you manners?"

Nate turned, seeing Noam approaching their table.

"How could you tell I was doing something rude when you were behind me?" Nate asked.

"Lucky guess," Noam said, pulling a chair back and sitting. "Sorry for interrupting your date, by the way."

"Didn't you hear?" Nate asked. "She's with Eduardo. She just came here to rub it in my face."

"Clearly I'm missing some context," Noam said. "No, no," he said, holding a hand up as Freya opened her mouth to explain. "I'm happy not knowing."

Freya pouted and Nate snorted out another laugh. The three of them then began talking about their time apart and what they'd accomplished while they were away.

"I made it all the way to Northveil Six," Noam said. "Made sure to spread the maps as far as I could. Last I heard on my way back, copies were already being made and distributed. Though, from what I understand, some people are starting to charge for them."

Nate's lips tightened to a line at that, but he didn't comment. He'd known that there would be people who would take advantage of his generosity for their own gain. He couldn't spread the maps far enough himself in the time they had left, so this would just have to do for now.

"How about you?" he asked, turning to Freya.

"Westray Four," she said. "I know, it's not as far in as Noam went, but I made sure to cover as much in both directions as I could. Ran into more than one large group, so I think I did my job."

"Did you run into any trouble?" he asked, addressing both of them.

"A bit," Noam said, clenching his fist and raising it, showing Nate the back of his right hand.

When they'd parted ways, the man had been at the 19th rank. Now, he was at 25, just one below Nate's.

"Same," Freya said, holding her left hand up and showing the same number.

"People?" Nate asked, tensing up.

"Monsters," Noam said.

"Same," Freya replied. "I took some shortcuts through the wilder areas to save time. I did manage to gather some ores and other items, though I began to run out of space in my ring, so I had to stop."

"I only tossed the corpses into my ring," Noam said with a shrug. "Didn't bother gathering anything."

"We'll have to get your stuff sold so we can get you some more points," Nate said. "We'll be heading out in the morning and going south, so we'll want you to be well-equipped. We also want to buy you something to help regenerate kanta. I know you have a technique that allows you to recover, but kanta recovery and cycling will help you grow faster."

"We're not going anywhere before you explain yourself," Noam said stoically, crossing his arms.

Freya bit her lip, looking suddenly uncomfortable but not disagreeing.

"I will," Nate said. "But not where people can hear."

"You have a room here. You can tell us there."

Nate sighed internally. It seemed the time had come to feed them the story he'd been working on. He hoped they'd buy it and not doubt him in the future.

They finished eating in silence – the inn was starting to fill up as night fell – after which, they headed up to Nate's room. It was small, just a bed with a nightstand and chair. Nate took the end of the bed closest to the wall. Freya took the other, while Noam sat in the chair, crossing his arms and staring at him evenly.

"Talk," Noam said, his voice hard.

Nate knew the man well enough to recognize the look. If he wasn't completely satisfied with his story, he *would* leave. Memories of their time together flashed through Nate's mind, including his friend's horrible death. He could not allow that to happen again.

"I have a sort-of technique," Nate said, letting out a breath. "I told you that I played video games before the end of the world and that I went looking for a map when I came into this one. Well, I found a map, but it wasn't those pieces of parchment I showed you both."

Noam watched him evenly, arms still crossed. Freya was looking at him with rapt attention, her expression a bit harder to read. Was she angry? Upset?

Nate plowed on, knowing it was best to get this all out in the open.

"The map is up here," he said, tapping the side of his head. "You're probably wondering why I didn't just tell you that in the first place, but I'm sure the answer is obvious."

"You don't just have a map of Warine," Noam said.

"Nope," Nate replied with a strained smile. "I've got a map of everything. The entire system is all crammed into my head. Locations of powerful monsters, items, portals and so on. I can see how dangerous things are going to become in the later planets and how doomed we truly are if we don't push everyone to become stronger."

"If it's a technique, let's see the scroll," Noam said, extending a hand.

This had been the one failing in Nate's plan. At least, it would have been if he hadn't had prior knowledge of this world.

"I did say it was *sort* of a technique," Nate said. "Think of it less like that and more like an item that can be inserted directly into one's brain. They're called Augments. You can find them at any shop if you're lucky enough. They're *extremely* rare but aren't all that costly. I happened to get lucky."

"That seems convenient," Noam said, seeming unimpressed.

Nate reached into his ring and removed an item that he'd hunted down in preparation for this moment. It was small, black, and twisted, looking a bit like a monocle with jagged edges and grooves running over its frame.

"This is an Augment of Magnification," Nate said, handing it to Noam. "I found it two days ago in one of the shops. It cost me a hundred points."

Noam turned the item over in his hands, his lips pursed. Clearly, he couldn't deny what he was holding, as it was right in front of him. However, seeing as he couldn't read a description, he was still skeptical. That was fine by Nate, as they had a third person present.

"Hand it to Freya," Nate said.

Noam did so, leaning over to hand the item over.

"Touch it to the side of your head," Nate said. "And think about absorbing it into your mind."

Freya, thankfully, didn't hesitate, touching the item to the side of her head. Before their eyes, the Augment began to glow, turning a bright white before disintegrating into particles of light and flowing into the woman's head.

"Woah," Freya said, blinking a few times as the Augment settled in. "This feels weird."

"Now, can you both look out the window?" Nate requested. They did.

"There's something etched into the city gates, right above the entrance when we walked in," Nate said. "Can you see it from here?"

"You know I can't," Noam said.

"Well, then, why don't you tell us then, Freya?"

Freya peered out of the window, concentrating on the gate in the distance. Her eyes squinted for a moment, then went wide in surprise.

"It looks like some sort of crude drawing, though I'm not sure what it is. A goat maybe?"

"Would you care to go and check?" Nate asked, feeling a bit proud of himself for coming up with all of this.

It was elaborate and could go wrong in any of about a billion ways, but so far, it seemed to be working.

"I believe Freya," Noam said. "It's you who I'm having a hard time believing. You claim that you can see what we'll be up against in the future," Noam said. "That still doesn't explain why we had to knock a city out of the sky."

Nate let out a long breath then and looked up to meet his eyes.

"It's not *just* a map. There's more still. You know how video games have missions and quests to reach specific goals?"

"You're saying that the maps in your brain are giving you future knowledge?" Noam asked, sounding skeptical.

"Not exactly, no," Nate replied. "It's more of a hint. An outline, if you will. A code to crack and decipher. There is a small bit of text at the bottom of the map, with the odds of our survival stamped at the bottom. Completing certain actions either increases or decreases those odds."

"I still don't think I quite understand," Noam said. "But I'm getting there. How did crashing the city help and how did you know to do it?"

"When we entered the world, do you know what our chances of survival were?" he asked.

Noam stared at him. He was clearly dodging the question.

"They were zero," Nate continued when he failed to answer. "Humanity had a *zero-percent* chance of survival. Do you know what our chances are now that Centrifuge is gone?"

"Don't tell me it's a hundred percent," Noam said. "Because there's no way I would believe that."

"It's not," Nate said. "It's closer to twelve. I know that sounds low, but it's still a chance, and I'm going to do everything in my power to make sure those odds become better. The first thing we need to do is make sure to get everyone off this planet before our time is up."

"You still haven't answered my earlier question," Noam said, pursing his lips. "How did you know that crashing the city would raise our odds of survival? Or was that just a lucky guess on your part?"

"As I said, the map gives me hints that I have to figure out," Nate said with a shrug. "I can't explain it any better than that."

"So, what you're saying is that we should just blindly follow you from now on and do whatever you say because a map in your head is giving you hints?" Noam asked.

"When you put it that way, I sound like a total lunatic," Nate said. "But yeah, that's pretty much it in a nutshell."

Noam's lips hardened to a line and his posture became defensive. He was closing himself off and Nate could see that he was losing him. He played his trump card.

"Do you have any idea what it's like?" Nate said, lowering his voice and looking down at the floor. "Being able to see possibilities of the future and not understanding what they mean? To see the terrifying monstrosities humanity is going to have to face, and knowing we might all die if we're not strong enough?"

Freya reached out a placed a hand on his shoulder. She, at least, looked sympathetic. Noam didn't look impressed.

"I don't know if I believe you," Noam said.

"Then what would your theory be?" Nate asked, meeting the man's eyes and allowing a bit of heat to enter his voice. "How could I possibly know anything at all about this world if what I said isn't true?"

"You could be the man in the sky," Noam said. "The one who dragged us all here, hiding in plain sight."

"He couldn't be," Freya said, coming to his defense. "He was unconscious when that man appeared again."

"Do you really think that someone powerful enough to do all of this," he said, gesturing to their surroundings, "couldn't be in two places at once?"

Freya appeared uncertain at that, looking between the two of them.

"Well," Nate said, crossing his arms, his voice heated and angry. "That works out conveniently, doesn't it? Anything I say or do won't be able to convince you that I'm *not* the man in the sky, so you're free to leave whenever you'd like with a clear conscience. You can tell yourself at night that you did the right thing in leaving.

"When you're drowning your sorrows at a bar, waking up in a gutter, or wandering aimlessly around the planet, watching death and devastation all around you, don't say I didn't try. So long as you can keep convincing yourself that *I'm* the enemy, you can fall into apathy and blame *me* for it!"

Noam was on his feet in an instant, hands clenched into fists and glaring. His muscles were tensed, and his eyes bore into Nate, daring him to keep going.

"Say one more word," Noam said. "I *dare* you."

"So what? You can have an excuse to attack me? Would that make you feel better about yourself? Go ahead then, hit me!"

For a few moments, it looked like he was going to, even as Freya stood and spread her arms out, looking a bit panicked.

"Enough! You shouldn't be fighting."

Nate and Noam continued to glare at one another for several long moments, then Noam abruptly turned and stomped out of the room, slamming the door behind him.

Freya looked between the door and Nate, clearly unsure of what to do. She looked afraid. This obviously hadn't been how she'd expected their reunion to go.

Nate sat back down, letting out a long breath and closing his eyes.

"I'm sorry I lost my temper," he said, massaging his temples. "It's been a long few days and I wasn't expecting the night to go like this."

"For what it's worth," Freya said. "I don't think you're responsible for all of this. Not after everything you did to help me."

She patted him on the shoulder and turned to leave the room.

"I'm going to talk with him and see if I can bring him around. We work well together. I'd hate to see our team break up after all we've been through."

Nate didn't say anything as she left the room, but once she was gone, he let out an explosive string of curses under his breath. He'd forgotten how stubborn and annoying Noam had been at this point in his life. The man was still clearly depressed over losing his fiancé and having to kill all those people had likely brought those memories rushing back.

He had been looking for an excuse from the start and now that he'd seen Noam's reaction, Nate was glad he hadn't told the truth, as the man likely wouldn't have believed that either. At least the story with the mental map had some merit and could theoretically exist. It explained things quite well, if not perfectly.

Coming back from the future, on the other hand, was an impossibility that he wouldn't be able to wrap his mind around. For now, Nate would have to leave the man to cool off. He doubted Freya would be getting anywhere with him after that spat they'd just had, but perhaps in the morning, cooler heads would prevail.

Nate knew he wouldn't be able to fall asleep, not with all the adrenaline pumping through his veins, so he dropped to the ground and began doing push-ups. He would go to the point of exhaustion and hoped that it would knock him out until morning.

His mind churned the entire time, refusing to give him even a moment of respite as the screams and crushed bodies returned to haunt him once more.

3

Nate finally threw the covers off himself at around four in the morning, having found sleep impossible. Tiredly, he stumbled his way down the stairs and into the main lobby, where he took a right and stopped before a locked door. His room key opened it, revealing a short corridor with two marked doors on either side. It showed one to be for men and one for women.

Nate entered the small bathing area, turning the nozzle and filling the room with steam. He got one bath here a day and was going to enjoy it. The water was steaming as he sank in, letting out a low groan as his abused muscles began to unknot themselves.

He sat there with his eyes closed, allowing his tired mind to try working out what to do next. If Noam decided to leave them, Nate would have to come up with a new plan. He hadn't been counting on that, so he honestly wasn't sure what he would do if things came to that. Freya was a great asset, but without someone to take the hits, dish out extra damage, and even heal when needed, they would be missing a crucial part of their team.

Time stretched on as his brain worked, and only when the water began to grow cold did he get out. He made sure to dunk his clothes from the night before into the water, working them with soap and wringing them out before storing them in his ring. He would have to dry them later that night. For now, he pulled a new set of clothes from his ring and quickly got dressed.

His boots, containing the technique of the lightning sloth were laced up and his Froster Drake leather armor was donned. He pulled a warm cloak out as well, draping it around his shoulders and fastening it with a clasp that could be easily popped should he need to enter battle. It would be cold out when they started and only begin to warm up as the day went on. If there was a single upside about Laybor, it was that the weather was milder and the days tended to be warmer.

Extreme climates wouldn't really start until the 8th planet, Solara, which was constantly plagued by terrible solar storms filled with radiation, which caused horrible and mutated monsters to roam the land. A light shiver ran down his spine as he remembered his group's first encounter with one of those nightmares.

Nate exited the bath, his mind still churning, and nearly walked right into Noam, who had his hand extended, reaching for the door.

For a moment, the two of them stared at one another, Nate wondering if the man was going to start throwing around accusations or try hitting him. Instead, Noam straightened himself, looked Nate in the eye and apologized.

"I'm sorry for what I said last night."

Nate was dumbfounded, so shocked that he couldn't think up an appropriate response.

"Freya came to talk to me last night after I left and made me see reason. She told me about everything you did for her. The way she spoke about you…" He trailed off, his eyes going distant. "What I'm trying to say is that I shouldn't have accused you of being the one who did all of this to us. Killing those people really got under my skin, especially when I couldn't see any reason for what we'd done.

"Don't get me wrong. Your explanation still has some holes in it. But if you're not a serial killer, then there has to be a reason why you did what you did. If I'm going to keep traveling with you, let alone trust you, you're going to have to prove what you're telling is the truth. If that Augment of yours can really predict events or at least give you hints as to what might happen, I want you to predict something for me. Show me you're not lying and then we'll talk."

With that said, Noam pushed past him into the bathing area and closed the door behind him, leaving Nate standing out in the corridor on his own. He let out a long breath, his mind beginning to calm itself as he thought. Noam had believed him – well, sort of, anyway – which meant he now had to hammer it home once and for all. With that thought in mind, Nate headed out of the bathing area. Instead of going back to his room, he left the inn, making straight for the closest world-operated shop.

"What can I do for you?" asked the female gnark at the counter of the small shop as Nate entered.

"I want to see the Limited list," Nate said, taking a seat.

The gnark tried to dissuade him as they always did, but after he insisted, the woman finally showed it to him, grumbling under her breath.

Nate needed to scroll down the list, going all the way down to those techniques that were limited to those under 25 in order to find it. To his surprise, there were hardly any left.

Kanta Sight 11/14 - 16,000

Kanta Sight: You may see the strengths of others, including techniques/spells as well as other insights.

Nate had been planning on buying this scroll sooner rather than later despite having come back from the future. Still, seeing how many had already been taken, he was grateful that Noam had forced the issue as he likely would have missed out on the opportunity while trying to hoard points.

"I would like to buy the Kanta Sight scroll," Nate said, placing his hand on the crystal.

He felt the points being sucked away, leaving him with a measly 5,700, but he would have had to buy this at some point, and he consoled himself with the knowledge that he at least got it this time around.

Kanta Sight would not only allow him to see specific techniques or spells but would also give him insight into their fighting styles. It had a total of 4 tiers, the highest of which would allow him a fraction of foresight into enemy movements. It was kind of like looking into the future, but he would need to be fast enough to act on that information, so upgrading the scroll past the 3rd tier before the 300th rank would be pointless.

"Would you like anything else?" the gnark asked.

"No, that's all," Nate said, rising from the chair.

There were other things he'd wanted to buy but simply didn't have the points for. His Cultivation Manual was currently at the 2nd tier, which would be fine for this planet and Laybor, but by the time he made it to the third planet, Raven, he would need to upgrade it again. Ideally, it would be done before he left Laybor, but the point cost was astronomical enough that it would be difficult to say the very least.

Nate exited the shop and headed back to the inn, slipping quietly up to his room and closing the door. Noam should still be bathing, as he hadn't been out long, which meant the man should be none the wiser to him leaving the inn.

Knowing he wasn't going to be falling back asleep, Nate began to move through martial arts forms, being careful not to strain himself to the point where he would break a sweat – he *had* just taken a bath, after all. The forms were simple enough, basic footwork and punches, no kicks or knees. He was careful to exaggerate each of the movements, continuing the process of ingraining them into his body. He'd failed many times due to his lack of muscle memory and practice, and Nate would make sure he did all he could to mitigate that weakness as soon as possible.

He continued his practice until a knock came at the door. It was still dark out, despite the time now being around seven in the morning, as the sun in Warine didn't rise for another hour.

"Good morning," Freya said, giving him a hesitant smile. "How did you sleep?"

"I didn't," Nate said with a sigh.

He was tired. Despite the manual boosting his physical traits, becoming tired was still very much possible and running on as little sleep as he'd gotten was affecting him.

"Same," Freya sighed. "It wasn't even fun stuff keeping my brain from letting me sleep."

She made a sour face.

Nate didn't bother asking what she meant by that, simply grunting in reply.

"I bumped into Noam earlier this morning," Nate said, standing aside and allowing her to enter.

He noticed her shoulders stiffen at that.

"He said you spoke with him last night."

"I did," Freya said, turning to face him as he closed the door. "I couldn't leave things the way they were. Not after what we went through together. What did he say?"

"He apologized," Nate said, still feeling a sense of disbelief that Noam had been the one to say he was sorry.

When he'd gotten older, the man had begun to bend more, but at this point in their lives, Noam was as stubborn as Nate had been.

"Did he say anything else?" she asked, fidgeting with her hair.

"Just that you made a very convincing argument," Nate said. "He doesn't believe that I'm the one responsible for all of this, but he wants proof of my Augment."

"I can understand why you didn't tell us about it," Freya said, relaxing a bit. "I mean, if anyone knew you had something like that, you'd become a prime target for everyone who wanted to survive."

"I'm glad you understand," Nate said, giving her a small smile.

This part of his plan had been the simplest. They were supposed to tell one another about everything they could do, but keeping a secret like this until he was absolutely sure he could trust them would make sense to both of them. Noam would especially understand, based on his background in the Israeli Special Forces.

It was well known that knowledge was power.

"Speaking of Augments," Freya said, seeming happy to change the subject. "I've noticed some pretty cool things about the one you gave me. Why not mention anything about them before?"

Honestly speaking, it had been because he'd forgotten. One person could only equip so many Augments before they hit their limit, so by the time Nate was on the 8th planet, no one was buying any new ones, as they'd been tapped out. Now that they were starting over from the beginning, he'd be *far* more careful about which he took into himself and which he gave to his comrades.

Sure, it had helped him prove a point and back up his story, but the Augment of Magnification was *perfect* for someone like Freya and her Tome of the Magigun.

Of course, he wasn't going to say that, so he gave a different excuse.

"I didn't mention it because I hadn't found anything suited to either of you," Nate replied. "I didn't want you trying to find something potentially useless and equipping it simply because it sounded nice at the time. Every person has an Augment limit. It varies from person to person, but the average is five."

"How do you know when you've hit your limit?" Freya asked.

"Oh, you'll know," Nate said.

In his previous life, the consensus had been that the individual limit was completely random. The lowest recorded he'd heard of was 3 Augments, while the highest had belonged to Liam Watanabe himself, at a staggering 17 Augments, which was unbelievable. Now, Nate was going to be doing some research to discover if the limit really was purely random or if there was something else behind it.

"I can see why you picked this for me," Freya said, tapping her temple. "But I already have good aim, and I don't have any spells that can hit a target at more than around twenty yards before starting to fizzle out."

"Firstly," Nate said. "There's more than one use for the Augment of Magnification, and secondly, we're going to fix that today."

"We...are?" Freya asked, raising an eyebrow.

"We are," Nate said, giving her a smile.

4

"I don't know about this, Nate," Freya said, staring at the spell scroll. "This will basically clean me out, and I worked *hard* to get all these points."

He, Noam, and Freya were currently inside the very shop Nate had visited earlier in the day after a large breakfast and long explanation about Augments, which he'd needed to repeat to Noam after giving Freya an explanation about all the functions hers would have.

After breakfast, they'd found a smaller shop where she and Noam had haggled for sale prices of their goods, netting them both a good number of points. Now, Nate was trying to convince her to basically spend them all to buy a scroll and upgrade it to the 2nd tier.

"Trust me when I say that it'll make all the difference," Nate said. "This will cover for a big weakness and will be very useful when combined with that Augment I got you."

Freya gave him a sidelong glance, telling him that she hadn't missed the subtle reminder of what he'd done for her. Despite that, she did as she asked. With a heavy sigh, she paid the 25,000 points for the spell scroll of Snipe Crack. Yes, it was a ridiculous name, and yes, there was a reason why no one had yet purchased this 1/1 spell from the Limited list, both of which Nate had already dealt with.

"Go on, then," Nate said, looking meaningfully at the scroll.

"I would like to upgrade this to the second tier," Freya said, the pain clears in her voice.

"Place your hand on the sphere," the gnark said mechanically.

Freya did, and the remaining 55,000-point cost was paid, bumping it to the 2nd tier. This left her with a grand total of 2,480 points, even less than what Nate had at the moment.

Freya sighed, opening the scroll and scanning it for a moment, then, her eyes went wide as saucers. She looked between Nate and the scroll several times before shaking her head in amazement.

"You know, when you pull things like this out of your nonexistent hat, I *can* believe that you can see the future."

Noam shifted a bit at that, clearly wondering what the scroll could do.

"Don't tell him anything," Nate said. "I think someone should be surprised, don't you?"

Freya nodded quickly, stashing the scroll in her ring and looking at Noam expectantly. Of them all, he had the most points by far, and that had been even before they'd spent what they had. At nearly 100,000, the man was the closest of the three of them to being able to upgrade his manual for a second time.

"So, you got anything for me?" Noam asked. "Going to tell me how to spend my points as well?"

"Yes, actually," Nate said. "You won't spend *anything*."

Noam raised an eyebrow.

"You're around thirty thousand away from being able to upgrade your manual again. You'll see a lot more following that path than anything else now. I don't think you'll find much of use on this planet, though that *is* just my opinion."

Noam stared at him for a long moment, then nodded. There was clearly still some tension between them, and he knew that needed to be resolved, but Nate was sure the man would come up with something soon enough.

"So, where are we off to now?" Freya asked as they exited the shop and walked out into the early-morning sun – or at least, what passed for it in this world.

"We're heading south," Nate said. "It's the only direction we've get to travel and will line us up with the best series of portals into the second planet once we're strong enough."

"How long will it take us to reach the first of the southern towns or cities?" Noam asked as Nate pulled his scooter from his ring, the others following suit.

"Only a couple of days if we move quickly," Nate said.

"Good," Noam replied. "I've thought of something you can do to prove you're not lying, but I won't say anything until we've passed the first of the southern towns."

Nate was curious – though he thought he already knew what the man would want – but he simply nodded and hopped onto the scooter, pushing off and heading for the gates.

Nate, Freya, and Noam were all lying on their stomachs, the hill sloping downward, and their bodies hidden by the swaying, blue-green grass surrounding them on all sides. Below, the speck of moving color was only visible due to the bright yellow coloration of its shell.

Despite not being able to see it, Nate knew what it was. The electric snail, a creature so rare it only showed up once every year or so, would be at the 27th rank, one higher than his own and two above his friends. Thankfully, it wasn't a starred monster, so it would be a bit easier to take down.

However, it also had three separate spells it could use, making Freya's new spell extremely useful in taking it down. Seeing as this world would be blowing up in less than 6 months, this was likely the only electric snail that would ever exist, and Nate wasn't about to pass up on the opportunity to take it down.

"Do you have a clear shot?" Nate asked as Freya extended her Magigun, sighting down the barrel at the distant target.

"Yup," Freya said, grinning to herself.

"Get ready," he said to Noam. "We're going to have to move quickly as soon as she fires."

"You still haven't explained what her spell will do," Noam grumbled, clutching his tomahawks.

"All right," Freya said. "Firing in three, two, one."

Her finger depressed the trigger of the Magigun as she used the Snipe Crack spell. A blaze of white power blasted from the muzzle, tearing into the air for a grand total of two feet before it shattered the world, disappearing into a crack in space.

"Let's move," Nate said, leaping to his feet and dashing down the hill.

He rose just in time to see another crack, matching the one next to Freya, appear near the snail. The blazing white projectile blasted from the rift in space, impacting the snail with enough force to crack its shell and hurling it off the ground. While it was still in the air, a ripple of force blasted out from the point of impact, flattening the grass for ten feet in all directions.

The snail hit the ground with a *thud,* blood oozing from the crack in its shell as a wave of crackling white spread out from its body, scorching the grass as it lashed out in blind rage.

The snail tried squirming to its feet, only for another spell to explode from a new rift that formed before the snail's prone body.

"Was that her Poisonshot?" Noam exclaimed, whipping his head back in Freya's direction.

She remained where she had been before, still hidden by the swaying grass.

"Yup," Nate said with a grin.

Two more Poisonshots followed, each lancing into the monster and vanishing without leaving so much as a mark. The snail wailed, its cry grating at their ears like nails on a chalkboard. He felt the mental assault as they approached, the monster's second spell trying to disorient them.

Now that they were close enough, Nate didn't need to focus to hit his target. He used his Gilded Skin, metal flowing over his body and shielding him from the crackling storm that blasted from the monster's body as he barreled into it.

Electricity coursed through him, locking his muscles and causing him to fall. Still, he'd put himself in the position where he'd been able to land a direct hit, so, even as he fell, he forced his kanta to flow, summoning his broadsword as he did.

The Gilded Blade sliced easily into the snail's fleshy hide, sending a spray of greenish blood across the ground as it tried to slither back. The snail itself was quite large, the top of its shell standing nearly three-and-a-half feet at its tallest, while its body was about half that again in length.

The monster backed away far faster than a creature of its species should be able to, but it was a monster and would hardly be a difficult one to take down if any cultivator could simply close it and prevent it from using the full power of its spells.

Nate was back on his feet in an instant, rolling over his shoulder and bringing forth his Goldshield as the snail unleashed its third spell. Twin streams of electricity blasted from its eye stalks, clearly aimed at Nate's chest. They impacted with his shield and were deflected back at the monster, though the shield didn't manage to take all the damage well.

While the snail was struck by its own spell, Nate took a hit too. The spell crashed through his defenses and slammed into his shoulder. Searing heat tore into his Gilded Skin, leaving a scorch mark in its wake as Nate spun from the spell's line of fire. His shoulder throbbed, but he'd managed to avoid taking a direct hit and the limb was still intact, which, to Nate, was what really mattered.

He dropped to his stomach as the snail unleashed a second spell, grimacing at the dip in his kanta. It had been a risk to bring the Goldshield out, as it drew on his strength in far greater amounts than his first two techniques. The spell breaking through had cost him even more, but he'd accomplished his goal of getting the monster to focus on him.

Noam pounced on the snail from behind, tomahawks clutched in both hands and his body wrapped in the kanta of his Brutal Guardian technique. Dense, red kanta flowed around the man's body, his eyes shining like those of a demon as he brought both weapons down. Some sixth sense must have warned the creature about its impending doom, and its fleshy body vanished into its shell in a flash.

Noam's blades smashed into the ground, sending up a spray of dirt and debris. He whirled, bringing both weapons up and around, crashing into the crack Freya had put into its shell. Nate noted the single eyestalk lying on the ground where the snail hadn't been quite fast enough, then grinned as Noam's tomahawks smashed into the snail's shell, hurling it off its base once more.

A larger web of cracks spread from the point of impact, leaving the creature lying on its side. A streak of purple slammed into the creature again as Freya came running up, skidding to a halt some ten yards from the battlefield proper and leveling her weapon.

The snail screamed as Noam hit it again and Freya used Poisonshot for a fifth time. Nate knew she was pushing it by now, having nearly exhausted her resources. If she wanted to keep being useful, she'd need to switch to her less costly spells.

Thankfully, she seemed to realize that as well, as she swapped over to her Blinding Buckshot, which slammed into the monster's ugly head as it slid from its shell, clearly intending to attack again.

The snail screeched, reeling for a moment, as stabbing needles of light forced themselves into its one remaining eyestalk. That was all the time Nate needed, lunging in and triggering his Steelshod. The kanta began draining quickly from his core as he blasted forward, his fist impacting with the side of the cracked shell, resulting in a low *boom*. His fist rocketed forward again, the additional force slamming into the shell and shattering it like hot glass.

He ripped his hand back, showing a pulsing mass of organs and innards. Thankfully, he didn't need to stare at it for long, as a rapier – summoned to his left hand – drove through the opening and deep into the snail's body.

Nate dismissed the weapon as the snail unleashed a final desperate attack, lightning ripping through him and Noam, who'd taken the snail's head while Nate had been stabbing it. His friend's technique held, though Noam was driven to his knees. Nate felt the uncomfortable buzzing pass through his body, causing his muscles to spasm and momentarily lose control over his techniques.

He still managed to catch himself before he fell, stabbing his backsword into the snail's side again to prevent himself from falling and make sure the creature really was done for good.

The snail let out one final ear-piercing shriek, then went still, its body flopping to the ground in a pool of spreading ooze. A wave of kanta crashed into him as the snail expired and Nate let out a low groan as he straightened, dismissing his Gilded Skin and feeling raw and tender all over.

"That was *not* fun," Noam said, rolling his shoulders and clutching at his head.

"Oh, come on. That wasn't too bad," Freya said, giving them both a wide grin. "Stop acting like such little ninnies. We won!"

They'd come out victorious, and with *far* fewer injuries than Nate had been expecting. It was all thanks to Freya and her new spell.

5

"So *that's* what it does," Noam said, finally understanding what the woman had done.

"Pretty sweet, right?" she said, running her fingers over the Magigun's stock, which poked from the holster at her hip.

"I'll say," Noam muttered. "Kind of makes me feel a bit obsolete."

"Oh, don't say that," she said, patting him on the shoulder. "But, yeah, I don't see why I need you two losers when I'm *this* awesome all on my own. I think it's time we break up the band for my solo career!"

"We all know how that went for Soltara," Nate said, naming a famous singer from back on Earth. "Do you *really* want to go that route?"

Freya winced visibly at that.

"You know, on second thought, I think I'll stick with you losers. Safety in numbers and all."

The aforementioned singer's career had not gone well after leaving her band, while her previous bandmates went on to become the single most successful group in the world.

"How much kanta do you have left after that battle?" Nate asked.

"Not much," Freya admitted. "That first attack took a *lot* out of me."

"It's the price you pay for something so powerful," Nate replied. "Next time, I'd recommend using one of your first two spells instead of Poisonshot. It'll make things easier on you."

Freya's new spell had several effects. The main attack would come in the form of a bullet made of pure force. It would be so powerful that it would tear a hole in the world, travel through the dead space between her and her target in the blink of an eye, and emerge from a second tear to hit the target.

The impact would be incredibly powerful in its piercing capabilities and its blunt force. The ripple of flattened grass after the impact would have knocked any bystanders off their feet, had there been any. The final effect of the spell was the one Freya had used to hit the snail from so far away.

The rift created by the spell would remain in place, allowing Freya to fire more spells through. A new rift would open each time in her targeted area. Each new rift that was opened would further destabilize the first she opened until it collapsed. Currently, the limit was three spells, but if she continued upgrading it, that limit would increase, along with the power of the actual spell. There was a reason it had cost so much to begin with, and the next tier would be more expensive.

"Care to explain why you wanted to kill this thing so badly?" Noam asked, looking down at the snail's body. "The amount of kanta I got from it wasn't anything special."

"For points, of course," Nate said, crouching by the monster's disgusting corpse.

"We can get points from this thing?" Freya asked, refusing to come any closer.

The ooze was spreading, and she clearly wanted to be nowhere near it. The smell wasn't exactly pleasant.

"Well, most of its body is useless," Nate admitted, pulling his knife from his belt and crouching by the snail's corpse. "Which is why I didn't ask you to avoid destroying anything specific."

He slid the knife in between the shell and the remaining flesh poking from the front, ignoring the gaping hole in its side. This would be a far easier way to get what he wanted.

"I think I'm going to be sick," Freya said, covering her mouth as Nate pulled the gooey flesh away from the shell, leaving a trail of blood and slime.

"Why, Freya," Nate said, affecting a tone of surprise, "don't tell me you don't like snail slime."

"If you take one more step, I'll shoot. Do *not* test me," Freya said, leveling her Magigun at Nate, who'd risen with a slimy hand extended in her direction.

Nate held his hands up in surrender, grinning broadly as Freya slowly lowered her weapon, staring at him suspiciously as though he would lunge at her without warning.

"That's disgusting," Noam said as Nate plunged his hand into the base of the snail's shell and began rooting around.

"It's a good thing I don't have to touch it then," Nate replied jovially.

He'd used his Gilded Skin the entire time, not wanting to go rooting through the snail's disgusting body with his bare hands. After a moment of searching through the still-warm mess, his fingers finally closed around a hard object. With a disturbing *squelching* sound, Nate pulled his arm free, clutching a slime-covered sliver of yellow crystal.

"Hang on to that, would you?" he said, tossing it to Noam.

He hid another grin at the man's exclamation and stream of curses as he fumbled the object in his hands. Nate, in the meantime, stuck his hand back into the snail and continued searching. He pulled his hand free several times, tossing slivers of crystal to the man before continuing to dig.

Finally, after what felt like ages, he emerged with a sound of triumph, clutching a squishy and twisted-looking organ. It was a pale pink, with seven valves branching from its center. It was twisted into a knot, with small swirls running over its surface.

Freya made a gagging sound as Nate lifted it to his nose and took an exaggerated sniff, while Noam looked at him like he'd lost his mind.

"Would you mind telling us what that is?" the man asked as Nate rose to his feet.

"This is the snail's heart," Nate said with a wide grin. "It's considered a delicacy here in Warine and is so rare that the wealthy will pay a literal fortune for the smallest taste."

"You're joking right?" Freya asked, looking a bit green. "He's joking," she said, turning to Noam. "Right?"

"I'm not so sure," Noam said, looking at the pulsing organ in revulsion.

Nate pulled it into his ring. He wanted to keep it fresh. The fresher the meat, the better the price he'd be able to bring when he went to sell it.

"This better be worth it," Noam said, looking at the collection of crystals in his hands. "What exactly are these anyway?"

"Kanta crystals," Nate said. "You'll typically find them in monsters on later planets, but the rare few can be found in particularly strong or rare monsters in the earlier planets."

"What do they do, though?" Noam asked, wrinkling his nose at them.

"Oh, they have loads of uses," Nate said, dismissing his technique, slime falling to the ground all around him and leaving him completely clean. "Uses we can talk about on the road since we still have a long way to travel, and I'd rather be somewhere safer when night comes creeping in."

Noam grumbled to himself, stashing the slime-covered crystals in his ring and crouching to wipe his hands clean.

Freya remained where she was at the very fringe of the battle and pointedly *not* looking at the dead snail.

"You know, that was quite unattractive," she said, as Nate came to join her.

"Hey, don't knock it until you try it," Nate said with a grin. "The snail's still right there."

"And ruin my nails? I think I'll pass," Freya said.

"Come on, stop being such a baby about it. Noam and I both did it, so you should too. For teamwork and solidarity stuff."

She slugged him in the shoulder in response then walked away, muttering under her breath about boys.

"Smooth," Noam said as Freya stalked away.

"What can I say?" Nate said. "My charm is irresistible."

The three of them spent the rest of the day hiking through the swaying grass, stopping occasionally to collect the bits of copper ore they spotted along the way. They got into a few fights with monsters as well, though none were as tough as the snail had been and gave them very little in the way of kanta or potential points.

By the time night rolled around, they'd covered a good distance toward Southnote Nine, the first town they'd come across on their journey. It wasn't a large town by any means, but from there, they'd have several pathways to potentially follow, which was why he was going there, instead of the larger city of Southbound Two.

"I miss real food," Freya sighed, biting into the bland protein meal around their small camp that night.

"We can always take the snail heart out and cook it up," Nate said, having already strategically put himself out of Freya's range.

"I'm sure you would enjoy swallowing something slimy," Freya retorted. "I, on the other hand, am classier than that."

"We're not eating the snail heart," Noam cut in before Nate could retort. "Not after all the trouble we went through to get it."

"It wasn't really all that much trouble," Freya said. "The only one who got hurt was Nate, so it's a win-win as far as I'm concerned."

"You know, that really hurts my feelings," Nate said, rubbing at his shoulder. "I could have been seriously injured."

"Pity you weren't," Freya said, popping the rest of the protein meal into her mouth and chewing as quickly as she could manage. "And on that note, I think I'll be turning in for the night. Nate, you get to take the first watch."

"Hey! I didn't volunteer for…"

Noam disappeared within the rigged tarp as Freya slipped into their tent, leaving Nate all alone.

He muttered under his breath about a lack of gratitude for all his hard work, though inwardly, he smiled. He was happy to see that things were returning to normal, even if he could still feel the underlying tension in the group. That would hopefully soon be addressed, but for now, the more he could keep breaking down barriers, the easier it would be for things to progress once he proved himself.

Sighing, Nate leaned back, staring up and watching the stars slowly vanish from the night sky. His mood darkened a bit at that, remembering Xavier Kent's final words.

You've killed us all.

How had the man known what would happen? Was it at all possible that Xavier Kent hadn't actually died in their previous timeline, but had instead gone back in time like he had, only from an earlier point in their history? And, if so, what had he known that Nate hadn't? Were there others who'd come back as well?

All those questions and more swirled around Nate's mind as the stars continued to wink out, counting down to the complete annihilation of this world.

6

Just as he'd predicted, the town of Southnote Nine came into view as the sun was setting the following day, the three of them having set a blistering pace to reach the town before nightfall so that they could stay at an inn. Nate hadn't wanted to waste the points, but he'd been outvoted, much to his annoyance.

"Well, isn't this quaint?" Nate muttered as they walked into the town's only inn.

It was a small, squat building set on the far side of town. It looked like it hadn't been updated in decades. The furniture was old and cracking, the paint flaking off the walls and ceiling, and even the winge standing behind the front desk appeared weathered and ancient.

Something about her fine features tickled at the back of Nate's mind, like a long-forgotten memory, but for some reason, he couldn't seem to put his finger on it.

"We'd like to stay the night," Freya said, though she sounded unsure about the proposition.

"How many rooms would you like?" the old woman asked, her voice creaking.

"That depends on how much it'll cost," Freya said.

"For the lady, it will be fifteen points," the old crone said. "For the boys…" Her eyes swiveled to them, and a small gleam flashed across them. "It'll be three."

"*Fifteen*?" Freya exclaimed, Noam leaning closer to Nate as Freya began a tirade. "That's ridiculous! In my world, we have a *word* for people like you. *Rude*. And you know what else…"

"Please tell me I'm not imagining things. This woman is *super* creepy, right?" Noam asked as Freya continued yelling.

"One hundred percent," Nate said, opening his Kanta Sight.

It was a unique skill, as it was specifically designed to give him information on sentient creatures and monsters. Simplistic ones, like the snail they'd fought, would give him nothing at all.

Noam and Freya both lit up in brilliant color, Freya shining a pale yellow, while Noam shone closer to a darker yellow, verging on orange. The way the skill worked was that it would show him color based on their friendliness toward him in particular. The range would run from white to black, over a spectrum of yellow, orange, and red. The darker the color, the less friendly they would be toward him.

It was imprecise to be sure, but that was only one aspect of the technique. It also highlighted their ranks, showing a glowing sigil floating on either hand, regardless of whether it was covered or not. Thirdly, the person's techniques or spells would appear in his mind, along with their descriptions.

It was extremely useful in just about every social situation, as it would immediately tell him if they were in grave danger.

Nate kept his eyes from widening as his heart began to race and cold sweat broke out across his spine. A dark red nimbus appeared around the woman, roiling and twisting around her form. A shiver ran down hid body as a rank appeared. It was not on either of the woman's hands, but stamped on her left shoulder, marking her as a monster.

Worse still, glowing stars appeared below the number, marking her as a 2-Star monster of the 45th rank, a creature that would obliterate their group before they could even begin putting up a fight.

Nate didn't even wait to see what technique or spells this monstrosity might have, instead, reaching out and grabbing Freya by the collar.

"You know, on second thought, we're going to stay somewhere else," Nate said, dragging a complaining Freya toward the inn entrance.

"Why leave?" the woman asked, her face beginning to contort as she rose above the counter.

Her face began to shift, growing longer, more angular as dozens of needle-like teeth formed within her mouth. Her eyes grew large, her pupils slitted, and her nose flattening as her hair grew wilder.

"You know, on second thought, I think I'll go with your suggestion," Freya said, turning and sprinting for the exit.

Noam was already at the door, holding it open and staring at the monster with ever-widening eyes.

A high-pitched screech echoed as Freya bounded through the door with Nate right on her heels. The instant he was clear, Noam slammed the door behind him, shoving his back up against it. A loud *crash* echoed as the monster slammed into the door, making the entire building shudder.

"Help me hold it!" Noam yelled, looking terrified.

"Don't bother," Nate said, leaning over, hands on his knees and his entire body shaking. "She won't be able to leave the inn."

"How can you be sure?" Freya asked, shaking as well. "I mean, did you *see* that thing? It was like one of my nightmares came to life and decided to pay me a visit!"

"It's a monster called a Kanta Leech," Nate said, straightening to his full height as he tried to calm his racing heart. "It's one of Warine's impossible to kill monsters. But, luckily for us, it's stuck inside."

Now that he'd seen it, the memories came flooding back. Every world had monsters in it that were far too powerful for anyone to handle until they went to subsequent worlds and became strong enough to return to kill them.

Humanity had given these creatures a name, lumping them all into a single category called the Dwellers. They were extremely powerful, gave out phenomenal rewards, and had a major limitation placed on them to prevent people from being slaughtered. That was why their territory was limited. In the case of this Kanta Leech, she would be forced to remain in the inn, unable to step outside, nor act until she was discovered or they were foolish enough to stay the night.

Unfortunately for many back in the previous timeline, they had fallen victim to this creature, who had only grown stronger with the human meals. Nate didn't think she was ever killed before the planet exploded, but if he remembered correctly, she had been upgraded to a 3-Star monster at the 70th rank at that point, growing as cunning as an average human and being quite adept at luring in prey.

A starred monster's intelligence level would rise as it increased. While the 2-Star monster had had rudimentary intelligence – enough for basic speech – they were able to sense that something was off. The way she'd looked and acted had been more than enough, especially when she'd given the price for a stay.

Kanta Leeches preferred to feed on those of the opposite gender. So, as a female, she would have preferred to eat him and

Noam over Freya. If she'd been smarter, the monster wouldn't have made such an obvious blunder.

Once she became a 3-Star monster, she'd be able to disguise herself far better. The difference between a 2 and 3-Star monster was like night and day, just as the difference between a 1 and 2-Star was.

A monster of this caliber would need at least three teams of five working in tandem to take it down, and the average ranking of the challengers would need to be in the 50s if they wanted to stand a chance.

"Are you *sure*?" Noam asked, still pressing his shoulder to the door.

"Yes, I'm sure," Nate said. "Otherwise, I wouldn't be so calm right now."

"You don't look very calm," Freya said. "In fact, I'd say you're on the verge of wetting yourself."

The statement was so utterly ridiculous that Nate burst out laughing. He was joined a moment later by Freya, and to his surprise, Noam joined in as well. They had just survived a brush with certain death and the relief of not having been eaten was overwhelming.

Their laughter soon died down as the three of them stared at the doorway to the inn.

"We need to find a way to warn people about this," Freya said.

"We can mark the door," Nate said, drawing his hunting knife and approaching the door.

He leaned in and began carving the warning. He stepped back a couple of minutes later to admire his handiwork.

"Well, that's ominous," Freya said.

"That's the point," Nate said.

He'd tried to come up with a way to warn people in as few words as possible, knowing the fickleness and impatience of human nature. He'd written only three words.

Death waits within.

If he'd written something like 'do not enter' he had the feeling that people would *definitely* enter. Now, if someone was stupid enough to go inside, it was on them.

"Seeing as the inn is out, where do we go now?" Freya asked, looking around the quickly darkening town.

"We leave," Nate said with a wide grin. "And break out the tent."

It seemed he'd gotten his way after all.

"I hate camping," Freya grumbled as they finished setting up the tent. "It's so uncomfortable."

"You're just complaining because you got used to beds," Nate said. "Once you've been in the great outdoors for long enough, you won't want to go back."

"I disagree," Noam said. "I've spent my fair share of time in the 'great outdoors' as you call it, and I was grateful for my bed every time I went back to it."

"We'll stay in an inn in the next town," Freya said. "Speaking of which, where are we headed exactly? You didn't give us much direction."

"We're heading for a city called Southnet Eight," Nate said. "There's a portal located there that will let out in a prime location on Laybor. The monsters will be strong, but not so strong that we'll be pushed back."

"Are you saying that there are portals that we would be pushed out of?" Freya asked.

"One hundred percent," Nate replied. "Some portals let out into some truly dangerous areas of Laybor. I'm pretty sure I marked them on the maps we were handing out."

Freya dug into her ring and removed one, giving it a glance.

"Oh yeah," she said, looking embarrassed. "I guess I didn't really look it over, since we have you. My mistake."

"There is somewhere I would like to go first," Noam said, his voice somber.

This was it. This would be the make-it-or-break-it point in their travels. Whatever Noam was going to ask for now, Nate would have to prove, without a shadow of a doubt, that he was telling the truth.

Nate leaned forward, listening intently as the man spelled out his demands.

7

"Are you sure about this?" Nate asked as they approached the gates of Southseer Seven, one of the smaller cities in the southern part of the planet.

He reflected on how lucky they'd been upon entering the planet, as he'd emerged near Centrifuge. It meant he and his team had access to all four cardinal directions. Had Nate come out further away in any direction, he wouldn't have been able to spread his warnings the way he had.

Over the last few days, they'd continued traveling, splitting up briefly a few times to visit smaller towns and cities along their route, distributing maps and leaving dire warnings about the imminent collapse of the planet.

By now, he was fairly confident that he'd averted complete disaster, despite his massive blunder, but there was always the chance he hadn't, which was why he continued in his mission to spread as much knowledge as he possibly could. He already had enough deaths on his conscience and didn't need to add the rest of humanity on top of that.

"If what you're saying is true, then yes," Noam said grimly. "I most certainly do."

Noam had demanded they stop another organization like Pavlov's here in the south. Nate was to predict where they would strike and come up with the best way to stop them. Unfortunately, if the timeline held true, they would be starting up with a nasty dark guild, one that he knew they couldn't beat on their own right now, given that the leader should be nearing rank 37 or 38 by now.

Of course, with the timeline on this planet altered, things might be a bit different, so he would need to keep a close eye on their surroundings.

"Death awaits you all if you leave this world!"

Nate's head whipped in the direction of the city square, where a man stood on a raised podium, yelling at the gathering crowd of curious people. It took Nate exactly two seconds to recognize the man and he swore under his breath.

The timeline had indeed moved up.

"Well, that doesn't look good," Noam said as the man continued yelling, his thick, Scottish accent apparent.

"My guild and I went through one of those so-called portals," the man continued, speaking vehemently as more people gathered. "We were met with death and destruction. We barely made it out with our lives. Better we all stay here, where it's relatively safe, to live out our days in comfort."

A low muttering began to sweep through the crowd as the three of them stopped just a few feet from the podium.

Colin MacDonald, leader of the MacDaddy Guild, was here early. He was still acting the same as he had back in the previous timeline – like a scared little toddler, too afraid to leave the safety of the playground. The problem was that last time, he'd only started spouting this stuff six months later, by which time many people had already crossed over.

People *had* listened to him back in Nate's old life, but not nearly as many as would listen to him now before any real information about Laybor came out.

"What about the maps?" Nate asked, drawing the crowd's attention.

He hated to do so, but someone needed to speak in opposition to this man. Otherwise, all of his plans would be for nothing.

"What maps?" Colin asked, clearly confused.

Nate reached into his shirt and removed one of the copies of his map, slightly crumpled from use.

"They've been going around everywhere in the north, east, and west," he said, passing it to the closest person standing nearby.

The man took it hesitantly, then opened it, looking within.

"It's a map of the entire planet," the man said, his eyes going wide.

"It can't be real," Colin said quickly, trying to regain the crowd.

"I have more copies," Nate said, pulling several more from his ring. "I was told to pass them along."

People eagerly crowded around him as he began passing them out, pulling their copies open and beginning to talk amongst themselves.

"This *has* to be real," someone in the crowd said. "There's a hidden cave on here that my group stumbled into. As far as we know, no one else was there."

"I've seen these portals with my own eyes!" said another person.

Soon, similar cries of agreement and confirmation swept through the crowd, the people doing all the work for him. Nate hid a smile as Colin glared at him, the man's black-bearded face going red with fury.

"Give me that!" he yelled, snatching a map from one of the passersby and ripping it open.

He scanned it briefly, then began shouting to the crowd once again.

"Don't you see what this is?" he bellowed, his powerful voice carrying over the noise. "That man in the sky is trying to get us all killed! I've heard of these maps," he continued, though he clearly hadn't. "They only started showing up after he did. Don't you think that's a coincidence? Because it certainly sounds like one to me!"

The crowd started muttering again, and Nate could tell that he was losing them.

"What do we do?" Freya asked in an undertone. "If he keeps spouting this stuff, we'll never get anyone off in time and all our work will be for nothing."

Nate scanned the crowd quickly, looking for another familiar face. If Colin was here, spouting his idiocy for all the world to hear, his sister Fiona had to be nearby. If they could talk some sense into her, then perhaps they could get Colin to back down. Nate didn't want to think about what he would have to do next if they couldn't convince her.

Suffice it to say that he would eliminate the threat to humanity, even if it did stain his soul once again.

Luckily, he spotted her standing right at the edge of the crowd. Fiona looked much like her brother, with the same dark hair, intense eyes, and hard features. However, her body language suggested that she wasn't exactly comfortable with what her brother was doing, which meant that they had a chance.

The crowd finally began to disperse after another minute, where Colin made sure to bring his speech to a close by telling the people to think of their families before running through a portal to certain death. With that said, he hopped off the podium and went to join his sister, the two of them moving away from the crowd and deeper into the city.

"Come on," Nate said. "We need to go talk to them."

"Are you sure that's a good idea?" Noam asked. "He seemed convinced. Also, isn't this city going to come under attack soon?"

"Soon isn't an exact timeline," Nate said. "And we need to try talking some sense into him. Otherwise, we may as well just give up. People are looking for excuses not to leave and they'll take it the second they get one."

"Okay," Noam said. "I'll concede on that point. But what are you going to say? How can you possibly convince someone who is so certain they are right?"

"By talking to the only person who can talk common sense into him. His sister."

"You mean the woman walking next to him?" Freya asked. "How do you know she won't be on his side? If I had a brother, I know I would be."

"Call it a hunch," Nate said. "Now come on, we're losing them."

He sped up, pushing through the crowd and following the pair as they wound their way through the city. He honestly wasn't sure where they were headed but knew that he needed to catch them alone before they joined the rest of their Guild. Once they did, Colin wouldn't listen to reason, and he'd have the numbers to force them to back off.

That was why, when they entered a narrow alley, Nate was quick to catch up.

"Hey, wait up!" he called, stopping them at the alley entrance.

Colin and Fiona turned, the former becoming hostile at Nate's appearance, while the latter appeared to be on guard. One could never be too careful.

"What do you want?" the man snarled. "Have you come to undermine me again with your devil's maps?"

"I haven't come to undermine anything," Nate said, taking on a neutral tone. He made sure to keep his hands by his sides and appear as non-threatening as possible. "Just to ask a question."

"I don't have time for-"

"Oh, just let him talk," Fiona said, cutting him off. "I'm sorry about my brother. We're all pretty sure he was cracked in the head as a baby."

Colin turned his glare on his sister, which she promptly ignored.

"You heard the man in the sky's message, same as everyone else," Nate said. "He said that if we make it through, we can all go back home. So, why are you trying to keep people here, in such an obviously dangerous world, when they all have a chance of going back to Earth?"

"Firstly, I wouldn't believe a *word* that sky devil had to say," Colin growled, turning his ire back on Nate. "Secondly, have you been to the next world? Because let me tell you something, sonny, I *have* and the monsters there are no joke."

"What's your rank?" Nate asked.

"Twenty-nine," the man automatically answered, taken aback by the sudden change in topic.

"And what about the rest of your group, assuming you're traveling with one?" Nate asked.

"Low-to-mid-twenties," Fiona said, answering in her brother's stead. "Why are you asking?"

"Because if you'll take a look at the maps I was passing around, you'll see that the minimum required rank to safely enter Laybor is thirty. You can't walk into a shark's maw holding a piece of bloody meat and then claim it isn't safe when you're almost killed, so why would you do the same here?"

Colin glowered at him, but once again, it was Fiona who answered.

"We're not basing this on a single trip," she said, looking nervous. "I convinced Colin to go back again after we'd failed the first time and things didn't go well."

"Did you run into more monsters you couldn't beat?" Nate asked. "Because judging by your ranks, you still wouldn't have been able to beat them."

"It was *people* waiting for us," Colin snapped. "Humans, from back on Earth, standing by the portals and waiting to kill us the moment we walked through!"

8

Portal Reavers.

That had been the term given to people in Nate's previous timeline who had camped out by portals so that they could kill people who were coming through. The portals between worlds were designed in such a way that only one person could walk through at a time. When you emerged on the other side, you tended to be disoriented for the first few seconds, and that was often enough time for someone to take a crack at killing you.

"Was anyone killed?" Nate asked, feeling his lips pulling to a hard line.

Once again, the timeline had been accelerated, but nothing had changed massively as far as he could tell, only sped up.

"No," Fiona said. "We were all able to make it back safely, but it was a near miss. One of our friends was badly hurt though."

"We were *lucky*," Colin snarled. "Many groups we've come across along our way weren't. I've heard stories of entire groups being wiped out while trying to make it through. It's not the monsters you have to watch out for. It's the people. That's why I'm going to keep warning people away from going so that they can live out their lives here, where people won't murder them just for walking on the streets."

He tried to push past Nate, but he stood firm.

"Are you telling people not to go because you and a few other people couldn't walk through a portal?" Nate asked. "There are fourteen-thousand different portals leading into Laybor and you're telling people to stay away from *all* of them?"

"Let me ask *you* something, mister high-and-mighty," Colin said, his face growing redder. "If you knew there was a chance that you'd be immediately killed just by walking through a portal, would you take it, especially when you know that if you stay put, you'll be safe?"

Nate stayed silent.

"Yeah," Colin said, shoving past him. "That's what I thought."

Nate remained where he was, watching the siblings walk away, Fiona throwing an apologetic look over her shoulder.

"So, now what?" Noam asked.

"I think you know what," Nate sighed, his mind already working.

In their previous timeline, there had been four Guilds who were notorious for Portal Reaving in this part of the world. They were Black Coffin, Rose Sombre, Ashland and Twilight Moon. The problem was that each had different strengths and weaknesses, and before taking them on, he would need to know who they were facing.

For example, if they had to fight Ashland, they would probably want some protection against fire magic, as their guild liked burning things. They would also need help against any of these guilds, as they were large. The smallest of them was Rose Sombre, though knowing his luck, it would be Black Coffin, whose membership should be somewhere around 300 by this point.

"Does that mean we're going after another organization?" Noam asked.

"Portal Reavers are a menace to society and enemies of the human race," Nate replied. "They need to be put down."

"What about the attack on this city?" Noam asked, looking around.

That would be the tricky part. If history held true, Ashland would be making a visit soon. Depending on how many of them there were, Nate would know if they were the culprits. Of course, they would still need to find a way to stop them, but that was a problem for future Nate. Present Nate had other problems to deal with.

Since Colin had already made his statement here, he would be moving on soon, so Nate needed to intercept the man before that and convince him to keep his mouth shut until he could deal with the Portal Reavers.

To make a convincing argument, he would need to prove to be capable beyond any shadow of a doubt.

"Nate?" Freya said.

"Huh?" Nate grunted, snapped from his thoughts.

"What are we going to do about the imminent attack on the city?" Freya asked, repeating Noam's question.

Nate's mind began to race. As far as he knew, no one had claimed this city yet. In fact, no one had claimed it for several years in their previous timeline, as more tempting cities had called the ambitious away from this region.

"Follow me," he said, having made his mind up.

"Where are we going?" Freya asked, hurrying to keep up with him.

"To the nearest shop," Nate said. "I hate to do this, but with what's coming, I can't think of any other way to make this work."

"To make *what* work?" Noam asked suspiciously as they rounded a corner and entered the main marketplace.

There were stalls lining the side of the road as per usual, but Nate headed straight for the official shop, knowing that he would get the best price for their precious cargo there. Had he had the time, he would have preferred to sell to a specialty shop, which would have netted more points.

This shop was quite a bit larger than the previous one he'd visited. It had six separate counters manned by as many gnarks.

"What can I do for you?" asked a bored-sounding gnark as they approached the counter.

"I need to sell this," Nate said, plopping the oozing snail heart onto the counter.

"Yuck! Get it off! Get it off," the gnark exclaimed, leaping back with a yelp.

"This is a very rare delicacy," Nate said calmly. "I would like to sell it."

"No! *No, no, no.* And just for good measure. *NO!*" exclaimed the gnark, backing all the way to the wall. "I am not dealing with slimy organs! No way, sir!"

Nate looked over to the gnarks at the other counters, all of whom had suddenly seemed to develop a fascination with the walls, ceiling, and anything else that wasn't in his vicinity.

"Yeah, I hate to say it, but I'm with them," Freya said, standing some fifteen feet back.

Noam remained where he was at Nate's side and raised an eyebrow.

"I was unaware that they could refuse to buy items here," the man said.

56

"They can't," Nate said, giving the man a hard stare. "It would be in everyone's best interest if we get this over with. Don't you agree?"

The gnark refused to budge.

"Are any of you going to step in?" Nate asked. "Or is this shop refusing to buy a perfectly legitimate item from me?"

"I can help you over by my counter, human," a gnark on the far end offered after several moments of silence.

"Excellent," Nate said, lifting the oozing organ and walking across the shop.

Slime trickled to the floor, eliciting sounds of dismay from the other gnarks.

"Hey, if you want to blame anyone for this mess, blame the guy who didn't want to buy this from me in the first place," Nate said, plunking himself down behind the furthest counter.

The glares leveled at him suddenly turned, and the gnark who'd refused to deal with him turned pale. Nate hid a smile, imagining the man cleaning up once he was gone.

"What can you give me for this?" Nate asked.

He didn't bother giving the description or trying to haggle. That was the one downside of selling in a shop like this.

The gnark pulled on a pair of gloves, then gingerly took the organ, placing it on a small scale he pulled from beneath the counter. He then lifted it, turning it from side to side and muttering to himself. He tallied some numbers, consulted some notes, then cleared his throat.

"This is quite the sizable heart," the gnark finally said. "The cuts are clean and precise, and this was harvested correctly to maintain the greatest...*ugh*...flavor."

The man audibly gagged when talking about the possibility of someone eating this thing.

"That being said, for this quality, we pay twenty thousand a pound. Your heart is exactly four point six-one-six pounds, bringing you to a total of ninety-two thousand, three-hundred-and-twenty points."

Nate hid a grimace when he heard that number. It wasn't enough. Even when adding his points into it, he wouldn't reach his goal.

"You don't seem happy with that figure," Noam said, noting his expression. "Care to tell me why?"

"We need a hundred thousand to buy our way into the city's manor and take control of it. I was hoping the points from the heart would cover it, but it looks like we're going to have to sell the kanta crystals as well."

He'd really wanted to hang onto them, but this was the only plan he had that might work.

"What if I covered the difference in points?" Noam asked. "We *can* pool them to unlock the doors, right?"

"We can," Nate said, noting no objection to selling the heart for this purpose. "But I'd much rather you save your points."

"Very well," Noam said, pulling the crystals from his ring and setting them down on the counter.

"How much for these?" Nate asked.

The gnark lifted them, turning the small shards one at a time.

"Low quality at best," he said. "Two-hundred points a gram."

The crystals all dropped onto the scale, showing that they'd managed to collect a bit over 25 grams, netting them a total of 5,065 points. It didn't quite make the mark, but it was close enough that Nate would be able to cover the difference. He hated wasting points like this. Once this was all said and done, not only would they be losing out on the points they'd collected by killing the snail, but he would also lose a sizable chunk of his remaining points.

He did the math as he placed his hand on the sphere, accepting the sale. He would be left with a measly 3,085 points, and all for a city that would likely be burned to the ground within the next few days.

"Finally," Freya said as they left the shop. "I never thought we'd be rid of that gross slug thing."

"It was a snail," Nate sighed, thinking of all the lost points.

"Aww, don't feel too bad," Freya said, giving him a wide smile. "At least you still have me."

"Oh, happy day," Nate grumbled.

Freya stuck her tongue out in response, earning a chuckle from Noam.

"Oh, real mature," Nate said. "See how well you'll be treated when I'm the lord of this city."

"Please, you'll be as much of a lord as I will," Freya said with a snort.

"Well, at least I'll own…" Nate trailed off as the trio walked around the corner, the city's manor coming into view.

He swore under his breath as a group of people dressed in red and orange robes stood before the open door.

They were too late. Ashland had already taken the city, but in a completely different way than Nate had been expecting.

9

"What's happening?" Noam asked, his eyes narrowing as he saw the robed figures heading into the manor.

"It looks like we were too late," Nate said, mind racing.

This was not supposed to happen. Ashland – because this was the Ashland Guild – didn't usually think in terms of tactics or with long-term rulership in mind. They simply marched across the land, burning cities and taking what they wanted before moving on. Taking control of the city spoke to a more cunning approach, one that would make things infinitely harder.

He would now need to figure out their plans, as well as who was in charge. Simon Dalefield, the leader of Ashland in his time, was a pyromaniac serial killer who had been serving multiple life sentences back on Earth for the numerous horrific crimes he'd committed. He was powerful enough to attract followers of like minds, and together, they had been one of the most destructive Guilds on the first few planets, before they'd inevitably been put down.

Simon was clearly not the one in charge over here, which meant that Nate needed to do some reconnaissance.

"What are we going to do?" Freya asked, all joviality gone from her voice.

"We'll need to scope out the place, see what we're dealing with," Nate said, his eyes flicking to the horizon.

It was late afternoon, but the sun wouldn't be going down for several hours yet. That meant that they'd be easily spotted if they tried sneaking around the manor. With the city now under their control, Ashland could pretty much do as they pleased. He thought for another moment, a plan formulating as he turned away from the manor, brows furrowed.

"We're going to find Colin and his Guild," Nate said.

The man might have been a coward, but he wouldn't stand by if he knew people were going to be killed. More accurately, his sister wouldn't, and where she went, he would follow.

"What good will that do us?" Noam asked.

"We need time," Nate replied. "We can't be worrying about attacks on both fronts. People need to get off this world, and Colin's fearmongering will really hurt our chances."

"What happens if they make a move while you're trying to convince him to stop?"

"Once we find him, you head back to the manor," Nate said. "If anything happens, come get us."

Noam grunted, then went silent as the three of them moved quickly through the streets, searching for where the man and his guildmates were staying. It didn't take long. A few questions to the right people led the group to a small inn located near the fringes of the city.

It was lucky for them that the entire guild was gathered in the dining area when Nate entered, as it would have been troublesome to try tracking him down.

"I'll be going then," Noam said as soon as he spotted the man, who was sitting at a table with a small group and looking sour.

Nate nodded as the man slipped away, leaving him and Freya to confront the group.

"How are we going to do this?" she asked, eyeing the group.

No one had looked in their direction yet, but it was only a matter of time. Even if none of the others recognized him, Colin and Fiona most certainly would.

"I thought I'd just wing it," Nate said with a shrug.

"Why do I follow you again?" Freya asked as Nate began walking directly to the table.

"It's my irresistible charm and charisma," Nate said.

"If that's what you have to tell yourself to sleep at night," Freya replied.

A member of the group saw them approaching and got Colin's attention. The man turned, his expression souring the moment he laid eyes on them.

"You can't seem to stop following me, can you?" Colin asked when they stopped before the table.

"How about a proposition?" Nate said. "I give you a location where you and your Guild can gain a lot of points and boost your ranks, and you take a break from your crusade."

"What is it with you and wanting to stop me?" Colin asked, narrowing his eyes. "It's almost like you want people to walk through those portals to be slaughtered."

The rest of the guild looked at him warily. There was a mix of men and women, all quite young and appearing battle-scarred in one way or another. It was clear that this was what remained of his guild after the ill-fated trip through the portal to Laybor.

"What I want is to go home," Nate said flatly. "The more people who make it to the end, the better my chances will be. Call me whatever you'd like, but I would much prefer to sleep in my own bed than a tent or rickety inn."

"I'd take that over certain death any day," Colin said. "Besides, it seems like you've already forgotten what I said last time. I won't stop because *I*, unlike *you*, value human life."

"If you value human life as much as you claim, then you'll take my offer," Nate said. "The monsters aren't going to be getting any weaker, and the longer you delay, the greater the chance of your team being wiped out."

A low muttering went through the group at that, all looking at Colin worriedly. Clearly, they'd seen it as well. The monsters on Warine were just as likely to kill them as ones on Laybor, and if they didn't raise their ranks, they would be prey not only to the monsters but to any would-be assassins.

"What's going on here?"

Nate turned and saw Fiona approaching the table, balancing a tray stacked with plates. He'd seen her at the bar when they'd entered but knew that they'd be spotted before she returned. That was why he'd taken the initiative.

"He's trying to bribe us to stay quiet about what's happening," Colin growled. "The only ones I know would benefit from that would be the ones ambushing people as they walk through the portals. You're one of them, aren't you?"

The man's voice slowly rose as he spoke until he was yelling loudly enough for everyone within the inn to hear him. A glowing gilded dagger appeared at Colin's throat, tickling his Adam's apple. A clatter of movement followed an instant later, as everyone at the table abruptly stood, gearing up for a fight.

"If I were part of some conspiracy to keep sending fodder through to my supposed comrades on the other side, why would I ask you *nicely* to stop?" Nate asked, pressing the dagger a bit harder into the man's neck before releasing it.

The dagger vanished in a puff of mist, though the gathered fighters remained tense. Nate ignored Colin and turned to Fiona, who looked equal parts murderous and relieved.

"There's a Guild in town called Ashland. I'm sure you haven't heard of them, but they're *bad* news. My friends and I are trying to stop them, but we can't do that if we have Mr. Doom over there running his mouth."

"What does one have to do with the other?" Fiona asked before Colin could start yelling again.

"Like I said before you arrived, I want to go home. If people get too comfortable here and refuse to move on, we'll be stuck here forever."

"What makes you think that you can't go back on your own?" Fiona retorted.

"If you've ever played a videogame, you'll know that the first level is always the easiest," Nate said. "This isn't a game, but if your experience on the second planet is anything to go by, things only become more difficult from here."

"Gain more ranks and you'll be fine," Fiona said, crossing her arms stubbornly.

It seemed she was trying to poke holes in his plan or find any weakness in his defense so she could pounce on it and deny him his request.

"Have any of you faced a Starred monster yet?" Nate asked, looking around the room.

"No," Fiona admitted. "But we *have* heard of them. A group we came across said they'd fought a monster with a gold star on its shoulder and that it was many times more powerful than anything at its rank."

"Well, it only gets worse from there," Nate said. "We've personally run across a two-star monster not far from here. Even if we gathered every powerful guild on the planet and attacked at the same time, we would all be wiped out, and that's not an exaggeration."

"You're saying there's an unbeatable monster just hanging out a few towns over and we're just supposed to believe that?" Colin cut in.

"I was there," Freya said, jumping into the conversation, her voice heated. "I've never seen anything like it. It was like a nightmare come to life. It looked like an ordinary woman tending an inn much like this one. It was only thanks to Nate that we got out of there alive. She turned into a monster as we ran, her skin slipping away like a suit to reveal the terrifying nightmare within. I still see it at night…" she trailed off, shivering lightly.

A single glance around the table was enough to show Nate that Freya's words had had an impact. Even Colin looked disturbed. It was the perfect time for Nate to jump back in.

"If you really want, you can go check it out for yourselves, though I would strongly advise against it. I don't have any proof of this yet, but I suspect that the starred monsters will only be growing more powerful as we go. If that nightmare was any indication, we're going to need a lot more help if we want to get out of here."

"If everyone on the planet can't beat a two-star monster, as you claim," Fiona said. "How are we supposed to make it through alive?"

"I said it's impossible to beat *now*," Nate said. "But it won't be forever. I've gotten a pretty good feel for the monsters in this world and people are going to have a very hard time moving up the ranks once you get into the mid-thirties. The only way to keep progressing is to move on. So, back to my original point. Will you back down for now if I give you a spot where you and your guild can benefit?"

"What makes you think we can't just find this supposed spot on our own?" Colin asked. "We have a map, same as you. I'm *sure* we could figure it out."

"This spot isn't on the map," Nate said. "We found it on our own, and let me tell you, it's unlike anything else you'll come across on this planet."

"How do we know you're telling the truth?" Fiona asked.

"If I lie, you'll know soon enough, and you can go back to your fearmongering and panic-spreading," Nate said with a shrug. "As you clearly know, I want to go back home. I miss my bed and I miss my family. Not all of us were lucky enough to come into this world with them by our sides."

He gave the pair of siblings a hard look.

"Fine," Fiona said, before Colin could say anything. "Give us the spot and we'll stay out of your hair. For now, anyway. But you're going to have to do something for us as well if you want us to stop our 'fearmongering' as you put it."

Nate raised an eyebrow.

"If you're going to insist people keep traveling, you're going to have to take care of whoever is attacking them on the other side. Do that, and we'll not only leave you be, we'll even join your little crusade to go back home."

"Fiona don't go making promises for us!" Colin exclaimed.

"What's the harm?" Fiona asked, turning on her brother. "Do you really think three people can fix everything?"

Colin hesitated, then relaxed as the reality of what Fiona was telling him sunk in.

"You've got a deal," Colin said. "But I'm adding another condition."

Nate was getting sick and tired of bending over backward for these people. Maybe he *should* just kill them.

"You have six weeks," Colin said, sounding smug.

"Fine," Nate said. "But it really seems like a lopsided deal to me with all these conditions you people keep heaping on, so I've got one of my own. If we accomplish everything you've set before us, you're going to owe us."

"Owe you what?" Colin asked with narrowed eyes.

"Oh, you'll see," Nate said with a cold smile. "You'll see."

"What was all that about?" Freya asked as they left the inn just a few minutes later. "All the 'you'll see' stuff? I was half expecting you to start rubbing your hands together and cackling like a madman."

"You watch way too many movies," Nate said.

"I'm not wrong," Freya replied with a grin. "I was totally getting some Dark Lord vibes from you. Care to share anything you've been keeping from us? Do you moonlight as an evil overlord or something?"

"Something like that," Nate answered, moving quickly through the streets and heading in Noam's direction.

He'd left the man alone for long enough. Dealing with Colin and his sister had been a pain, but he hadn't had to kill anyone, which was nice.

The pair moved through the city, slipping between buildings, and dodging through the milling crowds. It still wasn't anywhere near dark, but Nate had a bad feeling that something had gone terribly wrong.

When he arrived at the manor, he found nothing out of place. A quick look around revealed Noam standing with his back to a nearby building and glancing in the general direction of the manor every so often.

"Did anything happen while we were away?" Nate asked, approaching the man.

"A few more people showed up, all wearing the same outfits. Aside from that, nothing. You?"

Freya jumped in, explaining all that had happened, while Nate stared at the manor, wondering what was going on within. None of this added up.

"Woah," Freya said as a group of more than fifty robed figures entered the square, all heading toward the manor.

"We need to get in there," Nate said, watching the stream of people heading into the building.

"How?" Freya asked with a frown. "We won't exactly fit in, and *please* don't tell me we're going to knock a few of them out, tie them up, and sneak in that way."

10

"We're definitely going to be caught," Freya grumbled into Nate's ear as they followed the line of people into the manor.

They had done exactly what Freya had suggested they shouldn't do. Sure, it was cliché and seemed like it shouldn't work, but with over a hundred members gathered within the manor, it would be hard to pick them out. The previous owners of these robes were currently in a dark alley, bound, gagged, and being watched by Noam.

He'd wanted to come, but in the end, agreed to stay back as the guard. The last thing they needed was for the two they'd knocked out to come to, free themselves, and charge in while they were surrounded by potential enemies.

"I told you this would work," Nate said, hiding a grin as the robed guard at the door didn't even give them a second glance.

"Just because we got in doesn't mean we're going to be able to pull this off," Freya said. "Why did it let you talk me into this?"

"Because you trust me completely," Nate said. "Besides, when have I ever steered you wrong?"

Freya gave him a sidelong glare in response and Nate hid a grin as the two of them moved farther into the manor. It was nice enough on the inside. Maybe not the nicest he'd ever seen, but decent for the points needed to own and operate.

People dressed in matching robes were milling about, clustered in small groups and talking amongst one another. Nate was careful to keep Freya close by. He was far more nervous than he was letting on, as he spotted one notorious criminal after the next, their faces standing out in his memory of the past.

Shag Nighthorn had murdered sixteen people in cold blood, trapping them within a building and burning it to the ground. Allen Kirk had tortured his own mother to death. Samantha Pace had killed her entire family over *nothing*.

Right now, they were simply impressionable youths all eagerly gathering here for some reason but they would be responsible for the crimes in the future.

He only recognized a few criminals from back home, people who'd been notorious before coming to Warine. Those, he made sure to avoid, as well as any larger groups of people who might know them.

"How long do you think we have before someone realizes we're not supposed to be here?" Freya asked as Nate stopped by one of the doorways, finding a convenient corner to tuck themselves away into to wait.

"It's unlikely we'll be found out," Nate said, though he wasn't sure he believed it. "There are many people here who don't know one another. Just take a look around and you'll see."

Freya took in the room, noting how everyone was separated into groups. Many people were looking around as well, looking at the manor's interior and wondering what they were doing there.

"Ah," Nate said in an undertone and tilted his chin up. "Looks like things are about to get started."

In the large hall, a figure appeared at the top of the balcony overlooking the gathered people below. Nate frowned as he recognized the familiar and terrifying visage of Simon Dalefield. The man's hands were covered in burn scars, the scar tissue running up both hands and vanishing beneath the billowing sleeves.

The side of his neck was likewise covered in burns, though his face remained clear of any such deformity. His shaggy gray hair hung in snarls around his face, his unkempt beard still flecked with some of the black that had adorned it in earlier years. His face was lined and weathered, his nose crooked and mouth pulled to a hard line.

His eyes were what had always drawn people in. Deep-set and bright blue, they appeared manic, giving the man a haunted appearance. Nate's hand curled into a fist when he saw him, wondering if there was any chance of taking him out now, before he could cause any further harm.

That hope was dashed when the man's hands wrapped around the railing, revealing the mark on the back of his left hand.

Thirty-seven.

The man was beyond his reach for now.

"Who's that?" Freya asked as the noise quieted at Simon's appearance.

"The leader of Ashland," Nate said, keeping his voice down. "He's a famous American serial killer from back home. This is worse than I thought."

He added that last bit so that she wouldn't become suspicious.

"Why are people following someone like that?" Freya asked, her voice tinged with a bit of fear.

"Why did people follow Pavlov?" Nate replied.

Freya didn't reply to that, watching the man as he spread his arms, releasing twin jets of black fire from the tips of his fingers. It was more for show than anything, but it had its intended effect. Everyone quieted and those in other rooms joined, packing the area full of people and squeezing Nate and Freya up against the wall.

He didn't like having his escape route blocked off, but there was little he could do about it now.

Nate half-expected the man to begin speaking, but much to his surprise, Simon remained silent, watching the room with his manic eyes. Nate's frown deepened as the door behind the balcony opened and a woman stepped out, striding purposefully to the balcony and taking the spot beside the serial killer.

She was nearly as tall as the man himself, standing at around 5' 11''. She wore the same robes as everyone else, though they were cut differently, made to fit her figure in a more flattering manner. Long, dark tresses hung down her back, reflecting the sheen from the torches burning in brackets throughout the room.

Her nails were painted the same shade of red as her lips and her green eyes stood out, thanks to a heavy application of shadow around her eyes.

"Who's she?" Freya asked, eyeing the woman nervously.

Nate pursed his lips.

"I have no idea," he replied, feeling his heart rate increase.

He didn't recognize this woman. He'd never seen or even *heard* of someone like her within Ashland's ranks. Yet here she was, standing by Simon's side, and judging from the way the man watched her, *he* was the one deferring in this instance.

Still, Nate had his Kanta Sight, which *should* tell him more about her, but he wasn't going to risk using it until they had an exit. The back of the woman's left hand showed that her rank was equal to that of Simon's at 37, and if she somehow sensed the scan –

69

which was possible – they could find themselves in a bad spot with no way out.

"Welcome," the woman said, her rich voice resonating throughout the hall.

She carried herself with poise, and the way she talked spoke of someone who was used to giving orders and being a part of high society.

"I know that some of you initially opposed the idea of capturing this city rather than burning it to the ground and taking it for all it was worth, but I'm glad to see you all saw it my way."

She flashed a smile, her perfectly white teeth gleaming against her red-painted lips. A low chuckle went through the crowd at that, though Simon looked less than pleased. At this point in Ashland's history, this city should have been their first target. But, if this woman had somehow usurped Simon's authority, history would be changing unpredictably.

This could be so much worse than Nate imagined. He didn't like unknowns.

"Now that we have successfully taken this manor, the city is now under our control. It is the perfect base of operations from which we will begin our conquest. Under my leadership, Ashland will not be some low-level group of thugs who burn and pillage. We will be a guild to *fear*. One which others will flee from at the sound of our name. We own one city now, but in just a few short months, the entire southern part of the continent will be ours."

A low cheer rang through the room, though some seemed less enthusiastic than others.

"I can see that there are still some who doubt my abilities," the woman continued after the applause had died down. "That is perfectly understandable. A singular victory over a rival is not enough to prove myself when you've had such a capable and charismatic leader all this time."

Simon scowled a bit at that but didn't otherwise react to the woman's words.

"I can assure you, however, that just as Twilight Moon fell, so shall the others who think to control the underworld in our territory."

Nate felt his heart skip a beat at that. Twilight Moon had been defeated by *Ashland*? He kept his expression neutral as the

70

woman's eyes swept over the two of them. Nate did everything he could to remain calm as the woman's eyes locked onto him, narrowing ever so slightly as they did.

He felt Freya's grip on his arm tighten, the motion thankfully hidden by the baggy robes they both wore. For a moment, he wondered if this woman had somehow uncovered them despite the large number of people gathered there.

After several heart-stopping moments, her eyes continued to scan the room, allowing Nate to breathe a sigh of relief. It seemed they hadn't been recognized after all.

"I know many of you believe that this world is the one to conquer. That we should put all of our efforts into subjugating Warine to our collective will. I can promise you that far greater treasures await us on the second planet of Laybor."

A low muttering went through the room at that, the people talking amongst themselves. They'd clearly been caught off guard with this proclamation.

"I know this may seem contradictory to what I said just moments ago about conquering the southern part of this continent," she continued, her voice smooth and unbothered. "You have nothing to fear because once we have overtaken the next city in our path, I will lead the strongest of us through the portal to the next world and create a foothold for our future dominion.

"While we are away, Simon will continue our ultimate goal. The mission that drew us all together in the first place. We were dealt a terrible hand when the man in the sky forced us from our homes, but now that we're here, I can see that this was a blessing in disguise.

"Ashland wasn't meant to be some backwater guild of nobodies. We were not meant to be a group of wanton murderers who reveled in destruction. We were made for *greater* things!"

The woman paused, her eyes gleaming with the light of internal fervor, the very same that was reflected at her from the entire crowd, all enraptured by her speech.

"We will rule not only Warine, not only Laybor, but *every single planet* in the entire system! When all is said and done, Ashland will reign supreme!"

Nate felt a chill run down his spine as the room erupted into thunderous applause. It seemed the people here liked the idea of ruling everything and being part of the group that would be in charge.

Now, they had a bigger problem. Not only would they need someone to resist them here on Warine, but someone would need to follow Ashland into Laybor to stop them there as well. In his previous life, Ashland had been a pain. Yes, they'd been dangerous, but dangerous in the way of a wild animal on the loose.

This version of Ashland was far more so. With a cunning and unknown leader at its head and Simon's appeal, they could likely accomplish exactly what this woman was setting out to do.

"Come on," Nate muttered to Freya, as the woman raised her arms, a dazzling smile spreading her lips. "I think it's time to leave."

The pair of them began moving through the packed crowd, making for the nearest exit. There was enough movement in the crowd to mask their passage. The woman continued to turn, flashing her perfect smile at everyone, waving to the gathered fanatics and bowing gracefully.

Forget Simon; this woman was far more charismatic than he'd ever been. She knew how to work a crowd. Knew how to speak. To match their levels of energy and synergize with what they were all feeling. In other words, she was an amazing actor.

"Looks like we're home free," Freya said as they finally made their way to the open door.

Seeing as they finally had an easy escape route, Nate used his Kanta Sense to scan the woman. He had barely begun his scan when her head whipped in his direction, her eyes locking onto his and widening in both anger and recognition of what he was doing.

Her aura, which had been a pale yellow, rapidly began to darken, turning all the way to dark orange as she raised a hand, clearly intending them harm.

Thankfully, their backs were to the door. Whirling, Nate shoved Freya out, ducking behind the frame to put themselves out of her line of fire. No one else had noticed just yet, but he knew it would only be a matter of seconds.

"We've been discovered," Nate said, grabbing Freya's hand and running from the manor. "We need to get out of the city and *fast*!"

11

Freya pulled her hand from Nate's grip as they rounded a corner and began to outstrip him as she fell into her proper running form. Nate seemed to keep forgetting that the tall woman had been a runner back on Earth, and once again, his untrained body failed to keep up properly, forcing her to slow down for him.

It was embarrassing, though he didn't let it show. She had training. He didn't, so he needed to play catchup. The two of them didn't say a word, tearing through the city until they came to the alley where Noam was standing guard over the pair of Ashland Guild members.

"What happened?" he asked as they tore into the alley.

The guild members had come to and were struggling against their ropes. One of them had a nasty bruise on the side of his head, and the other's face and hair were caked in blood. They hadn't killed either of them, but they wouldn't be feeling too great over the next few days.

"We were made," Nate said, breathing hard as he came to a stumbling halt. "We need to get out of the city as quickly as we can."

"Calm down," Noam said. "Take a breath. They'll be looking for a couple of people in Ashland robes. Change back to your normal clothes and we'll be able to leave without being recognized."

Nate wasn't too sure about that. The woman had looked him right in the eye. If she saw him, she would recognize him.

"Would you mind holding up the tarp?" Freya asked Noam.

The man grunted, taking the proffered tarp and holding it up, giving her some privacy. Nate, in the meantime, quickly stripped out of the Ashland robes and into his normal clothes. The Froster-Drake hide armor was smooth and well-fitting, conforming to his body nicely. He felt much better wearing them, as the robes had flapped and tangled his legs as he'd been running.

Nate was ready faster than Freya and felt the passing of time like it was a physical force. He kept looking over his shoulder, half-expecting the terrifying woman to come barreling into the alley, hands raised and ready to cast her spells. She had been able to sense his scan, which meant she must have a sensory spell of her own.

There was no telling what type of sensory spell it was, as there was a massive range, from increased vision to being able to sense vibrations in the ground. One common thread they all had was that when someone used a sensory skill directed at them, they would know and be able to locate the source.

If she had used whatever spell she had on him, Nate would have known, just as she had.

"Ready," Freya said, allowing Noam to lower the tarp.

"Great," Noam said, eyeing the two tied-up Ashland members. "Now, we're going to leave the alley and walk calmly toward the nearest gate. Freya, take your scrunchie out of your hair. A change in style will further throw suspicion. Nate..." Noam pursed his lips. "Mess up your hair as best you can."

Nate did as he was told, running his fingers through his hair and intentionally messing it up until Noam seemed pleased. He looked over to Freya, whose long, golden-blonde hair now fell in a smooth curtain down her back. It looked nice out of her usual ponytail, allowing several thick strands to frame her face. She quickly tucked them behind her ears to allow a better field of vision.

"Good," Noam said, nodding in satisfaction. "You can tell me what happened while we're moving."

Nate didn't want to walk calmly. He wanted to bolt for the gate and run for all he was worth. Even if they could somehow stand up against that woman, the entire guild was here. As strong as their small group was, there was no way they could stand up to that many fighters. Heck, they would be hard-pressed to stay alive against the one woman.

If Simon decided to join in, they were toast, as the man would burn them all to death.

The three of them strode from the alleyway, walking calmly and leaving the bound and gagged members of Ashland for their comrades to find. Nate would have preferred to kill them, but he knew that the others wouldn't condone cold-blooded murder, so he'd let it go. If they came across them again, he wouldn't hesitate to end them.

"Stay calm and act natural," Noam said, as a trio of robed figures ran past, scanning the crowd for their quarry.

Nate had to fight the urge to fidget or speed up. He knew that this approach was much better than running. If they were spotted, they would be pursued even after they left the city. However, it went against his every instinct. Every second they stayed within the city was another in which they could be caught.

"Care to fill me in on what happened?" Noam asked. "Clearly, something didn't go your way."

"Everything was fine up until we were leaving," Freya said, glancing at Nate. "They had two leaders instead of one, which wasn't what we were expecting. It seems like they're bent on world domination instead of burning everything to the ground, though I did get the impression that they'd murder anyone who got in their way."

"That seems different from what you told me," Noam said to Nate.

"Like I said, it isn't exact," Nate replied, his lips pursed. "There was only supposed to be *one* leader of Ashland. He was there, as expected, but the woman was a surprise."

"Do you know who she is?"

Nate shook his head, his brows furrowing.

"I used a technique I have, something I acquired a few weeks ago but didn't mention. It's called Kanta Sight. It allows me to see things about people, and before you get mad that I didn't tell you, I kept it a secret for the same reason I did with my Augment. It's a dangerous technique to have."

Noam didn't respond to that, though Freya looked a little hurt that he'd kept yet another secret from them. He could have told them the truth, that he'd only picked it up a couple of days ago, but this fit his narrative far better. It would further explain how he knew things.

"Anyway," he continued. "The technique isn't perfect. If the person I'm trying to scan has a sensory technique or spell of their own, they'll be able to tell if I'm looking. The woman found out, so all I got was a name. Selena Maylard."

By the look on his companions' faces, neither of them knew who she was either. That was hardly surprising, given that they hadn't returned from the future like he had. What troubled him was the fact that he had no clue who she was. She had not even existed in the previous timeline as far as he knew. Definitely not to the point where he'd ever heard mention of her name.

Only Simon's name had come up in association with the Ashland Guild. If Selena was to be believed, then Twilight Moon, a guild that had *far* surpassed Ashland in power in the previous timeline, had been wiped out. The two guilds had clashed in his previous time, but in each and every instance, Twilight Moon had driven them off.

In fact, it was after one of these encounters that the allied force of the guilds struck at Simon's group when they were already reeling from a terrible loss. This was another unknown, one that threw yet another wrench in his plans.

Whoever this Selena was, she needed to die. They had only one lead right now and one opportunity to strike back at her. She would be leaving Warine with a smaller group and traveling to Laybor. Yes, the group would be strong, but it would be small in number.

"What's going on in that head of yours?" Noam asked as they approached the gates.

Shockingly, they had yet to be stopped, though Nate could see a half-dozen members of Ashland standing before the gates, interrogating people as they were trying to leave.

"The mission hasn't changed," Nate said. "Ashland still needs to be stopped; it's just going to take more work now. We'll have to enlist some help to at least slow them down on Warine, while we go to Laybor and handle them on that side."

"It seems like a lot of things are piling up here," Freya said worriedly. "Are you sure we can handle it all?"

Currently, they all had to reach the 30th rank and head over to Laybor, find out which guild was Portal Reaving and kill them all before Colin's six-week deadline. They also had to thwart Selena's attempt to spread Ashland's power and influence here, then find and deal with her group in Laybor *and* make sure the maps had continued to spread through the southern part of the continent before the eventual collapse of the planet.

Piece of cake.

The group went silent as they reached the gates, a pair of people in robes walking up to them, their postures aggressive.

"Why are you leaving the city?" one of them asked, sticking their face in Nate's.

"I was unaware that I had to ask random strangers for permission to go where I please," Nate replied coolly.

"Answer the question," the second man said.

"It's none of your business," Nate replied, crossing his arms.

He knew that there was a chance they would make a scene here, but they clearly didn't recognize him, so he was acting like anyone would in a situation like this. They were on the attack, so he was going to be defensive.

"Don't make us force the answers out of you," the first man said, narrowing his eyes. "You won't like what we do to people who don't cooperate."

Noam's ax was at the man's throat in an instant, the half-moon blade pressed to the side of his neck.

"Do you really want to start a fight over something so stupid?" Noam asked, sounding almost bored. "I don't know what you people want or who you think you are, but this world doesn't belong to you. So, we can come and go as we please without giving out our personal information to random strangers in creepy robes."

The others, who'd been interrogating people, came to join them when they saw the ax.

"What's going on here?" one of them asked.

He sounded aggressive and like he was looking for any reason to start a fight.

"We want to leave the city," Nate said calmly. "But for some reason, your buddy thinks he's entitled to know why. So, unless you want my friend here to give him a haircut, I'd suggest you step out of our way and let us be off."

For a moment, Nate wondered if this was going to devolve into a fight. It would be three against six, but a quick scan had already shown him that these aggressive and posturing people were all in the teens as far as ranks went. The difference in strength wouldn't be huge, but the difference in skill and technique would be, as not a single one of them had a 2nd tier tome or manual.

People were starting to look and stopped to watch the exchange by the gate. Several of them recognized Nate from earlier when he'd been handing out the maps and began to move forward. Seeing that they would be outmatched if they decided to start something, the third man decided to do the smart thing.

"Step aside, Mikey," he finally said, his lips pressed to a hard line. "Let these…fine people be on their way."

Noam slowly lowered his ax, though he kept it in his hand, as the first man stepped aside, glaring daggers at the three of them as they passed.

"This isn't over," Noam said as they walked through the gates, feeling the glares of the Ashland guild members following them.

"I know," Nate said, resisting the urge to turn around.

They'd hurt the group's pride, and that was far worse than simply throwing a punch.

12

"Well, that's a relief," Freya said once they lost sight of the city walls. "I'm honestly shocked we managed to make it out of there without a fight."

"I wouldn't celebrate just yet. They're going to come after us," Nate said.

"*All* of them?" Freya asked, going a bit pale.

"Not likely," Noam said. "If I had to guess, it'll be the group that we embarrassed. They'll probably come after us on their own, without telling anyone where they're going. We should be able to dispose of them without having the rest of the guild on top of us."

"While I don't like the idea of having to kill more people, I'm glad we won't be starting it. Though I will hold out hope that you're wrong," Freya said. "Speaking of, is there any reason we need to stop Ashland's advance through Warine if the planet is going to blow up in a few months?"

Nate had thought about that himself but hadn't had to think about it for long.

"Despite what that woman said about not wanting to burn everything down, they'll still kill anyone who gets in their way," Nate said. "The more people they kill, the stronger they'll become. We're trying to stop them in their infancy before they become too powerful to stop."

"I guess that makes sense…" she said, trailing off and her brows coming together.

"That didn't pan out how we were planning," Noam said. "But it seems you were at least right about one thing."

"Does that mean I'm off the hook?" Nate asked.

"Not quite," Noam replied. "We have yet to see how this is all going to work out. For now, I'm content to keep traveling with you, unless I come to believe otherwise."

Knowing that they were likely to be followed, Nate didn't bother with their scooters, keeping their pace light and easy, making sure their enemies could find them. If they were going to be attacked, they may as well get an easy rest of the day out of it.

"Where are we headed?" Freya asked as they wound their way down the road.

"We're going to Southside Eight," Nate answered. "It's about five days of good traveling, though it'll probably take us around a week, seeing as we'll be taking breaks to fight monsters to get our ranks up. Once we reach the city, we'll make our last drop of maps and then I'll go looking for a friend."

"How can you be sure this friend of yours will be there?" Noam asked.

"I can't," Nate said with a shrug. "But let's just say I've got a good feeling about it."

The group made camp as the last of the sunlight began to fade, though none of them went to sleep. Noam helped Nate rig up a series of snares around the perimeter to warn them of any incoming attackers or monsters. They weren't too far off the road, so the only ones who would be bothering them were likely those already on their trail.

Nate bit into his bland rations, staring into the gloom as the stars winked out overhead. He felt as though the weight of the world rested on his shoulders, and it was showing. Things had been rough over the last few days. Fewer fights and more scheming and travel. They were falling further and further behind, and he knew that if they were going to be contenders, they were going to need to buckle down and make some progress.

The only problems with that were their timeline, Ashland's conquest, and the unknown Portal Reavers who needed to be stopped. All of this needed to be done with just the three of them, as his fourth hopeful teammate wouldn't show up for quite some time. As far as he knew, they were off to the south, despite being not only from the US but the same *state* as Nate himself.

"What pervy thoughts are going on inside that head of yours?"

Nate started as Freya's face loomed before his, her lips twisted in a playful smile. She grinned wider at his reaction and sat back, looking satisfied.

"Looks like I caught you red-handed."

She *had* caught him off guard, that much was true. A snort of laughter escaped him as Freya shoved the last of her meal – more unappetizing protein mush – into her mouth, still grinning like a cat that caught a mouse.

"You know, if I said something like that to you, it would be considered rude," Nate said.

"Perks of being a girl," Freya replied smugly. "I get to say what I want and all you can do is stutter and fumble for a reply to my genius."

"You call what you just did genius?" Nate asked with a raised eyebrow.

"I *did* basically read your mind," Freya said, still grinning. "So, what was it? Give me all the juicy details. I don't want you to leave anything out."

Freya's hand flashed to the Magigun at her side as her eyes narrowed, the weapon already out of its holster and leveled to Nate's left before the light tinkle of the alarm they'd set went off.

Her index finger depressed the trigger and a blaze of burning red flashed past him. Nate and Noam were on their feet in an instant, the latter drawing his tomahawks, while Nate readied himself for battle.

There was a cry of pain as Freya's Blazing Bullet found its mark, though there was no thud of a body hitting the ground. Whoever she'd shot was still very much alive.

"Man, do I like this toy you got me," Freya said, already on her feet and depressing the trigger again.

It was unsurprising that she'd spotted the enemy before they had. With her Augment, her eyesight would be many times greater than the others on her team, especially with the magnification aspect.

"Incoming," she warned, firing several more shots into the gloom.

Nate's eyes flicked around, spotting shapes moving at the very edges of his vision. It might have been brighter at night in Warine than on Earth, but it *was* still nighttime, which meant decreased visibility.

Five figures appeared, all dressed in Ashland robes. They were approaching from the direction in which Freya had begun firing her spells. Two of the attackers raised their hands, one glowing silver and the other black.

Nate's Goldshield appeared as a beam of condensed sliver streaked toward them, the attack rebounding off the construct and streaking back at the one who'd fired it. The man let out a yelp, diving to one side as Freya's Blazing Bullet caught him in the face.

There was a horrible sizzling sound as the spell tore through the man's left eye, burning out the socket and cooking his brain. The man was dead before he hit the ground. The second magician's spell was a bit trickier, manifesting in a black line that wavered like a heat mirage on a hot day.

Nate's shield couldn't track it, and neither could he, so he did what anyone would do in a situation like this – he threw himself to the ground.

He felt the searing heat as it passed by overhead, missing him by inches. Thankfully, it wasn't a wide-ranging one spell, because Nate had once again been made the target. Noam's shout hit the charging group a moment later as he used Guardian's Draw. Immediately, the group's attention switched to him, the remaining four fighters all running toward him.

Guardian's Dread hit them a moment later, causing them to stumble in their tracks. Nate was back on his feet, with Freya continuing to fire her Blazing Bullet. She was aiming for the magician, while Nate and Noam fell upon the cultivators.

Nate dashed toward the lead man, ducking a clumsy punch and driving his fist into the man's stomach. The man doubled over, and a glowing dirk drove through the back of his skull. A rush of kanta flowed into Nate as the man's body toppled, blood spraying from the deadly wound.

He frowned as he noted the man's rank of 8, moving on to the next, who tried to brain him with a swing of a wooden cudgel. Nate raised an arm, his Gilded Skin appearing in an instant. His arm reverberated with the force of the blow, dull pain radiating through the limb. However, the difference in rank made up for it.

This man was even weaker than the last at the 7th rank, and while he could still cause damage – and kill Nate if he wasn't careful – the man's blows could be blocked one-handed even when swinging such a heavy weapon.

The man's eyes went wide for an instant before Nate's fist drove into his nose with a loud *crack*, blood spurting as he reeled. In a single motion, he swung his hand, his backsword appearing in a gleam of gold and slashing the man's throat wide. Blood sprayed in the air as he fell, kanta rushing into Nate as the body toppled.

He turned, prepared to continue fighting, only to see that Freya and Noam had finished the rest. The former was looking around, still holding her Magigun, while the latter was removing one of his tomahawks from a man's chest. It came free with a dull *crunch*, dragging blood and viscera along with it.

"That was too easy," Noam said, scanning the men's faces. "I don't recognize any of them, do you?"

"No," Nate said, eyeing the others.

None of these fighters had been at the gate during their confrontation, which could mean only one thing – they had been fodder, though Nate didn't know why.

"You see anything?" he asked, turning to Freya, who was now actively using her Augment to scan their surroundings.

"Nothing," Freya said, her eyes flicking around.

Nate pursed his lips. He didn't like this.

"We're moving out," he decided, grabbing the few belongings they'd unpacked when stopping for the night.

Neither the tent nor the tarp had been rigged, and now, Nate was glad they'd forgone that small comfort. It made it easier to get moving. He pulled his scooter from his ring and the others followed his example.

"Do you think there are more coming?" Freya asked, looking over her shoulder as Nate kicked off down the road.

"You can count on it," he replied grimly.

"Do you think that woman is onto us?" Noam asked, speeding up to match his pace.

"It's possible someone spoke to her and gave our descriptions," Nate replied. "She only saw my face for a second, but that might have been enough for someone like her."

He hated not knowing who this Selena woman was, or what her capabilities were. If there was one advantage he had in this timeline, it was that he knew what would happen. The fact that there was a complete unknown here was throwing him for a loop, but he had to remain calm and collected. Otherwise, things wouldn't end well.

"I think something's catching up to us," Freya said after about twenty minutes of silence.

"What is it?" Nate asked, not daring to risk a glance over his shoulder.

Freya squinted, turning her head once again.

"It looks like another group from Ashland. They're on...well, I'm not really sure *what* it is, but they're moving pretty quickly."

"Animals or objects?" Nate asked.

"Some sort of vehicle," Freya replied. "It looks like a bike, but it has five wheels and is carrying three passengers apiece."

He knew they were called Quinto Riders. It was a form of bicycle on Warine, adapted to the types of roads and rolling hills that dotted the planet. The five-wheel construction offered better balance, control, and a smoother ride. Each wheel was mounted to its own shock system that moved with the terrain. Additionally, the fifth wheel would move on its own if the Quinto Rider was charged with kanta. It wouldn't increase their speed by much, but it would make pedaling easier.

"How many are there?" Nate asked.

"Only two bike things as far as I can tell," Freya replied.

That meant six more attackers.

"Let's try picking up the pace," Nate said. "Look for a spot that'll give us an edge in battle. If you can, Freya, give us some cover."

They couldn't risk her using any of her powerful spells, as they needed to preserve their kanta. If Ashland were going to keep coming after them, they were going to need every ounce of power they could muster, which meant no burning out early.

Several tense minutes passed as the group leaned into their scooters, kicking harder to give them more speed, even when going downhill. However, the Quinto Riders had larger wheels and were built for greater speed. They continued to gain on them to the point where Nate could begin to hear the scrape of the wheels over the dirt road.

Freya's Magigun flashed as she fired her Blinding Buckshot a couple of times. Screams and curses followed as the group fell back, but seeing as no retaliation was incoming, Nate had to assume the group was made up entirely of cultivators.

"I can't hold them off forever," Freya said as she fired a Blazing Bullet that went wide.

Trying to hit a moving target while also moving was extremely difficult, and even the most skilled marksmen would have a hard time making a shot like that. Freya had plenty of practice with a gun, but even her aim wasn't *that* good.

"Found a spot," Noam called. "An eighth of a mile off the road. There."

He pointed and Nate followed the line of his finger, finding the spot easily. It was a raised ridge protruding from the side of a small hill. If they could reach it quickly enough, it would give them an edge, forcing their cultivator enemies to come up the hill to attack them. Additionally, it would give Freya free rein to unload on them without them being able to retaliate.

Nate kicked his scooter to the side, leaping off and landing in a sprint, pulling the scooter into his ring as he did so. Noam and Freya's dismounts weren't nearly as smooth, but they caught up with and overtook him within a handful of seconds, all making a mad dash for the hill.

13

Freya's Magigun blazed as she fired back at the approaching group, the six fighters from Ashland yelling and whooping as they closed the distance.

"Spot any ranks?" Nate asked, breathing harder as he fought to keep up with his two teammates – being the slowest in the group was starting to get old.

"I think I caught a two on one of them," Freya said, turning back and continuing to run.

That didn't really mean anything. The two could have come before or after, meaning they could be in the 20s or simply have the number 2 somewhere in their ranks. Freya *did* say that she didn't recognize any of them, which didn't bode well.

Noam was the first to reach the hill, sprinting up the small rise and whirling to face their enemies. His tomahawks were already in his hands by the time Freya reached him, and her first spell was already blazing by when Nate reached the crest of the hill a couple of seconds after.

He turned, his chest heaving from the exertion, and fought to calm his breathing. Freya backed further up the hill, putting the two of them between her and their enemies. The bikes stopped at the foot of the hill, the fighters forced off them by Freya's stream of Blazing Bullets.

Just as Freya had said, there were six in all – four men and two women, all cultivators. Now that they weren't running, Nate could see the markings on their hands, and he didn't like what he saw. The entire group ranged from 19 at the lowest to 23 at the highest. The one at the 19th rank might go down easier, but the others most certainly would not. Their group was only a tiny drop more advanced, and in this battle, numbers would be to their opponents' advantage. However, due to the slope of the hill, they'd only be able to attack two or three at a time, so if the fight didn't drag out, Nate knew his group could have a pretty good chance of winning.

The deciding factor would be experience and the tiers of their manuals and techniques.

Freya's Blazing Bullet tore through the air, whipping up a small breeze in its wake. The spell had been aimed at the man in the lead, a hulking brute who filled the Ashland robes quite well. His body shimmered and Nate swore, recognizing the telltale armor of Flameguard.

Ashland was famous for using a specific type of manual when it came to cultivation, as many had wanted to follow in Simon's footsteps. It was why so many of them had fire-aspect abilities. Of course, none of them had Simon's one-of-one Manual of the Hellfire Archdemon, but the one their guild picked was no joke.

For the cultivators, it was the Path of the Flame Titan. It was on the Limited list but was limited to 3,000 instead of being rarer. Still, it was a powerful manual if used correctly, and it seemed that this man had been doing things right.

Flameguard was a 2nd tier technique, one that was learned after advancing the Manual of the Flame Titan, and it was every bit as good as his own Gilded Skin. In fact, it was even better when it came to certain types of attacks – such as those made of fire, for example.

Freya's Blazing Bullet slammed into the man and exploded in a blaze of sparks against his skin. The man didn't slow down, continuing his rush up the hill.

Noam ran past Nate, his tomahawks clutched in his hands, his voice ringing with the power of his Guardian's Dread. It hit the hulking man like a physical blow, causing him to stumble for a second, and that was all Noam needed.

The tomahawks blurred in his hands, slashing and hacking at the man's arms, legs, and chest. The hulking man staggered back, throwing his arms up to defend himself. Small jets of flames exploded from his body at each impact and Nate grimaced at the paltry damage Noam was inflicting on the man. Still, he *was* managing to keep him occupied, which was good, as there were five more people to deal with.

Freya switched her target to the woman running for Noam, forcing her back. Flickering flames flowed across her skin, instead of the shimmering heat, meaning she only had the first-tier technique, Flameshield, which was far weaker and more easily overwhelmed.

"Don't use fire spells on anyone who's got a shield," Nate called back as he ran at the first attacker.

The woman raised an arm as Nate lashed out with a powerful kick, pivoting on his back leg to keep his balance and lend the blow more power. His Gilded Skin flowed over his body as he attacked, not wanting to risk physical contact with someone using Flameshield. As the name implied, it was a shield made of flames, which would protect the defender and hurt the attacker.

She crossed her arms as Nate's kick struck, trying to take the blow, but gravity and physics were working against her and the woman was tossed off her feet, tumbling partway down the hill. One of the men dashed in to take her place, his body also flickering with the Flameshield.

The biggest issue with the Path of the Flame Titan was its versatility. Everyone got the same shielding techniques, but the second ones were always different, as they depended on the wielder. When the man conjured a sword made of living flames, Nate was hardly surprised.

His Gilded Blade appeared in his right hand, the backsword flashing up to deflect the blow. However, it seemed that it was *he* who'd forgotten the laws of physics this time, as the blade of fire passed clean through his own sword, cutting down against his armored skin.

The man who'd attacked had already positioned himself in a way that would avoid Nate's strike, so while his sword bit into the ground, the man's slashed into his skin. The blade of flames didn't cut like an ordinary sword, splashing against his armor and leaving a glowing line of superheated metal in its wake.

Nate hissed in pain as his skin beneath the armor began to burn, forcing him to dismiss it. The man lunged at the opening, stabbing with the sword, only for Freya's Blinding Buckshot to explode in his face.

The man howled, staggering away and clutching at his eyes as his sight vanished in a blaze of white. Nate's armor flowed back into place in an instant, the metal having cooled the moment it had been dismissed. His broadsword appeared as he slashed down, using the full strength of both his body and gravity to bring it crashing down on the man's shoulder.

The man buckled, dropping to the ground as his armor flared, trying to keep the blade from biting into him. However, while the Flameshield excelled at blocking magical fire-based attacks, it was a bit less effective against physical ones – especially those made by a 2nd tier cultivator like Nate.

The broadsword sheared through the armor, sending jets of flames spewing in all directions. Freya's spells flashed past him as a third attacker tried to break the line, and he silently thanked her as he dismissed the broadsword and lifted his arms again.

A second one appeared, and he swung downward. The man lifted his blazing blade to parry, instinct guiding him more than anything, and it was that instinct that cost him his life. Nate's broadsword cleaved through the weakened section of his armor, sheaving at an angle through his collarbone and into the center of his chest.

The broadsword vanished as a wave of kanta slammed into him, filling his core further. Nate kicked the man's body back, hoping to buy himself a bit of time, only for the massive man to rush past Noam and charge him.

Blazing gauntlets appeared over his hands as Noam spun away, the man's body radiating heat as he charged. Nate prepared himself for a fight, only for a spell to smash into him. The man vanished in a flash, appearing halfway down the hill. He staggered, then leaned over and vomited as Freya's Tele-bang spell took effect.

However, it left the path wide open, and three more attackers charged them, the two women and one man. They all had the Flameshield active, showing they were all 1st tier cultivators, but one and all were in the 20s as far as ranking went.

One of the women came straight for him, her steps smooth and swift. She moved with an unnatural grace, and a single glance at the ground told Nate why. Small bursts of flame shot from her feet as she ran, propelling her forward at greater speeds and giving her far better control over her movements.

A pair of gleaming daggers appeared in her hands as she closed and Nate took a step back, his Gilded Skin flowing over his body once again. He swayed aside, avoiding the first dagger strike, but a shriek of metal-on-metal followed as a second found its mark, scraping along the underside of his armpit as she ducked a punch, trying to cut him open.

He whirled, throwing a back fist, but she was fast, slipping away from the blow and stepping forward. The dagger drove into his belly, forcing him back a step, but once again, the armor kept it from penetrating. He still felt the force of the blow reverberate through him. His armor might be good at stopping attacks from piercing him, but it wasn't designed to cushion any impacts.

The woman lunged at him again as he stabbed at her and missed, only for Freya's Tele-bang to slam into her as well. The woman was teleported off the side of the hill, swaying in place and clutching at her head. Suddenly free, Nate turned, seeing that Noam had his hands full. The second woman and man were both concentrating their attacks on him, and while he was holding his own, it was clear that he was having a tough time.

"Keep them off us!" Nate called as a third attacker came rushing up at them.

Freya's Magigun barked, and this time, it wasn't blinding white or red that fired from the barrel. The spell that flashed from her Magigun slammed into the ground in the midst of their enemies. The man who'd been advancing on Nate had slowed when the woman fired in his direction, but seeing as she'd seemingly missed, he advanced once again, grinning wickedly.

He held a curved saber in one hand and a round buckler in the other. No Flameshield flickered around him, but lines of red traced his arms and legs. It was an enhancer-type manual that Nate wasn't familiar with. Before he could look into it further using his Kanta Sight, Freya's Shattering Shrapnel went off with a *bang,* sending sharpened fragments of kanta tearing into the man's unprotected legs.

He wasn't the only one who'd been hit. As he dropped to his knees, screaming in pain as blood gushed from his torn legs, the woman hounding Noam was driven away as well, close enough to the explosion of shrapnel that it partially tore into her Flameshield. Small beads of blood appeared on her robes as she was thrown off her feet, leaving Noam clear to concentrate on a single target.

His opponent wasn't nearly as skilled as he was at hand-to-hand fighting, and with a few decisive strikes, Noam put the man on his back. Both tomahawks came down, crunching into his chest. The man twitched a couple of times, then stopped moving.

At the same time, Nate attacked his fallen opponent, driving a summoned backsword into the base of his neck. The man didn't go down without a fight, and although blood sprayed from his neck, he swung at Nate's ankle with his sword.

The impact was hard and left a visible dent in the metal covering Nate's foot. Worse was the loud *crack* that echoed as he staggered away, white-hot needles of pain shooting up his leg. Nate tried to catch himself, but his broken ankle flared and he toppled to one side.

A shadow loomed over him as he tried to right himself, and he turned in time to see a glittering blade just inches from his eye.

14

Nate's eye slammed shut by reflex and he felt a stabbing pain in his skull as the blade smashed into his sealed eyelid. His head smashed back into the ground, the world spinning as the blunt-force impact radiated through his skull. It was only thanks to his Gilded Skin that he hadn't lost the eye – or been killed, for that matter – as the metal covered even his eyelids.

The woman was clearly surprised that he wasn't dead, as she didn't react immediately. It was a good thing, as Nate was still stunned by the attack. She moved to attack him as he tried to clear his head, only for Freya's Blinding Buckshot to smash into her face.

She screamed, staggering back, giving Nate the opportunity to strike. He couldn't stand on his broken ankle, so he did what his enemy had and swung his summoned backsword into her ankle with all his might.

The powerful blade sheared through her Flameshield, slicing clean through the limb and sending the woman toppling over, blood fountaining from her severed foot. Nate rolled as she fell, summoning his dirk and jamming it into her thigh.

With a powerful yank, he dragged her body down, the woman still screaming and thrashing as she tried to free herself. Screams of metal on metal sounded as her daggers ripped across his armor. More spells flew above him, and he heard Noam yell again, but Nate was too busy concentrating on his battle on the ground.

The woman lunged at him as he dismissed his dagger, half-turning onto her side as she jammed it into his ribs. Pain flared at the point of impact, but he ignored it, using his Steelshod and driving a fist into her jaw. A small jet of flames escaped the woman's remaining foot, throwing her back a bit and preventing the blow from being lethal.

However, it clipped her hard enough to tear her cheek open and daze her momentarily. It was the instant Nate needed. With a yell, he shoved his body forward, using both his arms to drag himself. He then pushed up, summoned a dirk in both hands, then allowed his body to drop, using his full weight to drive the weapon into the center of her forehead.

The woman thrashed as her skull caved in under the driving force of his dagger, her arms and legs flailing. Then her body went still, allowing Nate to roll off her and onto his back, breathing hard. Kanta slammed into him in a wave, and he felt the advancement to the 27th rank hit him. He was forced to dismiss his Gilded Skin then, revealing a series of burn marks beneath. The woman's Flameshield had been going the entire time, heating up the metal cloaking his body. However, he'd forced himself to keep it active, knowing that releasing it would mean injuries that were *far* worse.

The battle wasn't over yet. There were two left and one of them was the hulking 2nd tier cultivator. Nate shoved up on his hands, trying to think of some way he could help, only to see the remaining two fighters running away.

The surviving woman and the hulking man were retreating, running for the Quinto Riders they'd left at the base of the hill. Much to Nate's annoyance, they took them both, each hopping onto one and pedaling away from the battle.

"Should we go after them?" Noam asked, coming over to his side.

He had a deep gash across his right forearm and his face was marred by an ugly burn.

"We'll never catch them," Nate groaned, forcing himself into a sitting position.

His body ached all over and he didn't even want to look at his ankle.

"Are you okay?" Freya asked, running over to join them.

Of the three, she was the least injured in that she hadn't been touched by the battle at all. That was good. It was how it should be. Magicians didn't belong on the frontlines, and it was only because of her that the battle had gone so smoothly.

"We'll live," Nate said. "Thanks to you."

"We need to keep moving," Noam said.

"I'm not going anywhere," Nate groaned, already concentrating on cycling his Kanta.

It would take a few hours to restore his ankle to pristine condition, though if he rushed it, he could make it manageable within the hour. It would hurt to travel on it though.

"I can help speed this up," Noam said, crouching and placing his hand on Nate's ankle.

"You need to reserve your kanta," Nate said. "This isn't over, and you know it."

"I have plenty to spare," Noam replied. "Besides, if we don't move now, we'll probably have to fight before you're ready and that'll put us in an even worse spot than me being low on power."

Nate couldn't argue with that, so he just shut his mouth, nodded, then closed his eyes and concentrated on healing. His kanta regenerated naturally, even in battle. He also had the Kanta Orb, which he hadn't had to dip into just yet, thanks to his natural regeneration. The others would be running out far faster than he was.

Freya's Mediation wasn't nearly on the level of his technique and Noam didn't have one. He would restore his kanta the same way everyone else would.

A warm sensation spread from where Noam's hand was pressed, soothing the swelling in the ankle. At the same time, Nate bent his will to restore himself. This was still going to take some time, given that Noam could likely only keep his end up for a minute or two without dropping to dangerously low levels of kanta, but it would considerably shorten the amount of time he needed to remain off his feet.

If all went well, they could be up and moving within the next ten minutes. His ankle would still hurt, but he could work on soothing it as they moved. It wouldn't be nearly as effective as when he was still and could give it his full concentration, but it was better than nothing.

Freya sat next to him and began recovering her kanta. She'd used quite a bit in her battle as well, his senses told him as much. She had perhaps a quarter of her usual capacity remaining, while Noam's was rapidly dropping. He'd had around half at the end of the battle, as he'd been relying more on his physical attacks than ones enhanced by techniques. The silence stretched until Noam backed away, letting out a slow breath.

"That's the best I can do for now," he said, wiping at his forehead and leaving a smear of crimson in his wake.

It was only then that he seemed to notice the cut. He placed his hand on his arm and Nate noticed the dark 26 stamped there. It seemed his rank had gone up as well. A glance to his left showed a matching number on the back of Freya's left hand. All of them had benefitted from the fight, but Nate knew it was far from over.

Two of their attackers had escaped and there would be a target on their backs. If, by some miracle, they'd managed to slip under the radar before, there was no chance of that now. Someone truly powerful would be in the next group and Nate didn't want to be anywhere near there when they came looking for him.

Southside Eight was still quite a distance from here, but now, it had not only become their goal, but in all honesty, their only refuge.

Well, the only safe *refuge anyway,* Nate thought as he concentrated on knitting the bone back together.

Noam's technique had already done most of the work, removing inflammation, soothing the torn ligaments, and repairing most of the bone. It was now his job to fuse it all back together and not rush, otherwise, he'd undo the man's hard work and be forced to start from scratch.

"Are you ready to get moving?" Noam asked around ten minutes later when Nate opened his eyes.

"Should be," he said. "Would you mind giving me a hand?"

The man took Nate's proffered arm, helping him to get to his feet. Nate was careful to keep the weight off his ankle until he was standing. Slowly, he allowed his weight to settle onto the ankle. It still hurt – just as he'd been expecting – and felt a bit stiff, but overall, it felt more like a mild sprain than a break by this point, which was good enough for him.

"I'm ready to go," Nate said. "Though I won't be running anywhere for the next few hours."

"Let's hope for all our sakes that we don't have to," Noam replied.

"Can't we catch a break?" Freya complained, swerving hard to one side as a streak of fire blasted into the ground, sending a shower of dirt into the air.

It hadn't even been an hour since they'd set off from the hill and Ashland was back on them. This time, they'd come prepared. A group of fifteen fighters were right on their tail, carrying several magicians within their ranks.

Additionally, at the head of the pack was someone Nate recognized — Sylvia Crawler, one of the higher-ups in the Ashland Guild. He'd had plenty of time to use his Kanta sight on her and discovered that she was currently at the 29th rank, several higher than their group.

Had she been alone, this wouldn't have been a problem. However, she had been joined by several fighters, all of whom were ranked in the 20s. Additionally, he still wouldn't be able to fight at his best, as his leg still throbbed when he put his full weight on it. He could walk – might even be able to run – but the sort of movement required of fight was beyond him at the moment, meaning that everything would fall to Noam and Freya, though they couldn't fight *and* protect him at the same time.

Another spell came whizzing up from behind and Nate was forced to swerve, feeling a twinge in his ankle as he ducked low. A flaming ball of tar splattered into the road to his right, sending liquid fire blasting in all directions. A small globule stuck to the back wheel of his scooter and as soon as he saw that, Nate knew it was finished.

His brain began to work in overdrive as the fire began to consume the man-powered vehicle.

Three against fifteen were not odds he liked. Even if by some miracle they managed to win, there was no way they would all survive.

They weren't going to reach any city or town, let alone Southside Eight. So, what were their options? Nate frantically tried to remember if there was anything in the area that could give them an advantage. He grimaced as his mind alighted on their one and only hope. The problem was that their 'hope' was just as likely to end up with the deaths as this chase was.

He could either take the definite death or the maybe death and knew which he preferred.

"Follow me!" he yelled, leaping off his flaming scooter and throwing it back at the approaching group in the vain hope of slowing them down.

Nate didn't reserve anything, triggering his Steelshod and kicking off, his feet pistoning out as he ran and lending him extra speed. His ankle began to scream in protest almost immediately, but it was this or die.

Freya and Noam were right on his tail, catching up with him quickly as they put their everything into the run.

"Where are we going?" Freya asked, sounding panicked.

Another flaming ball of tar splattered into the grass to their left and Freya threw her arm over her shoulder, firing off a spell. There was a dull explosion as her Shattering Shrapnel went off. Nate didn't spare a glance back, knowing it would only slow them down.

"There!" he said, pointing down.

They'd just crested a small hill, revealing the landscape below. About a quarter of the way down the hill and to their right stood a break in the world, a triangular slash of blue in the otherwise unbroken sea of grass.

"I thought we weren't ready!" Freya yelled.

Nate stumbled as his ankle twinged, and it was only thanks to Noam that he managed to retain his footing, the man's hand shooting out and snagging his arm.

"We're not," Nate said, regaining his balance.

His ankle was on fire, but that didn't matter right now. What mattered was getting off Warine and away from Ashland. There was little chance they would try following them through, but if they did, their group would be set up well to handle them. After all, Portal Reavers weren't the only ones who could kill people stepping through to another world.

Another spell exploded right behind them, threatening to toss them off their feet. A glance over his shoulder showed him that the enemy was nearly on top of them, the Quinto Riders flying over the grass. They were gaining on them quickly, but not quite quickly enough.

Sylvia raised a hand as she saw where they were headed, fire kindling in her eyes. Now that she knew where they were going, she could aim to hit them. Additionally, they'd only be able to enter the portal one at a time, which would mean they would be sitting targets.

He cursed silently but knew they didn't have a choice. They continued running, the portal growing closer with every passing second. A projectile exploded ahead of them, forcing the group to swerve out of the way. Nate's ankle screamed at him again, but thankfully held, thanks to the Steelshod technique he was channeling.

The technique encased his foot, acting as a sort-of brace. This was to prevent any undue harm during the explosive movements and now saved his ankle from snapping like a dry twig. Thankfully, the portal was right ahead. Sylvia lifted her hand again.

97

She knew she wouldn't catch them in time, so she was doing all she could to hit them before they entered. If one of those flaming tar balls hit them, they would go down and that would likely be the end of them.

"Don't slow down!" Nate yelled, doing exactly that to allow Freya through the portal ahead of him.

Thankfully, she didn't look back, plowing straight through and vanishing from Warine.

A blazing sphere of flaming tar shot from Sylvia's hand, trailing sparks and billowing smoke in its wake. His Goldshield flashed into existence behind him, catching the flaming projectile. Part of the attack was deflected back at the attackers. Part of it splattered across the shield though, sticking to the construct and beginning to burn away at its structure.

"Go!" Nate yelled as Noam hesitated.

The man grimaced, then dove through the glowing triangle of blue light. Another projectile slammed into the Goldshield, sending a spiderweb of cracks spreading across its surface.

Nate threw one last look back, dismissing the flagging shield. He gave Sylvia a little wave, then dove through the portal, narrowly avoiding a third attack.

The world bent around him, a rainbow of swirling color briefly flashing around him before he abruptly landed again. His ankle gave out as he landed, and he finally fell, his head spinning momentarily as he tried to orient himself to his new surroundings.

His head stopped spinning pretty quickly, his vision coming into focus and seeing Noam and Freya standing before him, breathing hard. Misty sunlight streamed down around them, painting everything in an uncertain light. Behind him stood the portal, a shimmering red curtain that would take him back to Warine. It was how people could differentiate between portals leading back to the previous world or forward to the next.

"Watch the portal," he told Noam, pulling himself out of the way. "Someone might decide to follow us. If they do, you'll have a couple of seconds to kill them before they can react."

Noam nodded, stepping up to the portal and drawing his ax, clutching the massive weapon in both hands.

Then, the wait began.

15

Several minutes passed that way, in tense silence. Nate had regained his footing quickly and had positioned himself on the other side of the portal, while Freya had taken a few steps back, drawing her Magigun and keeping it leveled at the opening. If anyone walked through, they would be dead in a matter of seconds.

Thankfully, no one did, and by the time the five-minute mark passed, Nate allowed himself to relax. It could have been a ploy by the enemy to get them to drop their guard, but by this point, he had to assume that they'd wised up and decided not to follow them.

"We're alive," Freya said, allowing her arm to fall. "I can't believe we're alive."

"For now," Noam said, finally turning to look around.

Nate turned from the portal as well, getting his first good look around the planet of Laybor for the first time in decades. They'd emerged – thankfully – near one of the many thoroughfares, an area populated heavily by the hard-working and industrious borers – the local inhabitants of this world. Had they come out in an unpopulated area, like the Untamed Wilds, they could have been in for a rough time. As it was, they still needed to get off this world as quickly as possible, as their bodies wouldn't be well adapted to this new climate until they hit rank 30, when they would cross the threshold to survive this world.

They were strong enough for now to survive here, but the harsh sunlight would begin burning them sooner rather than later. Contrary to what most might believe, the perpetual mists here actually increased the intensity of the sun.

The temperature was just as he remembered it. Humid. A light fog perpetually hung in the air on most of Laybor. The two suns floating in the sky above, one right next to the other, were to thank for that. That, and the abundance of water on the planet.

The twin suns, one yellow and the other orange, were the same size, but the orange was further away from the planet, giving it the appearance of being smaller. The blue-green sky, visible through the perpetual fog, looked watery, shimmering and rippling in the light.

"Ugh, this place is ruining my hair," Freya complained, running her fingers through her ponytail, which was starting to frizz.

"Would you perhaps like me to make it all go away, princess?" Nate asked with a grin.

"Can you?" Freya asked. "I would be extremely grateful. Who knows *what* kind of reward I might be willing to offer."

She winked.

"Gross," Noam said. "More to the point, where *are* we?"

Nate consulted his memory, scanning the thoroughfare before him and turning a slow circle in the calf-high grass beaded with moisture.

Behind them, he could see the field stretching for quite a distance, noting the looming shadow of buildings in the far distance. To his left and right, the thoroughfare stretched, a road some fifty feet across, teeming with traffic. Carts loaded with all sorts of building materials were being lugged by hulking drawrs – animals that appeared like a mix between an elephant and mule. Wagons peddling food and beverages were traveling as well, stopping occasionally at the center of the thoroughfare to sell to those borers who stopped for a break.

On the other side, the grassy field continued, this one stretching to the horizon. To his left, the access road stretched endlessly, and to his right, it continued until a hulking skeleton of a wall loomed in the distance, half-constructed buildings and massive mounds of dirt littering their surroundings.

In the far distance, he could see the peak of a mountain seeming to brush the very heavens. That would be Peak Silence, the tallest mountain on the planet, which meant they were exactly where he'd been hoping to come out. It was as safe an entrance into Laybor as they were going to get, short of warping right into an already-constructed city.

"Looks like we're on the fringes of City 1162-B," Nate said, pretending to look at his map.

"How original," Freya said, eyeing the borers with interest.

The borers of Laybor, much like the winges of Warine, were well adapted to their planet. They appeared like a mix of beaver and mole-man, the average standing around four-and-a-half feet, with wide, flat tails, six-fingered hands with short claws and wide, flared feet. Their faces were distinctly beaver-like – minus the massive teeth – and their small black eyes were appraising and cunning.

Their bodies were covered in a slick fur, which varied in color from stark white to pitch black, though they moved along a spectrum of tans and browns for the most part. They also had strange proportions, with massively wide and muscular upper bodies and thinned, finer hips and legs. This was where their tails came in, helping them balance the massive loads they tended to carry.

As far as Nate could remember, borers were indifferent to the humans for the most part. So long as they stayed out of their way and didn't interfere with their work, they were perfectly happy to ignore them.

If there was a single lesson he'd learned from his time here, it was *never* to mess with a borer's work. Do that, and you were liable to be murdered by a swarm of enraged beaver-moles who would rip you apart with their bare hands.

"Yeah," Nate said. "They're not the most creative when it comes to naming things. They're constantly building as well, so they simply number the cities as they go up."

"Wait, you're telling me that this planet has over eleven-*hundred* cities alone?" Freya exclaimed.

"That's not all that many," Noam said, sounding unimpressed.

"It's not a massive planet," Nate replied. "Plus, they have no heavy machinery. They build everything by hand. And no, it's actually not *just* eleven hundred. It's eleven-hundred cities in this quadrant. Note the 'B' at the end of the city name. Laybor is separated into sixteen quadrants, each with its own cities, towns, villages, and so on. I can also tell you that the number of towns outnumbers cities about five-to-one, and villages outnumber towns by about three times that."

"Okay," Noam said. "So they like building things then. *Why*?"

Nate shrugged.

"Beats me."

That was one thing no one had ever figured out. Why did borers constantly feel the need to build? No one knew. Stay out of their way and you would be fine. That was all that mattered.

"Where do we go from here?" Freya asked, still running her fingers through her hair.

"That way," Nate said, pointing in the direction of the city under construction. "We won't be able to last here indefinitely without sustaining damage. We also still need to reach Southside Eight. It'll be faster traveling this way."

"Why didn't we try this in the first place?" Noam asked as Nate began making his way to the thoroughfare, his ankle still throbbing.

"Because traveling through Warine would have been much safer," Nate replied, pointing down the road.

A creature had leaped from the tall grass, falling upon one of the wagons as it tore into the nearby borers. The creature's body was covered in slick and shaggy fur. For all intents and purposes, it appeared to be some sort of coyote, but its body was just a bit too large, its body too angular, and its fur appeared just *wrong*.

Even from here, the dark 33 was visible on its shoulder. Nate continued walking, while Noam and Freya stared at the monster as it dragged a borer into the grass, vanishing from view. The other borers simply picked themselves up, dusted off their torn clothes and went on their way, leaving the dead and dying to fend for themselves.

"Talk about cold," Freya said with a light shudder.

"Yeah, they're not exactly known for their compassion," Nate replied.

"Monsters here will attack you, even on the roads," Noam said. "That seems like a significant step up in difficulty from the last planet."

"That's it exactly," Nate said. "The planetary difficulty level isn't on a gradual curve from what I can tell. Sure, the overall rankings of the monsters will go up, but the safe areas will grow sparser. Camping on or near the road won't guarantee safety anymore. Only sleeping within a city would give you that."

"Will monsters attack even towns and villages?" Freya asked.

"As far as I can tell," Nate said. "I could always be wrong, but I wouldn't count on me being mistaken in this case."

Freya fell silent at that as the group walked down the busy road. borers looked at them with interest as they passed, but only briefly before they went back to concentrating on their work. It was unfortunate that he'd lost his scooter, as it meant they were stuck walking, but that was just fine with Nate. He didn't think his ankle would be able to handle anything more.

It took them nearly four hours of walking in the sweltering heat to reach the walls of City 1162B, by which point his skin was feeling particularly raw and his body was drenched in sweat. His hair was plastered to his head and his clothes hung off him, soaked through.

"Please tell me there's a way to avoid being constantly wet here," Freya complained.

"There is," Nate said, eyeing the woman. "We'll make sure to stop at a shop before heading back."

Her hair was as sad and soaked as the rest of them, her clothes equally soaked and face slick with perspiration. They were dressed for Warine, not Laybor, which was why they were having such a miserable time. All they had to do was buy clothing suited to this planet and they'd be fine. Well, in the sense of becoming soaked anyway. The searing sun wouldn't stop until they were all at the 30th rank.

"Good," Freya said. "And as soon as we return, we're finding an inn. I need a shower. A cold one at that."

Nate decided not to jump on the obvious opening. They were all tired, after having not slept the entire night, jumping into a different time zone, and being constantly assaulted by the environment alone.

They had seen dozens of attacks across their path as well, though none had come close to them as Nate had positioned their group toward the center. There was a reason the thoroughfare was considered safe and that was because there were other targets you could point the monsters at. If there was easier prey, the monsters would go for them rather than you.

"Does anyone else feel like they're getting the worst sunburn of their lives?" Freya asked as they passed beneath the half-constructed archway that would become the city gates.

"It's the sunlight refracting through the mist," Nate said. "It strengthens the UV rays and damages those who aren't strong enough to passively resist its effects. In other words, anyone below the 30th rank."

"That makes sense, I guess," Freya said, staring around the construction site.

Massive scaffolding made of wood rose into the sky on all sides, the tallest of which had to be well over a hundred feet. It was hard to believe these creatures could build such massive structures, given the limitations of their technology, but that didn't seem to stop them.

"There," Nate said, pointing to a small section of the city, untouched by the construction, muddy ground, or bustling borers.

The area was perfectly round, containing a series of long, low houses, obviously intended as living quarters for the builders. There were also several smaller structures, each serving a different purpose. However, there was one that immediately stood out, even to Freya and Noam.

"A shop!" Freya cheered, realizing where Nate was taking them.

"Yup," Nate said, steering them toward the building.

Once they purchased the goods he wanted, he would lead them to the opposite side of the city, where they were still busy excavating. There, on the very edge of what would one day become a city, would be a portal back to Warine, one that would cut their journey to Southside Eight in half. If there was a single perk of being here on Laybor, it was that travel here was *far* faster thanks to the planet's smaller size in comparison to Warine.

16

"Holy cow, it's freezing in here!" Freya exclaimed as they walked into the shop.

The chilly air within the shop felt like a well air-conditioned home on a hot summer's day. That was if the home in question belonged to a polar bear. For some bizarre reason, the gnarks there liked it freezing, likely to counteract the heat from the outside.

"Haven't seen your kind around here yet," the single gnark behind the counter said as the trio approached.

"I take it that we're the first in this quadrant," Nate said, taking a seat and trying not to shiver.

"Yes, sir," the gnark said. "So, what can I do for you?"

"We need clothes suitable for Laybor," Nate said. "Two sets each preferably and let's try and keep the cost down. We also want three Low-Kanata Scooters, and I would like a Transference Orb."

"The outfits will run you fifteen points apiece for the men's and twenty for the woman," the gnark said. "And before you say anything, the female outfits are more costly due to material. The Low-Kanta Scooters will be a bit more expensive at four-hundred-and-fifty each and the Transference Orb will be fifty."

As far as Nate was concerned, the new scooters were well worth the price, as they offered a significant upgrade compared to the regular ones they had now. He had paid a whopping 350 points for his, and the loss still stung.

"Before you make the purchase," Noam said, "is there any reason we're not trying to get those bikes that the Ashland Guild was using?"

"Scooters are cheaper," Nate said. "On top of that, they're more portable and maneuverable. Trust me when I say that that'll be important on this planet and the next from what I understand. We can also offset the cost by selling your scooters. These new ones will be far better."

"And I was just getting used to it too," Freya sighed, removing the scooter from her ring.

In all, they got 550 points toward the new scooters, bringing the grand total to 950 points. The gnark handed them the scooters one at a time and Nate felt a bit better about the expense after seeing them. They had four large wheels, like the previous models, but the braking system was far better and the frame itself weighed less. Additionally, there was a small node attached to each of the handlebars where they could pour their own Kanta into the scooter.

A small engine attached to the rear wheel would activate and assist in speed. It wouldn't be a huge difference, but as with the Quinto Riders, it would add enough extra torque to make their trips easier and quicker.

The clothes were handed over as well and Nate admired the fabric, running his fingers over the slippery-feeling sleeveless shirt. He was going to have to get his hands on something better, especially for Freya, who didn't have her own armor spell, but that was going to have to wait until they could find the proper monster hides to craft them.

"I'm going to change," Freya said.

"I wouldn't if I were you," Nate warned. "I know you want to, but we'll be returning to Warine within the next few minutes and it's going to be cold there."

Freya looked like she wanted to change anyway but, remembering the typical frosty temperature of the 1st planet, decided to listen to him.

"Won't the damp clothes just make the cold worse though?" she asked.

"Not if you wear your cloak," Nate replied. "Trust me when I say that Laybor clothes are ill-suited to Warine."

"Fine," she sighed. "But so long as we're here, I'm getting my hands on some second-planet goodies."

Nate bit back the automatic impulse to shout as Freya sat down and asked to see the list of nail polishes the gnark had for sale. To him, it seemed like she was taking her precious points and lighting them on fire. To her, this was a coping mechanism that she hadn't managed to shake. After making her selection – which took nearly twenty minutes – she asked to see *more* items.

Nate shared an exasperated look with Noam, who simply shrugged, crossed his arms, and continued waiting in silence. It seemed Nate's friend had more patience for this than he did. Finally, after what felt like ages, Freya finished, packing her items into her ring. She turned, seeming to be in a much better mood, and spotted the orb clutched in Nate's hand.

"What is that thing?" she asked.

"This is a Transference Orb," Nate replied, hefting the small item.

He hadn't wanted to buy it just yet, as he would have preferred to remain unknown for a while longer, but he currently had a surplus of points that weren't his. Noam and Freya knew this, and it meant that he would be stuck footing the bill for everything for the foreseeable future. He could always transfer the points through a shop, but he'd have to pay, and he needed every point he had.

"What does it do?" she asked suspiciously.

"Why don't you touch it and find out," Nate said, unable to resist.

He'd noticed that he'd been a lot more open to exchanging these playful back-and-forths with her as of late. Nate wasn't sure how he felt about it just yet, but he *did* know that it helped dim the crushing pain and sorrow of his previous life and the knowledge of all he still needed to do to save this world.

"So forward of you!" Freya said, putting a hand up to her mouth. "The least you could do is buy me dinner first."

"Your loss," Nate said with a shrug. "Noam?"

Noam placed his hand on the orb without complaint, his eyebrows rising as he saw the message flash in the corner of his vision. This would be a new experience for everyone involved. Nate knew exactly what Noam would be seeing right now. He could see it himself, clear as day.

Nate Chesterson would like to transfer 31,666 points to your account. Would you like to accept?

Noam accepted without preamble and Nate felt his total points decrease by the same amount as they were transferred over. It hurt to willingly give the points up, but they weren't his to begin with, and this way, no one could claim he didn't play fair.

"Thanks," Noam said, stepping away and looking at his hand.

"What just happened?" Freya asked, looking between the two of them.

"You'll have to come over and find out," Nate said, extending the sphere.

Freya looked at Nate, then the orb, then back up again at Nate.

"Fine, you charmer, I'll bite," she said, coming over and placing her hand on the orb. "Ooh, now that's what I call a present!" Freya said as Nate transferred the points over to her. "You really know how to charm a girl."

"They were yours to begin with," Nate said, tucking the orb into his ring. "Don't go blowing it all at once."

Freya eyed the counter behind them, clearly tempted to do just that, but in the end, resisted the urge to buy more beauty and hair care products.

"More importantly," Nate said, turning to Noam, "if I'm doing my math correctly, you've got enough to upgrade your Path Manual to the third tier. I won't tell you what to do with your points, but having a third-tier manual will put you leagues ahead."

"I have just enough," Noam said. "It would nearly deplete everything I have."

"Do you remember upgrading to the second tier?" Nate said.

"That's the only reason I'm considering this," Noam said.

Nate didn't rush the man as he stood in thought, clearly debating whether he should take the plunge or not. Had their positions been reversed, Nate would have done so without a second thought. He currently had nearly 60,000 points, thanks to the windfall with the snail, but he knew they wouldn't be finding anything that would award nearly that many.

He needed to save everything he had, and unfortunately, the 3rd tier of his manual would have to wait. His next big purchase would be the 4th tier of the Cycle of Regeneration. Once he had that, he would be able to speed his healing, recovering from injuries in battle *far* faster. Additionally, passive regeneration of kanta would rise and active cycling to increase rank would be far more effective.

"You haven't steered me wrong in this area so far," Noam said. "I'll trust you're not doing so now."

The man went over to the counter, removed his Manual of the Sacred Guardian, and spoke the words.

"I would like to upgrade my manual to the third tier."

"Place your hand on the orb," the gnark said.

Noam did and Nate could practically see the man's point total plummeting from over 129,000 to just over 1,300. It would be well worth it. Nate already knew what the man would be getting and watched as the gnark upgraded the manual, the book shining brighter as more detail appeared on the cover.

Noam's presence swelled and Nate felt the level of danger the man posed rise. His overall rank hadn't changed, but if the rippling muscle beneath his clothes was any indication, the man's physical and defensive prowess had just risen by a considerable amount.

"How do you feel?" Nate asked as the man took his manual back and stashed it in his storage ring.

"Strong," Noam said, rising from the chair and flexing his fingers. "*Really* strong."

Light crackled behind his eyes and he stood straighter.

"I got two new techniques, though I have to wonder about how they're named."

"Well? Don't keep us in suspense!" Freya said.

"The first isn't actually so bad," Noam said. "It's called Total Guardian. It allows me to summon a double of myself, made of kanta to defend on my behalf. I'm not entirely sure what that means, but if I understand correctly, this double of mine will serve as an additional shield. The other technique is called Maniacal Guardian. It does the same as the first but as an offense."

"I wonder how that would work," Freya said, placing a finger to her chin. "Maybe it'll be like the *Cloner* skill from Planetary Combat Sixteen, or…never mind. I guess we'll find out soon enough."

"Yeah," Noam said, looking at Nate. "Thanks for pushing me to get this. I needed it. I haven't been feeling like I've been pulling my weight in fights recently. With this, I'll be able to do *much* more damage."

"I don't doubt it," Nate said, remembering well the terrifying duo of kanta-Noam's in vivid detail.

It was such a powerful pair of techniques that it almost wasn't fair. The Path of the Sacred Guardian was a truly powerful one, but, like all powerful Paths, it had its price. The cost to increase to the 4th tier would be monstrous, just as he knew it would be for them all. In Noam's case, it would be nearly three times what the last had been at 361,000.

    If that was any indication, his was going to be much higher. The general rule was that the more something cost, the better it would be. That most certainly held true here in the System of Twelve. Despite the cost and current rankings, they were much further ahead than they'd been the last time around and Nate intended to keep it that way. The only area in which they were flagging were their actual ranks, and that was something he was going to have to address.

    "Before we go, I wanted to check if you had any augments available," Nate addressed the gnark.

    "Well, isn't this your lucky day? It just so happens that we do."

17

"If I didn't know better, I'd say you liked her or something," Noam grumbled as they left the shop.

"Well, I *am* the only girl in the group, so it's understandable that everyone would be fighting over me," Freya said.

She was in a good mood after receiving her second augment in a row. This one was called Deadeye, which markedly improved a user's aim. While it might have seemed redundant with her Magnification Augment, this one was different. While Magnification increased eyesight and allowed her to see at greater distances, Deadeye directly affected her aim with her Magigun.

It would coordinate between her eyesight and muscles to make adjustments on the fly. This meant that while moving or in the heat of battle, she would be hard-pressed to completely miss a target. If she was standing still, there was very little chance she would miss where she was aiming.

"I'm not fighting over you," Noam said flatly. "You're a nice girl, but too young and not my type."

"That's fine by me," Freya said, refusing to allow her good mood to be dampened. "At least Nate's still head-over-heels for me."

"Keep dreaming," Nate said, though with far less conviction than Noam.

In truth, he could admit that he *did* like her but knew that pursuing any type of romance would distract him from his ultimate goal and mission. He could not allow his feelings into the mix when there was so much at stake.

"Moving on from Nate's obvious infatuation," Freya said, unbothered. "I really hope we can find somewhere decent to sleep. I'm dealing with some serious portal lag right now."

"Portal lag?" Noam asked.

"You know, like jetlag," Freya said. "Only with portals."

Noam nodded, clearly agreeing with the sentiment.

Nate could well understand what they were dealing with. Though his mind had long since grown accustomed to jumping from one time zone to another, his body was not. It was one of the many things he needed to rectify after returning from the future. He was also exhausted, especially after the night they'd had.

"Not to worry," he said. "If I'm right, we should be emerging close to a small town. It'll be late, but just this once, we can sleep in a little."

He didn't want to give Ashland the opportunity to do too much more, nor catch up with them, so he couldn't allow them too much leisure.

"I'll take it," Freya said, pumping her arm in the air.

The group continued talking as they wound their way through the construction site, moving from areas of heavy work to more complete buildings. The roads became nicer, cobbled instead of mud and dirt.

"It's still hard to believe they can do so much," Freya said, tilting her head back to examine one of the towering buildings.

"Wonder how much one of these cities costs to take over," Noam said.

"A *lot*," Nate replied. "It's ridiculous how much borer work is worth."

They passed several more of the beaver-like creatures, Nate taking note of their ranks as they did. One and all, the creatures here were ranked in the low 40s, meaning that they were probably more advanced workers, creatures who'd been on the job for quite some time.

The suggested rank to move on to the third planet, Raven, was 62, but the more powerful borers would only appear in the Capital cities, which were City One of each quadrant. It was also in those cities where the best items, leads on monsters and so on could be found, but they were also all located in the most dangerous areas of the planet.

"Are we nearly there?" Freya asked. "I feel like my skin is actively burning and I honestly don't think I could get any wetter if I jumped in a lake."

"Almost," Nate said. "Just another block or so."

Sure enough, as they crossed toward the edge of City 1162B, a triangular slash of color appeared before them, this one colored a bright red.

"Home sweet home, here we come," Freya said, walking straight through the portal without slowing.

Nate followed right behind her, feeling the familiar rushing, followed by a wave of dizziness as he stepped through. He swayed on his feet but managed to remain upright, shaking off the nausea and shivering.

It was dark out, stars twinkling overhead. His breath steamed before him as he pulled his fox fur cloak from his ring and draped it around his shoulders. He was still cold, but it wasn't too bad.

"Please tell me we're not far from that town you mentioned," Freya said, rubbing her arms beneath her cloak.

"It's just down the road," Nate said, pulling his scooter from his ring.

They were currently near the side of the road, the portal sitting just a few feet into the swaying grass. Everything was quiet, though Nate could hear the normal night sounds of the planet and wasn't too concerned.

"For all our sakes, I certainly hope it is," Noam said, shivering lightly. "Though, if I'm being honest, the cold isn't bothering me as much as it should."

"You've got your third-tier manual to thank for that," Nate said, pushing off the grass and onto the road, the others following behind.

The chill air cut through the cloak, making the damp clothes clinging to him feel even worse. However, what he'd told Freya about Laybor's clothes being ill-suited to Warine hadn't been an exaggeration. They were designed to insulate cold and repel heat. In other words, the clothes actively attracted cold. If they'd worn them here, they would be suffering from hypothermia in just a couple of minutes, cloaks or not.

The small town of Southline Three came into view within five minutes of scootering down the twisting road. Nate didn't bother with using kanta, knowing that that was a chore for the morning, when they were less exhausted.

Only a small gate surrounded the town, but no guards were posted. The gate had been left open for travelers, so the three of them had no trouble entering the town. It didn't take them long to find the only inn, the three of them entering with an almost audible sigh of relief as the warmth of the building engulfed them.

"A bit late for visitors, isn't it?" the winge asked, rubbing at her eyes as she emerged from a back room.

113

"We didn't want to sleep on the road," Nate said. "So we kept going until we found this place."

The winge – an elderly woman – looked the three of them over. She was clearly tired and had been sleeping until the bell woke her. They'd had to wait nearly five minutes for her to show up.

"Fine then," she grumbled. "Fifteen points per room, and you're only getting one meal out of it."

It was late and none of them wanted to argue about price, even though the woman was clearly ripping them off.

"Fine," Nate said. "Two rooms then."

"Three," Noam said, crossing his arms. "I would like some privacy for once."

Nate was forced to pay the full 15 points for his room, grumbling all the while about the astronomical cost. He received a pleasant surprise upon entering the room though, finding that not only was the bed large and plush, but the room itself came with an attached bath.

Okay, so perhaps it was worth the 15 points after all, he admitted to himself.

Though he was exhausted, Nate took great pleasure in peeling himself out of his sodden clothes and falling into a hot bath, lingering there perhaps a bit longer than he should have, before finally going to bed.

Despite his exhaustion, Nate didn't have an easy time going to sleep once he lay down in the soft and unexpectedly plush bed. His mind continued to churn, trying to plan the next few days. Ashland had an unexpected leader, and he hadn't really had much time to think it over. Who was this woman?

As soon as his mind had finished churning through every possibility, his thoughts turned to his old friend and leader of the Warband Guild – the one that *should* be located in Southside Eight. However, with the changes, things could be different. It was entirely possible that he either wouldn't be there or would but wouldn't have formed his guild yet.

There was also the distinct possibility that he'd already moved on to Laybor, leaving Warine behind. Right now, there were just too many unknowns and things happening too quickly.

Once again, his mind turned to the reason for that occurrence – the fall of Centrifuge and all the people who'd died due to his actions. No matter how many times he told himself it had been for the greater good, his mind plagued him with images of the dead and pieces of human remains poking from the debris field.

Curse that Xavier Kent, Nate thought bitterly.

If only the man had listened.

Nate turned the other way, trying to banish the thoughts from his mind so that he might finally rest. God only knew how much he needed it after the day they'd had, yet his mind refused to allow him the comfort of rest.

A knock came at his door and Nate sat bolt upright, heart racing. His mind immediately went to the worst-case scenario – that they were under attack. However, after a few heart-pounding moments of inaction, a familiar voice floated through the crack in the door, hesitant and uncertain.

"Nate? Are you awake?"

Nate exhaled when he recognized the voice, rising quickly from bed and walking over to open the door.

Freya stood there, dressed in a loose-fitting set of pajamas that Nate recognized as Warine-made. He hadn't bothered spending the extra points, preferring to save them for something more valuable, but apparently Freya had decided she wanted the comfort.

Her hair was freshly brushed and reflected the lamplight in the hallway, the sheen of her golden-blonde hair showing yet another expense at the shop. Her nails had been repainted as well, a royal purple with shimmering flecks of white beneath the surface. Though her face was scrubbed clean, Nate could see that she'd applied some form of cream or cosmetic, as it looked glossier than it would have otherwise. He took it all in at a glance, noting the look of relief and apprehension in Freya's eyes.

"Couldn't sleep?" he asked, stepping aside to let her in.

"Not for lack of trying," she said, walking in and allowing him to close the door behind her.

She stood awkwardly in the center of the room as Nate went back to the bed. When he raised an eyebrow, she still hesitated, remaining where she was.

"What's wrong?"

Something was clearly up, as she wasn't acting at all like her usual self, meaning that she was once again showing some vulnerability.

"I can't stop thinking about it," she said, wrapping her arms around herself.

"About what?" Nate asked.

A lot had happened lately, so she was going to have to be more specific.

"My father," Freya said, forcing out the words.

"Do you want to talk about it?"

Freya bit her bottom lip, clearly uncertain, but when Nate patted the bed next to him, she accepted the invitation and took the proffered seat.

She sat in silence for several minutes, staring at the floor. Nate allowed the silence to stretch so she could gather her thoughts. Though they'd already spoken about her father before and she'd resolved to end his life, the trauma of what the man had done wouldn't simply *leave* because she wanted it to.

"Every time I close my eyes, I can hear his voice," Freya finally began, her voice somber. "How he knew what those men might do to me when he sent them. How they would have tortured me, beaten me and who knows what else. So long as I made it back alive, what did it matter, right?"

She began to cry as she talked, showing a side of herself that Nate had never seen in their previous lives once again.

"For years, I worried about him. I'd made it my mission to find some way of getting him out. I ran, hid, plotted, and schemed and all along, he was completely fine! I can't help but imagine what would have happened if you hadn't stepped in that day. Attacked those men for the sake of a stranger you'd never even talked to..."

She swiped at her eyes frustratedly, even as the tears continued to come.

"I hate him so much, but at the same time, I can't help but remember the good times. All the kind things he said and did for my sake. I know he's gone but...but..." The sentence cut off as a choked sob escaped her throat and she leaned to the side, into his shoulder.

Nate wrapped an arm around her, remaining silent and allowing her to vent her frustration. He could well understand the emotions warring within her. She couldn't correlate the memories of her father with the man she'd confronted only a few weeks ago. Her promise to kill him likely wasn't helping and the psychological damage Sean had inflicted was going to take years to overcome.

"I'm sorry," Freya said after several minutes, still keeping her face buried in his shoulder.

"Don't be," Nate said.

"I don't know what I did to deserve someone like you," she sobbed.

"Hey," Nate said, lightening his tone. "Don't sell yourself short. I was carrying around a lot of baggage when I ran into you. You make the days brighter and the nights more bearable."

"So, you *can* be sweet when you want to," Freya said, with a sniff, finally pulling away from him.

Her cheeks were damp with her tears and her eyes were red-rimmed.

"I'm only telling you what I feel," Nate said. "After what we did in Centrifuge, I couldn't sleep for weeks. Every time I closed my eyes, all I could see were the bodies. All I could hear were the screams of those I'd condemned to die. No matter how I told myself it was for the greater good, those lives were still my responsibility. I still hear them, but with you around, they're not as loud and things aren't quite as bad."

Nate realized he'd said a bit too much about how he felt when Freya's eyes widened. It was only a bit and she disguised it pretty quickly, but he cursed himself for allowing emotion to cloud his judgment.

"I didn't realize you cared so much," Freya said softly, placing a hand on his knee.

"I do," Nate said. "Just like I care about Noam. The three of us have been through so much together that it would be hard not to."

Contrary to what he'd hoped, Freya didn't remove her hand, keeping it where it was. She kept her gaze locked with his, light reflecting in her bright green eyes. Her fingers tightened, bunching into the cloth covering his knee and she leaned in a bit closer, lips parting subconsciously.

This was bad. If things kept on like this, they were liable to do something that Nate *really* didn't want. Well, he actually *did* want it, but at the same time, knew what was at stake — the lives of everyone on Earth, including his family.

With an effort of will, Nate looked away, breaking their eye contact and looking toward the darkened pane of glass set into the wall near his bed.

"It's getting late," he said, making sure not to turn back. "Unless there's something else you'd like to get off your chest, I think we should get some sleep."

Silence followed his words and he finally mustered up the strength to turn back and meet her gaze. She was smiling, though it wasn't her usual sly grin – the one she wore right before cracking some inappropriate joke or making a comment.

"I'm feeling a lot better, thank you. Would you mind if I stayed here tonight? I don't think I can go back to the silence of my room."

"It'll be quiet here too," Nate pointed out.

"Not with your snoring, it won't," Freya joked.

"I don't snore," Nate said.

"How would you know?" Freya retorted. "You're asleep when it happens. I, on the other hand, *would* know. You could wake the dead with that racket."

"Maybe you should go back to your room then," Nate replied.

"I can't," Freya said seriously. "I have a solemn duty after all."

"Solemn duty," Nate repeated, deadpan.

Freya nodded vigorously.

"Who else will be here to smother you with a pillow when your snoring starts an earthquake? If it weren't for me, the whole world would...*hey*!" Freya half-laughed, half-complained as Nate smacked her in the face with a pillow. "Mercy! Mercy," she said when Nate didn't let up, continuing to smack her with the fluffy weapon.

She collapsed backward onto the bed, giggling uncontrollably as Nate stopped. Her cheeks were still damp and her eyes still red, but the smile on her face spoke of a great weight lifted from her shoulders.

He knew it was only temporary and that she would need to talk this through again, but he would be there to listen when she needed him. Freya finally stopped giggling, her eyes still shining and the smile spreading wide across her face.

"Thank you," she said, her smile fading somewhat and a note of sincerity coloring her voice.

"Anytime," Nate said, and he meant it.

18

Nate awoke to the feeling of something sharp and familiar poking him in the ribs, as well as the heavy weight lying across his chest. He cracked an eyelid, finding Freya snuggled right up to his side, lying sideways with an arm draped across him. How her elbow was also jabbing him at the same time was a mystery and one he was sure he would never solve.

Light streamed in through the window, which was hardly surprising, given the time they'd gone to sleep the previous night. If he had to guess, they hadn't even gotten to the hotel until around five in the morning. It was only due to the late-rising sun in Warine that it had been dark by the time he and Freya had gotten to sleep around six.

He honestly wasn't sure what time it was. All he knew was that he wanted to do nothing more than go back to sleep. Nate fought that feeling down, then began to extricate himself.

"No," Freya groaned sleepily, clutching him a bit tighter.

"We have to get up," Nate said, trying once again to get up.

"But you're so warm and cozy," Freya said, her eyes still closed. "Can't we just pretend we're a couple on holiday for a bit longer?"

"I never realized we were playing pretend in the first place," Nate said.

"We don't have to pretend if you don't want to," Freya said, a smile cracking her lips.

Her eyes remained closed.

"Come on, lazy pants," Nate said, finally managing to tug his arm free. "Noam's probably been up for an hour already and will be wondering where we are. We don't want him getting any ideas, would we?"

"That would be so scandalous," Freya said with mock surprise. "Why, a proper girl like me messing around with…*gasp, boys*? Whatever will my socialite friends from the nineteen-forties say?"

Freya finally opened her eyes to see Nate giving her a dead stare. That didn't stop the grin on her face from growing wider.

120

"Oh, come off it," she said, turning to her back and stretching her arms over her head. "Stop being such a sourpuss."

"I'm not being a sourpuss," Nate grumbled. "We can't keep lying around and wasting the day. Not when there's so much that needs to be done."

"Fine," Freya said, rolling her eyes. "I'm getting up, but I have first dibs on the shower."

"You *do* realize that you have your own room with a shower all its own, right?"

"Yeah," Freya said, sliding out of bed. "But it's more fun to use yours. I can sit there in the bath, *right* where you were just a few hours ago and paint myself a pretty picture."

"You do that," Nate said flatly. "But if you're going to use mine, I want the key to your room."

"Gasp," Freya said, putting a hand up to her mouth. "Asking a girl for the key to her private-most chambers? Have you no shame, sir?"

Nate sighed as the woman chuckled again, rising from the bed and arching her back.

"You know, there's plenty of room for two in there," she said with a wink. "If you ask nicely, I might let you share."

"All right, we can share," Nate said. "It'll save us time."

"Taking me up on my invitation? I never thought I'd see the day," Freya replied, still grinning. "Well then, why don't you follow me?"

She walked toward the bathroom, a sway to her hips as she did. Nate followed her, knowing she was going to pull something at the last second. Freya entered the bathroom and turned, hooking her finger invitingly, grinning all the while, then slammed the door abruptly when Nate was just a couple of feet away.

"Real mature," he said, hearing her laughter from inside.

"Like I would let you hog all the hot water," Freya said, her voice sounding muffled from within. "Also, there was no way you were coming in and we both knew it. You're too much of a wimpy anime character when it comes to girls."

"I clearly remember someone trying to play that trick and it not working," Nate said, recalling back to the time when Freya had joked about him being an alien.

She'd been the one to chicken out that time as well.

121

The only reply he got was the faucet turning on and the sound of running water. Sighing, Nate decided he might as well use the time to sit and cycle. His ankle was still a bit sore and a little extra healing wouldn't hurt.

He'd barely situated himself on the floor when a knock came at the door.

"You alive in there?" Noam's voice asked, drifting through the frame. "Have you seen Freya?" he asked when Nate opened the door. "I tried going to her room but…"

He trailed off as Nate hooked a thumb over his shoulder to the bathroom, where the sound of running water was still evident. Noam raised an eyebrow.

"Oh, don't give me that look," Nate said. "She couldn't sleep and needed to talk to someone. She didn't want to sleep alone, so she ended up staying the night."

"And the reason she couldn't use her own bathroom?" Noam asked.

"Because she's Freya," Nate replied, frustration entering his voice.

"You know, when someone shows such obvious interest with no reciprocation, they might begin to wonder if the other party is even interested," Noam said. "Not to mix into your personal business, but to me at least, it seems obvious that Freya is interested in you as more than just a friend. Why do you continue to rebuff her advances?"

This question was very much in line with the Noam of Nate's previous life. The man was a romantic, so it only made sense that he would pry into other people's affairs as well. Nate had suffered through more than one awkward date and several relationships thanks to this man and wasn't about to fall for it again.

"Did Freya put you up to this?" Nate asked, crossing his arms. "Is this another one of her jokes?"

Noam blinked, clearly taken aback by his response.

"No, she didn't," he finally said. "I was just curious. That's all."

"Well, let's just say I have my reasons and leave it at that," Nate said, his tone saying that this was the end of the conversation.

"Fine by me," Noam said. "How much longer are you going to be?"

"I'll be in and out once she's done, so that will all depend on Freya. What time is it?"

"Around noon," Noam said, earning a wince from Nate.

"I knew it was late, but not *that* late."

Still, their upgraded scooters would give them a faster trip to Southside Eight. Once they were done there, they could concentrate on raising their ranks to the needed level and move on to Laybor. He already had a training spot in mind. It would be dangerous, but it would help them advance much faster, and at this point, it was the fast and dangerous route that was the safest, which he found to be quite ironic.

"I'll be waiting for you downstairs," Noam said. "Unless that augment of yours has anything useful for us?"

He raised an eyebrow.

Clearly, the man still wasn't convinced, which was unsurprising, given the recent turn of events.

"Nothing that I haven't told you," Nate lied.

Noam nodded, then turned, heading away from the room.

"Did you test your new techniques yet?" Nate called after him.

The man shook his head.

"If you leave the town's south gate and walk a hundred yards off the road, you should run into some monsters. It might be a good use of your time while we're waiting for Freya to finish."

"I might do that," Noam said, then left, disappearing around a corner as he headed down the hallway.

Nate closed the door behind him, letting out a breath, then moved to situate himself on the floor once again and regain his meditative state. Emptying his mind, Nate began to cultivate the energy of the world, feeling the kanta flowing into him and soothing his aggravated ankle. It only took around fifteen minutes of cycling to fully restore the limb and the sound of running water from inside the bathroom had still not abated.

Nate rose and began to stretch, running first through a series of exercises designed to loosen up his muscles, then fell into a more strenuous routine of push-ups, sit-ups, crunches and the like. There wasn't a lot of space to maneuver, so he couldn't work on any of his sword forms, but basic strength training was always a good use of his time.

The sound of running water finally stopped around twenty-five minutes after Freya went into the bathroom, but it took another twenty after that for her to emerge, her cheeks rosy and a towel wrapped around her.

Her hair once again had that lustrous sheen from the previous night and was somehow already dry.

"It's all yours," Freya said, motioning to the door with a sly grin.

"You used up all the hot water, didn't you?"

"Every last drop," Freya replied. "If you're quick enough, it might not turn to ice while you're in there. Oh, and don't come out of there without asking," she said. "Unless you want a peek."

Her grin widened as she tugged at the top of her towel.

"I'll try and resist the temptation," Nate deadpanned.

He was glad he'd warmed up, as this was not going to be a fun experience. Nate went into the bathroom and made sure the door was locked before stripping out of his clothes and getting into the tub.

Frigid water poured from the spout the second he turned it. It was so cold that it robbed him of his breath. It seemed Freya hadn't been lying when she'd said she used every last drop of hot water.

Uttering a stream of curses, Nate began the quick motions of cleaning himself off, all the while hearing Freya's barely suppressed snorts of laughter through the door.

I'm going to get her for this if it's the last thing I do, Nate silently promised himself, his mind beginning to work on a myriad of plots and schemes to make the woman pay.

19

"What's gotten into you?" Noam asked as Nate bit angrily into his egg and cheese sandwich. "Is the food that bad?"

"The food is fine," Nate said, grinding the words out between his teeth and glaring at Freya all the while.

The woman was still smiling from ear to ear, refusing to be cowed by the force of his glare. It annoyed him to no end, and he was *sure* she knew that.

Noam looked between the two of them, Freya happily munching on her sandwich as they walked down the road, away from the small town in the direction of Southside Eight.

After having wasted so much of the day, Nate was eager to get moving, so he insisted they take their food to go. The winge woman was more than happy to see them leave, which was strange, considering that guests were how she made her money. Still, the food was pretty good, so he wasn't complaining. Freya's treatment of him, on the other hand...

He'd have thought that after their talk last night, she would treat him differently, but it seemed she was back to her usual self – brash and unapologetic.

"If you say so," Noam said, still looking uncertain.

"Did you get to test your new techniques?" Nate asked, changing the subject.

"Yes," Noam said, clenching his fist. "They're strong. Stronger than I expected."

"The cost might be high, but the techniques are well worth it," Nate said.

Truthfully, a 3rd tier manual wouldn't strictly be necessary until the 3rd planet, Raven, but having it early definitely wouldn't hurt. Especially when no one had yet to acquire one to his knowledge.

There were many who'd moved to the 2nd, but the 3rd would be a large jump in cost and many wouldn't see the value when they could buy individual scrolls to supplement their fighting styles.

"I want to see," Freya said.

"I'm sure we'll all get to see soon enough," Nate said, thinking of the fighting they were going to have to do.

The day proved to be uneventful, the group mounting their scooters as soon as they were finished eating and speeding down the road. They ran into several groups, handing them copies of Nate's maps, along with the warnings to get off the planet as soon as they could.

They only stopped to make camp once the stars were twinkling in the sky and Freya began to audibly yawn and complain about how tired she was. They didn't have much energy to talk around their bland dinner – Nate was still insistent they finish the protein meals he'd brought from Earth – and they went to sleep without much fanfare after rigging up their early-warning system.

Ashland was still after them, and they knew their faces by now. There was a good chance they were asking around about their small group.

"I feel *much* better this morning," Freya said, stretching and arching her back.

Her hair was back in its usual ponytail, though she'd somehow found the time to style it a bit differently. The hair now hung lower on the sides of her head and several strands hung down to either side of her eyes, framing her face. Her nails were different as well, now painted a light green instead of the purple she'd worn yesterday.

Nate didn't comment on it and neither did Noam, the group continuing on through the early morning and into the afternoon without running across any people. They spotted more than a few monsters off the side of the road, but none of them were worth their time, as the strongest of them were at the 12th rank, meaning they wouldn't net much kanta, nor were they rare enough to garner more than a hundred or so points apiece.

Right now, their goal was Southside Eight, which, at their current speed, they should be reaching quite soon.

"There it is," Nate said, slowing down and gesturing to the top of a long hill, where a wall rose, blotting out the horizon.

"Well, at least this one's built at the top of a hill instead of the bottom," Freya said, twirling a lock of hair around her index finger.

126

"I'm just ready to get back to raising our ranks once this is done," Nate said. "We've been idle for too long."

"Idle?" Noam said with a raised eyebrow. "In case you forgot, we were literally fighting for our lives not two nights ago. In my experience, that's more than enough."

"In this world, there's no such thing as too much fighting," Nate said. "The more you fight, the stronger you become."

He paused, tugging the gloves on his hands a bit higher, making sure they were secure. When their group was on their own, he didn't bother wearing them, but seeing as they were about to enter a major city, it was the smart thing to do.

"Are we going to sleep in an inn tonight?" Freya asked.

"Not if I've got anything to say about it," Nate said. "We enter the city, spread the last of the maps around, and see if we can find my friend. Once we've been assured that someone will be working to keep Ashland in check here, we can go to the training area I have in mind to get our ranks up.

"Remember, we've got a limited amount of time before Colin starts going around and threatening doom and gloom for anyone who leaves this world, and we can't have that."

"You know, if I didn't know any better, I'd say you had an unhealthy relationship with sleeping on the ground instead of a normal bed," Freya said.

"I like beds just as much as anyone else," Nate replied.

"Do you? What is it you like about beds? Is it what people typically *do* in them?" Freya asked, waggling her eyebrows.

"Yes," Nate said. "I like sleeping."

With that said, he shoved off, squeezing the handlebars of his scooter and pumping his kanta into the small engine at the back. Immediately, his speed picked up and the effort he had to put into pushing himself uphill diminished.

"What's gotten into you the last couple of days?" Freya asked, coming up next to him. "You're acting like someone peed in your food or something."

"You *can't* tell me you're using that one again," Nate said.

"It's a saying we had back home," Freya said with a shrug.

Nate sighed and just shook his head.

"Come on, Groucho, what's got your knickers in a twist? You can tell me."

127

Nate glanced over his shoulder, seeing that Noam was staying back, giving them the room to talk.

No help there, Nate thought bitterly. *Thanks for having my back, pal.*

"I'm just tired and stressed, that's all," Nate said, trying to dodge the subject.

"We're all tired and stressed," retorted Freya, not letting him off. "Besides, I've seen you handle much more stressful situations without batting an eye. Something's been eating at you ever since we talked that night in the inn. Was it something I said?"

"No, it wasn't anything you said," he replied quickly.

He wasn't going to have her second-guessing her decision to trust him. That would destroy their current relationship and set them back months.

"Okay," Freya said, sounding audibly relieved. "Well if it isn't that, then *what* is it?"

Nate opened his mouth to answer, then paused. What *was* bothering him? Was it the fact that Freya had hogged the shower and left him stuck with the freezing water or that she'd been ribbing him more than usual?

Freya's ribbing had only gotten on his nerves in the beginning but once he'd gotten used to it, he just rolled with it. She would too once he got her back for that little stunt with the shower.

"I don't know, if I'm being honest," Nate said with a sigh. "All I know is that I've been all wound up and it's been getting worse over the last few days."

"Does it have anything to do with Noam?" Freya asked.

"No," Nate said.

He needed to find a way to build trust with the man, but that would come with time.

"If it's not any of us, then does it have anything to do with any of our fights?"

Nate thought about it, then shook his head. Fighting was fighting. He'd been the one who'd held them back in their last fight due to his broken ankle, but that was just the way of things. Injuries happened. It wasn't like he could have done anything differently.

"I wish brains weren't so weird and incomprehensible sometimes," Freya said in response.

"Yup, I'm a real mystery," Nate deadpanned.

"What I wouldn't give to know what's going on inside your head," Freya said.

She thought for a moment, then her face scrunched up, her nose wrinkling.

"You know, on second thought, I think I already know, and just thinking about it has officially scarred me for life."

Nate snorted out a laugh at that, feeling his dark mood receding somewhat.

They continued in silence, the sound of the wind and rushing wheels the only things to break it. As they drew nearer to the top of the hill and the city began to come into stark detail, Freya spoke again.

"This goes both ways, you know."

"What?" Nate asked, turning to her.

"If you ever need to talk, I'm here to listen," she said, giving him a genuine smile.

The genuine smile lasted all of two seconds, before twisting into her sly grin.

"That is unless you've decided you can't keep all those dirty little secrets to yourself anymore. In that case, I think you'd best go scar someone else."

"If anyone's got a head full of life-scarring material, it would be the girl who regularly makes inappropriate comments. That would be you, by the way, in case I wasn't clear."

"Fair enough," Freya said, her smile softening.

"Thank you," Nate said as he began to slow down.

"Hey, we were normal people, sort of, just a few months ago. Now we go around killing things and offing people daily. If that's not going to have a negative impact on our brains, then I don't know *what* will."

Nate nodded, thinking that it might be nice to just vent occasionally. He felt much better after that short exchange in which she'd acted maturely. It freed his mind to focus on more important things, like tracking down his friend, reaching the 30th rank and heading off to Laybor.

They were falling further and further behind by the day. The leaders would be closing in on rank 40, many of them already having moved on to Laybor. After all, there were parts of the world far removed from here, where Portal Reavers were already being dealt with. If they were going to stand a chance of catching up, they were going to have to walk the dangerous road for a while.

Southside Eight would be the last safe area they'd be in for a while. He hoped Freya and Noam were up to the challenge.

20

"I almost forgot what it was like to be in a crowded city," Freya said, looking around with interest.

All around them, traffic flowed, winges and humans walking down the main street, stopping at booths on the side of the road, talking with one another and shopping.

"So, who exactly are we looking for and how would we even go about finding them?" Noam asked. "This city seems quite large."

"Easy," Nate said. "We start handing out the maps and he'll come to us."

"Don't we want to avoid attracting attention?" Freya asked.

"Not from him and his guild," Nate said.

"You keep mentioning this word, 'guild,'" Noam said. "It's a strange term that I have heard used to describe groups, though it was uncommon back on Earth."

"It's a videogame reference," Freya said. "I'm not sure why it's caught on here, but that's the way things seem to be going. If I had to guess, a bunch of gamers started using it and others followed."

"Okay," Noam said, addressing Nate directly. "*If* this friend of yours is here, how can you be confident they have a guild? And, even if they do, how do you know they'll help us? It seems like there's a lot of guesswork involved in this, and you seem far too confident about it all."

"Like I said, I've got a good feeling about this," Nate said, tapping the side of his head.

Once again, Noam wasn't buying it, though Freya seemed to be perfectly fine with his explanation.

"This is a big city," Freya said to break the tension. "Should we split up to spread the maps around? Maybe then we should meet up in the square in an hour and see if any of us have run into this friend of Nate's."

"That sounds like a good idea," Nate said. "His name's Dirk, he's a short guy but built like a tank. Trust me when I say you'll know him when you see him."

They walked to the side of the road, where Nate split the remaining copies of the map. They continued together until they came to a split in the road, where the three of them headed off in different directions.

As soon as his companions were out of sight, Nate turned down a side-street and began backtracking. He knew exactly where Dirk would be and not having Noam or Freya with him, he wouldn't have to pretend otherwise.

He slipped through the crowd, moving through the familiar streets of the city and seeing older landmarks that he knew wouldn't be here in just a few short months. It was still hard to wrap his head around the fact that the Mystery had shown up again.

Perhaps he was making a mistake in thinking that everything would be the same this time around and it was that line of thought that had him so uncertain. Second-guessing every decision he made. Perhaps it was this that had him in such a bad mood. He had the same mission as before but didn't have the knowledge and tools he needed to make sure he succeeded.

It took Nate only a few minutes to reach the small building near the market district. No one had purchased Southside Eight yet, but Dirk would have taken this place as soon as he'd entered this world.

Sure enough, as he approached, a man and woman stepped from within the building, both holding modified rifles across their chests and staring at him suspiciously. Both wore the slick and highly durable army clothing that seemed to be able to survive anything and wore dog tags around their necks.

There was a reason their guild had been called Warband, and the reason was simple. Dirk had gathered every member of the US Army he could find. Soon enough, they would begin flocking to him.

In just a couple of years, he'd be leading one of the top guilds in the System, and that was saying something, considering just how many there would be.

Dirk had died long before reaching the 12th planet and hadn't been there when they'd battled against San-gu-oh. He hadn't made it off the 5th planet, dying in the raid against Blood Swarm. Mallory Lancer had killed him personally. It was why Nate's initial instinct upon seeing her when first entering Warine had been to end her right then and there. Dirk's fall had seen a major rift open in Warband and

132

they'd broken apart soon after into several smaller groups, all of which had fallen before reaching the 7th planet.

He hadn't seen Mallory since leaving her and her two children with Carver, but he knew he'd be running into her again soon and sincerely hoped that what he'd done had made a difference because Dirk was going to be crucial in the battle to come.

"Can I help you, civilian?" asked the woman, her voice hard and commanding.

A quick glance at them showed the woman to be a Second Lieutenant, while the man was a First. It seemed that Dirk's motto still rang true. No one was too highly ranked to do any task. It hadn't made him the most popular back home, but here in the System of Twelve, his way of doing things would keep his people alive.

"I'm here to speak with the colonel," Nate said, eyeing their rankings.

The woman was ranked at 26 and the man was at the 25th. Both markings were on their right hands, which meant they'd become cultivators, though the rifles they carried were probably their choice of weapon here.

Unlike Pavlov's gang, Dirk had been smart enough to realize that ordinary firearms weren't going to cut it here, so he'd had them all upgraded as soon as he could afford to. Everyone who joined him already knew how to use these weapons, so there was no need for training.

"Colonel Eagert isn't available right now," the woman said mechanically.

Nate reached into his shirt and removed one of the maps, extending it to the woman.

"I'll wait," he said, then crossed his arms.

The woman took the scroll, though she didn't open it, her training keeping her from doing so. If someone had a direct message for her superior officer, it would be bad form to look. It wasn't exactly illegal, seeing as they weren't on Earth, but she would refrain from doing so.

"Very well," the woman said, clearly intrigued. "Permission to deliver the message, sir?" she asked the First Lieutenant. It seemed she wasn't going to leave without permission.

"Deliver the message, lieutenant," the man said.

It seemed he was interested as well.

Nate didn't have to wait for long. The woman returned within half a minute.

"The colonel will see you," she said. "Are you carrying any firearms?"

"Nope," Nate said.

"Very well then, follow me," she turned, and Nate followed, heading through the doorway and into the small building.

There were several rooms within and each one was occupied by a small number of soldiers, all wearing their fatigues and running some form of training. Judging by the number of people here, he'd say that at least half the guild was out at the moment. He didn't recognize any of them, which made sense, as he was meeting Dirk far earlier than he had the last time.

She stopped before a heavy-looking door, where another man stood guard, the rifle held at the ready.

"He the one?" the man asked.

"Yes sir," the woman replied.

"Go on in then."

The woman knocked once, then pushed the door open without waiting for a reply. Nate followed, walking into a small meeting room. A single table occupied the space, with six chairs cramped around it.

Three people were already inside, pouring over the map when they entered, and to his relief, he recognized them all.

In the center, was Dirk, or Colonel Eagert as he would have to call him at the moment. He was a short, powerfully built man whose frame swelled within his decorated uniform. The Silver Eagle stood out most of all, marking him as the highest-ranked officer. His iron-gray hair was cut close to his scalp and his face was as hard and lined as Nate remembered.

To his left was a woman with black hair and eyes, wearing a similar uniform, though instead of the silver eagle, she wore a silver oak leaf. This was Lieutenant Colonel Ash Williams, Dirk's right hand.

To his right was a man with a similar-style haircut to Dirk, though his contained far less gray and his face carried fewer wrinkles. Captain Thomas Shelby wore the twin silver bars, his uniform looking a bit sparse in comparison to Dirk, though that was hardly surprising, given their difference in rank and experience.

Nate didn't know much about how the military functioned, and the one time Dirk had tried to explain it to him, it hurt his head.

The only thing he had gotten out of it was that there had been a major change to uniform design and placement of insignias in the 2060's. The movies still depicted military dramas and the like in their old uniforms, which annoyed him, as it undermined the radical shift in how the military operated.

Nate took it all in in an instant, the three figures continuing to stare at the map as Nate waited with the woman who'd escorted him here. Now that he was standing close enough, he could see her nameplate which had been hidden by the angle of her arm and the rifle.

Painter.

Nate's brow furrowed. Where had he heard that name before?

"You want to explain this, son?" Dirk asked, finally looking up from the map.

"Nate," Nate said, in way of introduction. "And I'll be happy to tell you all about it so long as it doesn't leave this room."

"Lieutenant Painter, that will be all," Dirk said.

"Yes sir," Painter said, snapping a salute before turning to resume her duties, making sure to close the door behind her.

"Mind if I take a seat?" Nate asked. "I've been traveling all day."

Dirk gestured to one of the chairs on the opposite side of the table, which Nate took. He made sure to remove his gloves, placing them in one of his pockets to show his rank. He had nothing to hide from these people. They would keep everything he said to themselves; he was confident of that.

A silence hung over the room, all three officers staring at him with an intensity that would have made any normal person squirm. Nate had dealt with them enough to remain relaxed.

"What do you any of you know of augments?" Nate said.

"Let me get this straight," Dirk said after Nate finished with his explanation. "You have knowledge of this world, meaning its inhabitants, layout, locations of resources, and more, and you're just handing the information out?"

135

"People are dying," Nate said, crossing his arms. "It would be cruel to keep this to myself, don't you think?"

"Son," Dirk said, rubbing at his eyes. "Do you *know* what our enemies can do with intel like this?"

"I don't know a nice way to say this," Nate said. "So, you'll have to forgive me if I'm a bit rude. The world as we know it is over. I understand that people we don't want to find this will get their hands on it. That's a risk I'm willing to take, so long as the majority are decent people who are just trying to survive."

Dirk stared at him for a few moments, fingering the map.

"Why are you here?" the man finally asked.

"I need your help," replied Nate matter-of-factly. "There's a guild called Ashland, have you heard of them?"

"Yes," Dirk said. "A small-time group led by a serial killer. They weren't causing too much trouble last I heard."

"Your intel is outdated then," Nate said. "Ashland now has over a hundred members and is already making their way across the continent. They have a new leader, or at least, co-leader. Her name is Selena Maylard, and she has grand plans for conquest."

"Where did you last encounter this woman?" Dirk asked.

"Southseer Seven," Nate said. "Around five days from here. My companions and I had to fight a couple of groups off before fleeing through a portal to Laybor."

"You went to the second planet, even though your own intel would advise against such a course of action?" Dirk asked.

"If it's you and two others against a group of fifteen, and one of you is injured, you take your chances," Nate said.

Dirk grunted in reply, then looked back at the map once again.

"I take it you want us to stop them in exchange for this information then," Dirk said.

"With all due respect, you won't be able to stop them," Nate said. "You don't have the manpower. What you *can* do, though, is keep them hemmed in. Stop them from getting free of Southseer Seven and wreaking havoc. Last I checked, Selena was headed to Laybor with some of their higher-ranking fighters to set up a base for themselves there. Warine isn't enough for a woman like this."

"You seem to know an awful lot for a civilian," Dirk said, eyeing Nate suspiciously. "You have an air of command about you, like you're used to giving orders and having them obeyed, but you're only a kid. Care to share anything else about yourself?"

"I was a raid leader," Nate said with a shrug.

"Raid leader?"

"In Epic Crawler Online," Nate said with a wide grin.

"It's an MMO, sir," Thomas said. "A videogame."

The confusion on Dirk's face cleared up in an instant, though he looked far less impressed.

"You can go," he said, waving a hand. "We'll keep an eye on Ashland, but whether we can take them out or not will be up to me. No one tells me how to run an op, especially not some videogame-playing kid."

"Don't underestimate them," Nate said, getting to his feet. "This isn't Earth, colonel."

"I know, son," Dirk said with a deep sigh. "I know."

Nate left the room as the three officers went back to staring at their map and talking in hushed tones. He was sure they were going to try and have him followed, but he knew Dirk well enough to know his tactics, so whoever they sent would be easy enough to shake.

Nate emerged from the building and immediately turned left, slipping into an alley as he noticed Painter on his tail, trying to remain inconspicuous. He grinned to himself, then broke into a run, slipping between two buildings and stabbing a summoned dagger into the wall, the flat of the blade supporting his weight as he dragged himself up.

He scaled nearly fifteen feet by the time Painter reached the mouth of the alley. She glanced in, but, seeing nothing, continued moving with the crowd, convinced he was still there. Nate waited for a few seconds, then lowered himself to the ground.

It had cost him some kanta, but he was already regenerating what he'd lost thanks to his technique. He'd lost his tail, and that was all that had mattered.

He ducked out of the alley, looking over his shoulder, and ran straight into Noam, who'd been standing there, waiting for him.

"We need to talk," Noam said.

By the look on the man's face, it was clear to see that he wasn't going to get out of this. So, with a sigh, Nate motioned him on.

"Lead the way."

21

"You know far too much," Noam said as soon as the two of them had ducked into a quiet alley near the border of the city. "Far, *far* too much."

"I don't know that much," Nate said, trying to deflect and diffuse.

Noam had been growing more and more suspicious as time went on, and while his explanations had worked, the fix had only been temporary.

"You knew this friend of yours was going to be here and *exactly* where to find him. Freya's suggestion worked to your benefit, didn't it?"

"It was a lucky guess," Nate said. "Nothing more."

"I followed you," Noam said. "If that was a lucky guess, then I'm Allen Porter."

Allen Porter had been a famous musician in the 2040s before his untimely death. He'd been extremely famous worldwide, and the members of his generation were as cult-like as the followers of the Beatles in the 1960s.

"I...um..." Nate said, his mind moving a mile a minute.

He needed to come up with something, but what could he tell this man to get him off his back? He couldn't tell him he was from the future. That was basically the *first* rule of time travel – don't talk about time travel.

"How could you have followed me?" Nate finally said. "I didn't see anything, and for all you know, I had to look for a while before finding them."

"In case you've somehow forgotten, I was in the Special Forces," Noam said. "I know how to tail someone without being seen. I worked in intelligence gathering as well and spotting a liar isn't hard. You might be a good one. Good enough to fool most people, but I'm not one of them. Either you tell me the truth, or I walk. You clearly want to keep me around for some reason, so I'm betting that whatever you're hiding isn't worth me leaving."

Noam crossed his arms, his jaw set in that stubborn way that Nate absolutely *hated*. Nate let out a long breath, looking around to make sure no one was looking or listening. It seemed he'd been cornered. He had two options. He could either come up with another lie and hope the man bought it, or tell him the truth and hope he bought it.

Those were terrible options, so he decided to go for number three: none of the above.

"Do you trust me?" Nate asked.

"Clearly I don't," Noam said. "Otherwise, we wouldn't be having this conversation."

"After all we've been through, you don't trust me?" Nate said. "After fighting side by side with me against monsters, the Russian mob, Xavier's men. You *really* don't trust me?"

Noam hesitated for a moment, a small crack appearing in his hardened expression. Nate spotted that weakness and pounced.

"Who got you out of that bar when you'd given up on life? How do you think we'd be doing without your help? Do you think we'd have been able to raid Pavlov's city or find Freya's father without you? What about our recent run-ins with Ashland? You can clearly see that what we're doing is good, so *why* the distrust? Because I'm keeping some personal things to myself? That hardly seems fair, given what we've all been through together."

"You can stop laying it on so thick," Noam said, raising a hand to stop him. "I remember everything we've done. *Everything.* Including the fact that you lied to us about how Centrifuge was going to fall. You made us both believe that there was going to be ample time for people to escape, but more than three-quarters of the population died in the collapse. I've killed for my country before. I've ordered drone-strikes, bombings, personally pulled the trigger on more than one high-profile target and caused unwanted collateral damage *many* times.

"I never lost a night's sleep over any of it, because I had my orders and I understood that what I was doing was for my county and the greater good of our people. So, *explain* it to me. Give me a reason why we did this and then, we can move on."

"I already have," Nate said quietly, his mind going back to the past, to the fall of Warine and the death toll in Centrifuge.

"Yes," Noam said. "You gave me the reason, but murdering hundreds of innocent people because of something that might potentially happen in the future *isn't* good enough. In my belief, no one is guilty until they have committed the crime, regardless of whether you have prior knowledge of it or not. In my eyes, you have committed the act, but I have no basis for why you did what you did. I want my answer."

Nate let out a long sigh, suddenly feeling very old. He hadn't felt this way since returning to his previous timeline, but now, with Noam demanding answers for his actions, the weight of his age and responsibility weighed heavily on his mind.

Noam noticed the shift, seeming puzzled, though he remained silent, waiting for his answer.

Nate knew he'd been backed into a corner. He could try one more thing, but if Noam still persisted, he would have to tell him the truth and deal with the consequences.

"Are you sure you want to know?" Nate asked seriously. "Because once I tell you, there's no going back. No undoing the knowledge or the burden that will follow you for the rest of your time in the System of Twelve. Once you know, you'll never see things the same again. So, I'll ask again, are you sure?"

To his credit, Noam thought it over. Clearly, the seriousness in Nate's tone had given him pause, but as the gears turned behind his eyes, Nate could see the man wasn't going to back down.

"Regardless," Noam said. "I still want to know."

"Very well," Nate said, letting out a breath. "Before I tell you anything, you need to swear to me that you will never repeat anything I'm about to say without my express permission."

"I swear," Noam said.

Nate knew that once the man gave his word, he wouldn't go back on it. He would take Nate's secret to the grave.

"Well, that's a relief," Nate said. "Because what I'm about to tell you will probably seem even more unbelievable than everything else I've told you up until now."

Nate took a deep breath, then began to speak.

"I am a man out of time…"

At first, Noam reacted how he thought he would, with skepticism and anger, but the longer Nate spoke, the less angry the man became. By the time Nate reached the end of his tale about the final battle and the losses they'd suffered, he was listening with rapt attention, his expression serious and his muscles tense.

"And that's pretty much it," Nate said, finishing up his tale.

He'd purposefully skimmed over the details of their friendship and how Noam had died, though the implication of the man's death was very much evident.

Noam was silent for several moments after Nate finished speaking, allowing everything to sink in. Finally, he spoke.

"You carry a heavy burden, my friend," Noam said seriously. "To carry the knowledge of future events, especially ones as dark and terrible as what you have described, is unthinkable. Knowing that you have already lived this life once, I can now understand your motivations and goals. I can also understand why you did what you did. You even gave Kent the opportunity to change, even though you already knew he wouldn't. That is the sign of someone with compassion and mercy.

"I will follow and support you in your mission, Nate Chesterson. It is a noble one. One worth fighting and even dying for."

Nate breathed a silent sigh of relief, though he still couldn't stop himself from asking, "What about the innocents who will die?"

"They are already dead," Noam said sincerely. "We will do our best to avoid casualties. Now that you do not need to carry this burden alone, I can act independently. You may give me warnings ahead of time, where you could not before. But, if innocents are lost, then I will console myself with the knowledge that a higher power is at work here."

"Higher power?" Nate asked with a raised eyebrow.

"Why else would you have been chosen to come back?" Noam asked. "Who but God could have sent you here? It is my belief that the pain was too great. So, you were sent to be our salvation."

"No," Nate said firmly. "I understand your beliefs and can respect them, but I won't have you treating me as some kind of divine messenger. I want you to be yourself. You should be angry with me if anything. I could have prevented Dalia's death but didn't."

"Now that I understand you, I know that you would have done everything you could, had you had the power," Noam said, though his face did tighten with pain. "Dalia..." he paused, composing himself as his voice cracked. "Did she die in the same way last time?"

Nate nodded.

"Then it was preordained, something that could not be changed, no matter the second chance we've been given."

Noam sighed, the pain still clear in his voice, even as a wry smile touched his lips.

"I will respect your wishes. Now, we'd best be off before Freya becomes suspicious of our absence. She's sure to be working up to a tirade by now."

"How much you wanna bet she makes a crack about the two of us sneaking off to get a room together?" Nate said.

"Nothing," Noam replied. "I'd lose that bet for sure."

"Finally!" Freya exclaimed as the two of them walked into the city square around fifteen minutes later. "What the hell took you so long? Is there something I should know about?"

"Know about?" Nate asked with a raised eyebrow.

Freya looked between the two of them meaningfully, her eyebrows raised. When neither said anything, she continued.

"Did the two of you sneak off to get a room or something? You know what, don't tell me, I can already see it. It's painting quite the pretty picture in my head right now."

Noam snorted out a laugh, while Nate replied.

"Is that how you pass the time when you're alone? Fantasizing about men hanging out together?"

"Hey, I like boys," Freya said with a shrug. "Thinking about two sweaty dudes going at it really gets me going, if you know what I mean."

"I think I do," Nate said flatly. "And I don't think I need that sort of imagery in my head."

"What imagery?" Freya asked innocently. "I was talking about watching a couple of shirtless dudes hammering at each other with swords, motivating me to train and better myself. What were y-*ohhh*, you naughty boy," she said, wagging her finger at him. "Naughty, naughty. Didn't your mama ever teach you about behaving properly around a young lady? For *shame*."

"I agree with her. For shame, Nate," Noam said, still doing his best not to smile too broadly.

Nate turned on him, feeling the sting of betrayal.

142

"Hey," Noam said with a shrug. "If you can't beat them, you join them, correct?"

Freya snorted out a laugh at his attempt, the difference in language and upbringing causing the saying to fall flat.

"Come with me, big guy," she said, wrapping an arm around his shoulders. "I have *so* much to teach you."

Nate stared at his two friends as they walked off, whispering conspiratorially between one another.

Perhaps he'd made a mistake in bringing Noam on as well as Freya. His timeline for finding their fourth teammate had just been moved up. He needed someone who would at least remain impartial to any ribbing, because Nate suspected that he would be ganged up on more than once in the coming weeks.

22

"So, care to tell us where we're off to now, fearless leader?" Freya asked as they trudged uphill through the swaying, blue-green grass. "And why we didn't stay in the city for the night?"

They'd been walking for nearly an hour, having left the city and the main road, hiking deep into the wilderness. The grass had grown progressively taller and thicker as the stars had risen in the night sky. Small wildflowers had begun growing as well, but Nate had ignored them, even though they were each worth a couple of points apiece.

The prize he was after would be worth far more.

"Our ticket off this planet," Nate said in reply, pushing his way through the heavy grass.

He could feel the ground underfoot becoming marshy, though he knew that as the cold continued to settle, it would freeze and become hard-packed, and that was what he was counting on.

Freya complained a bit more, but he could tell she didn't really mean it. She was tired, as they all were, and just wanted to lie down for a rest. Luckily for her, her opportunity would come soon.

After another half hour of pushing through the grass – which was now well above their heads – Nate paused, holding his hand up and motioning the group to be silent.

At the 27th rank, his perception field stretched roughly five feet in all directions. It wasn't much. He was used to his perception field sweeping out for hundreds of yards, but the real gains would only come once he topped the 100th rank and left all traces of humanity's weaknesses behind.

Immortality. Eternal youth. Immunity to pretty much all illnesses. Those were some of the lesser perks of reaching the 100th rank. Of course, the immortality had its limits. They *could* still be killed but, in theory at least, they could live forever if they managed to avoid something so unfortunate.

Nate didn't pause because he'd heard anything – the prey they were after knew how to remain silent. He'd had them stop because he'd recognized their surroundings, as well as the dense curtain of grass that stood before them.

The ground underfoot was wet, their boots sinking partially with each step.

"What is it?" Freya asked in a lowered tone as Noam crept up to his left.

"I'm pretty sure there's a monster up ahead," Nate replied. "We're going to move *very* slowly and peek through to see if I'm right. No loud noises or sudden movements. We'll be heard if we're too noisy."

"I guess we're doomed then," Freya said with a dramatic sigh. "Nate's constant grunting will give us away."

Nate debated slugging her in the arm but decided that the subsequent yelp would probably alert the monster. Ignoring her, he slowly inched forward, parting the heavy curtain of grass to reveal the sight beyond.

The sea of grass ended at the clearing, the ground before them was bare and covered in dozens of small lumps that Nate knew to be a mix of Nickel and, if they were lucky, some Orantium. Orantium was one of the many metals unique to the System of Twelve and could be used in anything from weapons to scooters. In other words, it was an extremely useful and versatile metal, one that would be in high demand. If mixed with the correct compound, it could make something twice as strong and half as light as steel.

Of course, the other materials couldn't be found on Warine, but that was beside the point. Orantium was better than iron in every way and Nate was sincerely hoping that there would be some mixed in with the nickel.

The bare and lumpy ground continued until it abruptly stopped at the edge of a sharp decline, one that Nate knew led to a sixty-foot drop filled with sharp rocks along the way.

At the very center of the muddy and ore-strewn area was a gnarled tree with several nasty-looking pieces of gray-green fruit dangling from its branches. The fruit itself would be worth its weight in points, but it wasn't the fruit Nate was interested in. It was the monster lying coiled around the tree's base.

For all intents and purposes, it looked like an alligator – if an alligator was twenty-feet long, had sharp ridges protruding along its spine, and a tail that could shatter bone. Maybe a regular alligator *could* do that last thing, but alligators from back on Earth couldn't move with the speed and flexibility of a striking Death Adder. For reference, that was faster than the average human could *blink*. It was a good thing that they were no longer average.

On top of that, its bite was highly venomous and could kill someone at his rank within 15 minutes if left untreated, not to mention that the bite itself could tear limbs clean off.

The black *25* on its shoulder was an indication of its current rank, but the gleaming star right under it marked it as a far more dangerous opponent.

Nate watched the monster for a few more seconds, making sure that both Freya and Noam got a good look as well, before retreating and motioning them back. He remained silent until they'd traveled some fifty yards back down the sloping hill, then turned.

"Are you mad?" Freya exclaimed, though she was careful to keep her voice down. "We barely survived our last fight with a starred monster, and you want us to tackle another one!"

"We're in much better shape than we were last time," Nate said calmly as he began pushing down the stalks of grass to prepare a camp.

Seeing this, Noam moved to help, though he seemed to have his misgivings.

"I remember how bad that last one was," Freya said, unconvinced. "And that monster was only at the sixteenth rank. This one is nearly ten higher."

"The Drake had the element of surprise last time," Nate said. "The Rattlegator won't. On top of that, it'll be sluggish once night sets in fully, and the ground is frozen solid. We'll have a pretty good shot at taking it down without suffering any injuries. Well, at least those that aren't too bad."

"There *has* to be another way," Freya said, her voice trembling a bit. "There has to be."

It had been hard for him to see why she'd been so against this at first, but now that he heard that tremor, Nate thought he understood. She was afraid.

"It's okay to be scared," Nate said in an understanding voice. "It's *good* even. Fear will keep you alive. Don't let that fear cripple you, though. You need to overcome it."

"I'm not scared for myself, you idiot," Freya muttered, then plonked herself down on the flattened grass and hugged her knees to her chest.

Nate shared a look with Noam, who shrugged and continued flattening the grass down to make them comfortable for the next few hours.

"I'm not planning on dying, if that's what you're nervous about," Nate said, going to sit next to her.

"I know you're not planning on it, but you always seem to end up on the brink of death every time we go into a fight," Freya said bitterly. "How am I supposed to feel about that? I know we can't help getting into some fights, but this is one we're actively looking for and I just don't see the point."

"This is the fastest way to Laybor," Nate said, placing a hand on her shoulder. "Also, remember that I'm not dead. Almost dying isn't the same as *actually* dying."

"But when's your luck going to run out?" Freya asked.

Nate shrugged.

"Who knows? It *could* be today. It could be tomorrow. I could be killed by a monster or a falling meteor. Regardless of how, I *will* die someday."

That much wasn't strictly true, but he decided to gloss over the details of immortality for the time being.

"I can either continue to fight every day, making myself stronger to ensure I'm harder to kill, or I can go off and hide in a dark corner, praying that I won't die some horrible death. I understand you're worried, but thinking about this will drive you insane as surely as watching all fifteen Night of the Living Zombie Bear movies in a row will."

Freya snorted out a laugh at that.

"Funny how you think I even know what that is," she said.

"A girl like you? There's no *way* you haven't watched them."

"I admit it," Freya sighed. "I did. Multiple times. But I watch it for the plot, I swear."

"Yeah," Nate said. "The plot."

Freya rolled her eyes, though she did give him a smile.

"I see your point, mister grumpy pants," she said. "I'll do my best to stop worrying, though I don't think I'll be able to get rid of it altogether."

"That much is expected," Nate said. "I worry about you too."

The scene of Freya's gruesome death flashed in his mind and sent a shiver down his spine, but he subdued that horrible memory and shoved it as deep down as he possibly could. This wasn't the time or the place.

"So," Noam said, moving over to join them. "What can you tell us about this Rattlegator?"

"It's got cultivator techniques, so no flying projectiles or fire," Nate said. "Which is a good thing. The bad news is that it's freakishly strong and fast. It can rip you in half with its bite, which is venomous, by the way, and its tail can break bone."

"Is that all?" Freya asked sarcastically. "Next thing we'll hear is that it's intelligent, can understand the intricacies of human conversation, and moonlights as a murder-solving detective named Dan."

"You have quite the imagination," Noam said, giving her a strange look.

"It's a gift," Freya said, tossing her golden-blonde hair.

"You seem to have a lot of those," Nate said.

"Jealous?" Freya said, smirking.

"Extremely," Nate replied dryly.

"Mister grumpy pants strikes again!"

"Back to the matter at hand," Nate said, ignoring her last comment. "It's strong, fast and has a flesh-eating venom that could kill you in under fifteen minutes. You'll want to watch out for the jaws and tail most of all. Its weaknesses are that it's cold-blooded, so it'll be sluggish in the dead of night. It's also vulnerable to Freya, since she can fire on it from a distance, which is good."

"So, am I going to be starting with my Snipe Crack then?" Freya asked, still grinning.

For some reason, she found the spell name to be funny, and with her odd sense of humor, Nate could understand why.

"Yes," Nate replied. "I would focus on using your Blazing Bullet after that, though. It's resistant to poison so it would be pointless to use Poisonshot."

"Works for me," she said. "I'll put a nice hole for you to stick your sword in."

"What about me?" Noam asked.

"You're going to be with me," Nate said, ignoring Freya's comment yet again. "You're going to try pulling that thing's attention. Use your new techniques sparingly, as I'm sure you know the cost. If it goes for Freya, I'll leave it up to you to defend her."

148

"Works for me," Noam said.

"Looks like we have a plan then," Nate said, rolling his shoulders. "We should get some sleep while we can. It's going to be an interesting night."

23

The air before Nate's lips steamed as his eyes cracked open, the stars above twinkling and the colors of the galaxies breathtaking. His nose was cold, as were his hands, though the rest of his body was warm.

Freya was curled up next to him, her face tucked into his shoulder, while Noam sprawled out on his back, just a couple of feet away. The man stirred as Nate did – not that he was surprised – and rose, seeming almost eerily alert. Nate supposed that when you were in the special forces for as long as he'd been, you learned to sleep light and be ready to move quickly when needed.

"Just a few more minutes," Freya groaned when Nate nudged her in the ribs to wake her up.

"Take all the time you want," Nate said, then moved away, getting to his feet.

Freya's hand scrabbled around on the grassy ground, searching desperately for the warmth, then cracked an eye, glaring at him.

"You are evil," she grumbled, then yawned widely as she pushed herself into a sitting position and rubbed her eyes.

It was well past midnight, which meant that the coldest part of the night would soon be upon them, when the Rattlegator would not only be the slowest but also the most sluggish to react. If they were lucky, they'd be able to take the monster out before it realized what was happening.

They got ready quickly, Freya still grumbling about getting up in the middle of the night just to 'kill some lizard.' Noam was silent, donning his Drake armor and strapping his tomahawks to his belt.

"You'll have better luck with the ax on this one," Nate said, when he saw that. "This thing's got a tough hide."

"I can hand them to my double if needed," Noam said, leaving the tomahawks where they were.

"Do you know your limits?" Nate asked, strapping his own Drake armor on and trying not to shiver.

"Yeah," Noam said. "Though I'm surprised by how little time I can keep the third-tier techniques going before I run dry."

"Don't worry about that," Nate said. "It'll all balance out as you grow in rank. It's why there's no point in pushing for a fourth-tier manual until at least the sixty-fifth rank. You'd barely be able to use them at all because of the massive amounts of kanta they use."

While the 2nd tier techniques would become less costly when he'd moved to the 3rd tier, they would still be more expensive than the 1st tier techniques were when he'd advanced his manual for the first time. In other words, while the cost *did* decrease, allowing him to use them more efficiently, they still cost more than the 1st tier techniques.

Similarly, the 3rd tier techniques were quite a bit more costly than the 2nd tier ones had been when he'd advanced to that point, so he'd be limited in how much he could use his new techniques without running out of kanta.

Nate made a mental note that once they moved over to Laybor, he would have Noam purchase a Kanta Orb of his own, as he'd gone without one for far too long.

"We all ready?" Nate asked, reluctantly removing his fox-fur gloves and stashing them in his ring.

"As ready as we'll ever be," Freya said, still yawning.

"Great, here's the plan," he began.

Nate crept carefully through the tall grass, his boots crunching lightly through the frozen ground. Frost coated the bottoms of the grass stalks, showing the rapid temperature change the area had undergone.

Beside him, Noam moved, silent as a whisper, his feet somehow making less noise than Nate's. Nate had been able to move like that in his previous life but his body was now clumsy and unwieldy in comparison. It was why he was working so hard to correct that and instill all the knowledge of his mind into his muscles.

The sheet of grass parted, revealing the Rattlegator once again. The monster had moved a short distance away from the tree, its tail wrapped around itself, and eyes closed. A low rattling echoed, rumbling through its body as it slept, its side rising and falling slowly.

Nate pushed through the grass, stepping out into the open. If the Rattlegator opened its eyes now, it would see them without a doubt. Still, that was why they were attacking now, instead of in the middle of the day.

His breath steamed in great smoky plumes, the brilliant galaxies overhead illuminating the open clearing in shades of blue and purple, reflecting off the many pieces of metal ore. It made the ground appear as though it were part of the sky and the Rattlegator was some ancient guardian of the stars.

Nate couldn't wait to turn its hide into points.

A rustle of movement came from their left and Nate turned, seeing Freya emerge from the tall grass some twenty yards away, at the very edge of the open battleground. Her Magigun was already clutched in one hand, aimed at the monster.

He raised his hand, stopping Noam in his tracks.

Let's see how good your aim is now, Nate thought as the woman raised the weapon, sighting down the barrel.

With her two augments, Freya should have a very hard time missing a vital point. He just hoped that she would be able to hit the target dead on, otherwise this could turn into an ugly and drawn-out fight.

He waited alongside Noam as Freya concentrated, then depressed the trigger. A bright flash of white lit up the night, vanishing into the crack in space. An instant later, it appeared through a second crack, the flash of white reappearing and slamming directly into the Rattlegator's left eye.

A massive explosion rocked the monster, blasting its head to one side and knocking it onto its back as a spray of blood showered the air. The gator roared as it was rudely awoken from its slumber, pain lancing through its head. Its legs and tail thrashed as it tried to right itself, its still-slumbering brain not yet comprehending what was happening.

Had this been an ordinary monster, Freya's shot would have killed it outright, especially with where she'd hit it. But this was a starred monster and even its eyes were strong enough to kill the momentum of an attack.

It was a good thing then that Freya still had three more shots, all of which came in rapid succession as Nate and Noam rushed in to attack.

Three Blazing Bullets appeared from cracks in the air, each one targeting a weak spot. The first slammed into the monster's belly, right where its heart should have been. The second caught it on the underside of its mouth, and the third hit its other eye.

The gator roared as each attack slammed home, sizzling across its skin and leaving burned flesh in its wake. The two that hit the belly and mouth didn't quite penetrate, but the one that hit its other eye did. Another roar echoed from the monster's mouth, though it was cut short as Noam's ax, emitting wisps of red kanta, slammed down on its throat, biting deep and lodging there.

Noam's Brutal Guardian would enhance not only his own strength and speed but also increase the severity of any injuries he inflicted while the technique was active.

With a grunt, the man ripped the ax free, sending a spray of blood across the frozen ground. The gator hissed and gurgled, its body thrashing, only for Noam's ax to come down for a second time, shearing deeper into its throat. The tail flashed around, and Noam released his ax, leaping back and avoiding the thrashing limb.

In the meantime, Freya had closed to within firing distance and began using Blazing Bullet again, blasting the monster in the same area repeatedly with stunning accuracy.

The gator finally got its feet under it, rolling to its belly, Noam's ax still lodged deep in its throat. The monster thrashed around, its tail and jaws snapping as blood continued to pour from its throat.

Nate, who'd been waiting for his opening, dashed in when the monster's head turned, his Gilded Skin cloaking his body and his Steelshod propelling him forward. The gator's tail swept for his chest, but he dropped to the ground, sliding beneath the swinging tail and snagging the handle of Noam's ax as he did.

With a grunt, he ripped the weapon free, then summoned a glowing dirk, jamming it into the monster's tough hide to arrest his momentum. It was thanks to his Steelshod that he was able to punch through the Rattlegator's thick hide, the piston-like effect of the technique driving the weapon in with extra power.

The gator roared again as Nate leaped back to his feet, dragging himself upright by using the handle of the dirk and hurled the ax back to Noam. The man caught the handle with a shocking amount of dexterity as he took a running leap in the air. The ax came down again as he caught it, Brutal Guardian lending him the power to shear into the top of the monster's spine.

The weapon didn't bite quite as deeply, but Noam still managed to lodge the weapon in enough to draw blood. The ax tore free as his momentum carried him over the monster, the man tucking into a roll and moving free of the gator's range.

"Stay back!" Nate called as Noam turned to attack again.

The gator was already dying, so there was little point in moving in for the kill.

Blood coated his hand from where he'd stabbed the gator, not actually having contributed much to this battle. Still, as the Rattlegator thrashed around, blinded and bleeding, he felt that he'd done more than his fair share.

This was a 1-Star monster. Had they attacked it during the day, it would have given them a real fight that would likely have dragged out over several minutes, opening them all to the possibility of real and crippling injuries.

Instead, they'd snuck up on this monster in the dark and used Freya to take its eyesight and Noam's superior strength to inflict a series of devastating blows to its exposed throat. He couldn't have planned a better fight if he'd tried.

He watched as the Rattlegator's movements slowed, its body growing weaker and weaker as the blood continued oozing from its neck. Finally, with one last rattle, the massive monster dropped to the ground. It lay there for several moments, its sides heaving. Then its breathing stopped and a rush of kanta slammed into Nate's Core.

24

"I wish every fight was this easy," Freya said, crouching before the downed body of the fallen monster.

"You and me both," Nate said, clenching his hand into a fist. Rank *30*.

It wasn't quite as much kanta as he'd been hoping for, but the Rattlegator was a less dangerous opponent than the Drake they'd battled. On top of that, he'd done less damage than the others, so his share would be smaller.

Looking at his two companions, he saw that they'd both closed the gap. Freya was now at the 30th rank, just like him, while Noam was at the 31st, taking a small step ahead of him. He must already have been close to the 27th when the battle started.

Nate examined himself from within, feeling the increased capacity and power within his Core. His perception field had increased once again and he felt stronger and healthier than ever before. It was easier to feel the changes when there were multiple rank increases, than when they came one at a time. He found that he quite enjoyed the sensation.

"The plan was well executed," Noam said, frowning as he lifted his ax.

The blade was chipped and warped, which was unsurprising, given how tough the hide of that monster had been. The ax was an ordinary weapon, and it was nearing the limits of what it could do.

Still, the man slung the ax over his back, despite the damage, thumbing the tomahawks at his waist and obviously wondering how much life they had remaining.

"We'll get those augmented when we go to Laybor," Nate said. "I had the same done to my knife so that it didn't break the first time I tried to stab a rank thirty monster with half-decent armor."

Noam nodded, though he seemed less than happy about his damaged ax.

"How much do you think we'll be able to get out of this baby?" Freya asked, running her hands over the leathery hide.

"If we go to the right shop, we can probably get somewhere in the range of forty thousand," Nate said.

"So little?" Freya exclaimed.

"That Froster Drake was a rare and powerful monster," Nate said. "I wouldn't get used to massive paydays like that one anytime soon."

Freya pouted, grumbling under her breath about it not awarding enough points for the effort.

"You *do* realize that forty thousand it a lot, right?" Nate said with a raised eyebrow. "Like, a *lot* a lot."

"Yeah," Freya said. "But we've got to split it three ways."

"That's still a lot, considering how much effort it took to kill," Nate said. "But, if that's not enough for you, why don't you take a look around and tell me what you see?"

"What would I s-?" Freya cut off as Nate pointed to the ground not two feet from where she was crouched.

Freya didn't have a hard time spotting the ore once it became obvious to her and she scooped it up, turning the lump of stone, the light of the metal veins reflecting the starlight above.

"I've never seen metal glow like this," Freya said, handing it over.

Nate grinned as he took it, recognizing the Orantium for what it was. It seemed that this was their lucky day.

A loud, hissing roar echoed through the night and Nate's eyes snapped up, his heart stopping in his chest.

"Oh, crud!" he exclaimed as a second Rattlegator emerged from the grass on the far side of the clearing.

Unlike the one lying at their feet, this one was very much awake and very much alert. Worse, judging by the shimmering haze hovering over its body, this one was burning excess heat to keep itself going.

Rattlegators were unique among cold-blooded predators in that they could store excess heat during the day for use at night. The reason Nate had been so confident that the first wouldn't give them too much trouble was the fact that it wouldn't have had much time to react, let alone think to burn its stored body heat.

"Oh, look at that. More points," Freya said, rising to her feet.

"Run!" Nate said, leaping to his feet.

"What? Why?" Freya asked, looking between the dead gator and the living one. "We took this one out, I'm sure we can handle another one, especially now that we're all over rank thirty. I feel stronger than ever!"

Red light gleamed within the monster's eyes as it continued approaching, its body winding from side to side, like that of a snake. The bright *28* marking its shoulder was bad enough, but the star once again marked it as a creature to be feared.

"Because," Nate said, grabbing her arm and dragging her back, "it's alert *and* enraged. We do not want to tangle with that thing. Now come on!"

It hurt to leave this monster corpse behind, but they needed time to break it down and the second Rattlegator wasn't going to give it to them.

"Are you sure we should run?" Noam asked, seeming to be on Freya's side with this one. "I think I can damage it, even if it's awake and a little stronger."

"Yes, I'm sure," Nate said, crouching and grabbing as many pieces of ore as he could reach. "We need to leave. Now."

With that said, he turned and ran, putting as much distance between himself and the enraged monster as possible. A sluggish and sleeping 1-star monster was one thing, an alert and enraged one was quite another. That thing was ready for a fight, and they'd already exhausted some of their reserves battling that last one.

They might be able to win, but he wasn't about to take that chance when he'd already achieved what he'd come here to do.

The Rattlegator suddenly stopped, body tense and staring between the group and the dead body. Then, it lunged forward with a hissing roar, covering the distance between them at shocking speeds.

"Holy cra-ahhh!" Freya yelled as Nate dragged her over the body of the dead monster, her feet leaving the ground for an instant before she crashed into him, the two of them falling to the ground.

The Rattlegator slammed into the body of its dead companion, the corpse flying into the air on a collision course with the two of them. Still clutching Freya, Nate pulled her tight and rolled hard to one side, the body of the dead gator smashing into the ground just inches away.

He leaped to his feet, dragging the woman up along with him and turning to run once again.

"Okay, we're running," Freya agreed, pale as a sheet.

The two of them took off after Noam, who'd already started running as soon as the monster had lunged.

Behind them, the Rattlegator hissed and roared, coming after them. Freya whirled, firing back over her shoulder at the monster. Her Blazing Bullets slammed into its face, bouncing off the monster's toughened hide and slamming into the ground at its sides. Thankfully, it slowed the monster somewhat, allowing them to run into the cover of the grass.

"How the *hell* is this thing so tough?" she exclaimed.

"Enraged monsters are much harder to kill," Nate said, keeping ahold of her hand.

The last thing he wanted to do was lose her in the forest of swaying grass.

"Nate?" Noam's voice echoed through the grassy forest.

"Here!" Nate called, despite the risk.

Another rattling roar shook their surroundings as the Rattlegator dove into the swaying grass, chasing after them.

A dark form came blurring through the grass and nearly collided with them, Nate's gleaming backsword appearing and very nearly skewering Noam as he staggered into view.

"Woah! Easy, it's just me!" Noam said, raising his hands.

"Stay close," Nate said, his heart thundering. "That thing can hear far better than we can. We need to find somewhere to hide and hope it gives up."

"There are plenty of hiding spots," Freya said, gesturing to the grass around them.

"The grass isn't good enough," Nate said, looking around quickly.

There was nothing other than swaying grass in all directions, the thick strands rising high into the air. Another rattling hiss sounded from off to their left. Standing still was *definitely* not a good idea.

"Come on," Nate said. "We need to keep moving. Just try and keep it down as much as you can."

The group took off running, shoving through the thick grass, and trying not to get it tangled around their feet. The only sounds that could be heard were their ragged breathing and the pounding of their feet against the ground. That, and the occasional rattling roar from the monster that was chasing them.

Nate turned hard to one side, pulling his friends along with him. They needed to shake this thing. It was far more suited to this terrain than they were and would undoubtedly catch them on a prolonged chase.

The hissing continued for several minutes, their group changing direction multiple times to try shaking the monster. Finally, after nearly ten minutes of running and backtracking, they slowed.

"Do you hear anything?" Noam asked.

He was breathing hard, though not nearly as hard as Nate.

"I don't hear anything," Freya panted. "Maybe we lost it?"

As soon as she said that, a blurring shape leaped at her from the surrounding grass, the Rattlegator's heavy body smashing into her and bearing her to the ground.

Freya let out a scream as she hit the floor, the monster's massive jaws snapping down at her face. Nate's summoned broadsword smashed into its side with all the strength he could muster, the Steelshod gauntlets cloaking his hands and feet lending the blow extra power.

The enraged monster was thrown off her, a line of blood marring its hide, and Nate grabbed her arm, dragging her to her feet.

"Are you okay?" he asked, seeing Freya wince as she straightened.

"I think my ribs are broken," she groaned, clutching at her chest. "That thing hits like a freight train."

The Froster Drake might have been physically stronger than any normal magic-based monster would be, but a *true* 1-star cultivator-based monster would be significantly more so. He was just grateful that the monster hadn't managed to bite her.

The Rattlegator righted itself and lunged once more, only for Noam to smash into it from the side, his massive ax cleaving into it. The monster roared as it was tossed off its feet once more, a small line of blood marring its side where Noam had struck.

Noam's ax, on the other hand, hadn't been so lucky. The strike had been echoed by a loud shriek of metal, as the blade had been bent to one side, a single, jagged crack appearing at the edge of the blade.

"Can you run?" Nate asked, eyeing the monster.

"I'll have to," Freya said with a wince.

The group took off once again, Freya using her Tele-bang as the Rattlegator lunged at them once more, throwing the monster fifteen feet away and disorienting it. The grass grew thicker, obscuring the stars and throwing their sense of direction. Had Nate been able to concentrate, he'd have known where they were, but seeing as they'd been running for their lives, he'd gotten completely turned around.

When they suddenly burst from the tall grass and emerged into a familiar clearing, he swore loudly.

"Come on," he said, turning toward the grass once more.

"I can't...I can't keep running like this," Freya wheezed, doubling over. "I feel like my lungs are on fire. I can't get a proper breath!"

Nate cursed again. She must have a punctured lung or even both, if she was unlucky. That Rattlegator lunge must have done more damage than he'd initially realized. That and the extra running probably hadn't helped.

A low, rumbling hiss came from within the grass before he could decide on a course of action and the Rattlegator slowly emerged, its body low to the ground and eyes gleaming. The telltale heat haze still shimmered around its body and its jaws were partly open.

Nate, Noam, and Freya slowly backed up, but Nate knew they were stuck between a rock and a hard place. Behind them was a cliff, and before them was a powerful monster. They couldn't run, not with Freya injured as she was, which only left them with one real option. They were going to have to fight.

"I have an idea," Noam said, watching the approaching gator.

"I'm all ears," Nate said, as they continued backing away.

"Back up to the edge of the cliff. We might be able to provoke it into a charge."

"There's no *way* that'll work," Freya groaned. "The monster can't be *that* stupid, can it?"

"Normally not," Nate said, continuing to back up. "But it's enraged. It might be stronger, but it won't be thinking as clearly. This might actually work if we're fast enough."

The Rattlegator hissed again as the group was backed right up against the edge. A quick glance over his shoulder showed Nate the steep and sharp descent to the bottom. If they fell, at least one of them would die. Right now, he gave himself fifty-fifty odds. Noam had a good shot of living. Freya, on the other hand, would *definitely* die.

"Here it comes," Noam said as the gator's body bunched up. "Dive!"

The three of them dove. Freya to her left, Noam to his right, and Nate forward, flattening himself as the Rattlegator's massive bulk sailed over him and over the edge of the cliff.

25

"Holy cow!" Freya exclaimed, dragging herself to her feet and looking down to the bottom of the cliff. "That thing's still alive!"

Nate turned, still on his hands and knees, and looked to the bottom of the steep fall. Sure enough, the Rattlegator had survived the fall. Its body had been punched full of holes and lacerations by the sharpened rocks, bits of flesh and gore clinging to the myriad of sharpened stones on the way down.

The monster looked like a wreck, but it *was* still alive and very much enraged.

"Do you think I can kill it from here?" Freya asked, her pain momentarily forgotten.

"You can try if you have the kanta," Nate said, watching the monster struggle to climb back up to them.

The heat haze no longer played about its body, and it was already looking more sluggish.

"I think I've got enough left for one more Snipe Crack," Freya said, drawing her Magigun.

The Rattlegator roared as Freya leveled her gun, then squeezed the trigger. A flash of white vanished into a crack in space, a matching one appearing near the monster's head. There was an explosion of force as the projectile impacted, smashing into its eye.

A chunk was blasted out of the side of the monster's head, even as it was thrown off its feet once more, rolling several times before going still.

Freya collapsed to her knees, her breath rattling and looking pale.

"Did it get it?" she asked, already pulling at the kanta in her surroundings to try recovering.

Unlike Nate, she wouldn't be able to heal things like broken bones, but if she could keep the injuries from worsening, they could make it to town for her to buy the upgrade.

"It's still alive," Noam said grimly as the ragged monster pulled itself to its feet.

"If it dies, we'll be rewarded, if it doesn't, we don't get anything," Nate said. "Right now, though, we can't worry about that. We need to get Freya back to the city."

"At least collect the body," Freya said as she tucked her legs under herself. "If we had to go through all of that, I'm not going to leave empty-handed."

Nate looked at her hesitantly but, in the end, agreed. He wasn't going to leave points laying around after all they'd been through.

"Noam can take care of some of your injuries," Nate said, but Freya shook her head.

"Let him save his kanta. I'll be fine."

Once again, Nate hesitated, looking to Noam.

"I can take some of the pain away at least," Noam said.

"I *said* I was fine," Freya snapped. "It's just a few broken bones. If I can't handle that much, how am I supposed to stand on my own in this group?"

So this was her pride talking. Nate felt that it was stupid for her to be so stubborn about this, but if she said she was fine, he wasn't going to push it and waste even more of their time.

"Very well then," he said. "You collect the ore, and I'll break down the body."

Noam nodded and began moving around the clearing, scooping up the pieces of scattered ore. While he did that, Nate crouched by the dead body of the first Rattlegator. It had been damaged by the second monster's attack, so the value would be less than what they could have gotten, but the fact they were getting anything at all was good.

He summoned a heavy-bladed knife using his Gilded Blade and began breaking the monster down. His kanta was already recovering, though he'd burned through more than he'd have liked in that last battle with the Rattlegator. If things had gotten any worse, he'd have been forced to use his Whitefire Injection, which was something he would rather avoid.

There was a specific augment he was after and only once he had it would he be confident in using the technique for any amount of time without dire consequence.

As he worked on breaking the monster down so that its parts could be carried in his ring, he was acutely aware of Freya's labored breathing. She was trying to put on a good show, but this kind of pain was something she wouldn't be used to. Nate believed he could handle injuries quite well, as he'd suffered his fair share, but Freya wasn't.

"How are you holding up?" he asked once he'd managed to remove the monster's head and stash it in his ring.

The thing had been over 250 pounds and it was only thanks to his current rank that he was able to physically lift it on his own.

"I've been better," Freya said, her voice tight with pain.

"You *sure* you don't want to ask Noam for help?"

Freya shot him a glare in response to that question.

"Noam, how are you doing?" Nate asked, calling to his friend.

"There's still plenty to gather," Noam said. "I...oh, *come on*!"

Nate's head jerked to his right, where Noam's eyes had turned. Emerging from the tall grass was a third Rattlegator. This time, *none* of them hesitated, the group abandoning whatever they were doing and making a mad dash for the grass. There were a few tense moments as they ran – Freya's breaths rattling audibly as they moved – where Nate was worried that the monster would be coming after them.

But, after five minutes of running downhill at a breakneck speed, he began to slow down. They'd lost Noam and he wasn't going to risk calling for him, as the last thing they needed was another fight on their hands. They would just have to continue to Southside Eight and hopefully meet him there.

"What in the hell is going on tonight?" Freya wheezed.

"We must have hit a swarm," Nate said, his mouth flattening to a line. "It's uncommon with starred monsters, but it can happen every once in a while. The smell of their dead kin attracts them. I wouldn't be surprised if another few show up before the night is out."

"Just our luck, huh?" Freya said with a pained smile.

"Just our luck," Nate repeated. "Come on, we've got a bit of a walk before we reach the city."

The two of them began moving, this time at a slower pace, allowing Freya an easier walk. She stopped about halfway to their destination though, letting out a low groan and sinking to her knees.

"I don't feel so good," she said, her stomach heaving.

"What's wrong?" Nate asked, beginning to feel worried.

Freya vomited in response, blood and bile splattering against the ground as she retched. She listed to one side then, her eyes rolling up in her skull and her body beginning to shake.

Now very worried, Nate seized her, holding her in place as her body thrashed, shuddering uncontrollably for nearly a full minute. Finally, she stopped, her eyes refocusing, and her brow beaded with sweat.

"Nate, I don't like this," she groaned. "I...I..." She trailed off, hunching inward and clutching at her stomach again.

"Come on," Nate said, helping her roll on her back, away from the pile of awful she'd expunged.

Freya rolled without complaint, keeping her hands clamped over her stomach.

"I'm going to take a look," Nate said, keeping his voice calm and even, though he was feeling anything but. "But I'm going to need you to move your hands. Okay?"

Freya nodded, slowly forcing her hands to her sides and clenched her teeth and Nate pulled her shirt up. At first, all he saw was the pale, unbroken skin of her waist, but as he pulled the garment up past her navel, he was greeted by an ugly sight.

Nate winced inwardly as he continued to pull the shirt up, revealing a series of black and blue markings tracing from her belly, all the way up to the bottom of her chest wrap – the system's equivalent of female undergarments. Nate ran his fingers over the bruises gingerly, feeling the lumps of broken bone beneath. This was much worse than he'd thought. Much, *much* worse.

"I'm going to pull your shirt up a bit higher, okay?" Nate said.

Freya just nodded, keeping her eyes closed, her breathing shallow. Nate carefully pulled the shirt up further, seeing blood staining the wrap near the top. He stopped once he could see her collarbone, fully revealing the extent of the damage that Rattlegator had managed to inflict.

Her right collarbone was cracked, a small shard of bone having punched through the skin. The skin that wasn't covered by her wrap was blotchy and bruised, dark red patches showing through.

Not only were her ribs and collarbone cracked, but she was also profusely bleeding internally.

"Okay," Nate said, his mind working quickly. "Here's what we're going to do. I'm going to carry you back to the city. While I'm doing that, you're going to keep cycling kanta and stay awake. Does that sound like a plan?"

Freya nodded once and Nate released her shirt, allowing it to fall back. He stood then, sliding his hands beneath her back and knees, then straightened, taking her full weight in his arms. He would have preferred to carry her on his back, but with the placement of her injuries, that would have been a bad idea.

"Don't...don't I feel like a...princess," Freya said with a dry chuckle.

"Oh good, you can still make jokes," Nate said, taking off at a slow jog. "And here I thought you were terribly injured."

"Guess you...were right. Should...have listened and taken the...the help."

"If you're admitting you were wrong, you've *really* got to be out of it," Nate said, forcing a laugh.

"It all worked out...pretty good for you..."

"I don't see how you being horribly injured would benefit me in any way," Nate replied.

"Enjoy...grabbing a...peek?" Freya said, forcing a half grin onto her lips.

"I think I'd have preferred seeing something less black and blue," Nate said in response.

Freya let out a dry chuckle at that, then winced again and went silent. Nate did his best not to jostle her as he ran, shoving through the heavy grass and silently cursing himself. They were going to have to get their hands on some emergency drafts once this was all over. Even if it was expensive, their lives were worth more than this.

Noam had his healing, but it cost him kanta he would need to use for fighting. He was a warrior, first and foremost. The healing technique was more of an emergency measure than anything.

Nate sighed to himself. This was going to hurt.

"A Healing Draft please," Nate said, placing his hand on the glass sphere within the shop.

166

"That'll be eight-thousand points," the gnark behind the counter said.

"Yeah, yeah, I know," Nate said, biting back a curse.

The points were removed, and Nate made his way over to Freya, who lay on the floor, barely conscious. The last few minutes had been touch-and-go, as the woman's temperature had begun rising rapidly. If not for her continued efforts to cycle kanta, things might have turned out differently.

"Drink up," Nate said, pulling the cork and placing the bottle to her lips.

He flashed back to the last time he'd done this when Freya had been injured in the battle against some of Pavlov's gangsters. This time, she was conscious and could drink the potion on her own.

She let out a groan of ecstasy as the pain vanished, her bones shifting back into place and her damaged internal organs restoring themselves. Any blood that had collected within her body was expunged and within a matter of seconds, Freya was back to full health.

"Looks like I owe you yet again," Freya said, giving him a tired smile. "I feel like I can sleep for a week."

"Come," Nate said, extending a hand and helping her to her feet. "Let's find you somewhere you can sleep it off."

Freya nodded, accepting his help, and leaning on him as they left the shop. They ran into Noam as they exited, the man looking bedraggled and worried.

"Oh, thank God, you're both still alive," he said, letting out a sigh of relief.

"Do me a favor," Nate said. "The next time this stubborn woman tells you not to heal her, *don't* listen."

"Oh? Forcing me to do things against my will?" Freya asked. "I thought better of you, Nate. For shame."

"Well, it looks like she's back to herself," Noam said. "So, care to fill me in?"

Nate told him what had happened as they walked the darkened streets of the city, heading to the closest inn. They were only around halfway there, when the entire group paused as a rush of kanta slammed into them all.

Nate grinned as he turned his hand, feeling new strength flood him once more. The black *30* on the back of his hand shifted, changing to a *32*. Freya's arm, which was hanging over his shoulder, showed the same number as his.

"Same," Noam said, showing the back of his right hand. "Seems like a smaller jump than the last."

"It only gets harder from here," Nate said with a shrug. "It's more difficult to train once you hit thirty on Warine. It's still doable, of course, but we'd be much better off on Laybor."

"We can go after I sleep," Freya said, yawning widely.

"Good evening, welcome to the…"

"We need three rooms for the night," Nate said, cutting off the warbling voice of the female winge who'd approached them upon entering.

With the way she was dressed, as well as the decorations surrounding him, he already knew this was going to be expensive.

26

Freya let out a loud moan, her eyes rolling up into her head and attracting a lot of unwanted attention.

"Do you see what I have to deal with?" Nate asked, trying to pretend he didn't exist as half the restaurant turned to see what was going on.

"Yes," Noam said, hiding a smile. "I can see that this can be embarrassing."

"Oh, shove it up your bunghole," Freya said, chewing slowly and relishing every bite. "I'm just enjoying some good food in the proper manner."

"There's nothing proper about this," Nate said.

If the meal hadn't been included with the outrageous 40-point stay at Hotel Fancy, he would have stood up and left right then and there. It was a good thing that it was later in the morning and most of the patrons had already cleared out, as he couldn't imagine how much more embarrassing this would have been if the place had been packed.

Now that she knew it bothered him, Freya continued to make all sorts of noises throughout the meal, which Nate did his best to ignore.

Once they were done, they left the inn, heading for one of the nearby tanneries where Nate believed he could get the best price for the parts of the Rattlegator they'd killed.

"Why don't we sell this on Laybor?" Noam asked as they walked towards the closest of the tanners.

"Because they'll give us less for it," Nate said. "Monsters like this are less valuable on the second planet."

"How much are we going to lose out on since we don't have the whole body?" Freya asked.

"Not much," Nate said. "I got the most valuable parts and they're in pretty good shape."

Sure enough, the tanner offered Nate 31,000 points for the parts. Noam got his share, but Freya received a much smaller one because she once again owed Nate points.

"This is so unfair," she pouted as they left the tanner. "I only got a measly three-thousand points."

"It could have been less," Noam pointed out. "We didn't have to give you the extra thousand."

Freya stopped complaining.

"How much ore did you manage to get?" Nate asked.

"A good amount, actually," Noam said, checking his ring. "About sixty pieces of the nickel and four of another metal that I cannot identify."

"Orantium ore," Nate said. "We can sell the iron, but we'll want to keep that. If we can get our hands on some sandstone and pumice, we'll be able to get some Ortium ingots."

"Ortium?" Noam asked.

"An excellent metal for a new ax," Nate said, pointing to the wrecked ax on Noam's back.

The man soured a bit at the mention of the broken weapon.

"Will it hold up any better?"

"Have you ever felt the weight difference between titanium and steel?" Nate said in reply.

"I have," Noam said.

"Imagine a metal lighter than titanium but twice the strength of steel and you'll get Ortium."

"Call me intrigued," Noam said. "But will it be easy getting our hands on both sandstone and pumice?"

"Nope," Nate replied with a wide smile.

"Thought so," Noam sighed.

Their group stopped by a smelter where they traded in their nickel ores for 250 points apiece, netting them a total of 15,000, which, split three ways, totaled 5,000 each. Now in a considerably better mood, Freya began chattering about the battle as they headed out of the city, Nate noting a tail on their group as they left.

"Don't look, but someone's following us," Noam said when he noticed it himself.

"It's one of Dirk's men," Nate said dismissively. "They won't bother us."

"Your friend?" Freya asked. "Why would he be sending men to follow us?"

"Good question," Nate said. "I'll have to ask him the next time we run into him. Take your scooters out. Let's see if we can give them the slip."

As casually as they could, the group stopped, removing their scooters from their rings.

"Do you think it'll work?" Freya asked.

"No idea," Nate said. "But whether it works or not doesn't really matter. I doubt they'll follow us into Laybor, which is where we're headed right now."

He shoved off, Freya and Noam following him. He didn't look to see if they were being followed, speeding down the road toward their destination about a mile-and-a-half from the city.

"Looks like we lost him," Noam said once they stopped.

"Good," Nate said, stashing his scooter and stepping off the road.

"So we're really going to Laybor this time," Freya said, taking one last look around as they headed up the slight incline, grass brushing at their ankles.

"We'll probably be back at some point," Nate said. "We'll have to let Sean and his clan know once we've dealt with the Portal Reavers, but yeah, we'll be gone for a while."

"I'm really not looking forward to what this place will do to my hair," Freya sighed.

"Don't worry," Nate said. "The portal we're going through leads right into a village. We'll be able to find somewhere to change quickly."

"Well, that's a relief," Freya said, giving Nate a smirk. "That's not the kind of hot and sweaty I like, if you know what I mean."

Nate chose not to say anything, seeing the trap for what it was.

"It's rude to ignore people like that, you know," Noam said.

Nate shot the man a glare, while Freya laughed.

Still, despite outward appearances, he was happy. He'd been afraid he might lose her last night with how badly she'd been injured, but once again, Freya had managed to pull through. He would rather endure a thousand of these terrible comments a day than lose her.

"Age before beauty," Freya said as they stopped before the portals.

"I think she means *you*, Noam," Nate said, seeing his chance to get back at the man.

"I am the senior-most member of this group," Noam said, nodding sagely. "It is only right to respect your elders."

With that said, he walked through the triangular streak of blue breaking the horizon. Leave it to Noam to find a way to spin it back.

"Looks like it's your turn then," Nate said, gesturing to the portal.

"Last I checked, you were the older one and I, the beautiful one," Freya said, "but just this once, I'll concede."

She stepped up to the portal, then turned, her sly smile turning sincere for just a moment.

"Thanks for saving my life again, Nate. I honestly don't know what I'd do without you."

Before he could reply, she'd turned and walked through the portal, leaving him on his own. Nate turned, examining the sprawling landscape of Warine, the first planet. It would indeed be a while before they returned here. Things would be far more dangerous on the other side of this portal, but he knew that in order to succeed in his mission and hopefully find his family, he was going to have to keep moving.

Nate inhaled one last time, enjoying the pleasant air of Warine, before turning and walking through the portal.

It was dark out when he emerged on the other side, the air hot and humid, with thick clouds hovering overhead. Perspiration began beading on his brow almost immediately as the stifling heat of the planet assaulted him.

"This is *so* much worse than the last time," Freya said. "I feel like I'm swimming through the air."

On Laybor, there were no starry galaxies to illuminate the darkness, so visibility was low at night. Thankfully, they were on the very edge of a village, where bright lanterns lit the central road, spilling out into the wilderness where the three of them had emerged.

"Let's go find an inn and get changed," Nate said. "It'll also help us get our bearings."

Although he knew *roughly* where the portal would have let out, he wasn't sure *exactly* where on Laybor they were. So, getting some help from the locals would give him a good sense of which way they needed to travel in order to begin their investigation into the Portal Reavers.

Their group began walking down the road – they'd landed a couple of minutes outside the village – their feet thumping oddly against the hard-packed road.

"What's this thing made of?" Freya asked, looking down to her feet, where the ground shone strangely.

It didn't appear to be wet, but the lantern light did shine off its surface.

"You can't expect me to know everything," Nate said with a shrug.

He knew a lot comparatively, but such an obscure detail was beyond him, mainly due to the fact that he hadn't bothered to find out in his previous life.

"Gasp! Something the all-powerful Nate *doesn't* know," Freya said.

"I'm shocked," Noam chimed in, doing a very poor job of hiding his grin.

It seemed the man was glad to see that there were at least some things that he didn't know about this world. Noam hadn't asked him for any specifics since he'd revealed the truth to him, and Nate doubted the man ever would. It was probably best that way, as knowledge of the future was, as he'd said, a heavy burden to carry.

"Wow, this village is even stranger than that half-finished city we saw the last time we were here," Freya said, as they finally reached the entrance to said village.

A low-slung fence made of clay ringed the perimeter of the village. As far as defenses went, it may as well have not even been there, but Nate knew that the borers would have constructed it simply as a border to show where the village started and ended.

A gateway stood around ten feet tall, two rounded pillars of stone having been driven into the ground, with a piece of the same shining material the road was made of having been slung between the two.

"Can you read what it says?" Freya asked as they paused on the threshold of the village.

"The lanterns are shining the wrong way, so no," Nate said. "Unless one of you wants to give me a boost so that I can read it."

"I think just asking works fine for me," Freya said, swiping an arm across her forehead. "Any longer out here and I'll turn into a raisin."

Nate was glad she saw it that way. He may have adapted to many climates in his previous life, but here and now, he was just as susceptible to the heat and damp as any of them. He was sweating buckets, just as he was sure Noam was. The difference between them was that they saw no point in complaining. Freya's chatter was more than enough for the three of them.

Walking through the gateway, Nate was greeted by the familiar sight of borer houses, all built in neat, uniform rows down the main street.

Borers had three kinds of settlements – villages, towns, and cities. Each was classified by its size and population. Villages were almost always a single-street settlement, with all houses and shops running along the main road. There were a few exceptions, but a village was never more than three streets in total.

Towns were built differently, typically constituting anywhere from eight to twelve main streets and a couple dozen side streets. Here, taller buildings were more commonplace, though he knew that the maximum height for a building in a town would be no more than thirty feet. It was how one could differentiate between a large town and a small city. That, and the fact that all cities had a surrounding wall no shorter than ten feet in height.

Cities could literally be anywhere from eleven main streets and up. The largest of the cities – the cities with the number 1 in their designation – sprawled to such massive proportions that they put even modern cities on Earth to shame.

Though he hadn't personally crossed from one side of a number 1 city to the next, he'd been told that one of them had spanned some 7,000 square miles in total area. It seemed like it would ordinarily be impossible to get around in such massive cities.

However, the borers were master builders. Having constructed cities on such a scale, they'd also worked heavily on the infrastructure, assuring that there were fast ways of getting from area to area, though it still took time to traverse the entire expanse.

"I have never seen houses like these," Noam said, pausing to run his hands over the smooth stone of the first structure in line.

The house was low-slung, standing no higher than fifteen feet at its peak. Its roof was domed and covered in bundles of densely packed straw of a kind that only grew on this planet. It was well adapted to the humidity and didn't fall prey to many other building materials that would wither and fall apart due to the excess water and sunlight.

While it was night here, Laybor was the exact opposite of Warine when it came to the day and night cycles. It was only dark here for around five-and-a-half hours each night, the first of the suns creeping up over the horizon at around two in the morning. By the time a normal person would wake, both suns would already be hanging in the sky and the temperatures would have soared well into the 90s, a fairly cool temperature for Laybor that wouldn't last for long.

While Noam and Freya didn't know this, the average temperature of this planet sat near the 140s. With the humidity, it felt even worse. But, as they'd advanced in rank, their bodies had grown hardier to the point where they could now bear it, if not a bit uncomfortably where the humidity was concerned.

At the moment, it was only around 85 degrees. It was the humidity that was killing them right now.

"Yeah," Nate said as Freya shot him a look, clearly wanting to see if this was something else he didn't know about. "Houses here are constructed out of a special cement made of local soil and minerals. From what I understand – and mind me, I don't know the specifics – they construct massive molds and pour the mixture in. When the house hardens to the point where it can stand on its own, the expanding stone shatters the scaffolding and all they have to do is clean it up.

"The only things not made of the stone mixture are the roof and door, which are made of weather-resistant materials also found only on this world."

"And Mr. Encyclopedia is back," Freya said.

"What era are *you* from?" Noam asked with a snort. "Encyclopedia?"

175

"What?" Freya asked, going a bit redder in the face. "Using encyclopedia is no different than calling a communicator a phone, even if the term *is* outdated."

"Except no one calls it a communicator," Nate jumped in, grinning. "No matter how badly Primo Corp wants people to."

"Yeah, well, there's nothing wrong with using older terms, is there?" Freya said.

"Sure," Nate said, grinning from ear to ear. "If you want to sound like an old geezer."

"Yeah, well…*You're* an old geezer!"

Freya stuck her tongue out at him, then sped up, walking faster down the main street.

"Does she realize that she has no idea where the inn is?" Noam asked.

"Just give her a second," Nate said, his grin undiminished.

It wasn't often that he got one over on the woman and he was enjoying himself immensely, even if he'd done it with Noam's help.

"Gah! All these blasted buildings look the same!" Freya yelled as she came storming back down the street just a minute later. "Which one's the inn?"

"I'll tell you only if you ask nicely," Nate said, crossing his arms.

"Just remember that we sleep together in the same tent most nights," Freya said. "Now, which one is the inn?"

"If you'll follow me, I'll be more than happy to show you the way," Nate said.

"Well?" Freya asked when he didn't move.

"What's the magic word?" Nate asked, turning his head to one side, and cupping his ear.

"Here's your magic word, you limey bushwhacker," Freya said, then stepped closer and whispered something into Nate's ear.

He stiffened, feeling a cold shudder run down his spine.

"I'll be happy to show you the way," Nate said.

"There. Was that so hard?" Freya asked, giving him a sweet smile, then turning and heading down the road.

"You look pale as a ghost, my friend," Noam said. "What did she say?"

"It's probably best you don't know," Nate said. "You'll never sleep the same if you do."

Noam gave him a serious look, then nodded. "Perhaps some things are better left unknown." Nate could not have agreed more.

27

They reached the entrance of the village's inn just a couple of minutes later, Nate stopping the group at the exact halfway point down the road and pointing to a small symbol etched above the doorframe.

"That's the sign for lodging in Laybor," Nate said. "You see that over a doorway, it means you can stay there."

Freya squinted against the light coming off the lantern set right by the inn's doorway, which washed out most of the symbol's detail.

"You'd think they'd have found a more obvious way of marking it," she muttered.

"They do, during the day," Nate said. "They'd normally set a sign out. At night they don't typically bother, as borers aren't much for going out in the dark. It's why no one's come out to see what all the racket is, despite all your shouting."

"I was *not* shou... Okay, I see your point," Freya said, cutting herself off partway through. "Let's just get inside. I'll be in a much better mood when my hair isn't trying to turn into a poofy clown wig."

Nate led the way inside, pushing the rounded door open and setting off a small bell near the top, tinkling in response.

"Oh, blessed cool air," Freya groaned as she walked in behind him, the blast of cold hitting them like a refreshing drink on a hot day.

"Why would they bother keeping it cool?" Noam asked as he followed Freya. "Not that I'm complaining or anything, but it seems to me that this world's inhabitants would be well-adapted to the heat and damp."

"Why did we have AC back home?" Nate responded in kind.

"Ah. I see your point," Noam said.

While the borers could stand the heat and humidity better than most, it didn't mean they particularly enjoyed it and built cooling systems into all their structures. The construction was more complicated than Nate could explain, but he knew the source was powered by kanta crystals, which made them highly sought-after on this planet – something he was keenly aware of in that they'd had to sell all of theirs back on Warine, where they'd been worth *far* less.

"This place looks stranger on the inside than it does on the outside," Freya noted, looking around. "How is this place an inn? It doesn't look nearly big enough."

Sure enough, the room they'd just walked into was just that. *A* room. As in, singular, though it was divided into sections. The area they'd just walked into was well-lit, with a small stone desk built directly into the wall. To their left was a dining area, with tables and chairs – also made of stone – divided into perfectly spaced rows.

A bar ran the length of the far side of the inn, though there was no seating. Instead, a series of small couch-like beanbag-looking things covered the floor, taking up the majority of the space. Nate didn't answer her question, preferring her to be surprised more than anything.

Just a minute later, the floor behind the desk shifted, then slid aside to reveal a female borer dressed in their world's version of a nightgown. She had long, shaggy brown fur that was longer atop her head, which was currently adorned by about two-dozen neon-pink hair-curlers, several wisps having escaped to trail down the sides of her beaver-like face that appeared *very* grouchy at having been woken.

"*What?*" she asked, glaring up at the three of them, her dark eyes narrowed and puffy.

Her voice was uncannily light and feminine, though there was a growling undertone that he knew all of her race would have.

Like the males of her race, this borer was built like a bodybuilder who constantly skipped leg day, narrower at the bottom and wider and bulkier up top. Though, where the differences in anatomy were concerned, the differences between male and female were obvious.

For one, all of the females had long hair sprouting from the tops of their furred heads. If that wasn't an obvious enough sign, the four bulges in the front of the borer's nightgown were an obvious giveaway.

"We'd like some rooms for the night," Nate said.

"Aliens," she muttered, crouching beneath the counter. "*Freaking* aliens."

Freya gave him a look, but Nate shook his head.

179

The woman rose, plonking a glassy orb on the counter.

"It's twenty points a night," she said, glaring at the three of them. "And you'll need at least two rooms. Unless I see a ring on that female's finger, I'm going to assume neither of you are married to her. You'll behave properly while under my roof."

"Two rooms it is," Nate said, pressing his palm to the orb and paying the 20-point cost.

This was to be expected here on Laybor. The further along one went in the system, the more things were going to cost. For this planet, 20 points wasn't all that bad.

"You only paid twenty points," the borer said, narrowing her eyes once again.

"As you said, none of us are married to her," Nate said with a shrug. "She can pay for her own room."

"You aliens disgust me," the borer said, spitting to the side. "Come here, my dear," she said to Freya, her voice softening. "The room's ten points for you."

Nate didn't bother complaining as Freya stepped forward, giving him a wide grin as she placed her palm on the orb.

"Here's your key, my dear," she said, handing Freya a piece of square stone with a number etched into it.

She looked past her then, glaring at Nate and Noam.

"Best come get your key before I decide to throw you both out on your lazy, non-courtestial behinds!"

"Courtestial?" Noam asked. "Is that even a word?"

"It is to them," Nate muttered as he went to retrieve the key.

"Rooms are right down the hall," the borer said, pointing to the hole behind the counter where a winding staircase led underground. "If I hear *any* fiddle-faddling or any of you boys trying to sneak into this poor girl's room, I'll tan your hides and send you packing! Am I understood?"

"Yes," Nate said.

"Perfectly," Noam affirmed.

The woman wasn't making idle threats. The ranking on the back of her left hand marked her as being ranked at 45. She was *not* someone Nate wanted to tangle with.

Nate felt her glare on his back the entire time he descended the stairs, the woman's eyes only leaving him once he dropped out of view. The staircase was longer than it should have been, Nate noting the small lip of stone they passed around halfway down.

He emerged into a stone corridor just a couple of seconds later, the floor polished and the ceiling sitting at just seven feet in height. Lanterns flanked both sides of the corridor, illuminating six doors, all of them closed.

"She's not going to follow us down here, is she?" Freya asked, looking back up the winding staircase.

"No," Nate said. "They live right beneath the inn, we're another level down."

"How could we have missed an entire level?" Noam said, sounding doubtful.

"The borers are master builders," Nate said. "Is it any wonder they've managed to do that when none of us could spot where the rooms were located?"

"That *is* true," Noam said. "I didn't see so much as a single seam in the stone. I wonder what *else* might be hidden down here."

The hatch above closed a moment later and the stairs spiraled up, pulling away from the ground, the metal construction flattening itself against the ceiling and leaving their view of the other side of the corridor unobstructed. Six more doorways became visible down the opposite side, marking this inn as being large.

A small indentation in the wall with an arrow pointing up would call the staircase back down.

"Okay," Freya said in a lowered voice. "What in the bloody hells was up with that woman? She was weird, right? All that stuff about acting properly under her roof. Also, did she have four breasts!?"

"Yes to that last question," Nate said, grinning. "They're a completely different race, what did you expect?"

"Not *that*!" Freya said.

She paused for a moment, giving Nate a meaningful look, a sly grin spreading across her lips.

"Don't even go there," Nate warned.

"Go where?" Freya asked innocently.

"To answer your *other* question," Nate said, glossing that particular line of conversation over. "The borers have a very hierarchical society. The men do all the heavy labor, while the women tend the homes and shops. Men are expected to be providers, so when we didn't offer to pay for you, it was seen as an insult. They're also *very* strict when it comes to the rules of marriage.

"If you're not married, there'll insist you sleep in separate rooms, maintain proper distances, and show no open displays of affection. Though, that's true even if you *are* married."

"What would happen, if say, that woman caught the two of us…fiddle-faddling?" Freya asked with a wicked grin.

"She'd throw us out on our fiddle-faddling behinds," Nate said flatly. "She'd probably also try to kill me. So, unless you want me dead, I'd recommend you keep your fiddle-faddling hands to yourself."

"I am still very confused," Noam said as Freya snorted out a laugh. "What is all this fiddle-faddling you are going on about?"

"Just think about it in these terms when it comes to the rules of borer society when the interaction of male and female is involved," Nate said. "If it wasn't okay in the '30s, it's not okay here."

"Oh," Noam said. "Well, that explains things pretty well."

In the '30s, the world had had a radical shift, as people had grown tired of the direction society was taking. Things had gone back to how they were nearly a century before and there had been a massive shift in the world as a result.

As with everything politically motivated, there were both advocates and detractors. Things in the '80s, when the world had ended, were a bit more relaxed, though nowhere near as contentious or divided as the world had been before the shift.

"In other words, they're a bunch of prudes," Freya said. "Guess that means you'll have to stop sneaking into my room in the middle of the night."

"I remember things happening a bit differently than that," Nate deadpanned.

"Hey, whatever you need to tell yourself to sleep at night," Freya said, shooting him a grin. "Now, if you'll excuse me, I'm going to get out of these sweaty clothes and into something more comfortable. Try not to let your imagination run *too* wild, Nate. See ya!"

A laugh floated back to him as she slammed her door, leaving Nate and Noam alone in the corridor.

"A man would have to be both blind and deaf to miss such obvious hints," Noam said.

"I have my reasons," Nate said. "Let's leave it at that. Also, I don't fancy being skinned alive."

"They would really do that?" Noam asked, sounding appalled.

"Maybe," Nate said with a shrug.

He'd once seen an angry mob of female borers string someone up by their ankles and beat them to death with clubs over something similar. As zealous as the males were about their construction, the females were equally insane regarding their rules.

Noam just shook his head, following Nate to the far end of the hall, where their room was located. It wasn't lost on either of them that they'd been placed several doors down from Freya, instead of across the hall or the next room over.

"This is strange," Noam said as Nate let them into the room.

"It's pretty standard," Nate said, eyeing the room.

If there was one thing he hadn't missed about Laybor, aside from the climate, it was the spartan inn accommodations.

The room was hewn from the stone, though it didn't look nearly as nice or polished as the corridor outside. The ceiling was even lower in here, forcing them to crouch in some areas. There were two beds, both set on the floor. They were also round, instead of rectangular, and Nate knew they would be almost as comfortable as sleeping on the ground.

Aside from the two beds, there was a single curtained-off area, where a bare stone tub and a literal hole in the floor sat. This would be their bath and toilet while here.

"This was not worth the points," Noam said, eyeing the place with distaste.

"I'm sure you've been in worse places," Nate said.

"I have," Noam said. "But I never had to *pay* to stay there."

"Well, hopefully this'll change Freya's mind about inns," Nate said. "None of the accommodations here, short of commandeering your own house, will be any more comfortable."

Noam sighed.

"Did you have to drag me into this?"

"Yes," Nate said. "I distinctly remember you taking Freya's side against me multiple times. Just call this payback."

"You are one vindictive son of a-"

"Can't hear you!" Nate said, ducking behind the curtain. "I'm too busy not listening."

Nate grinned to himself as he stripped out of his sodden clothes, turned the water to lukewarm and hopped in to give himself a quick scrub. He'd lied. There was *one* reason to stay in an inn over the outdoors – the bath. Sure, it wasn't luxurious, but it *did* have water that wasn't steaming hot.

Also, if they bathed in the outside world, they'd need to take off the clothes that protected them from the damp, which would completely defeat the entire point.

"I feel like a new man," Nate said, emerging a few minutes later.

He was now wearing his new climate-friendly outfit, the one that would keep him from feeling the oppressive damp. It had been worth every point in his opinion. The sleeves were missing, as would be considered normal, and the slick fabric clung to him like a too-small shirt. It didn't *feel* like it though. It felt breathable and comfortable, which was all that mattered to him.

"You look ridiculous," Noam said as he emerged.

"It's either tight clothes or walking through a perpetual swamp," Nate said with a shrug. "Your choice. Now, if I were you, I'd hurry up. We're only going to get a few hours to rest before we have to move again."

They'd decided to acclimate themselves to Laybor as soon as they came through. Despite it being around noon in Warine, it was well past midnight here in Laybor. Borers were early risers and would expect the same of anyone sleeping in their inns. Nate hadn't warned Freya about the wake-up call.

That would be his small revenge for the stunt she'd pulled with the shower. He could hardly wait to see her reaction.

28

"By the freaking gods! What the hell is wrong with these people?" Freya exclaimed once they were out of earshot of the inn's owner.

"I don't see anything wrong," Nate said innocently. "All they did was wake us up so that we didn't oversleep."

"It can't be any later than five in the freaking morning!" Freya yelled, throwing her arms in the air. "What person in their right mind gets up so early?"

"Everyone here, apparently," Noam said, gesturing around them.

The street was already bustling with activity, the male borers getting onto their world's version of mine carts – basically large wooden boxes mounted on tires – and heading to the village's exit. They were, more likely than not, off for a day of quarrying stone in the mountain that loomed in the east.

"Weird how they ignore us," Freya said, stopping to watch the borers rushing around, dragging small lunch sacks or saying goodbye to their families for the day.

"They don't really care about much other than their work," Nate said.

A few had looked in their direction at Freya's first outburst, but after that, they'd minded their business.

Despite the early hour, the suns were already blazing, and a thick mist hung heavy in the air. Thankfully, the clothes they wore prevented the hazy film from settling on their bodies, leaving them to only have to combat the actual heat, which their bodies were well able to handle.

Noam filled his clothes quite well and Nate found himself feeling just a bit jealous of his older friend's physique. Despite their time in the System and the changes to their bodies, Noam had already been in great shape – unlike Nate – when they'd entered. Freya too, looked good in her outfit, the fabric clinging as tightly to her as it did to Nate and Noam.

He would have to be careful not to glance in her direction too often, as he was *sure* she already had a dozen or more comments ready the moment she saw him looking.

"So, what's the plan for today?" Noam asked.

"Easy," Nate said. "We just ask one of the borers if they've seen anything out of the ordinary and go from there."

After asking the irritable innkeeper where they were, she told them that they were in Village 212D, on the border of four intersecting quadrants. They couldn't have come out in a better place, as it likely meant that the borers here worked with others from the other quadrants. In other words, there would be a lot of information crossover.

"Excuse me," Nate said, walking up to a borer who was rushing to catch his cart.

"I'm late," the borer said. "If you want something, make it snappy, alien."

"Have you heard of any disturbances nearby?" Nate asked. "Anyone like us showing up and causing trouble?"

The borer gave the three of them a once-over, then shook his head.

"I haven't heard of anything, sorry," he said, then turned and began rushing to his cart, which was already picking up speed.

"Could one of your friends or workmates have?" Nate asked, chasing after the borer.

Many times, these creatures were literal. Ask a question, get a literal answer. He might not have heard of anything, but one of his friends might have.

"Yeah," the borer said, waddling faster as his workmates called for him to hurry. "Friend of mine from the F-quadrant by the name of Jebber."

"Could you introduce us to him?" Nate asked.

"Sure," the borer said. "But that means you'll have to come with us to the mines and there are no freeloaders. You'll have to work if you come."

"What if we guard your cart on the road?" Nate offered.

Borers were not fighters. If they were attacked, they would run, leaving the slowest to get eaten while they made their escape, so the offer would be a good one.

"If the three of you can hold the monsters back, I'll gladly give you an introduction," the borer said, seeming pleased by this arrangement.

"Hurry it up, Bobbonius!" shouted one of the borers. "We're already falling behind, and I don't need the boss chewing us out again for being late!"

"Good news, chief," Bobbonius said as he grabbed the side of the cart and hauled himself in easily. "These three are going to keep the monsters off us today."

"Will they?" the gray-furred borer said, looking at them dubiously. "Are you sure you aliens can hack it? You don't look very strong."

Nate removed the glove covering his right hand and showed it to the borer. He knew chief was the title given to anyone who led a work-crew, and wouldn't be his actual name.

"Not bad," the borer said. "But not great either. Where were going, we'll run into monsters well into the thirties."

"We're combat trained," Nate said.

"Suit yourself," the chief said with a shrug. "We bear no responsibility for injuries on the job though. Company policy."

"We understand," Nate said, pausing to remove his scooter – the others following suit – as the cart began speeding up.

"How fast will that thing go?" Noam asked when he caught up with Nate.

"Not too fast," Nate said. "No more than ten to twelve miles per hour, depending on terrain."

"So, tell me, alien," called one of the six borers. "What brings you to our planet?"

"Business," Nate said, making sure to keep it vague and work-related.

If there was one thing the borers admired, it was a good work ethic.

"Really?" the chief asked, becoming interested. "What *kind* of work?"

"Policing, actually," Nate said. "We're looking for some alien criminals who are causing some trouble near the portals. We've been sent to stop them."

"Trouble near the portals?" Bobbonius asked, sounding shocked. "Who would dare?"

"That's exactly what we're here to find out," Nate said.

"Snare Worm, three o'clock!" called a smaller, dark-furred borer standing at the front.

"Well then, alien, time to earn your keep," the chief said, pulling out a rounded wooden stick and placing it in his mouth. "Best of luck to you."

He chuckled to himself, as though making a funny joke, and the cart swerved away from the monster that exploded from the ground, doing its best to avoid taking any hits.

"Freya!" Nate called.

"On it," Freya said, her Magigun flashing from her holster and finger depressing the trigger in a smooth motion.

A Blazing Bullet slammed into the five-foot cross between an earthworm and beetle, the monster screeching as it was blasted off course. Nate and Noam closed, leaping off their scooters and stashing them in their rings as they did.

The Snare Worm righted itself in an instant, beetle-like legs writhing and undulating as it did. Its body was a dark, mottled color, a segmented exoskeleton covering its form and giving it a sort-of armor. Freya's first attack had merely scorched its hide, but her second and third fired in rapid succession, first cracking the shell, then punching a hole into it.

The stench of cooking worm flesh wafted into the air and made Nate gag, though he didn't slow in his headlong rush. A dark *34* marked the left side of its circular mouth, one filled with needle-like teeth.

The worm rushed at the two of them, Nate summoning his Gilded Skin in anticipation of the fight ahead. The worm reared up as Nate neared, moving faster than Noam, its body towering in the air as it slashed at him with its legs.

Nate's backsword appeared in a flash of gold, parrying the attack. He felt the worm's strength in that blow, one that stopped him in his tracks. Two more legs blurred in, and Nate's Goldshield materialized on his open side. The legs were deflected, though Nate was forced to take a step to his right to maintain his balance under the tremendous force of the blow.

The worm lunged with a screech, its mouth gaping open and intending to swallow him whole. Nate swung the shield around, catching the blow and nearly losing his footing as the worm struck, sending him staggering. By that point, Noam had closed the gap. Wielding his two tomahawks and cloaked in his Brutal Guardian technique, he let out a cry, drawing the monster's attention.

The worm froze in place as the man's technique washed over him, a shudder running down its body as the fear effect of his Guardian's Dread engulfed it. The first tomahawk smashed down, driving the monster's head into the ground, chiton cracking and splintering beneath the mighty blow. The second came down an instant after, blood spraying as the monster shrieked.

"Watch out!" Nate warned as Noam lifted the first tomahawk, only for one of the worm's back legs to extend with the force of an arrow, slamming into Noam's chest and hurling him away, blood streaming from the puncture wound.

A Blinding Buckshot smashed into the monster's face as it tried to follow, but the monster was completely unaffected.

"It doesn't have eyes!" Nate called to Freya, who swore, then used her Tele-bang, driving the monster back fifteen feet.

Nate chased after it as Noam dragged himself to his feet, pressing a hand to his shoulder to close the wound.

The worm whirled to face him, bloody mouth opened wide as it swayed from the aftereffect of Freya's Tele-bang spell. Nate's broadsword appeared in his hand, the massive blade clutched in a tight grip. The monster lunged at him as the blade came crashing down on the weakened area Noam had already damaged.

Nate's muscles flexed under the force as the reverberation of the impact traveled up his arms. The worm's head smashed into the ground, Nate's Gilded Blade cleaving clean through and burying itself into the earth. He dismissed the blade, crossing his arms quickly as the monster's back half smashed into him and he felt the kanta rush into his Core.

The monster's heavy body slammed into his crossed arms, knocking him to his back and sending a loud ringing echoing through the air. His forearms smarted with the force of the blow, but he'd managed to avoid taking too big a hit. Dragging himself back to his feet, the worm's body went still, its legs curling in and body seizing up.

Nate let out a slow breath, dismissing his Gilded Skin. The entire battle had taken maybe twenty seconds in all, which was nice, to say the least. It meant they could easily catch up with the moving mine cart. He was also grateful to have an actual team with him now. Had he had to tangle with that monster alone, as he had done when he'd first entered the system, it would have taken him much longer and he'd have accrued several injuries.

Placing his hand on the corpse, Nate pulled it into his ring. The corpse wouldn't be worth much, but every point counted.

"Are all the monsters in this world that tough?" Noam asked, still rubbing his shoulder.

"That, or more," Nate said with a grin as he pulled his scooter from his ring.

"Well, that sucks," Freya said, scootering over to them. "And here I was hoping we'd be mowing through them as easily as the monsters on Warine."

"Yeah," Nate said. "Our days of one-shot kills are over. At least for the time being. But if we work together as well as we did here, nothing should give us *too* much trouble...probably."

"Why doesn't that fill me with more confidence?" Noam asked, pushing off.

"Probably because we're going to be tangling with more of these creepy worm things," Freya said with a grimace.

"Don't be so sour," Nate said. "There's no need to feel ashamed that it took you a few tries to get through its armor."

"I'm not," Freya said, a grin stretching her lips. "After all, I only have a gun, you're the one with the big sword."

"Not your best work," Nate said.

"Hey, they can't all be winners," Freya replied with a shrug, then shoved off, chasing after the retreating cart.

"You should give up while you still can," Noam said. "The sooner you accept that, the happier you'll be."

"Never," Nate said, pushing off with his right food. "I'll keep fighting until my last breath."

Noam shook his head and let out a long sigh.

"You will be remembered fondly, my friend."

Nate wasn't sure he liked what his friend was implying.

"Are you saying I can't get the best of her?"

"You may be good at many things," Noam said. "But when it comes to cleverness with words and witty retorts, you're falling further behind by the day."

190

With that said, Noam sped up, moving to catch up with Freya.

Perhaps, Nate thought to himself, *I should start dedicating more time in my day to another sort of training.*

It could doom the human race to extinction, but if he could get one over on Freya, it might well be worth it.

29

The group fought six more worms on their way to the mine, all of them sustaining a collection of minor injuries during their many battles. The one upside of the fighting was the increase in rank, which came to the three of them almost simultaneously after defeating the fifth rank *34* worm, bumping them all to *33*.

"I feel like I can knock a horse out with a single punch," Freya cheered when she'd grown.

"I don't know if you could do quite that much damage," Nate said. "Though I'd pay good money to see you try."

"How much do you want to bet I could do it?" Freya asked with a grin.

"Nothing," Nate said. "You won't find a horse anywhere in the system, at least not to my knowledge."

"There are things you don't know," Freya said. "If we *do* find a horse, how much would you be willing to bet?"

Nate thought it over. Freya was a magician, which meant she was physically weaker as far as brute strength went. Magicians and cultivators would be equally as hardy, but the tradeoff between the two was brute force in combat, versus at range. Freya was far more powerful when it came to any attacks at a distance, but weaker at melee.

"A thousand points," Nate said, sure that it would be an easy win. "But this only applies until you hit rank forty, and after that, the bet is off."

"You've got a deal," Freya said. "Now all I have to do is find a horse. I can't wait to buy a curling iron and that gold-collection nail kit. I can see it already."

The woman was practically drooling at the idea of spending his points on something so beyond ridiculous. If Nate won this hypothetical bet, he'd use the points to acquire a new technique scroll, one that he'd been wanting to get his hands on for quite a while now. He couldn't justify the additional cost at the moment, as it was more convenience-based than anything else, but if the points were free, he would gladly spend them.

"Hey, Bobbonius," Freya called, scootering closer to the mine cart. "You guys have any horses around here?"

"We have a few draft teams in the mine," Bobbonius said, surprising Nate. "We use them to lug some of the heavier blocks of granite that our carts can't handle on their own."

"You have *horses* here?" Nate exclaimed.

He'd never even heard of horses in the system, let alone in Laybor of all places. He would have killed for a horse. The distance they could cover in comparison to the scooters was monumental.

Freya turned her head, flashing him the widest grin he'd seen from her yet. It seemed their bet was about to be put to the test.

Cart traffic increased as they fell into the mountain's shadow, multiple carts coming together to form a much larger group that the snare worms didn't bother. Once the element of surprise was gone, the worms were much more susceptible to injury than other monsters. It was thanks to Freya's sharp eyes and the lookout posted by the borer team that they'd spotted as many as they had and avoided being caught.

The cart stopped before a massive hole in the mountainside, in line behind nearly two-dozen others. There were several lines here, in fact, and looking ahead, Nate could see a borer with a clipboard signing each of them in.

"Chief Six from V212D," the chief stated when it was their turn in line.

"Acknowledged," the borer said, making a mark on his clipboard. "You're working in Shaft 944 today. Report to your boss for exact detail..." The borer trailed off when he saw the three humans there with them. "Who are these undocumented workers?"

"Hired contractors," the chief said smoothly. "They kept monsters off us during our trip in exchange for an introduction."

The borer signing people took this in stride.

"Ranks?"

Nate showed him the back of his hand, motioning for Noam and Freya to do the same.

"All personnel below the thirty-fifth rank must wear safety equipment in all heavy-mining areas," the borer said robotically. "As a hired contractor working for Crew Chief Six from V212D, he is

193

responsible for any and all workplace injuries that may occur due to lack of safety equipment. Do you agree?"

"Acknowledged," agreed the chief.

He'd grown considerably more friendly after the first attack had been warded off, especially so when they'd driven off the third, which had capsized their mine cart and nearly chewed the head off one of his workers. Though, knowing the borers, the man couldn't have cared less about the man's life and more about the composition of his team and decreased productivity, which would reflect poorly on him as a chief.

"Go on through," the borer said, waving them in.

The work crew pushed the cart through, entering the darker tunnel lined with flickering torches. This was the first time Nate had seen an open flame in Laybor since returning and knew they didn't bother for the most part, due to the damp air. Inside the mine, though, things would be nice and dry.

"Oh, praise whatever overlords decided to make this place," Freya said, fanning her face. "I could use more of this cool air. Any chance I can take some with me when I leave?"

"Air does not work that way on this planet, alien," Bobbonius said.

"It was a rhetorical question," Freya said, rolling her eyes.

She had discovered the borer penchant for taking things literally and was not enjoying it. Nate wondered if he should adopt a similar strategy when dealing with her. It seemed to be working well.

"So, how deep is this mine?" Nate asked. "And where will we find this friend of yours?"

"The mine is quite deep," Bobbonius said, seeming more than happy to talk about his work. "There is a vast network of tunnels, some going as deep as three miles underground and others as far as four miles upward. If you're worried about proper tunnel support, don't worry. Our engineers are quite capable. As for Jebber, he's likely working in a different tunnel today, but we should be able to find him at lunch."

"Oh, yeah?" Freya asked. "And when is that?"

"Lunch is a two," the chief said. "Now, less jabbering and more walking. It's a long way to our section and I don't want to be late."

194

"*Two?*" Freya exclaimed. "But it's barely six in the morning!"

"Yes," Bobbonius said. "Our Overboss is quite generous with his breaks. Some of the other mines don't get lunch until four, though the average is around three."

"And they only get fifteen minutes," another of the crew chimed in. "We get twenty."

"Oh wow," Freya said, the sarcasm clear in her tone. "Twenty whole minutes. Lucky you. How long is a workday?"

"Workdays are typically over between eight and nine, depending on where you're located near the mine. The further you are, the earlier you finish," Bobbonius said. "We finish at eight because it takes about an hour to get here and back."

"You work from six to eight every day?" Noam asked, sounding appalled. "And only get twenty minutes for lunch?"

"It's only fourteen hours," the chief said with a shrug, as though it was completely normal.

"Yeah, Noam," Freya said with a grin. "Only fourteen. Talk about lazy."

Dead silence greeted her as every borer in the group turned steely eyes in Freya's direction. The group went from being friendly to extremely hostile in the blink of an eye.

"What did you call us?" asked the chief, his voice low and edged with anger. "Because I think I must have misheard. You didn't use the L-word, did you?"

Freya balked at the sudden shift, looking at Nate in a panic.

"Of course not," Nate said, clapping the chief of his massive back. "You must have heard wrong. No one would call your crew of hard-working and industrious men something so offensive."

The borer stared at Freya for another long moment, before relaxing, the tension leaking out of the air.

"Come on," the chief said. "We can't be late."

With that, he pushed past Freya, pretending she didn't exist, and ordered his team to get moving again.

"What did I say?" Freya hissed in an undertone as the cart began moving again.

"Just think about what kind of people these are," Nate said, keeping his voice low as well. "A race of creatures who call a fourteen-hour workday normal, are up at the crack of dawn, and are constantly working… What's the most offensive thing you could call someone like that?"

Freya's eyes widened, her lips pulling to a rounded O as she realized what she had said. In Laybor, the most offensive thing you could call a borer was lazy. Had they not defended the group and assured they'd made it to work on time without losses, they probably would have attacked her for such an offense.

They carried on in silence, moving through one rough-hewn tunnel after the next, following the line of carts as they made their way deeper into the mine. It took them nearly thirty minutes to reach their section – one of the furthest points in the area, it seemed – where several other teams were already hard at work.

"Man, is it loud in here!" Freya all but yelled over the sounds of hacking and sawing.

"What did you expect?" Nate yelled back. "They're quarrying as much as mining here!"

Sure enough, while some teams were attacking the walls with picks, furthering the tunnel, others were using massive circular saws made of big-toothed bronze blades to cut slabs of stone from the walls. The saws were handled by four borers each. One maneuvered the mine cart, while the chief yelled orders and directions.

The saws they used were massive, nearly ten feet tall each, and the blades – seeing as they were made of bronze – constantly needed to be swapped out. Every couple of minutes, the team would lower the saw, remove the chewed-up blade and replace it with a new one. The scrap bronze was tossed in a pile, where it would likely be recycled to make new ones.

It was fascinating, but Nate wasn't here to watch them work. He was here to find out what information Bobbonius might have for him. Unfortunately, they were going to have to wait a few hours for that to happen, as once the group was checked in with the boss overseeing this section of the mine, they had technically completed their mission.

"You can feel free to wander the mines as you like," the chief said as his crew outfitted themselves for the day's work. "Just make sure not to get in anyone's way and meet back here at a quarter to two. Otherwise, you're liable to miss us when we head to the mess cave."

"How can we tell time down here?" Noam asked. "We are in perpetual darkness."

The chief pointed up to where a massive hourglass sat mounted near the ceiling of the tunnel. The top and bottom of the hourglass were covered with rings. Currently, the sand in the top was just below the sixth line.

"They flip them at noon," the chief said. "Just keep that in mind. Now, I've got to get a move-on. We have a quota to meet."

With that said, the borer trundled off, already shouting orders to his team.

"So," Freya said, watching the work teams all around her. "What now?"

"Now," Nate said, grinning, "we go exploring."

30

Nate had had the opportunity to explore several Laybor mines in his previous life, searching for treasure like everyone else. The problem was that by the time he'd reached this area, it had already been picked clean by the stronger guilds that had already begun emerging. As far as he could tell, no one else had been to this mine just yet, which meant there were thousands of points in potential materials to discover.

"Do you have any idea where you're going?" Noam asked as Nate led them through a series of tunnels, moving away from Bobbonius' team.

"No idea," Nate said.

"Should we stop and ask for directions?" Freya asked.

"Nope," Nate said.

She snorted out a laugh.

"Typical guy answer. *I'm* going to ask for directions then. What are we looking for exactly?" she asked, realizing that she had no idea what they were looking for.

"We're heading for the abandoned parts of the mine," Nate said. "Places the borers have given up on for various reasons."

"You mean *dangerous* reasons," Freya said.

"Yes," Nate replied. "The more danger the better."

"You know, with the way you talk about running headlong into an area you know is dangerous, one might come to think that you're a bit of a masochist."

"You know me," Nate said. "I *love* being a monster's chew toy. It was always my answer when they asked us in grade school."

"And they didn't put you in a special home or anything?" Freya said.

"For some reason, they didn't think I was being serious," Nate said with a shrug. "I wonder why."

"Perhaps it's because you come off as insincere and a bit moronic," Noam suggested.

"I'd believe that," Freya said.

"Excuse me," Nate said, tapping a borer on the shoulder. "What would happen if I were to push those two into the path of one of those massive saws?"

"I wouldn't recommend doing that," the borer said seriously. "Their bodies would be ripped in half, their bones crushed, and their innards shredded. It would make a terrible mess and the paperwork…" The man shuddered visibly, then shook his finger at Nate. "Don't push anyone into the saws."

The entire warning was so strange that it shocked both Noam and Freya into silence. Nate nodded seriously, fighting the smile that was trying to force its way onto his face.

"I'll do that. Thank you for warning me."

The borer nodded, then went back to hacking at the wall with his pick.

"One more question, if you don't mind," Freya said, finally getting over her surprise. "You wouldn't be able to point us to any abandoned sections of the mine, would you?"

"I would," the borer said, then turned and went back to work.

Freya raised her arms to the sky, fingers curling in as she shouted in silent frustration. Once she'd vented her anger, she tapped the borer again.

"*Could* you please direct us to the closest abandoned section in the mine?" she asked sweetly.

The way she asked the question sent a shiver down Nate's spine. It was eerie how nice she was being. It was wrong somehow, like seeing a 5-star demon offering someone a batch of freshly baked cookies.

"Sure," the borer said. "Just take six rights, two lefts, walk fifty yards past the nineteen tunnels…"

It took everything Nate had not to laugh at the look on Freya's face by the time the borer finished with his directions. She turned away, looking dumbfounded.

"See why I didn't want to ask?" Nate said.

"I'll take your advice next time," she said, sounding to be in shock.

"Come on," Nate said, steering her by her shoulders. "Let's let the nice borer get back to work."

He'd noticed her fingers twitching toward her Magigun and didn't want to get in trouble for murder. The borers might have been fine with ignoring attacks by monsters, but a sentient creature murdering one of their own in broad daylight would be very frowned upon. After all, they would have to fill out all that paperwork, and there was nothing they hated more than paperwork.

"If they're not going to give us anything, how are we going to find an abandoned section?" Freya asked.

"Oh, that's easy," Nate said. "We just walk until we notice fewer borers. The fewer we see, the closer we'll be to an abandoned section."

"That sounds more like random chance than anything else," Noam said doubtfully.

"Hey, random chance is as good as anything down here," Nate said.

"Great," Freya muttered. "We're following a madman."

"Hey, *you're* the ones who agreed to follow me. You have no one to blame but yourselves."

"He has a fair point," Noam said.

"I hate it when he makes sense," Freya said. "Makes me feel like I'm losing my mind."

"I know what you mean."

"Hey!" Nate said. "Easy on the injury to my sensitive ego. Who *knows* what I might do if you keep insulting me like this?"

"Probably something perverted," Freya said, with a wide grin.

"I...*What*?"

She snorted out a laugh as Noam shook his head as if to say: 'I did warn you, didn't I?'

They continued wandering the tunnels for nearly an hour before Nate finally noticed the worker population decreasing.

"Well, it's about time," Freya said. "My feet are killing me. I could use a rest."

That wasn't a bad idea. None of them had had anything to eat yet, so taking seats on knobs of stone, the group had a small breakfast of unflavored protein meals. Nate was nearly out, having only about a dozen or so of them left, something that Freya was very happy about.

Nate, on the other hand, was not. It meant that soon, he would have to pay for rations with his precious points. It wasn't something he was looking forward to.

They washed their gross meal down with swigs of water, though Nate was sparing with his. Just as water was sparse in certain areas of Warine, it would be sparser still here on Laybor. There *would* be water practically everywhere. In abundance, actually. Drinkable water, on the other hand, would be much harder to find.

Pretty much all the water on Laybor was too sulfurous to drink, on account of underground rivers accounting for much of the supply here on the planet. It didn't rain often and when it did, the rain didn't last long. So, they would be relying on water packs from the shops while here. It would be a bit more affordable, due to the fact that it was the only reliable way to get a drink, but still more expensive than finding it for free.

It was why Nate had taken that bet with Freya. If he won, he would purchase the Iron Stomach technique scroll, allowing him to drink from any water source and eat almost anything without suffering adverse effects. Of course, this had its limits. It wouldn't nullify poison, which was why the cost was so low at a thousand points.

It would also end up costing more than buying water individually, which was why he wasn't springing for it. The third planet, Raven, would have no such water shortage.

Once they were finished with their lunch, the group rose to continue their wandering, finally coming across an abandoned series of tunnels some fifteen minutes later.

"I can see why they ditched this place," Freya said, rubbing her bare arms. "Gives me the creeps."

Torches flickered in brackets along the bare stone walls, reflecting the glittering mineral deposits within. Nate could care less about those, as they would take more effort than they were worth to extract. What he was looking for was an ore vein or similar that they could make a profit on.

"That's strange," Nate said as the tunnel came to an abrupt stop, a series of long boards nailed across to prevent them from going any farther.

"Well, that's a sign to turn back if I've ever seen one," Freya said, already turning away.

She stopped at the sound of splintering boards and turned to glare at Nate as he dragged the remains of the barrier aside, leaving the way forward open and clear.

"You know, there are reasons people put those things up," she said. "What if the tunnel is unstable? Have you ever thought of that?"

"If it was unstable, they'd have filled it in," Nate said. "Otherwise, it could compromise their entire operation. Besides, I've got a good feeling about this."

Freya seemed less than happy with his explanation, but Nate wasn't about to give up just because she was scared. There was something good down here, of that, he was sure.

Unsurprisingly, the torches continued further down the tunnel, though none were lit. Noam ran back, snagged one of the lit torches, and he and Nate took turns lighting them as they went. The tunnel was damper than expected, though the air seemed only to be growing colder the further they descended.

"How much further does this tunnel go?" Freya asked.

She'd pulled her blanket from her ring and wrapped it around her shoulders. If Nate had to guess, it was somewhere in the region of 65 degrees down here, which was practically freezing by Laybor's standards.

"Beats me," Nate said. "Though I'm sure it'll have to end eventually."

"We've seen nothing but bare stone walls for the last thirty minutes," Noam said. "They boarded this place up for a reason, yes? So, why have we seen nothing in all that time?"

Once again, Nate shrugged. The further they went without encountering anything that looked like treasure, the more convinced he became that there was something amazing down here. All they had to do was keep moving and they would find it.

The group continued moving for several minutes longer when Freya noticed something.

"Is it just me, or is it getting brighter up ahead?"

She had the best eyes out of the entire group, so it was unsurprising that she'd noticed it first. Sure enough, as they continued moving, the tunnel began to glow, a dull red light coming from the other end. Additionally, the air began to grow warmer, rapidly rising from the mid-60s to the 90s in under five minutes.

"This tunnel just can't make its mind up, can it?" Freya grumbled, stashing her blanket once more.

"I think we're close to the end," Nate said, feeling excitement creeping into his voice.

Sure enough, just a minute later, the tunnel widened out, a jagged hole in the wall showing where the borers had smashed through the wall and into the underground cavern.

"Okay," Freya said, staring around wide-eyed. "I take all my complaining back. This was *so* worth the trip."

31

The cavern had to measure some hundred yards across and around half that in width at the widest sections as far as Nate could tell. However, it wasn't the size of the cavern that had captured their attention. That belonged to the dozens of vents littering the floor. which were currently blasting out spouts of molten yellow stone.

The magma hit the ceiling of the cavern, splattering off and raining to the ground below, where it collected in large pools around the bases of the vents.

Small streams of the stuff wound their way through the room, covering it in a haze of shimmering heat and yellow-orange light. The cavern ceiling was smooth and glassy, though the stone itself remained dark. The air smelled as well, and it smelled *bad*.

"Okay, who did it?" Freya asked, pinching her nose. "I have to warn you that as a girl, I will murder anyone who accuses me of causing this god-awful stench."

"It's sulfur," Nate said, feeling the acrid smell burning its way into his nostrils. "You have all the vents to thank for that."

"I understand that this cavern is quite the sight to behold," Noam said. "But what was the point of coming here?"

Nate pursed his lips as he scanned the room. Noam had a good point. They might be strong and hardy, but *none* of them could survive a magma bath just yet. His eyes scanned the area, looking for any possible way to cross.

"Can you see anything on the other side?" Nate asked.

Freya squinted around the room, then shook her head.

"As far as I can see, this is just one big cave with no other ways out."

"I could try using my Gilded Skin," Nate mused, staring at the glowing floor before him.

"I don't know if that would be such a good idea," Noam said.

"You're probably right," Nate agreed, letting out a sigh.

This room was worth exploring if for the singular reason that he could see small bits of pumice scattered throughout the room. It was exceedingly rare on this planet and one third of the recipe needed to craft ortium. If they could get their hands on it and some sandstone, there would be enough metal to not only forge Noam a new ax, but also to augment their own clothing with some pretty epic armor.

"We're going to have to come back," Nate finally decided.

"When?" Freya asked. "Also, how in the world are we going to be able to enter?"

"We'll have to buy the means to do so from the shop," Nate said, grimacing.

It would cut into their profits, but the pumice alone would be worth a fortune on this planet, especially if sold to a shop run by a local instead of to the one run by the system's gnarks.

"We can buy something at the shop that'll let us walk through magma?" Freya asked, sounding disbelieving.

"A general rule of thumb in the system is that you can buy anything for a price," Nate said with a shrug. "What we'll be after are Magma Resist Drafts. They'll be significantly cheaper than the Magma Proof ones, and since we've already got some good physical resistance, I think we'll be able to manage it."

"How much will this cost?" Freya asked.

Nate grimaced again.

"Sixty-five-hundred apiece."

Freya winced.

"It seems like an unnecessary gamble to me," Noam said, rubbing his chin. "To risk so much for potentially nothing."

"Trust me when I say it'll be worth it," Nate said, giving him a meaningful look.

Noam still seemed skeptical, though he reluctantly agreed in the end. That was good. If he just went right along with it, Freya might have become suspicious. This way, if the man continued to act as he had, she wouldn't notice that anything was up.

"All right, here's the plan," Nate said. "We come back here tomorrow with Bobbonius's crew. We kill some more of the worms and hopefully offset the cost some more. Then, we'll retrace our steps to explore this place without the fear of dying a horrible death."

"I like not dying a horrible death," Freya said. "You can count me in."

"Very well," Noam said, agreeing as well. "Though I do have to remind you that we're on the clock. We only have so much time to stop whoever's killing people by the portals."

"I know," Nate said grimly. "I'm really hoping this friend of Bobbonius can tell us something useful. For now, we'll turn back. I'm sure there's plenty more to see."

"Don't forget about our bet," Freya said with a grin.

"If you can find a horse to knock out without pissing off every borer in the area, you're free to try," Nate said.

Freya cracked her knuckles, still grinning.

"Ow! *Ow.* By the mother of all unholy…ow! That freaking *hurt!*"

Nate watched as Freya doubled over, swearing up a storm as she clutched her left hand, occasionally waving it, groaning, then clutching it to her chest once again.

"Well, you've got to admire her spirit," Noam said, watching the woman's antics.

"What did she think was going to happen?" Nate asked, unable to hide the grin that stretched from ear to ear.

Freya had somehow managed to find a horse and convinced the owner to allow her to try knocking it out. The borer had thought she was joking at first, but when she'd convinced him she was serious, he'd called all of his friends over to watch. Freya had made a big show of winding up and stretching, before delivering a stunning punch to the side of the horse's jaw.

The animal had staggered, screaming and neighing in pain, while Freya had doubled over. Nate wouldn't have been surprised if she'd broken her hand with that punch. He knew that he was messed up for laughing at his friend's misfortune, but if anything, the borers around him were even more messed up – especially the owner of the horse who'd allowed her to attempt something so insane in the first place.

"All right, the show's over," the borer said, wiping his eyes. "Let's get back to work."

Dragging the unfortunate horse behind him, the borer led it away, chattering among his workmates about how crazy aliens were.

"Well," Nate said when Freya finally looked up, tears beading the corners of her eyes. "I think we both know who's won our bet."

Freya nodded, still clutching her hand, her bottom lip quivering. She looked like she was about to cry.

"Oh, stop," Nate said. "I'm not falling for it."

"Fine," Freya said, straightening to her full height. "Can't blame a girl for trying."

She extended her hand to Noam – it did look like she'd broken it after all.

"Would you mind? Please?"

"I should leave you with the injury to teach you a lesson about considering the consequences of your actions," Noam said.

Freya glared at him.

"But, seeing as you have been so entertaining, I will heal you."

The man took Freya's hand and she let out an audible sigh of relief, her shoulders slumping as Noam's healing began repairing the damage she'd done to herself.

"How does it feel?" Nate asked.

"What, my broken hand?" Freya asked. "It freaking hurts. I thought it would be obvious."

"Not that," Nate said, grinning wider. "I meant losing a bet to me."

"Eh, not as much as you might think," Freya said with a shrug. "What really hurts is knowing that my hair will remain woefully uncurled and my nails unpainted. A real shame too. I look pretty hot with curly hair."

"As nice as I'm sure that would be, it would be extremely impractical to have your hair flying all over the place when fighting for your life," Nate said. "The way you have your hair right now is far better."

Freya stuck her tongue out at him and Nate grinned, removing the Transference Orb from his ring.

"A deal's a deal," Freya said, placing her hand on the orb and transferring a thousand points from her total.

This brought her total down to an even 40,000, while it brought his up to nearly 68,000. Nate reconsidered spending those points on the ability to drink or eat anything, as he was now only

7,000 away from the 4th tier of the Cycle of Regeneration. Once, he might have resented having to spend the extra points instead of boosting his Manual. Now, after how many times it had saved his life, he knew that having the ability to speed heal would be invaluable.

"A pleasure doing business with you," Nate said, stashing the orb.

"That feels *so* much better," Freya said, flexing her fingers as Noam released her hand.

"The next time you decide to punch a horse, I hope you have your own method of recovery," Noam said flatly.

"I will," Freya said, looking at her hand. "I'm going to buy that upgrade so that I can heal bones. It'll definitely be cheaper than buying healing drafts, that's for sure."

"If you're going to spend the points, may I suggest you take it all the way to the third tier?" Nate said. "The total cost would be ten-thousand, and while that is a lot, the difference between them is well worth it."

"How so?" Freya asked as their group began retracing their steps back to Bobbonius's crew's workspace.

"You'll have passive kanta regeneration," Nate said. "It'll regenerate on its own half as fast again as before, even while fighting. It's why I haven't run out in the middle of a fight, even though we're all at the same rank, and the two of us have the same Kanta Orb."

Speaking of Kanta Orbs, his and Freya's had hit their limit when they'd reached the 30th rank. Now, he could hold more in his own core than the Orb could match. The Orb would only be able to hold as much as he'd been able to at rank 30, while he was currently at 33. The upgrade would be 50,000 points, and for now, he was going to leave it.

"Wait a minute," Noam said. "Have I been missing out on this valuable skill the entire time?"

"You already have a healing technique," Nate said. "I didn't think it mattered."

"I can heal, but I don't have passive regeneration," Noam said thoughtfully. "This sounds like something very useful. If you don't think it a hinderance, I think I would like to purchase this technique from the shop."

"They *are* limited to seventy-two in total," Nate said. "There's a good chance they've all been claimed, but who knows? We might be lucky. If not, there are alternatives, though they *would* be less potent…"

Nate trailed off, trying to think of what Noam had in the way of self-healing. He'd assumed that Noam wouldn't want to spend the points, as he could recover on his own. Then again, it would cost him kanta, rather than him being able to use what was around him. On the flip side, it *was* much faster. To get a similar result, Nate would have to pay a whopping 85,000 in upgrades to get the same thing.

"I think I'm liking the sound of this," Freya said, flexing her arm. "Think of all the practice I could get for our next bet."

"If you think you can knock another horse out after a bit of practice, you're on," Nate said with a grin. "I'll gladly take more of your points."

"Oh, I don't think you'll be winning this time around," Freya said. "I have a plan."

"Well, we will all have to wait for this plan then," Noam said, rolling his eyes. "Because there will be no further horse-punching today. We have wasted enough time as it is."

"Agreed," Nate said. "Now come on, it's going to take us a while to get back to Bobbonius and I'd rather be early than late."

32

As it turned out, it hadn't been necessary to rush, as they returned to the borer tunnel within three-quarters of an hour. By the time they returned, it was barely half-past ten in the morning, meaning they still had several hours before the borer's lunch break. However, instead of going off and exploring, Nate decided he would simply train instead and advised Freya to do the same.

He began going through his usual routine, doing his morning strength exercises and finding that he could do twelve more pushups than he had before they'd left Warine – 6 ranks of growth *did* make quite the difference after all. Once he finished strength training, he moved on to forms, moving through his Martial Arts first, then his weapons.

He'd just begun with his weapons training when Freya interrupted him.

"Hey, Nate?"

"Yeah?" Nate said, not wanting to break his concentration.

"Would you be able to teach me how to punch like that?"

Nate turned with a raised eyebrow.

"You're a magician, why do you want to learn how to fight at melee?"

"It's like you said," Freya said, placing her hands on her hips. "I might be *weaker* at melee, but that doesn't mean I can't fight in close if I must. I've done plenty of training in firearms and track, but I haven't done anything in hand-to-hand."

"If you want training, I'd speak to Noam," Nate said. "He'd be a far better teacher than I would."

"I disagree," Noam said from across the tunnel, having overheard their conversation. "My fighting style isn't suited to bare-knuckle brawling like you. I might have focused on that once upon a time, but it has been so long that I'm rusty."

The grin the man flashed Nate as Freya turned to him told him the man was lying through his teeth. Noam was a perfectly capable and dangerous hand-to-hand fighter. He just didn't want the responsibility.

"It'll make the team stronger," Freya said, trying to appeal to his combat side.

"You *are* manipulative, aren't you?" Nate grumbled. "You would have made the perfect popular girl in high school."

"Aww, you say the sweetest things," Freya said.

"That wasn't a compliment," Nate said.

"Admit it. You're just jealous that I didn't have to go through the wringer of teenage angst and drama like you did," Freya replied.

"You have no idea what high school is like," Nate said, shuddering at the memory. "Fine, I'll teach you, but we'll be starting with basics. Once I show you a form, I'll leave you to work it on your own until you think you've got it down. After that, I'll show you the next."

"Sounds good to me," Freya said, raising her hands and throwing phantom punches into the air. "So, what are we starting with? Knockout punches? Kicks to the face? How to break someone's neck?"

"We're going to start with how to stand," Nate said.

"Stand," Freya said, dropping her hands. "Seriously?"

"Yes, seriously," Nate said. "Why don't you go ahead and take a stance for me?"

Freya seemed skeptical but did as he asked, sliding her feet out and raising her hands. Nate walked around her, nudging her elbows up and in, widening her base and having her bend her knees.

"Good," Nate said, then shoved her in the chest, forcing her to take a step back.

"Hey!" Freya said. "At least give me some warning before you get all handsy."

"That's your equilibrium," Nate said. "If someone or something knocks you off-balance, it's important to find it quickly."

Nate then demonstrated how to get in and out of the stances quickly, as well as how to move while remaining in said stance.

"Now repeat that until you can do it with your eyes closed," Nate said, once she got the idea.

"But this is so boring," Freya said. "Give me the good stuff. Just a hint. Please."

"You'll hurt yourself like you did with that horse," Nate said.

"Ouch," Freya said. "I guess I deserved that. Wait, are you saying that if I'd punched right, I wouldn't have hurt my hand?"

"You might still have hurt it," Nate said. "But you definitely wouldn't have broken it. Now, stop jabbering and start practicing."

With that, he went back to his side of the tunnel and began working on his forms. Freya came to him several times over the next few hours, while Nate was working forms, cultivating, or resting. Each time, he showed her something new. By the time lunch for the borers came around, Freya was working on basic jabs and crosses, as well as front and back kicks.

"Okay, aliens," Bobbonius said, trundling up to their group. "If you'll follow us, I can give you that introduction."

Their group followed the borers as they all headed out of the tunnel, Freya throwing punches in the air and grinning.

"I'll be a one-woman army before you know it," she said. "Just call me the Slick-Southpaw, terror of the cage fights. I would've kicked some major booty in the cages, don't you think?"

"I think you would have ended up on your booty a lot, if that's what you mean."

"Well, it's a good thing it's so fantastic then," Freya shot back. "Otherwise, that might actually hurt."

"You haven't started training for real yet," Nate replied. "Just wait until you begin exercising. Technique can only get you so far, especially with your disadvantage as a magician."

"I've trained all my life," Freya said. "How hard can it possibly be?"

The look that Nate and Noam shared had her looking a bit worried.

"You'll take it easy on me, right, Nate? We're such good friends, after all."

"Hey, you asked for this," Nate said.

"But I'm just a girl. You wouldn't be mean to a girl, would you?"

"You're a devil in a woman's body," Nate said. "It's too late to try selling me on the whole 'I'm just a poor girl' act."

"Gah! I'm too awesome for my own good," Freya said, throwing her hands up in the air. "Well, it was worth a try. Wait a minute," she said, a sly smile creeping onto her lips. "You're not going to do this to see me get so hot that I'll have to take my shirt off for the rest of our training, are you?"

"I think that's your fantasy, not mine," Nate said.

Freya opened her mouth to retort when they entered the borer's mess cave. The words died in her throat when she saw just how many of them there were.

"Stay close," Bobbonius said. "It's easy to get lost in here."

Nate and the others did just that, sticking to the borer like glue as he wound his way through the thronging beaver-like creatures, making for the center of the cave. More than once, Nate heard someone shout, "It's horse-punch girl!" to which Freya replied by waving and throwing punches in the air, much to the amusement of the psychologically damaged creatures.

It didn't take long for Bobbonius to get them to the center of the room, where he approached a smaller work team sitting on a log.

"Hey there, Jebber," Bobbonius greeted a hulking, brown-furred borer.

"How's it going, Bobbonius?" Jebber asked, raising his thumb to his nose and twiddling his fingers.

The motion was so ridiculous that Freya burst out into hysterical laughter, while Noam did his best to stifle a grin behind an upraised hand. Only Nate, who'd seen this exchange before, remained impassive. Bobbonius returned the gesture, while Jebber gave Freya an odd look.

"What brings you here? Shouldn't you be getting lunch?"

Bobbonius quickly explained the deal he'd struck with the three of them, Jebber seeming particularly interested by the fact that they'd kept his entire group alive.

"So, you're looking for information on some aliens in the area?" Jebber said.

"That would be correct," Nate replied, already seeing the price they were going to have to pay.

"I do have the information you're looking for, but I can't just give it away for free. Here's the deal. You escort my team and I back tonight and to the mines tomorrow morning, and I'll give you all the information you want."

"Where are you from?" Nate asked.

"From Town 90F," Jebber said. "It's only about twenty-five minutes from here."

"Hey! Don't go filching our guards, Jebber. We need them," Bobbonius complained.

"You have a whole crew," Jebber said. "We only have four, so you can afford to lose some."

The callousness of the borers would shock many people, but having seen how their race operated, Nate was hardly surprised.

"We can do the escort job, but if the introduction was only worth a one-way trip, it hardly seems fair for us to have to go both ways," Nate said. "You're going to have to sweeten the deal."

Jebber seemed to think for a moment, then shrugged.

"What do you want?"

"Sandstone," Nate said.

Jebber's face scrunched up at that and he shook his head.

"No way. That's too rare a resource to give you for twenty-five minutes of guard duty."

"Is it really not worth your life?" Nate asked. "You've already lost two of your crew. Do you want to lose even more? Think of all the work you won't be able to finish."

"You do have a good point," Jebber said. "Missing our daily quota would tarnish our reputation. Fine, I'll give you some sandstone, but only one pound. No more than that."

"Deal," Nate said, shaking the borer's hand.

"Great," Jebber said. "You can follow us to our section of the mine once lunch is over. We leave at half past eight."

"Great," Freya sighed. "An entire day of being stuck in here."

"Hey, look at the bright side," Nate said, giving her a grin. "You'll be able to practice for that cage match now."

Freya stuck her tongue out in response.

33

They left the mine with Jebber's crew at exactly half past eight, the four-borer team pushing the cart out onto the rough road, with Nate's group in tow. They'd passed the rest of the day by training, resting, and doing some more exploring. They'd discovered a few caves with some mildly interesting items, such as gemstones, which had excited Freya until he'd told her they were basically useless here.

While gems might have been worth a lot back on Earth, the system apparently didn't place much stock in them. Freya had still insisted on keeping them, saying that when they eventually made it back to Earth, she would be the wealthiest girl on the block.

They had found some other small items, mainly pieces of ore, though none as rare or valuable as the orantium currently stashed in Nate's ring. They found some iron and nickel, which was nice, but nothing along the lines of what he'd heard about in his previous life, where people had talked about uncovering rare crystal veins or the like. Someone had even claimed to have come across a rare stone tablet with a special technique carved into it.

It was something Nate could only dream of finding, as no one had wanted to divulge where they'd found said tablet, so he was just as lost in this as anyone else.

"So, what do you guys normally run into on your trips here and back?" Nate asked, keeping pace with the slow-moving mine cart.

"Oh, you know, the typical stuff," Jebber said. "Slick worms, dune foxes, barren-pedes. Though I have heard a rumor that a pack of fire foxes has been seen around here recently."

Nate became grim when he heard that. Fire foxes were dangerous, as they tended to attack in packs of eight or more. Additionally, they didn't stick to one type or another, the packs containing both magician and cultivator types. They were *not* an enemy Nate wanted to face, at least, not without another teammate.

Once again, he bemoaned the fact that the next person on his recruitment list was nowhere near their current location, as their help would be greatly appreciated.

Luckily for them, they didn't come across anything more dangerous than the dune foxes – small, sandy-furred monsters with too-large eyes and a penchant for causing the ground to turn to sand beneath their feet. They were annoying but with the three of them working together, it was nothing Nate couldn't handle.

By the time they reached Town 90F, Nate had reached the 34th rank, with Freya and Noam falling a bit behind. This was likely because Nate had spent time cultivating today, while the others had not.

"Thanks for the escort," Jebber said, hopping out of his cart. "We leave at exactly half-past-five, so you'd best be on time if you want that info."

The borer rummaged around in his bag for a moment, then pulled a small blocky piece of sandstone from within and handed it over. He seemed almost reluctant to do so, but a deal was a deal and Nate's team had kept the monsters off them, likely saving them from a total wipeout at one point in their trip.

"A pleasure doing business with you," Nate said, grinning as he took the sandstone.

Now all he needed was to explore that volcanic room in the mine, fetch some pumice, and they would have all they needed to get some ortium.

"I can hardly wait," Noam said when Nate told him. "This ax is on its last legs."

One side of the double-bladed ax was useless, the blade cracked and bent beyond recognition. The other side wasn't looking too great either. His tomahawks had fared a bit better, but they could see the metal beginning to warp. Before long, Noam's weapons from Earth would be completely useless, meaning that crafting him new ones was of the utmost importance.

"Let's go find a tanner to sell these monster hides first," Nate said. "Then we can see about buying the other supplies and items we need for you and Freya."

"Shopping!" Freya said, pumping her fist in the air. "Also, where are we staying tonight? *Please* tell me there's a better inn in this place than that last village."

"There might be," Nate said with a shrug. "There might also not be. We can always try staying somewhere and seeing how it is."

"You know, it might be worth it, just to get clean," Freya said, looking down at herself.

Her bare arms were coated in dust and dirt, just as they all were. Her face was smudged and her hair clung to her neck in sweaty strands. Just because their clothes protected against the damp didn't mean they couldn't become hot, sweaty, dirty, and all-around gross on this planet. Nate felt about the same. The inns here sucked, but having a bath might be worth it.

"Let's go do our shopping first, before things start closing down for the night," Nate said. "It'll be dark soon and the borers don't leave things open once the suns go down."

If he was right, they had less than half an hour to sell their goods to the locals, which meant they had to move quickly.

Town 90F was far larger than the small village they'd stayed in the night before. Borers bustled through the streets, closing up shop, coming back from their shifts at various workplaces, or taking well-deserved breaks in small roadside pubs.

These were basically carts acting as bars that served wares out under the open sky. The aroma of food tugged at them, but Nate kept them on track. After asking around for a few minutes, they were directed to a tannery four blocks in.

"The buildings here are definitely more varied," Freya said, noting the different structures. "Though nothing as tall as what we saw in that first city."

"It's a town," Noam said. "If I had to guess, there's a distinction between a village, town, and city. There might be more gatherings with even larger buildings."

"Huh, yeah, guess that makes sense," Freya said, rubbing her chin. "I wonder what something like that would look like."

Her gaze drifted off, obviously trying to imagine how a city larger than the one they'd seen under construction would look.

"All I'm getting are major cities back on Earth," she finally said with a shrug.

"I don't know if the borers are buildings skyscrapers like those just yet," Nate said.

The tallest building in town was visible from where they were, a thirty-foot-high complex – likely housing many single male Borers who were here from other settlements. If someone wanted to take over a village, town, or city here, they could need to purchase the largest building in the settlement, and unlike in Warine, they would have to purchase it directly from its owner.

In other words, it would be *far* more expensive and, in Nate's experience, not worth it.

"Here we are," Nate said, stopping outside a square stone structure half the size of a typical house.

The door was open, which meant they were still seeing customers for the day. Nate had already seen places closing and had been nervous they wouldn't make it in time.

"What can I do for you?" asked the female borer behind the counter. "I'm closing in five minutes, mind you, so make it snappy."

"We're here to sell some monster bodies," Nate said, beginning to pile the corpses onto the counter.

Unlike the winges of Warine or the gnarks of the system, the borers didn't really balk at the sight of blood. When various fluids began coating the counter and the shop's floor, the borer didn't even bat an eye.

She examined each of the worm corpses, as well as the other animals they'd brought in.

"The kills look clean on most of them," she finally said, prodding at the worm that Nate's sword had split in two and another that Freya's Shattering Shrapnel had punched full of holes. "Do you want any of the parts for yourselves?"

"No," Nate said, knowing that none of these monsters had parts that would make for good armor. "We want to sell the lot."

The borer nodded, then began counting up the figures.

"I can give you four thousand for the lot," she finally said.

"Come on," Nate said. "That's a miser's bargain and you know it. This is worth at least five."

"The cuts on these ones aren't clean," she said, motioning to one of the foxes. "If they were, I'd have offered five. I can go as high as 4200, but that's it."

After another minute of haggling, they settled on 4,400 points. Divided evenly, that made for 1,466 apiece. Since their points were a bit skewed due to the numbers, Nate was awarded 1,470 for his haggling, while the others each took 1,465 each.

"Tell me, how much were those corpses really worth?" Freya asked once they'd left the shop.

"About what we got for them," Nate sighed.

"So what was the point of all that haggling?" she asked.

"If we'd gone to a system shop, they would have given us thirty-five," Nate said. "They're worth around forty-five, but that borer was a tough negotiator. Still, I'm happy with how much we got."

"We killed eleven monsters," Noam said. "That means they were each worth an average of four hundred each. I don't know exact figures, but that doesn't seem exceedingly high for ordinary monsters at their rank."

"Monster ranks only play a part in how much their value is," Nate said with a shrug. "Rarity makes a big difference, as well as difficulty in defeating them. The monsters we fought were neither rare nor difficult to kill. Four hundred apiece isn't too bad when you think about it that way."

"I guess you've got a point," Noam said, still seeming thoughtful.

They wound through the streets of the city, noting the absence of any humans whatsoever. It seemed none had made it to this town, though, if Jebber was to be believed, he had heard of something, and Nate was sincerely hoping that it would lead them to whichever guild was causing so much trouble for people trying to cross through.

They found a shop not five minutes later, the entire group shivering as they entered. There were four counters, each manned by a mix of male and female gnarks.

"Do you know what to ask for?" Nate asked as Noam approached one of the counters.

"Yes," Noam said. "I must insist they show me the limited list two times, then try and find the same technique you have. If I do not, then I will ask for the Cultivator's Gas Tank, as ridiculous as that sounds."

"And you?" Nate asked Freya as Noam went off to his counter.

"Two upgrades for my Kanta Meditation scroll," Freya said. "And any augments if they have."

"I'll see you in a few minutes," he said, then headed over to the farthest counter in line.

"How can I help you?" asked the seated elderly gnark.

He was the oldest gnark Nate had ever seen, looking so withered and small that he thought it a miracle the man was still alive. His voice was reedy and ancient.

"I need to buy a Magma Resist Draft," Nate said.

In the end, it was decided that instead of all of them buying the drafts and exploring the room, only one of them would. This way, they could save their points and still reap the same reward. After playing rock, paper, scissors, Nate had been the lucky winner. Freya had said he'd cheated and demanded a redo, but seeing as she couldn't prove it, his victory had stood.

"It's quite expensive," the reedy gnark said. "Are you certain?"

"Yeah, I'm sure," Nate said, placing his hand on the sphere.

"Very well," the gnark said, charging him the 6,500 points. "Is there anything else?"

"Yeah," Nate said. "I need some Water Packs, a hundred meal rations, some rope, a lantern, and a large tent."

The gnark added everything up, the total coming to a whopping 680 points. The tent – which would be able to fit up to five people – was 300. The food was another 325 and the rest had been the water, rope, and lantern.

The results of his shopping took him from nearly 70,000 all the way down to 62, taking him further away from his goal, but he knew that the investment would be worth it in the end. For one, if they had a comfortable tent, Freya might be okay with sleeping outside, especially once she discovered that the borer inns were basically all the same.

They already had a washtub, and seeing as they had a second tent, they could set it up in there for some privacy. Additionally, the larger tent would have more room to move around in *and* offer a modicum of privacy if they rigged Nate's tarp across the inside. In his mind, they were points well spent.

Food and water were necessities he couldn't go without, and he could always use more rope. The light source hadn't been needed on Warine, but here, they would need a way to see in the dark, especially if they were going to be camping instead of staying in the settlements.

"Is there anything else?" the man asked when Nate finished packing everything away.

"Yes, actually," Nate said. "Do you have any augments?"

34

"I'm officially a master of the healing arts," Freya said, clutching her scroll in triumph.

"I wouldn't exactly call you a master," Nate said. "But you'll be able to heal yourself if you're ever stupid enough to ignore sound advice."

"I am wise enough to make my own decisions, thank you very much," Freya said, stashing her scroll in her ring.

"How about you?" Nate asked, turning to Noam.

"The Cycle of Regeneration scrolls had all been taken," he said sourly. "But they still had a few of the Cultivator's Gas Tank scrolls remaining."

"That's great," Nate said. "Have you already tested it?"

Noam nodded. Though he was annoyed that he hadn't gotten the same technique as Nate and Freya, he shouldn't be too disappointed in what he'd gotten. If anything, this suited him far better than the Cycle of Regeneration.

Cultivator's Gas Tank was limited to just 180 pieces, so it was good that Noam had been able to get his hands on it. Unlike the Cycle of Regeneration, it didn't work immediately. Instead, Noam would cultivate, storing the excess kanta in a separate space – the gas tank in this instance. When he needed to heal, he could burn off the excess and feed it to his body.

The scroll had a total of four tiers. The higher the tier, the more he could store and the faster he could burn it. In addition to burning for healing, he could burn the excess to empower his techniques as well. In essence, this took the place of both the Kanta Orb and the Cycle of Regeneration.

The downside was no passive recovery of kanta, speed healing, or passive healing. Passive healing was the ultimate form of the Cycle of Regeneration. At the 5th tier, Nate's injuries would recover on their own while he battled. There were other benefits as well, but that was the main one he was after. Though, after pushing his scroll to the 4th tier, it would be quite some time to hit the 5th as it was significantly more expensive than the 4th.

"Did you upgrade it at all?" Nate asked.

Noam shook his head.

"Good," Nate replied. "The first tier should suit you just fine until rank fifty."

The scroll would have cost him 3,000 points, and seeing as Noam was a bit low right now, it was good not to waste any, especially seeing as the smelting of the ortium ingots was going to cost them, in addition to upgrading their armor.

"You two find any augments?" Nate asked.

"No," Noam said.

"Not a one," Freya sighed.

"Me neither," Nate said, though he was hardly surprised.

"All right, let's go find somewhere to stay, get some dinner and some rest. It's going to be a long day tomorrow."

"By all the freaking…gah!" Freya yelled, clutching her head. "Nate, we are *not* staying at another one of these accursed inns. Do you understand me? *Never* again!"

It was morning and the borer wake-up call had gone out, jerking the unprepared from sleep once again.

"I understand," Nate said, keeping a straight face. "We'll camp out like we did before. Luckily for us, I just bought a new tent too, so we'll have loads of room."

Freya gave him a suspicious look, then groaned and clutched her head again, wincing and yawning at the same time. It was just past five in the morning, the three of them having met up in the hallway after the wake-up call had sounded. Jebber and his crew would be heading out to the mine soon, which meant they had to get ready.

"Do you think they have anything remotely like coffee in this world?" Noam asked, stifling a yawn.

He looked far better off than Freya did, though he looked like he could use some more sleep. They all could.

"We can always check," Nate said.

He'd never been much of a coffee person, so he hadn't bothered trying to find out, and by the time they were on the final planets, things like coffee didn't really matter. Imminent death seemed to have that effect on people.

"Coffee sounds wonderful right around now," Freya groaned, straightening to her full height.

The three of them headed above ground, Nate taking special care to hold the door for Freya as they entered.

"Oh, my hero," Freya sang, giving him a half-hearted smile. "Would my prince like a kiss for his heroic...gah, forget it, it's too early for me to be putting any effort into this."

Nate smiled to himself as he watched Freya walk up to the counter, the area already bustling with the morning rush, and asking the overworked-looking borer woman if they had any coffee. They did not.

They did have something called burac, which was a greenish liquid that smelled of vanilla. The three of them eyed a borer sipping on the concoction and Noam suddenly decided that he didn't need a coffee after all.

"You know what? I'm too tired and desperate to care," Freya said. "You ninnies can go without. Give me a cuppa that stuff."

"Of course, dear," the borer woman said kindly, filling a mug with the steaming liquid and handing it over to Freya.

"Are you sure about this?" Nate asked. "It's not too late to put it down and walk away."

"When you commit to something, you follow through," Freya said, then lifted the mug to her lips and took a slow sip.

Her eyes went wide as the liquid hit her tongue, her lips puckering and knuckles going white.

"That good, huh," Noam said, watching her.

"So good," she wheezed, setting the mug down.

A shudder ran up her entire body and for a moment, it looked like she was going to be sick. Then, she straightened her shoulders, set the mug down and thanked the woman.

"Well, it *did* wake me up," Freya said as they left the shop.

"What did it taste like?" Noam asked. "You seemed quite surprised by what you experienced."

"Imagine the sourest candy you've ever had, then, times that by ten, add fifteen shots of something that almost tastes like vanilla but reminds you more of how manure might taste. Stick that in a liquid that is somehow both chunky and liquidly at the same time, and that should give you a pretty good idea."

Noam shuddered this time.

"You are a braver woman than I," Noam said.

224

"I should think so, seeing as you're a dude and all," Freya shot back. "Now, Nate, why do I get the feeling that you knew what that stuff was?"

"Hey," Nate said, raising his hands. "I warned you. Even gave you the chance to back out, but you insisted."

She continued to glare for a few moments, then her countenance cracked and she grinned.

"Bet you were wetting your pants laughing at how I reacted." She tilted her head, as though trying to see.

"No pant-wetting for me," Nate said. "But yes, it *was* funny."

"You know, I feel like I've been making myself the butt of too many jokes lately," Freya said. "If the two of you weren't so boring and sour-pantsy then I wouldn't have to try so hard."

"Is that even a word?" Noam asked.

"No, it is not, in fact, a word," Nate said.

"Sourpuss," Freya said. "You need to lighten up. *Him*, I can understand, he's basically fifty, but you, Nate, don't look a shade over forty-five."

"Ouch, my ego," Nate said, clutching at his chest in mock pain.

"*Fifty?*" Noam asked, touching his face. "I don't really look *that* old, do I?"

The man was in his mid-30s, though he looked to be in his late 20s

"No, you don't," Nate said. "Freya just has a sick sense of humor."

"At least I *have* a sense of humor," Freya said. "Unlike you two. Now, if you'll excuse me, I need to go powder my nose."

She turned and headed back toward the inn.

"I am very confused," Noam said. "I have dealt with many women in my time, but she is…"

"Different?" Nate said.

"Different," Noam agreed. "She is strange, but has an odd ability to make me feel…good? Yes, I think that is the word I am looking for. Is that why you chose her for this team you are building?"

"Partially," Nate said, watching as she entered the inn. "Though in truth, she was nothing like this when I knew her. I mainly wanted her because of her abilities. We were also friends

225

before..." Nate cut himself off, marshaled himself, and continued. "Anyway, I like this version of her better. She's had a hard life, as you well know, but her ability to see the positive and stay upbeat is a very special character trait of hers. One I am very happy she has."

The two of them lapsed into silence, waiting for Freya's return. She emerged from the inn just five minutes later, her face looking freshly scrubbed and some shadow applied to her eyes.

"Powder your nose?" Nate asked upon her arrival.

"Hey, just because women in ancient times used that as an excuse to go to the loo doesn't mean I have to," she said with a grin.

"Oh good, you're early."

The three of them turned to see Jebber standing there, a group of five borers gathered behind him.

"And a good morning to you as well, Jebber," Nate said.

"That's Chief to you," Jebber said. "I got a promotion due to our last chief's untimely demise. Anyway, we'll be heading out in another couple of minutes. I've heard some reports of carts who've headed out earlier not making it, so you'd best be on your guard. The last thing we need is a wipeout right after I got my promotion. My first day as a chief would look bad if we didn't meet our quota because a few of my crew got eaten."

"Cold-hearted little bastards, aren't they?" Freya said, eyeing the borer with distaste.

"It's just the way they are," Nate said. "It's a culture thing. But yes, they're all pretty messed up."

Once again, Nate had to wonder if it was the Mystery himself who'd created these creatures or if they were actual natives in a world that he had commandeered. Whatever the case, the borers were borderline sociopathic at best and not to be relied upon.

"Well, you heard the man," Nate said, checking his kanta. "This may very well be where we earn our info."

"Like we haven't already earned it with these creatures," Freya said. "I call dibs the rear guard."

They'd divided up their positioning around the cart, placing one at the back and one to either side. This way, they could increase their chances of spotting monsters, especially those who hid.

"Any reason you're insisting on the back?" Nate asked, already thinking he knew the answer.

"I don't need you staring at my butt the entire time," Freya said. "Gives me the creeps."

"Right," Nate said. "Instead, you get to stare at *my* butt the entire time."

"I wouldn't think too highly of yourself," Freya said, patting him on the shoulder. "I've seen much better."

"You haven't seen any," Nate said as she walked past.

"I've seen that beaver-guy's," Freya said, pointing to some random borer and laughing.

"Well, in her defense, none of them wear pants," Noam said when Nate turned to him.

"I don't like the implication," Nate said.

"What? That your keister looks worse than the furry beaver behinds waddling all around us?"

Nate nearly jumped as Freya's head popped in between them, the woman having managed to sneak back without either of them noticing.

"Geez! You're going to give me a heart attack!" Nate exclaimed, clutching his chest.

"Guess I better be careful then. Can't have your pacemaker going out on you, old man."

She laughed again but stopped when she saw the sour expression on Nate's face.

"What?" she asked. "Too far?"

"A bit," Nate said, still feeling his heart racing.

"Sorry," she said, seeming to mean it. "I was only joking around with you. Was it the pacemaker joke, or the old man thing that set you off?"

"The you popping out of nowhere thing, actually," Nate said. "I don't like surprises."

Nate had had far too many experiences where someone had leaped out at him or surprised him and every single one of them was associated with death. If someone threw him a surprise party, he was more likely to kill everyone there before they had time to react.

"I'm sorry," she said, taking his hand and giving it a squeeze. "I'll keep that in mind for next time."

Nate nodded, seeing that she meant it. Regardless of how immature and annoying she could be, she was a good person under all of it. He knew this was a bit part of her personality, especially when she was covering up pain.

The fact that she continued to escalate her little pranks meant that she trusted him more. When they'd first met, it was only inappropriate comments, but now, she was initiating contact and apologizing. She was comfortable around him and strangely enough, he felt comfortable around her as well.

"Thank you," Nate said, squeezing her hand in return. "Now come on, it looks like they're getting ready to leave."

"I'm still keeping to the back," Freya said, her voice still missing that usual teasing tone of hers. "And I lied about your butt."

"Yes," Noam said, as Freya moved into position. "She is definitively different."

35

The sweltering heat of the day had already begun by the time they set off, their group spaced around Jebber's cart. Several others were leaving at the same time, apparently wanting to stay in a group. Not because it would deter whatever was attacking their carts, Nate knew, but because it would give the monsters other targets.

"How are things on your end?" Nate asked, swinging around to Noam.

"The air is very still," Noam said, frowning. "I feel as though we are headed into the shadow of some giant monster, yet I see nothing."

"I feel the same," Nate said. "I'll go see if Freya's spotted anything."

"Be careful," Noam said. "Something is not right here."

Nate nodded, then slowed and moved over, allowing himself to come level with Freya's scooter.

"You see anything?"

"Nope," Freya said. "You can feel the tension in the air though. It's so thick you could cut it with one of your Gilded Blades."

It was a bad play on an even worse saying, but everyone was tense. Seven other mine carts were within view, all of them having heard that Jebber's work crew had hired alien mercenaries to protect them. Several more were trying to catch up but were too far by this point.

"Keep an eye out," Nate said, then moved back to his previous position.

It was just a 25-minute ride to the mountain, which already loomed before them, its shadow vast and far-reaching. They were a little over halfway there, but every minute felt like it stretched endlessly. They were moving too slowly, inching their way closer to the entrance of the mountain, visible now on the mostly flat landscape.

The road was rougher here, less paved stone and more hard-packed dirt, the effect all the carts had after riding over the same area for as long as they had. To Nate, this meant that they were far from an established road and smack dab in the middle of the wilderness. Not that that really mattered on this planet as far as monster attacks went. But the further from the road you got, the more dangerous the potential monsters would be.

If there was a single thing that stood out to Nate, it was how quiet things had been. Not a single monster had attacked them, despite the tempting target of so many carts. The same trip yesterday had seen multiple attacks, yet now, there was nothing. Then, the cry came, echoing back down the road.

"Fire fox! Scatter!"

Nate swore, speeding up and kicking his scooter forward.

Freya came rushing from behind as Noam moved to the front of the cart.

"You see anything?" Nate shouted, frantically scanning the horizon.

"Not yet!" Freya replied, sounding tense.

Several moments passed and everyone held their breath. Then, out of a near-invisible hole in the landscape, came the fire foxes. Well over a dozen of them streamed out of the hole, their red fur trailing flames behind them as they ran.

In overall size, they were just a bit larger than the average red fox, appearing similar in many ways. The main differences were in the glowing orange eyes, flickering flames cloaking their bodies, and the orange glow emanating off their forms. They had the ability to murder their way through vast swaths of people as one of the most dangerous pack hunters on the planet.

"Keep moving!" Nate yelled back at Jebber. "We'll keep them off you."

Jebber didn't look back, urging his workers to move the cart faster, yelling, "We will not miss today's quota! Move it!"

"What a great guy we're guarding," Freya said as she stashed her scooter. "What are we going to do?"

"We only need to keep Jebber's crew alive," Nate said. "But I don't want to leave these things alive for our return trip to town. We take them now, before they grow any stronger."

By the time Nate came up with a plan, the lead foxes in the pack had closed more than three-quarters of the distance between them.

This fight was going to be a hard one. Pack hunters in the system were *always* more difficult to take down than single hunters.

"Freya," Nate said. "Let's see how good that aim of yours is. No fire magic."

They seemed to be facing a lot of enemies immune to her fire spells lately.

Freya's Shattering Shrapnel slammed into the area between the monsters, going off in an explosion of white shards. The foxes ranged in rank from 30 to 36, five of them Magician-based and the other dozen being melee fighters.

Freya's first spell pulled the pack's attention away from the slow-moving carts to focus on a greater enemy. Two of the foxes stopped in place, their mouths opening wide, fire kindling in their throats.

"Firebomb," Nate yelled. "Get out of the way!"

He dashed right, while Noam ran left. Freya dropped to her stomach, continuing to fire spells at the approaching group. Two balls of orange fire blasted from the foxes' mouths, racing through the air and splashing against the ground where Nate and Noam had just been standing. As soon as they landed, they exploded upward into a funnel of flames before vanishing an instant later.

The three other fox magicians paused, taking up positions at varying range, all beginning their own Firebomb spells. In the meanwhile, the first of the foxes closed to melee range and Nate didn't have any more time to plan. His Gilded Skin flowed over him, drawing on his kanta.

The first fox leaped at him, its body trailing fire, while a second and third circled to his right and left. Nate summoned a dirk, stabbing at the fox's face as it leaped. The heavy monster crashed into him, his armor growing warm as the flickering fire coiling over the monster's body began affecting him.

The fox let out a yelp as Nate's dagger drove into it, punching deep into its shoulder as the monster's teeth snapped at his face. He shoved back, rolling backwards over his shoulder as one of them snapped at his ankle. He could not allow them to bite him, seeing as their Firejaw technique would punch through his armor and leave him with very painful injuries.

The third fox pounced on him as he rose and Nate's backsword appeared in his left hand, swinging for the fox's throat. A

Firebomb hit him as he swung, blasting him off his feet and forcing him to give up his Gilded Skin as it became superheated.

He hit the ground hard, scraping his shoulder, but forced himself upright regardless. Another fox leaped at him as he rose, and his Goldshield appeared before him. The fox slammed into it with a loud *gong*, rebounding off the barrier. Nate dragged himself to his feet, dismissing the costlier shield and resummoned his Gilded Skin.

A fox was right on top of him as he rose and not having the time to summon a blade, Nate punched it in the jaw. It bit down on his raised forearm, and burning pain seared into his arm as the fox's powerful jaws punched through his armor, sinking into skin and muscle beneath.

Superheated teeth burned him from within, but only for the instant in which the fox remained latched. Nate's fist smashed into the side of its face, the crunch of metal breaking bone audible as the fox's jaw shattered.

It fell to the ground with a yelp, and Nate rose to his full height, already breathing hard. His Cycle of Regeneration was going, working to heal the burning in his arm, but it would be of diminished use to him until this battle came to an end.

Freya and Noam weren't too much better off, the former running and firing, even as spells hammered her, and the melee foxes continued to close. She already sported several burns and was favoring her right arm. Noam, on the other hand, had completely lost his two-handed ax, the weapon lying on the ground in a melted pile of slag.

His Guardian's Draw and Dread were keeping many foxes rooted in fear, and focused on him, while his Brutal Guardian cloaked his body, protecting his warping tomahawks from falling apart. None of the foxes were dead yet, the injured ones falling back and the fresher ones taking their places while the others recovered.

Nate growled as he shoved back another fox using his Goldshield, then used his backsword to fend another off as it nipped at his ankles. Blood sprayed as another fox lunged at his waist and Nate got a solid hit in, his backsword appearing an inch from the fox's belly and slashing it wide.

The monster was thrown away, yipping as blood poured from its open stomach. In response, three of the pack's ranged attackers focused on him, using their Firelances instead of Firebombs. Javelins made of raging flame blasted from their mouths, one after the next.

His Goldshield sprang up, Nate feeling the pull on his core once again. His planted feet were driven back through the dirt as the first spell struck, partially rebounding back at the enemy. The strain increased as the second spell hit, then the third.

Another spell came right on its tail, a fourth pulling away from Freya to attack him. This one wasn't stopped by the shield and Nate swore, throwing himself to the side as the lance struck, then punched through his defenses. It scored along his ribs, slicing through the metal of his Gilded Skin, and scorching the flesh beneath.

He rolled over a shoulder, summoned a dirk, then drove it up and into the open mouth of the fox who'd been waiting for him in ambush. Nate felt the searing heat of its fangs through his armored hand as he drove the dagger deep into its brain, feeling the rush of kanta pour into him.

He dismissed the dagger, pulling the monster's corpse into his ring the moment it died to preserve it in its current state. Fire foxes were valuable due to the danger in hunting them and their fur was prized beyond almost any other monster's on this planet.

"Nate!" Freya yelled. "Help!"

Nate whirled, seeing Freya being mobbed by three foxes at once. She was firing Blinding Buckshots and trying to put some distance, but they were persistent. One vanished with a loud *bang*, reappearing fifteen feet away, but Freya was breathing hard and he knew she had to be straining with so many spells one right after the next.

She had regeneration now, but it wasn't nearly enough to keep up with how much she was depleting.

Nate's Steelshod appeared over his legs, and he blasted forward, narrowly avoiding another Firelance that slammed into the ground at his feet, sinking deep into the earth. Two foxes gave chase, heading him off and snapping at his ankles. Nate kicked at one, driving it off, but the other leaped, sinking its jaws into his calf.

Nate howled and was forced to stop, whirling as the fox landed, twisting its head from side to side as it tried to rip the chunk of flesh from his body. Blood began pouring from the wound, smoke and steam rising as well. The nauseating scent of cooking meat filled the air and Nate knew where it was coming from.

His backsword plunged down, the golden blade punching through the top of the fox's head and into the ground. The monster released him and Nate dropped to a knee, sweating profusely. His calf felt horrendous and heavy. It didn't feel right.

"I can't keep them off me!" Freya yelled, blasting another and sending it back.

They were swarming to Freya's location, even with Noam's shouts to keep them on him. The foxes had left him be, all homing in on the woman who was flailing, blasting away with her Magigun. She was causing injuries, but no kills just yet.

Noam had managed a couple, just as Nate had, but the man's tomahawks were now just twisted lumps of molten metal that could no longer be called weapons. He'd resorted to fighting with his hands and, cloaked by his Brutal Guardian, was managing to cause some damage.

Nate had to do something quickly or Freya was going to be overwhelmed and die. She was already bleeding from bites all along her bare arms, the cloth of her torso having been torn open, where a blackened set of teeth marks were visible along her side and abdomen. They'd gotten her legs as well, which was why she was slowing down, making it easier for them to get her.

Had it not been for her Tele-bang, she would already have been overrun. As it was, she could do no more than send one fox away, then another two were on her.

Nate dragged himself to his feet, feeling his leg protesting the movement. Her kanta would be running out at any moment, what with how many spells she'd already used. She was probably on her reserves and burning through what was in her Kanta Orb at the moment. Nate hadn't wanted to use this, but he knew he had no choice.

Letting out a slow breath to calm himself, he allowed the shimmering heat to suffuse him. White light began leaking from his body, his eyes changing color to match as the flames turned to points and sank into his muscles, lighting him ablaze from within as he used Whitefire Injection.

The ground at his feet bubbled then shattered as he hurled himself forward, closing the distance between himself and Freya in

234

the blink of an eye, backsword cleaving down and shearing the head from a rank 35 fire fox.

36

Nate spun around the falling body of the fox, his backsword streaking through the air in a blur. His aim wasn't great and lopped off the second fox's shoulder, burning the flesh within. It was a good thing these monsters were so fire-resistant, or his technique would have caused their bodies to burst into flames the moment they died.

This way, their corpses would still be intact to sell if they made it out of this alive.

Nate jabbed down with a summoned dirk, nailing the head of the second fox to the ground in a spray of blood and sizzle of burning flesh. While their exteriors would remain unharmed, their insides were just as flammable as everyone else's.

In the blink of an eye, Nate had killed three of the foxes. He turned to confront a fourth, but his calf screamed in pain, causing him to fall, crashing hard to the ground, which immediately began to bubble and melt as he did.

"Nate! What the…What in the world *is* that?" Freya exclaimed, momentarily shocked when she saw him appear.

The foxes, seeing so many of their comrades go down in the blink of an eye, turned their attention to Nate.

"I can't keep this going for long," Nate said when the burning began.

He forced himself to his feet, Goldshield appearing as spells rained down on him.

Freya nodded, backing quickly away and raising her Magigun. She couldn't have had much kanta left, but she was still in this fight.

Nate's backsword slashed through the air as a fox leaped at him, seemingly in slow motion. At the same time, he sidestepped another, then summoned his Steelshod and stomped down, driving its head into the ground, and shattering its skull.

Bloody bone fragments and bits of brain matter clung to his boot as he pulled it back. His leg burned as he spun to confront the spell-slinging monsters, two of whom had fired on his turned back. He avoided one, but caught the second in his gut, the lance burning through his defenses and lodging in his stomach.

Nate dropped like a log, the burning intensifying further. His body was on fire from within as the summoned white flames continued to consume him. He didn't know if he could keep going. A fox sank its teeth into the side of his neck. Nate's hand flashed up, driving a burning dirk through its eye.

Blood seeped from the wound as he lost his hold over Whitefire Injection, the technique having already begun breaking down his muscles. He sighed in relief as he released it, noting that the damage wasn't as extensive as the last time he'd used it. He knew he had his higher rank to thank for that.

Still, he was in bad shape, just like the rest of them. The five spell-casting foxes were still alive and he didn't know how many he had killed.

Nate groaned as another fox appeared, lunging at his face. He raised his arm, prepared to take the hit, only for a monster of crimson kanta to smash it in the side, driving it away. The monster ran on all fours, though it was clearly capable of walking upright. Its crimson form was made of dense kanta, its fingers and toes elongated into claws.

Ridges covered its entire form, massive muscles bulging unnaturally, yet somehow seeming to fit. Its face was vaguely humanoid, mouth open in a silent roar as it smashed into his attacker. The fox's bones shattered like dry splinters as it was sent bouncing across the ground.

Finally dragging himself upright, Nate was treated to the sight of Noam's new techniques in action. A monstrous version of Noam, with a massive upper body, stood before Freya's prone form, tanking the hits from the spell-casting foxes. She seemed to be suffering the backlash of using more kanta than she had.

At the same time, the eight-foot-tall creature who'd just saved his life, finished the fox who'd attacked him. Noam stood twenty feet away, trying to close with one of the spell-casting foxes, but having little luck. Nate took a moment to look around, seeing one dead fox lying near Freya, a series of holes having been punched through its body.

Eleven down, five to go, he thought, dragging himself painfully to his feet.

His body cried out as the wounds accumulated over the course of the short battle protested the movement. Still, this wasn't over. He needed to keep moving.

Noam's summoned attack construct, the Maniacal Guardian, faded from view as soon as the monster was dead, though the defensive one remained in place.

Five monsters to go. Noam was trying to gain some traction, but all the foxes were focusing their attention on him. Despite all of his experience and expertise, he'd already taken a few hits. One across his ribs, another on his cheek, and a third on his foot. Noam had managed to minimize the damage each time, but the wounds had to be paining him, or he'd have been able to close with at least one of the foxes.

Okay, Nate thought, gathering himself. *Here goes nothing*.

His kanta flowed down to his boots, triggering the technique that lay within. The Lightning Sloth fur that had been worked into them by Geary flared, triggering the Lightning Lunge technique pilfered from the monster's corpse.

His body blurred as he was thrown forward, wind tearing at his hair as he closed the distance between him and his closest opponent in a blink.

The fox whirled as Nate appeared before it, mouth already open and prepared to cast a spell. Nate's Backsword swept out in an arc, appearing in his hand just inches from its face.

The glittering blade of gilded steel sheared into the monster's open mouth, removing the top half of its head. Nate fell once again, his calf screaming as a Firelance streaked at him. His fall saved him, the attack going wide, but Nate's interference had had its intended effect.

Now that the monsters were distracted, Noam was finally able to make some headway, closing with the nearest of the foxes and tackling it head-on. It hit him at point-blank range, but seeing as it was a spellcaster, the effects of the attack were drastically weakened.

Noam barely staggered before smashing a crimson fist into the monster's face, crumpling its bones with an ugly series of crunches.

Nate rolled quickly to his right as a Firebomb dropped from the sky, splashing into the ground and exploding into a pillar of fire.

His Gilded Skin flowed over him as he rolled, but the explosion of force still tossed him a good five feet.

He hit the ground again, a loud *clang* ringing as he did. Nate forced his knees under him as two more spells streaked at him. His Goldshield appeared once again, driving him back, though the technique held. He gritted his teeth, feeling pressure began building in his chest.

"I don't have much left!" he yelled, breathing hard.

He'd already been pulling on his Kanta Orb, and with so many uses of his Goldshield, he was beginning to run low.

"Neither do I," Noam called back, also breathing hard.

Three left, Nate consoled himself. *Just three left.*

Nate dragged himself to his feet, releasing his Goldshield and feeling the pressure leave him. His Gilded Skin remained, and he crossed his arms as a third spell smashed into him. The Firelance splashed over his body, scorching his metallic skin and leaving him feeling hot.

The foxes were spread out, the closest around ten yards away and the furthest fifteen. A quick check showed him that they were at the 32nd, 35th and 36th ranks. So far, not a single rank 36 had been killed, which meant that this was likely their leader.

Nate felt his legs shaking as he regained his footing. If it had been his actual foot that had been injured, he could have compensated, but that bite to his calf had been so nasty that he could barely put any weight on it.

"I'm going to try something," Nate said. "But I'm going to need you to cover me for just a couple of seconds!"

They were desperate and on the verge of running out of kanta. Once that happened, they would be all but helpless against these monsters.

"What are you going to do?" Noam yelled.

"What I have to," Nate breathed, then dismissed his Gilded Skin, feeling himself sway on his feet.

"I don't have much left," Noam warned. "This will be it."

"So be it," Nate growled, gritting his teeth.

A light burning already suffused his muscles and he knew that what he was going to do would hurt. But what choice did they have?

Three spells flew at him as he stood there, only for the towering construct representing Noam's defensive power to appear before him, tanking all three spells. It shattered a moment later as Noam hit the ground, eyes rolling up in his head.

That was more than enough time for Nate to use his Whitefire Injection for the second time. Though he'd been too distracted to notice before, his ranking had jumped by two during the battle, bringing him up to 36. If he could sustain this for just a few seconds, they could still get out of this. If not, the foxes would kill them all.

It was a dangerous gamble to be putting everyone's lives on the line for one attack, but Nate knew they were out of options. His body burned from within as a shimmering heat haze surrounded him, white flames flickering off his skin in small bursts.

"Okay," Nate whispered. "Round two."

He exploded forward, ignoring the screaming in his leg each time it hit the ground and forcing himself to remain upright, no matter how badly he wanted to buckle. The world blurred around him as he closed with the first fox, the creature seeming to move in slow-motion as it opened its mouth to attack.

His backsword flashed, shearing the monster's head in two and sending a sizzling spray of blood into the air. He turned, intending to charge the next monster, but his leg gave out and he hit the ground, scraping his forearms in the fall. Blood coated his limbs, but Nate forced himself to roll, avoiding the Firebomb and leaping back to his feet.

His body was on fire as the technique consumed him from within, but Nate didn't stop, throwing himself at the next creature in line. The Firelance smashed into his chest as he charged, knowing that he'd fall if he dodged. This was a spell, not a bullet, so although his technique lessened the impact, it didn't entirely block it. A piercing, burning pain lanced through him as the spell punched into his chest, missing his heart by mere inches.

The spell vanished, leaving a bloody hole in its wake, one that began to sizzle and steam the instant it vanished. The pain was some of the worst Nate had ever felt. He ignored it, rapier appearing in a flash of gold to skewer the monster through the eye. If anything, he'd been lucky with how that spell had hit.

It had struck him when he'd only been around eight feet from the monster. Had he been just five feet further, it would have gone right through him. Without the ability to keep his Gilded Skin going, he was relying on his speed.

Nate whirled on the last monster, making sure to take the weight on his good leg.

One to go, Nate thought, breathing hard.

His muscles were screaming despite the fact that Whitefire Injection had only been going for around twelve seconds. He had maybe five or six more before his muscles would begin tearing themselves apart. Using it for a second time like this had been a truly desperate move.

Nate's family flashed before his eyes as he ran at the fox, a Firebomb taking him in the stomach. He ran through the explosion, burning heat scorching his skin and leaving it red and blistered. Some parts he couldn't even feel, which he knew was a bad thing.

The fire fox turned to run, trying to put distance between them, but Nate was faster. He closed with the monster, who unexpectedly turned and lunged, smashing into his chest and knocking him to the ground.

The monster's weight was slight as it landed on his chest, jaws lunging for his throat. Nate got an arm up and a loud *sizzle* sounded as the fox's mouth burned at the contact. Still, it punched through his skin as easily as a hot knife through butter, piercing to the bone.

A dirk flashed up, slamming into the monster's ribs with enough force to shatter them. It wasn't a fatal blow, the monster releasing his arm and lunging for his face. His right arm was trapped beneath it and his left would be too slow.

Nate jerked his head to one side, the fox's jaws snapping just an inch from his ear. He wheezed as his Whitefire Injection died, his body no longer able to sustain the massive strain. Nate lay there, panting and his vision blurry, as the fox lunged at him again. He was having a hard time focusing, but his senses were still sharp.

Guided by them, he managed to avoid the second attack, then punched the fox in the side. It was an ordinary punch, unpowered by anything other than his human strength. The fox staggered a bit but retained its perch. It seemed the monster wasn't going down easily.

Fire kindled in its jaws, and although the attack would be greatly weakened due to their close proximity, Nate knew it would still hurt. He tried to reach for his Gilded Skin but felt the strain immediately. It was like a tight cord on the brink of snapping. If he did this, he would be out of the fight for at least the next thirty seconds, if not more.

Nate's mind was working frantically for an answer, when the fox's body was suddenly hurled off him, a streak of red slamming into the side of its head and disrupting its spell.

Nate's head whipped to the side to see the hazy outline of Freya, propped up on one arm, aiming her Magigun in his general direction.

"Kill the blasted thing!" she yelled.

Nate didn't need to be told twice.

His hand flashed to his belt, where his combat knife lay. He rolled to one side, drawing the blade as the fox rolled to its feet. Fire kindled in the monster's jaws once again, cut off when the knife plunged through the top of its brittle skull and deep into its brain.

Nate released the blade as he slumped, the monster staggering for an instant before collapsing onto its side. A rush of kanta flowed into him, pushing him to rank 37. He let out a slow breath, feeling the collective aches and pains of the battle wash over him. He knew he was in a bad spot as he fought to remain conscious.

Kanta was already trickling in from his surroundings. He had to remain conscious or he would die, and that would be a seriously terrible ending to such a desperate battle.

"You still in one piece?" Freya asked as Nate cracked his eyelids.

The woman looked about as bad as he felt, though she'd managed to avoid injuries as terrible as his. Still, the burns that marred her body were as red and painful-looking as his own.

"Still kicking," Nate rasped, not even trying to sit up. "How long has it been?"

"Only around fifteen minutes," Freya replied, tucking a stray lock of hair behind an ear – it had come loose in the desperate battle.

"The carts?"

"Made it to the mine as far as I can tell, but we'd have to check."

"Any monsters?"

"A couple," Freya said. "But I managed to drive them off. Seems like a bad idea to hang around here though."

"I agree," Noam said, coming into view.

The man was limping, though of the three of them, he appeared to be the least injured.

"Yeah," Nate groaned. "We should definitely leave. I don't think I've got the strength to move though, let alone walk."

"I don't think any of us do," Noam said, looking around. "But others will be attracted by the smell of blood."

Nate grunted in reply, then turned – painfully – onto his side, revealing his calf.

"Oof!" Freya winced when she saw the messy state of his leg.

"Okay," Noam admitted. "Maybe you can't walk. I've managed to recover a bit. Let's see what I can do for that."

A hand clamped around his calf and Nate felt soothing warmth flow into it, washing away the worst of the pain as it removed the destroyed muscle and began restoring it to full. Unfortunately, that only lasted for around twenty seconds, as Noam was forced to cut it off after that.

"I haven't felt an overload before," Noam said, swiping at his forehead. "And I don't think I want to ever again."

"I can agree with that," Freya said. "It felt like I'd been hit by a train, and I don't mean one of those slow-moving ones."

"It gets worse as you grow," Nate groaned, forcing himself shakily to his feet.

His calf still protested the movement, as did his entire body, but it wasn't nearly as bad as before. He could stand, and if he could do that, he could walk.

"Did you collect all the corpses?" he asked.

"I got some, Noam got the rest," Freya said, taking his arm and steadying him.

Unfortunately, he couldn't lean on her, as she had also sustained a leg injury. That was how these monsters hunted. Take out the legs so the prey falls, then go for the throat.

"Those little beasties were harder to kill than that Rattlegator," Freya said with a wince as they began plodding towards the mine.

"They work well together," Nate said, cycling his kanta, just as he felt Freya doing. "That's what makes them so dangerous."

"Hey, at least we got something out of it," Freya said. "I mean, aside from horrible PTSD and lifelong nightmares."

"Yes," Noam agreed. "I jumped to rank thirty-five. Not bad for a single fight with a group of regular monsters."

"Thirty-seven," Nate said with a groan.

"Well, I guess that means that I'm the new leader of this group," Freya said with a wide grin, though the effect was a bit lost as it turned into a wince.

"What?" Nate asked.

"Read 'em and weep, boyos," she said, tugging the glove from her left hand. "Thirty-*eight*. Whooo!"

"Wait, why am I now the weakest?" Noam asked, confused.

"Because you participated in the least number of attacks," Nate said. "Remember the start of the fight, where they were mobbing her, and she kept driving them off?"

Noam nodded.

"Since she dealt damage to every single monster, she got kanta when they each died. You and I, on the other hand, didn't."

"But she only killed one," Noam protested.

"Hey, I don't write the rules," Freya said. "All I know is that you're all going to call me Queen Freya from now on. I expect to be waited on hand and foot, and as your first decree as queen, I demand chocolate."

Nate snorted out a laugh despite the pain. It was nice to see she was still herself.

"I think we've all earned a treat once we get back to town," Nate groaned. "The queen can have her chocolate from her share of the points. For now, I say we concentrate on getting to the mine alive."

They continued their plodding and painful walk in silence, only occasionally making a comment or calling out a monster. For the most part, they managed to avoid them, but when any looked like they were getting too close, Freya would scare them off with her Magigun. A few insisted on ignoring the warning shots and came closer, though they were met by Noam's Guardian's Dread, sending them fleeing in terror.

It took them thirty painful minutes to reach the entrance to the mines, where they were met by the same borer from the day before.

"What happened to *you*?" the man asked, balking at their condition.

"Work," Nate groaned. "Where is Jebber's crew? He owes us for our labor."

"Chief Jebber you mean?"

Nate nodded.

"Hmm, let me see." The borer lifted his clipboard and began leafing through sheaves of parchment. "Ah, here we are. Section D, tunnel 505. I can show you the way if you'd like. I don't think anyone else is making it today. There have been some nasty attacks by a pack of fire foxes out on the open plains."

"We know," Nate winced. "We killed them."

The borer stopped dead, then turned to look at them appraisingly.

"You did?"

Freya produced one of the corpses from her ring, the monster's still-flaming body hitting the ground before him.

"Remarkable," he whispered, prodding the creature's corpse. "And you three did this all on your own?"

"Yes," Nate said.

The borer looked between the dead fox and the three of them several times, then straightened.

"If you're open to more work, I've got a job for you," he said seriously.

"Would you mind giving us the pitch after we've had some time to heal?" Nate asked. "I feel like I'm about to pass out."

"Oh, of course," the borer said, looking a bit embarrassed. "Please, why don't you three use my bunkhouse? I won't be needing it until tonight anyway."

Nate grunted in thanks and the three of them entered the small house built near the tunnel entrance. He slumped to the ground, his back pressed to one of the walls.

"Well, that was interesting," Freya said as she joined him on the ground. "I didn't realize so many of the borers would be handing out quests."

"They're not quests, per se," Nate groaned. "They're more like opportunities. If you do something impressive enough, the locals on the friendlier planets will give you the chance to tackle something dangerous, typically a monster. If you kill it, all the parts and rewards are yours. If you die…well, I guess it doesn't really matter in that case."

"Sounds like a quest to me," Freya said with a shrug.

"We can debate this later," Nate said, closing his eyes. "For now, I would *really* like to *not* be in agony, so please excuse me."

He went silent, concentrating on the kanta in the air to suffuse his body with healing power. He didn't know how long he sat there, but at some point, his stomach began growling. He opened his eyes, feeling the pain had greatly diminished, though it wasn't gone just yet.

Freya lay slumped against the wall opposite him, her mouth open and a line of drool trickling from the corner of her lips.

"Well, that's attractive," he muttered.

She looked to have been completely healed, which was a good thing. It seemed that she'd chosen correctly when deciding to listen to his advice on purchasing the additional tiers of her meditation scroll.

"You're awake. How do you feel?"

Nate turned to see Noam, the man sitting with his back propped against the wall and looking weary.

246

"Like I got hit by a train, and not the slow kind," Nate said, repeating Freya's earlier assertion. "The train was also on fire when it hit me, by the way."

"You've been out for nearly five hours," Noam said. "I've recovered quite a bit. I think I can help with what's left."

Nate nodded, hating how much time it took for him to recover. He couldn't wait to get to the shop with their items and upgrade the scroll to the 4th tier. Noam placed his hand on Nate's still injured arm, the warmth flooding through not only his arm, but his entire body.

He relaxed, releasing a long, slow breath as Noam's power worked its way through him, soothing the remaining injuries. They washed away burns, healed puncture wounds, and restored torn muscle.

"Do you have any *other* hidden techniques you want to tell me about?" Noam asked.

"That was the last one," Nate sighed. "It's my trump card."

"I can see why," Noam said. "The cost to use it seems quite steep."

"It doesn't use much kanta," Nate said. "It exacts its toll from the user's body. There are ways to counteract it, but the easiest is to increase your rank. The last time I used it, I could only keep it going for a few seconds, and even then, it was only the one time. The fact that I was able to use it twice shows that I'm getting stronger."

"Well, that's unsurprising," Noam said. "With how many ranks you've jumped ahead."

The man removed his hand, having nearly healed all of his remaining injuries. The last one was the worst of the burns sustained by the fire fox's Firebomb that Nate had basically taken head-on. It was a burn on his stomach that had eaten through flesh, muscle, and nerves. It was slow in healing, though the nerve damage had been healed, which meant that it hurt.

"Don't you worry about that," Nate said, removing one of his meal packs from his ring.

The reason the food had cost him so much was that he'd sprung for the good rations this time. A sandwich stuffed with sliced meat and condiments appeared in his hand and Nate bit into it with enthusiasm. If he'd been healing himself for over five hours, then it was well past eleven in the morning and he hadn't eaten all day.

"Are you going to share any of that with your best friend?" Noam asked, eyeing the sandwich with obvious envy.

"Oh, so you're my best friend now?" Nate asked, raising an eyebrow.

"For the person that healed you of your injuries?" Noam tried.

Nate took another bite of his sandwich.

"For the one who's likely to be healing more of your injuries in the future?" Noam tried.

"Fine," Nate sighed, removing another of the sandwiches from his ring.

"I smell food. Your queen demands you hand it over."

She has a nose like a freaking bloodhound, Nate thought as Freya's hand flashed out, snagging the sandwich from his grip.

"Your queen is happy," Freya said grinning through a mouthful of sandwich.

"Hey, what about me?" Noam asked.

"Take it up with the queen over there," Nate said, biting into his own.

"Queen, my rear end," Noam muttered. "Dictator is more like it."

"And here I was about to share," Freya said. "Talk about rude."

"No, you weren't," Nate said.

Freya paused for a moment, sandwich halfway to her mouth. Then, she shrugged, grinning widely.

"Yeah, I wasn't going to share."

"Here," Nate sighed, pulling yet another sandwich from his ring and handing it to Noam. "But this is the one and only time I'm sharing. They were very expensive. Understand?"

"Yes, completely," Noam said, taking the sandwich.

"Absolutely clear," Freya said through another mouthful.

For some bizarre reason, he didn't believe them.

38

After their early lunch, Freya and Noam talked while Nate concentrated on relieving himself of the last of his pain. Seeing as there was only a single burn remaining, he was able to mostly close it up with half an hour, and with Noam's help after that, it was completely healed. A small scar remained where the burn had been. Attacks that severe didn't just go away with healing.

And so it begins again, Nate thought.

He'd had quite the collection in his previous life, and it had felt weird having a body so free of blemishes. Now he had a few. The one on the side of his neck, a couple on his forearms and now, on his stomach.

"I need to change," Nate said, standing up.

His outfit was in tatters, the expensive clothes having been thoroughly destroyed in the battle. They were made to keep them cool, not offer protection from monster attacks.

"Go on," Freya said. "No one's stopping you."

"Come on, you little minx," Noam said, placing his hands on her shoulders and steering her out. "Give your subject some privacy."

"The queen demands to see-" Noam closed the door before Freya could finish her sentence.

Nate just shook his head, then proceeded to change, removing his burned and bloodied clothes, and donning his spares. He used a bit of the water he had to wash his face and hands, though he knew that a proper bath would be needed if he wished to be truly clean.

"That took a bit longer than expected, I apologize," Nate said to the borer as he emerged. "I'm Nate, by the way."

"Coronius," the borer introduced himself, shaking Nate's hand in an iron grip. "And that's not a problem, I'm always happy to help someone promising."

"We need to speak with Jebber," Nate said. "Would you mind telling us what's on your mind while we walk?"

"Of course," Coronius said. "Multitasking is always a good way to make the most of one's time. Follow me."

The borer headed off into the main tunnel, the three of them following close behind.

"There have been some attacks on our construction sites lately," Coronius said as they walked. "I've been getting reports from all over the G-quadrant that someone or something has been messing with them. Multiple building sites have been shut down and important projects have ground to a halt. We don't really know what's going on or what's causing these delays, but many borers are ending up dead."

"So, you need someone who can handle themselves to go check it out," Nate said.

"I've never met anyone who could take down a pack of fire foxes before," Coronius said admiringly. "If you could do that, I'm sure you could handle whoever's been ruining our work."

As usual, the borer seemed more concerned with the delays in construction than the piles of corpses they were likely dealing with.

"Where exactly has this been happening?" Nate asked.

"In the central area of the G-quadrant," Coronius replied. "Between Town 150G and City 180G. There are half a dozen villages, towns, and cities that've been affected as well."

Nate wracked his memory for what monsters might be in the area, but he couldn't remember exactly where it was in comparison to Warine. His memory wasn't perfect, and he sorely wished it had been better. Laybor was one of the planets that he'd spent the least amount of time on, having spent too much on Warine before moving over.

By that point, he'd learned the errors of his ways and moved on to Raven a few short months after coming to this planet. And though he had visited on occasion after that, it hadn't been for long stretches of time. In fact, most of what he knew of Laybor was secondhand knowledge he'd gained from speaking with his comrades.

"How far is that from here?" Nate asked.

"About a week, give or take a day," Coronius said. "The attacks have been moving closer and closer, which is why we've been getting nervous. Do you think you'd be interested in going to have a look?"

"We might," Nate said. "But we need to speak with Jebber first."

"Right you are," Coronius said, taking a hard right down a tunnel and walking a bit faster.

More borers soon came into view, working on the walls, quarrying stone, mining ore, or widening the tunnels. Nate took note of the various metals being mined. It was mostly copper and iron, though there were some veins of nickel mixed in with the bunch. No orantium was to be found though, which was hardly surprising.

The metal was just as rare on this planet as the last. It wasn't until the fourth planet, Sorcer, that it would become more readily accessible, and by that point, he would be looking for better materials.

It didn't take them long to reach Jebber's work crew, Coronius leaving them with a wave and telling them to stop by on their way out.

"You're alive," Jebber said, scratching his stomach as the three of them approached.

"We held up our end of the bargain," Nate said. "We'd like our payment."

"Actually, you didn't," Jebber said, gesturing to his crew. "How many workers do you see here?"

Nate looked, counting silently as his eyes roamed over the small group. He swore under his breath. There were only five, including Jebber. Someone had gotten killed in the time they'd been fighting the foxes.

"What happened?" Nate asked.

"Ambush Worm," Jebber said. "Snagged Francer right out of the cart and he was my best worker. Thanks to you, there's no way we're meeting our quota. Get lost."

"Wait a minute," Freya said, a bit of heat coloring her voice. "We almost *died* taking those foxes down and now you're sending us off without payment?"

"You didn't do your job," Jebber said, turning flinty eyes on them. "And now, you're disturbing our work. Either you leave or we'll *make* you!"

It was amazing how quickly things could go from cordial to hostile when it came to these borers, but as Nate had already known, if you disturbed their work, they had no mercy.

251

"As much as I would love to leave," Nate said. "She's right. We almost died saving your hides. If it wasn't for us, your entire group would have died, not to mention all the others who were traveling with you. I wonder how your overboss would react to the news that you're refusing payment to the people who assured he didn't lose over sixty workers."

"The overboss doesn't have time for the likes of you," Jebber said, though he seemed suddenly less hostile and more nervous.

He had every right to be. The overboss was someone who had zero patience for things not running smoothly. He would likely be some massive brute at the 50th rank or higher, someone who would squash Jebber like a bug for causing this disturbance.

Nate had once seen an overboss tear a chunk of stone from the wall and use it to splatter an offending borer across the floor. It was quite disgusting.

"No, I think he'd be very interested," Nate said, pressing his advantage. "I think I'll go find Coronius and ask him to take us to him."

Nate turned as though to leave.

"Wait!"

Nate hid a grin, then turned back with a raised eyebrow.

"Even though you didn't technically complete the job, I can give you the information you want, but only because I don't want you wasting the overboss's time, understand?"

"Completely," Nate said with a straight face.

Neither Freya nor Noam said anything the entire time this was happening, watching with interest as he coerced the information out of the unfortunate chief.

"About a week ago, a work buddy of mine was transferred over from a jobsite in the G-quadrant. He was put in my crew before our last near-wipeout, but he did a good day's work beforehand, so it was alright. Anyway, he told me that their jobsite had been shut down due to some aliens coming in and messing the place up. They did so much damage that they decided to abandon the site and move on."

"Where in the quadrant was this?" Nate asked, feeling a small surge of excitement.

It seemed that his hunch had been right after all.

"The site was going to be City 159 G," Jebber said. "Now it's been decommissioned and the name will be transferred somewhere else."

"Did your friend have anything else to say about them?" Nate asked.

"Only that a bunch of them appeared female, which he thought was strange. Females should be home, tending the children and running the shops, not out and about, getting their hands dirty."

He sneered at Freya when he said this, then turned his glare back on Nate.

"Now, I've given you everything you wanted. You can leave now."

"Thank you for your time," Nate said, then turned and motioned the others to follow.

"One thing before we go," Freya said, turning toward the borer, a smile plastered on her face.

"*What?*" Jebber asked, his voice clipped and hard.

"Did you hear that rumor going around? You know, the one about an alien who tried to knock a horse out with their bare hands?"

"Yeah, why?" Jebber asked, seeming confused.

"That was me," Freya said, the smile never leaving her face as she struck.

Her back leg pivoted perfectly, her hips swirled, and her hand was clenched into a fist. The punch was marvelous, catching the borer square in his beaver-like jaw. There was a dull *smack* as her fist impacted, Freya continuing the motion as she turned.

Jebber howled in pain, spinning away and smashing into the wall, clutching at his jaw, eyes wide.

"You hit me!" he exclaimed, as though not believing the gall.

"Yes," Freya said, holding up her clenched fist. "I did."

39

"That hurt like a mother!" Freya exclaimed, shaking her hand out once they were out of earshot of the stunned borer. "You said it wouldn't hurt!"

"No," Nate said, grinning from ear to ear. "I said you wouldn't break your hand, and, if you take a look, your hand is still in one piece."

Freya narrowed her eyes, still shaking her hand. Her knuckles had split and blood coated them, but none of her bones had broken, despite the stunning punch.

"That was quite impressive," Noam said. "Though you *do* know that punching someone in the face, simply because of an implied insult, is a bit extreme."

"Your face is extreme," Freya said, then grimaced. "Ugh, I'm off my game. Do you mind healing this?" she asked, extending her hand to Noam.

Noam grinned as he took her hand, the skin flowing back together and the blood crusting over.

"Ahhh, that's much better," Freya said, flexing her fingers. "Now, what was I saying? Oh yes, your *face*…You know what, it's too late. The moment's gone. Anyway, why didn't that knock him out?"

"You're kidding, right?" Nate said.

"Obviously not," Freya replied.

"He's like three times your weight," Nate replied. "And a rank 35 cultivator. You'd need to be at least twenty ranks stronger than you are now if you wanted a clean knockout."

Freya sighed.

"The queen will return to exact her revenge," she vowed.

"I think you already have," Noam said. "Did you not see how hard his crew was laughing when he hit the ground?"

"They're clearly a bunch of sickos to laugh at their boss like that, but I see your point."

"Great. Now that that's settled, I believe we know where we're heading next," Nate said.

"The magma cave?" Freya asked.

"The magma cave," Nate affirmed.

The group retraced their steps, heading down through the opened tunnel. It became cold before the warmth began to set in again, though this time, Freya had a blanket ready to wrap around her shoulders.

"How long will this thing last?" she asked as Nate removed the bottle from his ring and popped the cork.

"It should be around five minutes," Nate said, mentally preparing himself.

It was going to get really hot. Still, the Draft should do its work, which was what mattered.

"Wait, what if we end up on a planet with loads of volcanic activity?" Freya asked.

"As far as I can tell, we will at some point," Nate said. "And by then, we can hope that we'll be tough enough to just waltz through without having to take any drafts."

"Good luck," Noam said after Nate upended the bottle, swallowing down the orange-flavored draft in two big gulps.

A soothing cool began pouring off him in waves, pushing back against the heat.

"I'll see you soon," Nate said, then stepped into the room.

A barrier of cool air enclosed him as he stepped over the first of the magma streams, the heat already feeling oppressive. His clothes should remain safe, as the effects of the Draft would cover him entirely. The last thing he needed was for it to burn off and give his friends a show.

Nate moved quickly, crouching and snagging every piece of pumice he came across. They were small, porous stones, so light they felt insubstantial. It was exactly this lightness that would help the ortium remain strong and almost weightless.

He took a path straight through the room, leaping over the larger streams and having to walk through several. Stone was denser than the human body, even in liquid form, so his boots only sank a few inches into the surface but easily held his weight.

The heat was oppressive and heavy, weighing on him like a physical force. Sweat beaded his brow and small fires tried to start on the hems of his clothing. The draft continued to do its work, exuding a cold air around him, keeping anything from being set ablaze.

Nate found several metal ores within the room, the glowing metal being unlike anything he'd seen before. He recognized some of it as iron, though he had no idea what else was mixed in with it. He would have to take it to a smelter or smith to be told more. These were tricky to get into his ring, as he needed to tap it against the burning stone.

The draft worked well, but his skin became unbearably hot every time he did it. In all, he collected eight lumps of the ore. Nate crisscrossed the room several times, finding nearly fifty pieces of pumice, which, while not as rare as sandstone, would still fetch a fairly good price.

By the time he began making his way around the perimeter of the room, he was beginning to feel disappointed. He only had three minutes left before the draft's effects would begin to wear off and he didn't think he'd found anything of true value.

Nate reached the halfway point and began running, the blazing stone around him spraying into the air as another of the small vents went off. Droplets of molten stone splashed against his skin and slid off, leaving burning trails in their wake. Nate ground his teeth together, shaking his hand to release the cooling stone. He would need some healing when he got out of here, but right now, he needed to keep moving.

He began to turn past the deepest part of the cavern, when he paused, noticing something gleaming out of the corner of his eye. Turning quickly, Nate made his way back to the center of the cavern, an area tucked behind one of the spewing geysers of magma.

It was a small nook, dark and barely large enough for him to squeeze into, but the fact that it was so dark told him that the area was cool, which was strange, given how blazingly hot this cavern was.

Nate looked along the perimeter, knowing that if he tried to jump the vent, there would be no time to explore the rest of the room. Freya would have been unable to see this spot from their vantage, as it was tucked behind a stone pillar, conveniently placed at the center of the room.

He hated giving up potential finds, but he had a good feeling about this. Mind made up, Nate waited. A low rumbling echoed through the cavern, then a geyser of magma plumed before him, spraying into the air. He waited until the stream stopped, then broke into a run.

His Steelshod cloaked his boots and he took a running leap, the pistons on his feet blasting him forward as he hurled over the six-foot mini crater, landing on the other side. His momentum continued to carry him past the rumbling geyser and into the narrow nook.

Blessed cool washed over him as he entered, the oppressive heat vanishing in an instant and leaving him feeling refreshed, like walking into an airconditioned house after an hour in the burning sun.

He knew he didn't have much time to stay, as he still needed to cross back over to the other side and exit the cavern before the draft ran its course. Not able to see very well in the dark alcove, Nate removed his lantern from his ring, lighting the small script on the handle with a small pulse of kanta.

A yellow light shone from within the source, illuminating the area before him. As it turned out, the nook was quite a bit deeper than he'd first realized, the shadows having played tricks on his eyes. The nook was more of a tunnel, running for some twenty feet before it appeared to open up.

Nate moved quickly, the lantern light bouncing off the walls. He emerged on the opposite side, entering a smaller cavern. It was completely unremarkable, aside from a single pedestal of stone at the center. Nate ran up to it, his eyes widening as he recognized the stone tablet sitting upon the pedestal.

"Yes!" he cheered, pumping his arm.

Knowing he didn't have time to stay and examine it, he grabbed the tablet, stashing it in his ring and turned to leave. Then, he paused, grimaced and ran for all he was worth to the opposite side of the small cavern. He knew he was coming down to the wire, but he had to explore the rest of this space before leaving. He wouldn't forgive himself otherwise.

His lantern lit up the craggy walls, and Nate grinned when he saw several small nooks, each containing a glass bottle. He snatched them as he ran, not looking at their contents. Each took up an additional slot in his ring, which meant none were the same. Five in all entered his ring before he ran from the room, down the narrow tunnel, and into the magma cavern.

He had half a minute left at best, and a low rumbling was already coming from the sloping geyser before him.

Nate dashed up the side of the geyser, summoning his Steelshod once again. The rumbling intensified as he reached the crater, the glow of molten stone showing within. Nate leaped as the geyser erupted. He screamed, the tail end of the blast having caught him in the back, scorching his skin as it tore through his shirt.

He hit the ground on the other side, rolled several times, splashing through molten rock, then leaped back to his feet. He was seventy-five yards from the exit, with less than twenty seconds remaining.

His Lightning Sloth boots, which Nate had made sure to recharge, crackled as he threw himself forward, the burning air blurring around him as he covered around a third of the distance. He used his Steelshod to try and keep his speed up.

Seven. Six. Five. Four.

Nate could see Freya and Noam standing by the entrance, urging him to run faster. Clearly, they'd been keeping track of time as well.

The draft wore off when Nate was five feet from the tunnel. Gathering himself, he leaped, sailing over the burning magma at his feet and landing on the edge of the safe area, teetering for a moment on the edge. Noam and Freya moved in to help and their powerful hands seized him.

"Talk about cutting it close," Freya said.

"I'll say," Nate said, dropping to his knees and breathing hard.

He looked at Noam with a pained smile.

"Feel like patching me up again? I think I might have injured myself in that run back."

258

40

"The shirt's ruined," Noam said. "But you're good to go."

"Thanks for that," Nate said, deciding to leave the remains of the shirt on, despite it missing its back half.

"Boo! Take it off. Your queen demands it," Freya said when Nate elected to keep it on.

"How long are you going to keep up this queen shtick?" Nate asked with a raised eyebrow.

"Until I'm deposed, of course," Freya said with a grin. "But that's not going to happen. Power suits me and I won't give it up without a fight."

"What did you find?" Noam asked, changing the subject.

Nate pulled all the items out – though he only pulled one each of the pumice and ore from his ring – and lined them up on the ground in the tunnel.

"I found a bunch of these," Nate said, gesturing to the pumice. "We'll be able to get that ax made for you. I also found some ore that I don't recognize but figured it was probably worth something."

"An item the all-knowing Nate doesn't recognize?" Freya asked. "Whatever will happen next? A shirtless pillow fight perhaps?"

"What?" Nate and Noam both asked at the same time.

"What?" Freya asked. "That's a thing guys do, right?"

"In what world do you think that's something anyone in their right mind would do?" Nate asked.

"I knew she was lying," Freya muttered.

"What?" Nate asked.

"Oh nothing," Freya said. "Just remind me that if we see Cordelia to slug her in the arm."

Nate opened his mouth to ask the same 'what' again, but then closed it.

"You know what? I don't want to know. Moving on," he continued, going over to the glass jars. "I found these in a hidden cave behind one of the magma vents."

259

Nate lifted the first, revealing a glittering blue-green liquid within. When he shifted it, sparkles of silver appeared within, dancing like motes of sunlight through the surface of a lake.

"That's pretty," Freya said. "What do you think it does?"

"If I'm not mistaken, this looks like an Ocean Breath's Bomb," Nate said, turning the vial this way and that.

"A bomb?" Noam asked. "I was unaware this world had such items."

"Yeah," Nate said. "Just like they have Drafts to heal, or cause different effects, they also have liquid bombs like these."

"Why haven't we been buying any then?" Freya asked.

"Because they're extremely expensive and often not even worth it," Nate said. "The strongest bomb we can get right now won't have a radius of five feet. This, on the other hand – if I'm right about what it is – should give us a good twenty-foot area or effect."

"How exactly would it work?" Noam asked.

"I'm not going to spoil the surprise," Nate replied with a grin. "Who wants it?"

Freya and Noam both raised their hand.

"Well, seeing as you both do, you'll have to play for it," Nate said.

"As your queen, I demand you hand it over," Freya said, extending her hand.

"Scissors," Noam said. "You have paper. Looks like I win."

"Wait, what?" Freya asked as Nate handed the bomb over to Noam.

"Hey, I said you'd have to play for it," Nate said. "I clearly saw you throw paper, so, Noam is the clear winner."

"Now, that was dirty," Freya said. "You two are horrible to your queen. I should have you executed for treason."

"This vial looks like a Healing Draft…" Nate said, lifting the next.

"Dibs!" Freya shouted, snagging the draft before Nate could even finish his sentence.

"Next up," Nate said, lifting the next container and examining the contents within.

This time, it wasn't liquid, but rather a small magnet suspended in midair. Nate's eyes went wide when he saw it.

"No way," he whispered, looking between Noam and the jar.

"What? What is it?" Freya asked, already having lost interest in her Healing Draft and craning her neck over Nate's shoulder.

"This is one of the rarest Augments in the…that I've ever seen," Nate said, quickly catching himself.

He was about to say one of the rarest in the System but had stopped himself in time. He could get away with plenty around Freya, as she seemed to trust him, but if he started spouting off information he had no right to know, she might ask for an explanation.

"What does it do?" Noam asked, crouching next to him.

"This is a Magnetization Augment," Nate said.

"So, I could what, magnetize things?" Noam asked. "That doesn't seem all that useful to me."

"I'll take it if you don't want it," Freya chimed in.

"Without even knowing what it does?" Nate asked.

"It's an Augment. I'm sure it'll be useful," Freya said.

"Think of this as a pairing device," Nate said, turning back to Noam. "Just like you could pair a set of headphones to a device, this will allow you to pair any one object with yourself as long as it's made of metal."

"I still fail to see how that would be useful," Noam said.

"Let me give you an example, then," Nate said. "You get a new ax and link the ax with the augment. You could summon the ax directly to your hand without having to draw it. You could throw the ax and retrieve it with a thought. You could throw it past an enemy, then call it back, attacking from behind…Get the picture?"

Noam's eyes lit up as Nate went through his explanation, nodding vigorously.

"I'll take it, thank you very much for explaining its functions to me."

Freya pouted as Noam opened the jar, snagging the magnet with his fingers. The Augment turned to light as he did and sank into his hand, vanishing from view.

"There are only two items left now," Freya said with a pout. "I should get the next one."

"Have you forgotten that Nate has yet to claim anything for himself?" Noam asked. "Even though he was the one who dove into the magma room to retrieve them in the first place?"

Freya opened her mouth to retort, then shut it.

261

"Good point," she said. "So, Nate, what do you want for yourself?"

"The tablet," Nate said without a second thought.

"Are you sure?" Freya asked. "Nothing else?"

"The tablet will have a spell or technique," Nate said with a shrug. "If I can use it, I'll learn it, if not, I can sell it for a ton of points. I'll be happy with just that."

"What if I want it?" Freya asked.

"Well, that would be too bad then, wouldn't it?" Nate said.

"Yeah, but what if I *really* want it?" Freya asked again, a grin playing at the corners of her lips.

"Give me a quarter million points, and it's all yours," Nate said.

"A quarter million?!" Freya exclaimed.

"That's around what I'd get for it if I went to sell," Nate said.

"And you're giving us Augments and bombs when you have that?!" Noam asked indignantly, joining in with Freya's protests.

"Fine, I'll make you a deal. If I go to sell it, I'll give you each fifty-thousand points. What you're getting is already worth plenty, not to mention the fact that I was almost burned to a crisp in there."

"That sounds fair," Freya said. "But since Noam is getting an ax out of this, I should get the last two items."

Noam looked like he wanted to protest, but a single glance at the last two jars changed his mind.

"They're all yours," Noam said, giving them up without a fight.

"Woo!" Freya cheered, pumping her arms. "Gimme, gimmie!"

"Here you go," Nate said, plonking them into her palms.

Freya stared at the contents for several moments, then looked at Nate.

"Um, what are these?" she asked, staring at the two jars in confusion.

"I think you'll enjoy them," Nate said with a grin. "The one on the right is this world's version of a porta-potty. The one on the left is a carrying case."

"I'm all good with the portable bathroom," Freya said, looking at the small, rectangular blue box. "So long as I don't have to clean out the mess inside. But what in the world is a carrying case?" she asked, peering at the miniaturized metal briefcase in the second jar.

"Typically?" Nate asked, grinning even wider.

"Yes," Freya said, sounding suspicious.

"Why don't you go ahead and take it out. See for yourself," Nate said.

Freya looked at him with narrowed eyes, then carefully pulled the thick cork from the top of the jar. Reaching in, she pinched the handle of the case and removed it from the jar. The moment it was free of the jar's confines, the case expanded rapidly, going from a toy-sized briefcase to something a typical businessman would carry with him on a daily basis.

"Woah, this thing's heavy," Freya said as it thumped to the floor.

"Why don't you try opening it?" Nate suggested.

Still suspicious, Freya placed her two thumbs on either side of the catches. However, when she pushed down to open the case, she jerked back with a squeal of pain.

"Ow! What the hell, Nate? You could have warned me."

She sucked on both her thumbs as small beads of blood appeared. The top of the case had a circular depression, which turned crimson as she drew her hands away.

"No," she said, looking at the case. "Please don't tell me this is what I think it is."

"I'm not telling you anything," Nate said.

Freya went to open the case, and this time, nothing stabbed her. It flipped open, revealing a padded interior with nothing else inside.

"It *is* what I thought it was, isn't it?" she deadpanned.

"Yup," Nate said. "A Soulbound briefcase. Enjoy your loot!"

"You're horrible, you know that?" Freya muttered, slamming the case closed and trying to pull it into her ring.

It didn't work.

"Oh, yeah," Nate said. "I forgot to tell you that Soulbound storage items can't be kept inside other storage items. Sorry."

"Then what use *is* this rubbish when I can buy a ring that stores fifty times the amount of stuff and weighs next to nothing?" Freya exclaimed.

"Hey, not all loot can be great," Nate said with a shrug. "But, if you'd like to unbind it, you can sell it when we get to the next shop."

"I think I'll do that," Freya said, lightening up a little. "So, what did you get your hands on? And what's up with this whole tablet thing?"

"Tablets are like technique or spell scrolls, but found out in the world, rather than in a shop. They're all one-of-a-kind, like the limited one of one on the list in the shops, only these are guaranteed to be powerful. Nothing even remotely like this will be purchasable."

"Well, don't keep us in suspense," Freya said excitedly. "What is it?"

Nate lifted the tablet, the smooth stone now clearly visible in the tunnel. He hadn't gotten a chance to examine it closely, but now that he could, he could see it was beautiful. It was made of pure obsidian, the glassy surface smooth to the touch.

Seven circles ringed the tablet, six smooth and blank, while the topmost was covered in an intricate pattern. Lettering was chiseled above the ring.

Magma Body.

Nate stared, his eyes going wide. He blinked several times, wondering if he were imagining things, but no matter how he looked at it, the words at the top remained the same.

"Well?" Freya asked again, breaking the silence. "What is it?"

"It's a technique," Nate said, feeling like he was in some sort of dream.

There was no way could this be the same Magma Body technique, yet here it was. This technique was one of the most devastating and powerful he had ever personally witnessed.

It had, of course, belonged to one of their most bitter and hated enemies – The Yorkie, Captain Ray Cook. The Italian man had been a terror on the battlefield, and with this single technique, had caused such mayhem that the top ten guilds had formed a coalition on the ninth planet to take him down.

Unlike many others, Cook hadn't worked with a guild. Though the man had never fully upgraded the tablet – he'd only gotten it to the 4th tier due to the tremendous point cost – it had been

264

said that he would have been able to raze an entire planet with it if he had.

"I take it you want it then?" Noam asked, sounding disappointed.

"Without a shadow of a doubt," Nate said, concentrating on the tablet.

For a moment, nothing happened. Then the dark lettering within the first circle began to glow. A moment later, the knowledge flooded Nate's mind, imparting to him one of the single-most powerful techniques in the system.

When it settled, the letters within the first ring remained glowing, shifting between a bright yellow and dark orange, mimicking the movement of molten stone.

"Care to show us what it does?"

"*Gladly*," he said, grinning and feeling a sense of giddiness threatening to overcome him as he stood.

41

"You know, I feel like I really got the short end of the straw with that one," Noam said as the three of them approached the mine entrance.

"Hey, fair's fair," Nate said. "Don't pretend you aren't happy with what you've got."

"Fine," Noam sighed. "I'm happy with what I got."

"Well, I'm not," Freya said, pouting. "With that technique, you'll overthrow me by tomorrow."

"Don't worry, your majesty," Nate said, sweeping into a mock bow. "I would never."

"A girl could get used to this," said Freya, grinning.

"Ho there," Coronius called as they approached the exit. "Have you decided what you're going to do?"

"Just point us in the right direction and we'll be happy to go take a look," Nate said.

Coronius seemed pleased by that, giving them directions to the next city, where they would be able to follow the road to the area with the trouble.

"Best of luck to you, aliens," Coronius said, waving as they mounted their scooters and headed away from the cavern.

"He seems nice," Noam said.

"You know he doesn't care if we live or die, right?" Freya said, looking over her shoulder.

"I know," Noam said. "But courtesy has a way of disarming people. You should look into that sometime."

"Ouch," Freya said, grinning. "That was a good one, ya pompous geezer."

The three of them set off, making a good pace toward City 144G. According to Coronius, it took around three days by cart, so if they moved quickly, they should be able to get there by the end of the following day. Nate was eager to make it there, as without the protection of his shirt, he was already starting to sweat.

Still, the discovery and learning of the Magma Body technique washed away any notion of being in a bad mood. Never had he dreamed of finding something so powerful and with the

266

technique now in his possession, Cook would never be as dangerous a threat.

Nate would still kill him if he crossed the man's path, but his own Path of the Wandering Eel wouldn't pose much of a challenge, even *if* the man had been theorized to be ranked in the 40s at this point.

Despite them still being behind the leaders, Nate knew they were catching up quickly. Coming to Laybor had boosted them further than they would have been able to advance on Warine and despite the heightened danger, Nate knew this was the right decision.

The group continued traveling throughout the day with little trouble. They had to stop and fight a few times, killing a few monsters and raising Noam to the 36th rank. Neither Nate nor Freya advanced by the time they set up camp that night, which was fine in Nate's book. It had been a long day.

"I am so looking forward to not being woken up by a complete maniac in the morning," Freya said as she helped Nate stake the tent down.

Seeing as it was a larger tent, it took around ten minutes for the team to set up.

"You and me both," Nate said, swiping a hand across his forehead.

He was drenched up top, though thanks to the intact pants, things weren't quite so bad from the waist down. A bath sounded nice right now, and seeing as they were camped by the side of a flowing stream, they had a water source for bathing, even if it would be warm.

"Oh wow," Freya said, as she crawled inside. "It's so nice and roomy in here!"

Sure enough, there was plenty of space within. The roof was high enough at the center that Nate could stand at a crouch, though it would be more comfortable not to.

"Let's get that tarp rigged up so we can wash up," Nate said, removing it from his ring.

It didn't take long to get things set up and Nate – having won their go-to game of rock, paper, scissors – was the first in.

It was nice to play for turns instead of Freya just leaping ahead in line and though she did complain when she lost, she was still a good sport about it.

Nate's sleep was okay for the most part, though he was a bit warm. Noam and Freya were both on their spares, so no one had had anything to give him. With enough space, one might have thought that Freya would stay on her side, but when Nate awoke the next morning, it was to find the woman practically on top of him, snoring away.

"I do *not* snore!" Freya said, wind whipping her hair out in a stream behind her.

"How do you know?" Nate asked with a grin. "You're asleep when it happens."

"Queens don't snore," she said matter-of-factly, as though that were the end of the argument.

They ran into several more monsters that day and Nate jumped to the 38th rank, matching Freya's and officially removing her as the group's highest-ranked fighter. This had happened when she hadn't been quick enough on the draw a few times when monsters had appeared.

"You must have cheated somehow," Freya said as they stopped before the gates of City 144G, getting into the line of borers heading into the city.

"How could I have cheated?" Nate asked, curious how she would explain this away.

"Well, it's obvious, isn't it? You got in the way of my shot."

"Or," Noam interjected. "He was valiantly placing himself in harm's way to stop you from being attacked."

"Oh?" Freya said with a sly grin. "Nate, is there something you're not telling me?"

"Yes," Nate said. "Many, *many* things."

"Like the fact that you snuck some of your private stash along with you?" Freya asked.

"Stash of what?" Nate asked.

"Oh, I think you know," Freya said, waggling her eyebrows.

"I don't think anyone's sold a physical copy of that stuff in, like, four decades," Nate said. "Electronics stopped working, so I guess I've thoroughly disproven your theory."

"Oh, Nate," Freya said, shaking her head in mock sorrow. "It's okay to admit you have a problem. We're your friends. You don't have to lie to us."

"If anyone were to sneak a stash like that onto Warine, it would have been you," Nate said.

"Me?" Freya asked, widening her eyes. "But I'm just an innocent girl."

"Yeah, no one's buying that act."

"I second that," Noam said.

"Eh," Freya said with a shrug. "That's because the two of you know me. But still, we're getting off topic here. If you brought a stash, I'm just curious why you're not sharing."

"You would want this theoretical stash?" Nate asked, wondering where she was going with this.

"Of course," Freya said. "I could make a killing selling it to all the pervs out there. Who knows what they'd be willing to pay for something like that?"

"Well, as fascinating as this conversation has been, we're here," Nate said, slowing his scooter before the towering gates of the city.

"Don't think this is over, young man," Freya said, shaking her finger at him. "We'll discuss your punishment later."

"Okay, this just got really weird," Noam said, giving Freya a look.

Freya blinked, then flushed a deep crimson as she realized what she had implied.

"I'm not...that's...hold on...ahhh! Fine, you got me. I'm no one's mommy, least of all *Nate's*."

She shuddered at the mere thought, making gagging and retching sounds.

"Now that makes me feel all warm and fuzzy inside," Nate said, hiding a grin.

"Let's not even go there," Freya said, still making a face. "There's such a thing as taking it too far."

"I wasn't the one who did it," Nate said.

"I know," Freya said. "How about we just wipe this entire conversation from our memories and pretend it never happened."

"Works for me," Noam said.

"You know, if we forget this, I won't be able to use it against you in the future," Nate said, now grinning openly.

"Fine, let's make a deal," Freya said, sounding a bit desperate. "You get one free shot. I won't say anything in response."

"I'll take that deal," Nate said, extending his hand.

Freya took it quickly and the deal was struck.

"I'd like to cash that in right now," Nate said.

"Shoot," Freya replied, then mimed zipping her mouth shut and crossed her arms.

"You know," Nate said. "I think I'd like to treat you to a very expensive dinner. I might even call it a date if you want. All you have to do is say 'I want you to take me out on a date, Nate,' and I'll do it. Just keep in mind, this is your one and only chance."

Freya just about went blue in the face holding herself back from replying.

"Well, that's a shame," Nate said. "Guess no matter how often you imply that you're into me, you don't want it after all."

"You're horrible," Freya said with a glare.

"Hey," Nate said with a shrug. "It's the price you pay for convenient amnesia."

Freya continued muttering about being cheated out of a meal as they reached the front of the line, facing a pair of borers who looked like they'd rather be anywhere else. They were waved through without so much as a glance, earning a confused look from Noam.

"What's the point of having people stand guard if they're not going to be doing their jobs?" he asked.

"They don't like this sort of work, remember?" Nate said. "They consider it beneath them. It's not work involving construction of some kind. They probably did something to anger one of their superiors and now they're stuck on guard duty."

"Poor them," Freya deadpanned, having no empathy for the twisted race as a whole.

Nate looked up as they entered the city proper, walking onto the main street lined with buildings of various sizes. The smallest of the lot stood only twenty feet, but the tallest loomed at the city's center, over a hundred feet in height.

"Do you even know what we're looking for?" Freya asked, covering a yawn.

"An ore smelter, a tanner, a blacksmith and the shop," Nate said. "We'll also want to ask around and see if anyone's heard anything about strange happenings in the area."

"Please don't tell me we're staying in the city tonight," Freya said, looking up at the sky.

It was already around half-past-seven, and in a city this large, it would take a while to run all their errands.

"We're staying in the city tonight," Nate said. "It's the only way we'll be leaving tomorrow."

Freya let out a long sigh.

"If some creepy borer comes smashing on my door and shouting like a hooligan again, I'm going to shoot them."

"Knowing them, they'd probably find that funny," Noam said.

"Yeah," Freya sighed. "They probably would. Maybe I'll knock something over so that they'll have to fix it then. That'll show em."

Nate didn't say anything, though secretly, he knew that the borers would enjoy nothing more than to repair something that was damaged.

42

It took them nearly fifteen minutes to reach the market district, and from there, another ten to find a good smelter.

"Why are we coming here first?" Freya asked as they made their way through the bustling crowds towards the shop door.

"Because we still need to visit a blacksmith," Nate said. "And since they don't do busy work like ore smelting, we need to get this finished before they can start working on Noam's ax."

"Huh. Guess that makes sense," Freya said. "So, are all the smelters and blacksmiths also going to be women?"

"Nope," Nate said. "They consider this 'man's work' so no women will be seen anywhere near their shops."

"Of course they do," Freya sighed. "The sooner we get off this rock, the better."

"I couldn't agree more," Nate replied, though in his case, it was less about the borer race as a whole and more the fact that he didn't like the perpetual heat and damp.

If they were off this planet, it also meant they were strong enough to go to Raven, pushing humanity ahead by leaps and bounds.

Their group entered the smelter's shop just a couple of minutes later, making their way through the shelves containing various ingots for sale and to the front counter, where a female borer was standing and looked bored. Clanging metal sounds emanated from the back of the shop.

"I thought you said females wouldn't be around here," Freya said.

"She'd be the one handling customers," Nate said. "Not doing any of the physical labor."

"What can I do for you?" the borer asked as they approached.

"We need to have some ore smelted into ingots," Nate said, gesturing to Noam to place the orantium onto the counter.

"Hmm, we don't get this around here too often," the borer said, now sounding a bit more interested.

"We'd like them mixed with these," Nate continued, placing the block of sandstone and several pieces of pumice next to them.

This time, her eyes went wide.

"Just a moment," she said, looking between the materials and their small group. "Let me go fetch my husband."

With that said, she lifted her skirts – she was wearing a heavy-looking dress – and ran through the back.

"This can't be real," Freya said, staring after the woman in disbelief.

"Alien planet," Nate said. "Just consider yourself lucky that they aren't hostile. Can you imagine how hard things would be if every borer attacked us on sight?"

Freya opened her mouth to reply, then paused, thought about it, then gave her answer.

"You know, I feel like I'd still prefer that to this."

"Clearly, you have never been in hostile lands before then," Noam said. "I, for one, am grateful that the indigenous people are indifferent to our presence. It allows me to sleep better at night, even if monsters might attack at any moment."

The female borer came back, dragging a much larger and more muscular one behind her, before their conversation could really get going.

"'Sup, aliens," the borer said. "Ma wife says you're here for some work?"

He had a strange way of talking, like the slang used on the streets in the early 2000s. It was a bad imitation, like someone who knew what it was supposed to sound like but had never actually heard it. It ended up sounding part southern, part Brooklyn, and part street slang.

"We want these smelted into ortium ingots," Nate said, gesturing to the pile on the counter.

"I can work it, but it'll cost, ya dig?"

"How much?" Nate asked.

"Two and five pazzizles per," the borer said.

"Is the language filter broken?" Freya asked. "I can't understand a thing he's saying."

"No," Nate said. "Some borers are just weirder than others."

"Ah can hear you," the borer said flatly.

"Yes, we want the work done. Two-fifty per ingot. How many can you make?"

"Wit dis lot? I can get a deuceey!"

"I feel like he's doing this on purpose," Freya said.

"That's fine," Nate said, ignoring Freya's comment as he gestured to Noam. "He's paying."

"Touch the ball," the man said, gesturing to the sphere on the counter. "We get it done, baby!"

"Are you sure we can't take our business elsewhere?" Noam asked, eyeing the borer distastefully.

"This is why I don't bring this lug to the front," the female borer said. "He always scares away the customers, but I wasn't sure how to price it. Sorry."

"That's fine," Nate said. "We have more ore to show and I'd like these smelted as well. I'm really not sure what they are though."

He pulled the eight lumps of twisted ore from his ring. The lumps had cooled by now, the bands of metal having taken on a silvery sheen with striations of blue, purple lining them.

"Ooh," the borer moaned, leaning forward and placing his face *far* too close to the metal.

He sniffed loudly, then let out a creepy sigh as his body shuddered.

"I think I'm gonna be sick," Freya said, raising a hand to her mouth.

"You know how rare this be?" the borer asked Nate, a creepy smile plastered on his face.

"I don't even know what it is," Nate said.

"Of course, you not," the borer said. "This be vollter, supersteel compressed by volcanic activity. See the color, dog? It be flalalalahhh! Woohoo!"

The man pumped his arms in the air, doing a little dance, while his wife placed her face in her hands, as though praying for a swift and merciful death.

"I think I'm going to wait outside," Freya said. "Any more of this and my sense of humor will be gone forever."

She walked out of the shop, muttering about creeps and people who should be in jail.

"Can you turn it into ingots?" Nate asked, when the borer had finished with his dance.

"That I can do, sonny," the borer said, his accent going full-on southern for a moment. "You can bet your alien keister I can!"

"How much?" Nate asked.

"Fi-shelly a pop, bro!"

"How many can you get?" Nate asked, finding his patience wearing thin.

If they weren't already so committed, he would definitely have already walked out and begun his search for another.

This time, the beaver-man held a hand up, showing four fingers.

"Great," Nate said, slapping his palm to the orb and paying the 2,000-point cost to work the ores.

At 500 apiece, he was sure the metal would be valuable and that the blacksmith would be able to give him a better answer than this raving lunatic.

Noam paid 500 points for his share and the two of them promptly left, with promises that it would be ready in the morning. Nate wasn't happy to hear that, as he'd wanted to leave by morning, but it seemed they were going to be stuck here part of the day as well.

"Finally," Freya said, when the two of them emerged. "Sorry to ditch you, but I was actively losing brain cells in there."

"I can understand the sentiment," Nate replied. "Now, let's head to that tanner. I could really use some points and we can all use better armor."

The three of them reached the tanner just five minutes later and thankfully, the woman who worked there was far more accommodating. She expressed awe at the entire pack of fire foxes they brought her and promised to make them some armor. She also bought all of the rest for an average of 2,500 per fox, which was fantastic compared to the 400 they'd gotten for the worms and other monsters.

After getting armor for the three of them and having techniques worked into them, the cost was more than covered by the trade-ins. In addition to the promised armor, they also received a whopping 30,000 points to split between them.

"That was so much better than the last place," Freya said as they emerged from the shop.

She was grinning from ear to ear and Nate could understand why. They had just scored big time. Even he hadn't been expecting such a good price for the foxes.

They headed to the shop next, the official store of the system located within one of the taller buildings. They had to walk up four flights of stone stairs and down several corridors to find it. If it hadn't been clearly marked on the outside of the building, Nate wasn't sure they ever would have found it. He would have to start spreading the word about the possibility once people started coming through.

"What can I do for you?" the gnark asked as Nate sat behind the counter.

Freya and Noam had taken their own again, likely trying to pawn off unwanted items, buy food and water, or in Freya's case, more makeup or hair products.

"I'd like to sell these," Nate said, scattering most of the remaining pumice on the counter.

He still kept some in case they ran across more sandstone and orantium in the future. The last thing he wanted was to find some and not have the resources to turn it into ortium.

"Hmm," the gnark said. "I can give you eighty points per piece."

Nate was selling 40 pieces, so that only netted him a total of 3,200 points, which was unfortunate, as it still put him a bit short of the amount needed to advance his Cycle of Regeneration technique.

With a sigh, he gave up on it for the time being and purchased another set of clothes. He wouldn't need them once he got the armor back from the tanner, but it would still come in handy at night, and for the hours between now and then.

"Just out of curiosity," Nate said. "How much would it cost for an upgrade?"

He pulled the tablet from his ring and placed it on the counter, having the distinct pleasure of seeing the gnark's eyes go wide in shock.

"Where did you get this?" he asked, looking between Nate and the tablet.

"In a cave filled with molten stone," Nate replied with a shrug.

The gnark continued shaking his head, even as he pulled the cost up for Nate.

Upgrade Tablet of Magma Body, Tier 2: 680,000

Nate tried not to show the shock and disappointment that raged through him at the sight. Six-hundred-and-eighty-thousand points was insane for a second-tier technique. Then again, when he thought about it, it now made sense why Cook had never gotten it past the 4th – it was too freaking expensive.

This was like 5th or 6th Planet-expensive, not 2nd.

"Thank you," Nate said, placing the tablet back in his ring, knowing it would be a while before he could afford the upgrade.

It made the 150,000 he needed for his manual seem like a joke. He finished up before the others and had time to go change into his new clothes, breathing a sigh of relief that he would now be dressed normally.

The others finished up fairly quickly, allowing them to leave earlier than expected.

"What did you end up getting for the briefcase?" he asked a sullen-looking Freya as they headed out of the shop.

"Only fifty points," she grumbled. "But at least I got some new nail polish out of it."

"What sort of nail polish would cost such an exorbitant sum of points?" Noam asked.

"This one," Freya said, removing a clear bottle filled with golden polish and a gem-studded cap.

She seemed quite happy with it, grinning from ear to ear. Despite the expense, Nate wasn't going to begrudge her for getting it.

"You know, if I got any more, I would-"

Freya cut off as Nate slammed her against the wall, clamping a hand over her mouth. Noam, spotting what he had an instant later, stuck himself to the wall as well, crouching to peer back around the corner.

"What's the big idea?" Freya shout-whispered.

Nate silently pointed around the corner, then placed a hand to his lips. Freya, clearly curious, peered around as Noam had and went absolutely still. Nate joined a moment later, keeping himself pressed to the wall.

Approaching the store from the opposite end of the corridor was a pair of humans. They appeared to be teenagers, no older than seventeen. Nate didn't recognize either of them, but what he *did* recognize was the emblem stitched into the lapels of their official-looking outfits.

It was a stylized rose with a bloody knife stitched beneath.

"Well," Nate said in an undertone, as the pair entered the shop. "Now we know which guild is responsible for all that death."

43

"Who are they?" Freya asked, speaking a bit louder now that the pair were out of sight.

"No idea," Nate lied.

"Then why did you say you knew which guild was responsible?" Freya asked.

"Because they're both wearing the same symbol," Nate replied. "They don't look like they're related, and I don't know of any companies who have a logo like that. So, the obvious conclusion is that they're part of a guild. Seeing as the only one in the area would likely be the one murdering people who tried to come to Laybor, it only makes sense."

Noam grunted in agreement, his lips pursed.

"I don't like the idea of kids being involved in this," the man said.

Nate could not have agreed more. Rose Sombre – because this was without a doubt them – was led by a woman named Colette Bellecourt. She had been a teacher in an elite private school in the French countryside back on Earth. When she'd come through, it had been with nearly half the students, whose ages would range from around fifteen to twenty if he was remembering correctly.

The biggest problem was that she'd begun brainwashing them the moment they'd stepped through, and by this point, they would all believe in her dogma. Despite being children, they would be merciless in their attacks, even more so than many of the other dark guilds.

"What are we going to do?" Freya asked.

"Follow them, obviously," Nate said.

"You know, unlike the two of you, I'm not exactly a super-spy. I'm not good at all this sneaking around and following people."

"She has a good point. I can tail them without being caught," Noam said.

Nate wanted to follow them personally, but in the end, agreed to Noam's proposal. At this point in his training, he wasn't nearly as good as the man when it came to stealth and trailing people, and though these two were teenagers, they would spot another human from a mile away.

He risked using his Kanta Sight as the pair exited the shop. Neither turned in his direction and Nate was able to glean plenty of information from the pair.

"The girl's name is Claire, and the boy is Jean," he said. "Both at rank thirty-seven. Both magicians. They each only have a single spell, so they'll be at the first tier."

Noam nodded, then slipped from behind the wall and followed silently.

"We'll be in the inn across the street," Nate called after him.

A nod was the only confirmation that he'd heard and only once Noam was out of sight did Nate rise to his full height, letting out a breath.

Of all the guilds to face, Rose Sombre had *not* been the one he'd wanted to fight. He didn't like the thought of having to slaughter children, no matter how brainwashed they were. On the plus side – if there was one – it would be the smallest organization of the lot, at only around forty people.

That was still a lot, especially considering how dangerous Colette was, but if they could kill her, the others might disband. If he could get Carver here, the man might even be able to talk some sense into them.

"Nickel for your thoughts?" Freya said.

"Really? A nickel? Is that all they're worth?" Nate asked wryly.

"Oh, come on, I was being sincere for once and you had to go and ruin it," Freya said, placing a hand on her hip. "Way to go, Mr. Sourpuss."

"I'm worried, that's all," Nate finally said. "I feel like we don't have enough information, especially seeing as the first sighting of murderers is just a couple of teenagers."

"I'm a teenager," Freya said.

"Yeah, but you're an adult," Nate said.

"Barely," Freya said. "Also, I feel like the concept of children and adults is going to become really muddled in this world. If someone's trying to kill me, I'm going to kill them before they can finish the job, whether they're a toddler or geezer."

"You wouldn't really try and kill a toddler, would you?" Nate asked, feeling a small flash of worry.

"Ugh, I was joking," Freya said, rolling her eyes. "You *do* know what a joke is, right? Or have you forgotten in the midst of all that brooding you've been doing?"

"Unfortunately, that would be impossible, what with you sticking around all the time," Nate said.

"Someone has to keep the mood up around here. Otherwise, we'd just be a bunch of mopey sourpusses and there's only so much depressing garbage I can take. Now, come on, I believe you owe me a dinner."

"I specifically remember asking and you saying nothing. So, I, in fact, do not," Nate countered as they headed for the stairway.

"Well, I must have had a temporary bout of insanity to refuse, so I rescind my earlier refusal."

"That's not how this works," Nate said. "Unless you want my spontaneous bout of amnesia to suddenly wear off."

"You know, on second thought, I'd rather not," Freya said. "I'm suddenly feeling *very* tired, so I think I'll go turn in for the night."

"Right," Nate said. "Sounds like a plan to me."

The pair exited the building and crossed the street to the hotel, where they paid the ridiculous 25-point fee for the one-night stay – and by *they*, it meant Nate was stuck footing the bill – the two of them separating in the hallway and heading to their rooms.

Once Nate was alone, he let out a long sigh and allowed himself to slide to the ground with his back against the door. The screaming was starting again, the sounds of death and carnage echoing in his thoughts as he imagined himself slaughtering his way through a bunch of school children to get to their leader.

The idea appalled him more than he could put into words. Colette Bellecourt was a monster, worse than Pavlov was. She was damaging these children permanently, twisting them to her whims and desires for a bit more power.

The crazy thing was that almost all of them ended up dead before making it to Raven, *including* Colette. Perhaps he should simply allow history to take its course and leave it be. The problem with that was that he only had a few weeks until Colin began running his mouth again, not to mention the fact that that strange woman, Selena Maylard, was likely already here, working on establishing the Ashland Guild.

The screams continued in his mind, until Nate remembered something Colin had told him. People had been killed. Yes, it had been under the direction of Colette, but these people, teenagers or not, had committed murder more than once. Maybe ending their lives wouldn't be such a heinous crime after all. Hadn't he killed far more in the collapse of Centrifuge? If it was for the greater good, who cared if he had to kill some murderers?

However, no matter how he thought of it, the idea still appalled him. It wasn't the children's fault, it was Colette's. If killing all those faceless people in Centrifuge was affecting him this badly, how would the murder of brainwashed children make him feel? Additionally, could he make Freya go through with it?

Noam might do it without question if Nate told him it was necessary, but would Freya be okay with something like this?

Killing people who were after you was one thing, and her revenge against Pavlov was a long time coming, but going after children she had no qualms with and killing them was another thing entirely.

Nate continued to pace as the sun set and darkness fell over the city. His mind continued to race, trying to find some way out of this predicament. No matter how long he thought, his mind turned back to Carver. The man was kind and strong. He could see the best in people and was very charismatic. If they had him along, they might be able to make the difference.

With his mind made up, Nate left his room, slipping down the hallway and out of the building. The city was quiet, the lanterns lining the streets the only light in the area. Nate slipped silently through the streets, making for the far side of the city to a building he'd noticed when they'd first entered.

He reached the building without trouble, entering through the front and heading for the stairwell. It was a long climb to the roof, nine floors up, but his rank-38 body was able to handle it well. Nate emerged onto the roof of the tower, taking a moment to examine the city from there.

He could see pretty much everything.

He turned in a slow circle, his lips pursed and eyes peeled. This would have been much easier if Freya had been there, but she was tired, and he hadn't wanted to wake her. Recovering from a fight the likes of which those fire foxes had put up would not be easy, even a day later.

Thankfully, Nate was able to find what he was looking for after only a couple of minutes of searching.

Near the western wall of the city, hidden in a nook between two alleyways, was a buzzing red triangle, a slash in space that seemed to be sucking in the surrounding light.

Nate descended from the building at a jog, making his way swiftly through the streets. He got lost a couple of times but managed to find the portal back to Warine within twenty minutes. Taking a moment to toss a cloak over his shoulders, Nate braced himself and walked through.

Bright sunlight assaulted him as he stepped back into Warine, cold immediately beginning to adhere to his clothes. He shivered, allowing the nausea to fade and his eyes to adjust to his surroundings.

He stood around fifty yards from the road, swaying blue-green grass surrounding him on all sides with small wildflowers dotting the landscape. In the distance, he could see the walls of a city, though which one he couldn't be sure.

If his math was correct, they should have moved farther east than south after they'd entered the last portal, but areas between Warine and Laybor could get messy. There were plenty of times where he could step into a portal at the very south of the planet, then take the next portal over on Laybor and end up halfway across the continent when he returned.

For the most part, it was never that extreme, but in this case, it most certainly was. The grass grew darker the further south one traveled, and this grass was definitely more common in the east than anywhere else.

Nate jogged to the road, not even slowing as a spotted bobcat threw itself at him with a yowl. His hand snapped out, and a dirk formed of gilded steel. It crushed the rank 13 monster, piercing its skull and killing it in an instant. The kanta hit him as Nate pulled the monster into his ring, not breaking his stride as he moved.

He reached the road a few moments later, pulling his scooter from his ring and hopping on, pushing off down the road. Here, unlike in Laybor, there were people about, many traveling in groups and sticking to themselves.

Nate stifled a yawn as he scootered down the road, knowing that if he was going to get help and get some rest that night, he was going to have to be quick.

44

Nate recognized the gates of Eastfringe Six as he approached, sending a silent thanks that his memory had not failed him. There had indeed been a portal close by where Carver had set up shop at the central area of Laybor's G-quadrant.

Much to his surprise, he found a small line of people waiting to get in and human guards standing by the gates. It seemed that someone had bought the city since he'd last been there, which was unusual, as no one had done so in the previous timeline. He stopped and dismounted, stashing his scooter and listening to the people in line ahead of him, a couple with two small children.

"…sure this place will be safe, Molly?" the man was asking. "After what happened in Centrifuge, nowhere feels safe enough."

"I don't know, Steve," the woman said, sounding tired. "All I know is what Brittney told me. She said that this place is as good as it gets if you've got a family with small children, and seeing as we're already here, the least we can do is go look."

"Mommy, Mommy! Look at that!" one of the children – a four-year-old boy with a very snotty nose – said, pointing to the side of the road.

Nate followed the boy's pointing finger and felt his heart skip a beat.

No! What the hell are they doing here? Nate thought as panic began to rise.

A group of twenty people, all dressed in the robes of the Ashland Guild appeared from over a small hill, the rise having hidden their advance. He didn't recognize any of them, but the fact that they were here, so far from the southern part of the continent, could only mean one thing: they were fighting for expansion way ahead of schedule.

"Who do you think they are?" Steve – a man with thick glasses and a stubbly beard – asked, looking curious.

"Who *cares*, Steve," Molly said, sounding annoyed. "They could be a freaking circus for all I care."

The guards at the gate looked up curiously as the group marched onto the road. Clearly, they were all from the same Guild, otherwise, they wouldn't all be matching. They obviously hadn't seen them around here before though, as they didn't react with the hostility Nate expected. That was, until the one in the lead raised her hands, fire kindling across her palms.

"Down! Get down!" Nate yelled, tackling the family in front of him as a lance of fire blasted from the woman's hand.

It burned over Nate's head, and Steve and Molly screamed. The children didn't say anything, having been buried under the adults. The attack continued past them, slamming into the back of an elderly man waiting in line and piercing straight through him.

The man screamed in pain, dropping to the ground and rolling as his body was consumed by fire. Nate was back on his feet in an instant, whirling on the group and knowing that the response time of whoever was inside the city would not be fast enough.

One against twenty, Nate thought grimly.

Those were not odds he liked, especially seeing as he'd yet to upgrade his Cycle of Regeneration technique to the 4th tier.

Oh well.

Nate summoned his Goldshield as he ran at the group, several of them raising their hands and casting their spells. His Kanta Sight took the entire group in at a glance, showing numbers floating above their heads. The entire group was in the low 20s, with the leader being 26. That was good. With his rank of 38, he would have a bit of an advantage when it came to just about everything.

Four spells slammed into his Goldshield at once, and Nate ground to a halt, having to brace himself against the impact. His kanta flared as the shield held, the spells rebounding and scorching those who'd fired the,. Unfortunately, they all had their Flameshields active, so they did little damage.

Two more spells streaked at him, but Nate dodged around one and easily blocked the other, finally closing with the front of the line. Instead of attacking right away, he lowered his shoulder, used his Gilded Skin, then plowed directly into the group of gathered fighters.

He heard a scream and crunch of bone as he smashed his way through the lead fighters, emerging right in the center of the group. He planted his feet then and spun, summoning a broadsword using his Gilded Blade. Steelshod cloaked his hands, giving him extra power as he did.

He felt the blade shear through muscle and bone as he completed his turn, sending a shower of blood into the air as more screams abounded. The Flameshield was a good shielding technique, but a tier 1 technique cast by a rank-20 or 21 wasn't going to be able to block his swing.

Nate dismissed the blade, watching as nearly half the group staggered away, some with shallow cuts, two with missing limbs, and four falling to the ground, their bellies, chests, or necks opened. Nate felt the rush of kanta as he whirled, driving a Steelshod fist into someone's face. He felt the bare resistance of the Flameshield before his fist crashed through.

Blood sprayed as the crunch of bone reverberated through his arm, the woman's skull shattering like dry kindling. More kanta flowed into him as he turned again, feeling someone drive a blow into his back. His Gilded Skin warmed, but not nearly to the extent that he'd had to deal with in his last battle with Ashland.

Nate spun, seizing the offending man and slamming a dirk into his eye. The blade punched through the Flameshield even easier than his Steelshod. Blood covered his arm as the man fell dead at his feet. Two attacks slammed into Nate's back simultaneously, the spells knocking him forward a step.

Neither pierced his technique, but these were far hotter. Whirling, Nate saw two Magicians had put some distance between them and the group and were in the process of casting again. He ran at them, only for two cultivators to get in his way. Nate punched one in the gut but was then tackled from the side, someone's arms wrapping around his ankles.

With a curse, he went down, though not without taking another swing with a summoned backsword. The man who'd stood in his way was carved from shoulder to groin as he fell, hitting the ground and dismissing the blade, only for a fountain of blood and gore to rain down on him.

"Oh, gross!" Nate complained, as intestines flopped onto his chest.

He scrambled back as the man who'd snagged his legs tried to gain the upper hand, summoning his Steelshod over his legs and kicking him in the face. Nate actually had to do so three times before the man's nose *crunched,* and he let go with a scream. He frowned, trying to figure out why the man wasn't dead, when he spotted the Magician standing in the center of the road.

Of course. He was casting a shielding spell of his own, having seen that Nate could get through the ordinary ones.

He would have to kill him quickly before he became too much trouble. The problem with that was that now that he was on the ground, people began dogpiling him. A man leaped on one of his arms, using his bodyweight to pin it. Nate began to turn to punch a hole in his back, only for another man to seize his left.

A woman jumped on his legs, and another dropped across his chest. Nate could begin to feel the heat from their Flameshields working against him, heating the metal coating his skin. While he was being pinned, struggling to free himself, three of the Magicians began casting, all aiming for his head.

The path for them was clear.

Nate could hear the sounds of shouting from the direction of the city, but at this rate, he was going to have to really push it. The spells flashed, and his Goldshield appeared, tanking all three but taking a toll on his kanta. Worse, he was getting hotter, the metal covering his skin beginning to burn as the steady, applied heat continued to leech into him without abating.

This was why attacking a group of fighters, even those nearly 20 ranks below your own, was a bad idea. It was just unfortunate that Nate hadn't really considered that before diving in.

He strained, flexing his arms and legs and bucking his hips, but the combined weight of so many people pinning him was preventing him from getting any kind of leverage.

He now had a choice. Either lie there and hope he could last until help arrived from the city or pull his shiny new technique out and reveal to everyone here that he had it. Seeing as he didn't really want to die today, Nate chose option B.

Letting out a quick breath, Nate dismissed his Steelshod, Goldshield, and even his Gilded Skin. For just an instant, the heat was unbearable, then, it was gone as his body transformed. Lines of red appeared, cracking across his skin as it took on an almost stony appearance. That was until the rock began to melt, flowing into his body.

Now, the screams were coming from those lying on top of him as the burning magma from Nate's transformed body burned through their Flameshields and into their skin. No matter how they sliced it, molten stone would be far hotter than whatever flames they could conjure.

The fighters leaped off him, screaming in agony as horrific burns marred their bodies. Nate rose smoothly, the road around him beginning to melt as he took a quick look around. Two spells splashed off his skin as he was looking, doing absolutely nothing as the superheated stone his body was now made of absorbed the bolts of flame without any trouble at all.

"Let's make this quick," Nate said, his voice sounding strange even to his own ears.

He'd only ever seen this technique in action once, so he was going to have to hope that it all worked as he imagined. Nate moved forward, his leg elongating as he did, the bubbling stone stretching as he extended himself. His fist blasted out, also extending far more than was natural.

The man he was aiming for tried to run but didn't make it even a foot before the fist smashed into his back, ripping through his shield and spine and emerging out the other side. Nate ripped his hand free, leaving the man to fall to the ground in a dead heap. He spun his upper body, whipping both his arms out and felt them stretch once again.

The burning stone smashed into those in his immediate surroundings, hitting even those Magicians who'd placed themselves farther back. The best part of this technique was that since the magma was still a part of his body, the strength of the blows was not diminished.

In a single sweep, more than half the fighters went down, screaming in pain and suffering horrendous burns. Several more spells lanced into him, but Nate ignored them, slowly walking over the fallen Ashland guild members, his burning feet melting around their bodies as he put his weight on them, charring flesh and cracking bone.

More kanta rushed into him, pushing him another rank forward as he continued to attack. He punched, his fist flashing a good twenty feet and catching a fleeing magician in the back of the head. Magma bubbled up and around as his fist stuck in place, and the man screamed as his hair burned away, his flesh melting and skull cracking.

It was a truly gruesome death, one that even Nate felt sick seeing, but he knew he was running short on time. A handful of seconds using the technique had emptied half his core, and seeing as he'd been going for around ten, he was already drawing on his reserves.

The remaining Ashland Guild members broke as he turned on them, skin bubbling and popping, sending spatters of molten stone to the road below. Shimmering heat rose around him, the road steaming and melting under the extreme heat. Bodies burned as Nate turned to those who were running.

They would not get away. The magicians were all dead, their bodies burning or charred beyond recognition. Nate dismissed the Magma Body technique, feeling the immense strain vanish in an instant.

His Steelshod reappeared and he blasted after them, leaping from the steaming puddle he'd created and closing the distance in a matter of seconds. A rapier punched through one's back, a backsword swept through a second's neck, and a dirk pierced through a third's skull.

"Please don't kill me!" the last remaining member of Ashland pleaded, falling to his knees as Nate approached.

"Who sent you here?" asked Nate, the edge of his backsword tickling the man's throat.

"Our leader, Simon Dalefield!" the man cried, tears streaming down his cheeks and the front of his pants growing dark.

"Dude! That is so nasty," Nate said, wrinkling his nose in disgust.

"S-sorry," the man sobbed, snot running from his nose. "P-please! I don't wanna die!"

"What about Selena Maylard?" Nate asked, keeping the blade where it was. "What can you tell me about her?"

"She's a fortune teller," the man said. "She knows things before they even happen. Managed to convince Simon to let her join up."

"Where is she now?" Nate asked.

"I d-don't know," the man sobbed. "I'm just an initiate. A nobody."

"Is she on Warine?" Nate asked, seeing people running in his direction out of the corner of his eye.

"I think she left to the second planet," the man said.

"Is there anything else you can tell me about her?" Nate asked, pushing the blade a bit harder to his throat.

"She likes cats," the man tried weakly.

Nate narrowed his eyes and the man's blubbering redoubled.

"Hey! You there! Don't kill-"

Nate slashed his blade across the man's throat, leaving him to bleed out on the ground. His eyes went wide and he clutched at his neck as his blood gushed onto the street.

Nate turned, seeing a man dressed in leather armor and carrying a proto-sword.

Interesting, he thought as he examined him.

He was young, with long shaggy blonde hair and a jawline that would make most girls back on Earth swoon at the mere sight.

"Why did you kill him?" demanded the man, glaring at Nate.

"He's still alive if you want to save him," Nate said, standing aside.

The man on the ground struggled feebly for another moment, then went still, his eyes glazing over in death.

The expression of terror was still plastered across his face.

45

Nate drummed his fingers on the table, staring up at the position of the sun through the narrow slats of the waiting room he'd been shoved in nearly thirty minutes ago. The man hadn't been happy with Nate for killing a potential witness and he and his cohorts had escorted him into the city to await the decision of whoever had taken charge.

While Nate had been waiting, he'd had time to think. The man had claimed that Selena was a fortune teller, but as far as he knew, future sight wasn't a thing in the system. He still had no idea who she was and hadn't seen her in his life before.

He'd also turned over the fact that Simon was now sending people to burn cities while she was away, which suggested that he didn't really agree with her way of thinking. If Nate had to guess, that would likely mean a split in the Ashland Guild at some point unless they managed to eradicate them before they grew much larger.

When he'd grown tired of thinking along those lines, he'd worked on restoring all the kanta he'd lost in that short battle. It had been a shocking amount, especially once he'd used his Magma Body, but it had been well worth it.

He just had to remember that while it was powerful, it had its drawbacks. Number one was obviously the massive cost. It would drain his core and reserves in under forty seconds, especially now that his Kanta Orb was firmly stuck with rank 30 capacity. It would cost 50,000 to upgrade and right now, he had more important things to consider.

The second drawback was in dexterity. He had no use of his hands or fingers while the technique was active. The third was his movement speed. While his body could stretch to nearly 25 feet in total, he wouldn't be able to do more than a slow walk. It was why he'd dismissed the technique to chase after the fleeing members of the guild.

The positives were well worth those temporary limitations. For one, most spells and techniques would be unable to physically harm him. His body was made of molten stone, so anyone stupid enough to hit him would be severely burned and pretty much any spell would bounce off of him.

He could still be killed while it was active, so he had to be careful, but so long as he could injure his enemies before they could find any weaknesses, he would be fine. Another major advantage was his range. This was one of the few cultivator techniques that allowed him to hit targets outside of his normal attack range.

The best part about this technique was that this was only the first tier and Nate remembered the sort of damage Cook had been able to do with it at the 4th. The man had seemed near-invincible in their encounters, which spoke to how fortunate Nate had been in getting his hands on it.

Nate tilted his hand, sliding the glove back and staring at the dark number 40 that lay there. Twenty lives for just two ranks. It seemed like a poor tradeoff, but the higher one's rank became, the less kanta those of lower ranks would award.

He was just beginning to wonder if he should leave, when the door finally cracked open, revealing a familiar face.

"So, Damon tells me that you're the one who…Nate!"

Nate barely had time to brace himself before Mallory Lancer, one of the most notorious mass-murderers from his previous timeline, tackled him in a hug. The chair tilted back dangerously as it rocked, but thankfully didn't flip over, as that would have been awkward.

"Oh my gosh, what are you doing here?" Mallory exclaimed, finally letting him go and giving him a chance to breathe.

"It's nice to see you too," Nate said, returning the woman's wide smile. "I actually came here looking for Carver, though I *was* planning on visiting. How are your kids?"

Mallory's smile grew even wider at that.

"Jamey is…wait, we don't need to stay in this dingey place. Come on, I'll take you to the house where we can be more comfortable. Oh, everyone will be *so* excited to see you!"

She gave him another tight hug, squeezing so hard he thought she might be trying to crack his ribs.

"Mallory, have you…?" The door opened and the blonde-haired man – Damon, apparently – paused as his eyes flicked to their hands.

Mallory had seized Nate's in a powerful grip and had been dragging him toward the door when he'd opened it.

"Unhand her!" the man said, drawing his blade, a look of anger and hatred crossing his features.

Jealous much, Nate thought, hiding a smirk.

"Put that thing away Damon," Mallory snapped. "Nate is the reason that we all made it here safely and I won't have you treating him this way."

Damon looked like he wanted to attack, his eyes flicking between their clasped hands and Mallory's face. Finally, he shoved his sword back into its sheath and stepped away from the door, his back stiff as a board.

"Sorry about him," Mallory said, throwing another glare at the man, as she led him out of the room and into the street. "He's a bit overzealous when it comes to my protection."

"He clearly has a thing for you," Nate said. "You know that right?"

"Yeah," Mallory said. "But he's not my type. Too hotheaded. The kids don't need someone like that as their father figure. Anyway, that's beside the point. So much has happened since you left."

Nate listened as Mallory walked him through the streets, the woman occasionally waving to random passersby. The way they were moving, toward the manor set at the center of the city, soon had Nate convinced that it was she who'd taken the city as her own.

"When did you buy it?" Nate asked.

"The city?" Mallory asked.

"Yeah."

"About a month ago," Mallory replied. "Carver and I thought it was a good idea and since I'd gathered enough points, I decided to pull the trigger. Things have been much better since then and people have been coming here in droves. Don't worry though, we've been making sure to keep the training up. Anyone who wants sanctuary here, has to earn their keep and I'm proud to say that the average rank is sitting at twenty as of this morning."

That wasn't bad, considering that everyone who came here was looking for refuge for their families. Still, 20 wasn't nearly high enough to move on to Laybor and time was ticking.

"How far have you gotten?" Nate asked, as Mallory pushed the gate of the manor open – it didn't escape his attention that she hadn't released his hand the entire time, but he didn't comment on it.

Mallory bit the end of the glove covering her left hand and dragged it off, twiddling her fingers and grinning.

"Thirty-two?" Nate said. "I'm impressed."

"Been working hard, just like you said I should," she said, flashing him a toothy smile. "How about you?"

"If I could have my hand back, I'd be happy to show you," Nate said.

Mallory pursed her lips, as though pretending to think about it, then grudgingly let go.

Nate pulled the glove from his hand and her eyes went wide.

"*Forty*? How in the world did you get so strong?" she exclaimed.

"Keep it down," Nate said, looking around nervously.

"Sorry," she said, lowering her voice. "It's just that…*Forty*!"

"My friends and I went to the second planet, Laybor. You've already been hitting a wall, haven't you?"

"Yeah," she admitted. "It's been getting increasingly harder to grow in rank, but I thought that was normal."

"The monsters on Laybor are much more challenging," Nate said. "Growth is faster there. I was only at thirty-eight when I came through the portal though."

"That fight of yours pushed you up, I take it?" Mallory asked, pushing the front door to the manor open, revealing an opulent entryway within.

"Yup," Nate said.

"Do you have any idea who they were?" she asked, her smile fading.

"A dark guild by the name of Ashland," Nate said. "They're a menace and a scourge, and should be wiped out to the man."

"Is that why you killed that man when Damon asked you not to?" Mallory asked, closing the door behind her.

"He's likely murdered dozens of people," Nate said. "I have no mercy for someone like that. He was also coming to torch your city."

"They could have *tried*," Mallory said, a bit of steel entering her voice. "We know how to deal with criminals around here, even the superpowered ones."

"I can believe that," Nate said.

"Enough about them," Mallory said, shaking off the dark mood. "Tell me about yourself, how have things been going?"

As she talked, she led him down a corridor and into a small office, where she sat on the couch, rather than behind the desk, patting the spot next to her.

He gave her the abbreviated version of what had happened. Of his meetings with Freya and Noam, their destruction of the Rusband Guild. Discovery of Warine's imminent destruction and so on. He left out their involvement in Centrifuge's collapse, only vaguely saying they were in the city a bit before it had happened.

As he spoke, he paid attention to the woman. She seemed different than when he'd first met her on the road, clutching her children and looking afraid. Not only had she gained a lot of confidence, but that sadness that had clung to her like a shroud seemed to have lifted. It wasn't gone entirely, but she seemed far more relaxed. Her smile was easy and she laughed more readily.

No longer were his instincts screaming at him to run or attack this woman, despite their shared past. This Mallory was nothing like the monster who'd killed so many of his friends and comrades.

"Wow," she finally said when Nate had finished with his story. "I can't believe you did all that. Makes what I did seem sort of sad by comparison."

"How many families are in the city right now?" Nate asked. "And how many orphaned children?"

"Over a hundred-and-fifty families," Mallory said. "And last I checked, we had over two-hundred orphans."

"And they're all still alive thanks to you," Nate said. "I think that's a bit more than nothing."

"Carver does most of the work with the children," Mallory said with a smile. "But thank you nonetheless. Speaking of, where are your friends? You mentioned them, but no one is here with you."

"They're in Laybor," Nate said. "One is sleeping and the other is tailing two members of a dark guild who've been murdering anyone who tries to cross over in specific areas. It's making a real mess."

"Why did you want to come looking for Carver?" Mallory asked, seeming confused.

"Because the people in this guild are teenagers," Nate said grimly. "They've been brainwashed by their teacher and guild leader, and I need someone to try talking sense into them before going to war."

Mallory's features darkened at the mention of someone exploiting children.

"I'm sure he'd be happy to help," Mallory said. "And so would I."

"What about Lily and Jamey?" Nate asked. "Speaking of, where are they right now?"

Mallory broke into another grin, the anger leaking from her features.

"Lily's down for a nap and Jamey is playing with some of the other children. Don't worry about them, I can have someone watch them while I'm gone."

"You have someone to feed Lily?" Nate asked, not wanting to get too into this.

"Oh, she's already been weaned," Mallory said. "It's too much trouble trying to feed her in this crazy world. We just buy food for her from the shop."

"Will I get to see them before I go?" Nate asked.

"When were you planning on leaving?" Mallory asked.

"As soon as I speak with Carver," Nate said. "The time difference between here and Laybor are extreme. It's smack in the middle of the night there and I need some sleep before morning."

"You could always stay here," Mallory said, sounding disappointed.

"My friends will be worried if they can't find me," Nate explained.

"Oh, all right," Mallory said, sitting back in the couch with a sigh. "If I am coming to help, I guess it won't be too long before we can meet up again. Believe it or not, I've missed you."

"We only traveled together for bit," Nate said.

"You saved my family," Mallory said, leaning a bit closer. "Agreed to help a complete stranger and her children without asking for anything in return. You're a good guy, Nate. A really good guy. That's rare these days, especially in this world."

She leaned a bit closer, her long, curly brown hair tickling his cheek. Her green eyes were partly lidded, and Nate could see that like Freya, the woman had wasted points on makeup. Her pale cheeks were rosy with blush and her lips shone in the reflected sunlight streaming in through the window. She smelled nice as well, likely some perfume she'd blown more points on.

"Um, thanks," Nate said, suddenly feeling a little awkward.

He wasn't used to compliments, especially ones that were given so sincerely. Sure, he'd helped Mallory, but it had been out of self-interest more than anything else.

"Jamey really likes you," Mallory continued. "He didn't take to any of the other adults around here. He's always so shy around anyone not his own age, and I'm sure Lily would like you once she's old enough to get to know you."

"I can only hope," Nate joked as she leaned even closer.

Mallory licked her lips, her breathing coming a bit faster and her heart rate increasing.

"You...You're not...seeing anyone, are you?" she asked, her voice low and questioning, a hint of nervousness in her tone.

Nate could sense what was happening here, though by no means had he been expecting a reception like this. Apparently, he must have left a pretty good impression of himself, and it was only now, with this woman's face just inches from his own, that he realized how pretty Mallory actually was.

"I...uh," Nate said, considering lying, his mind working frantically to make sense of the situation.

A knock came at the door then, shattering the silence and Mallory leaned away, albeit reluctantly.

"Come in," she said, smoothing the front of her shirt.

"Sorry to bother you," Carver said, opening the door and stopping, surprised to see Nate sitting there. "You..."

"Me," Nate said, giving the man a small wave.

"Is this a bad time?" Carver asked, looking between the two of them.

Mallory clearly wanted to kick the man out, but she smiled and shook her head.

"Not at all," she said. "Nate actually came here looking for you."

"Did you now?" Carver asked. "Well then, I'd be most interested to hear about this."

Nate uttered a silent sigh of relief as the man sat and he began to explain his presence in the city.

46

Nate stumbled into his room in City 144G, collapsing onto the bed in a heap and letting out a groan. It was well past 3 in the morning; the sun had already begun to rise. He was sure Noam had taken a room somewhere in the hotel for the night and they would be talking about his discoveries in the morning.

After speaking with Carver at length, the man had agreed to come to Laybor the following day. He, Mallory, and a few of their fighters would come through the portal in the early evening – their morning – and meet up with their group in the city.

Carver was already past the 30th rank as well, and Mallory assured him that her top fighters would be at the 30th rank, or very near 30 when they crossed over. This meant that he and the others would need to remain within the city limits for the day. He would tell Noam and Freya of his escapades and what the plan was. One, because it would be impossible to hide the fact that he was now at rank 40, and two, because everyone was coming and he didn't want any surprises.

Nate slept like a rock, waking to the horrible pounding-screeching noises coming from his door as the evil borer woke him from his slumber. The pounding and screaming at the door made him want to leap from bed, dash from the room and throttle whichever unfortunate moron had thought to wake him from his sleep and for the first time since coming here, he thought he understood Freya perfectly.

Groggily, he forced himself from bed and stumbled into the washroom, where he proceeded to douse himself with liberal amounts of cold water. Staring into the foggy mirror, he could see that his eyes were bloodshot.

Yawning, he quickly got dressed, did some short exercises to get his blood pumping, then stepped from the room. Noam was already waiting out in the hall, his back to the wall and arms crossed.

"This is unusual for you," the man said. "Late night?"

"Something like that," Nate said, rubbing at his eyes. "You?"

"Got back around midnight," Noam said. "No later than expected."

Nate grunted in reply, then covered another yawn.

"What do you know about these people?" Noam asked.

"They're a bunch of brainwashed schoolchildren being led on by their psychopath teacher," Nate said with a shrug. "Can't say much more than that."

"Why not?" Noam asked.

"Because having knowledge of things that have yet to pass is hard enough to keep track of," Nate said. "There's a reason I didn't tell you about it beforehand and this was exactly it."

Noam raised an eyebrow, but Nate just shook his head.

"Look, the less you know the better. You know my secret, so you're just going to have to trust that I have all our best interests in mind."

Noam pursed his lips, but in the end, nodded in agreement. Nate let out an internal sigh of relief. He could only hope that the man didn't bring this up again in the future. Having one person potentially screw up the timeline was one thing, but having multiple people do so could throw a wrench in his plans.

Freya didn't emerge for another twenty minutes and when she finally did, Nate could see why. The woman had, once again, taken the time to style her hair with the short braids on one side of her head, using them to twine her hair into its usual ponytail instead of the small scrunchie she'd been using.

"Morning," she said. "I'm glad to see that my subjects have been loyally awaiting my presence."

In response to that, Nate removed his right glove and showed her the back of his hand. The response was exactly what he'd been hoping for. Freya's jaw went slack, her eyes went wide and turned suspicious.

"You snuck out to do some training just to overthrow me, *didn't* you? Well, I won't have it! I am still the queen."

"Drama queen maybe," Nate said.

"I'll give you points for that," Freya said with a grin. "It was a terrible pun, but the timing was on point. You're learning."

"How about we talk about all this over breakfast?" Noam suggested. "I don't know about any of you, but I am quite famished."

"Same," Freya said, despite not having done anything but sleep all night.

They headed up the stairs, winding their way above ground and into the common area. The room was already bustling with borers grabbing food and rushing for the exit, preparing for another long day of work.

The three of them moved more slowly, taking their plates of blue-tinged eggs, cheese, and bread to the furthest table from the door. They made sure to grab mugs of water, Freya's experience with the borer's hot beverages having been enough for them all.

"The food here might look weird as all hell, but it sure is tasty," Freya said, shoveling a spoonful of eggs into her mouth.

"I have never seen a woman eat as you do and yet somehow *not* become fat," Noam said, shaking his head in amazement.

"You're eating nearly twice as much as I am," Freya said. "And you still look the same."

"We all have our heightened metabolism to thank for that," Nate said, noting that he had also been eating more than was usual lately.

Their meals were going to become more expensive from now on, it seemed. It was the price for going up in rank. Higher ranking meant more calories burned to sustain such a powerful body. They wouldn't need to eat truckloads of food with each meal, but they would need to eat like serious athletes in training.

There was a cap to how much one would need to eat, but that came at the 150th rank, with around four times the normal portion for men and women. After that, the body became more efficient at using whatever they ate.

"Who would like to go first?" Freya asked, looking between the two of them.

"I think Noam should," Nate said. "What I did correlates to his tracking of those two."

"Oh, now I'm interested," Freya said, interlacing her fingers. "Did you sneak off for a secret rendezvous with a secret lover or something?"

It was hilarious how close to the mark she was, and at the same time, so *very* far away.

"I tracked them out of the city," Noam said, diving straight in.

Knowing how Freya could get once she was on a roll, this was probably a good idea.

"They moved swiftly, as though they knew this area well. I was expecting to have to follow them for a while, but before an hour had passed, they walked off the main road and headed to a small depression on the side of a hill. I had to be careful, as I did not want to be spotted, so I had to increase my distance between them and was unable to hear their conversation after that point.

"Beforehand, however, the pair spoke of their mission. Apparently, their leader, a woman by the name of Colette, had instructed them to remain here, guarding a portal within the city. But they were told to move on and rejoin the group, which was why they stopped at the shop. They were on their way out and needed to resupply.

"Both had killed people trying to come through and while the boy seemed a bit hesitant about it, the girl fully believed that we were all fake. Strings of code, she called them. Said they all deserved to die so that they could become stronger."

"Talk about cold and heartless," Freya said, looking appalled.

"She did not speak of us like we were human," Noam said grimly. "In all, they killed six people before they stopped coming. No one has come through in a week, so I guess that's something to be grateful for.

"They didn't talk about much of importance after that and I didn't really discover anything else of interest until I came across the cabin set into the nook between two hills. I stayed back to ensure my cover wasn't broken. Once they were inside, I moved closer. The building was large enough to house a group of forty or fifty.

"Almost everyone was asleep when they arrived. The building was basically a shell, a single, large room with several dozen cots spread throughout. The pair spoke to a woman who looked to be quite young, perhaps a year their junior, before going to sleep themselves.

"I stayed in the area for a bit longer, hoping to hear more but got nothing. So, I marked their location and returned."

That was interesting. If the entire Rose Sombre Guild was just an hour's journey outside the city, what was happening in the central location of the quadrant to halt all their work?

"Well, now that Noam's finished, I believe it's Nate's turn to share," Freya said, turning her eyes on him. "I'm *very* interested to hear about what you got up to last night."

Nate launched into an explanation of where he'd gone. His sleeplessness and a 'hint' he'd gotten from his 'augment' to find a portal and go back to Warine. He spoke of his battle with Ashland and his meeting with Mallory and Carver.

"So, you *did* sneak off to meet a girl," Freya exclaimed. "Am I not good enough for you, Nate? Is she prettier than me?"

"She might be, depending on who you ask," Nate said with a shrug. "I guess that would come down to personal preference."

"And what's your preference?" Freya asked, interlacing her fingers and propping her elbows on the table.

He could see the smirk she was hiding behind her hands.

"Mallory has two children to take care of and has recently lost her husband and her sister," Nate said flatly. "Her sister passed before she came, and her husband refused to walk through the portal with her. I expect you to treat her well."

"Oh, calm down, grumpy pants," Freya said. "I know how to behave. But you're avoiding the question."

"I didn't realize this was a contest," Nate replied.

"Are you kidding? *Everything* is a contest!" Freya said. "Have you never seen Contest Island?"

"No, I don't watch trashy reality shows," Nate sighed, rubbing at his temples. "And we're getting *way* off topic here. What I was trying to say was that we're going to have some help, but it won't be here until tomorrow morning due to the time difference."

"Can we afford to wait?" Freya asked.

"We don't really have much choice," Nate said. "The three of us alone can't take that guild down. We're going to need all the help we can get, *especially* if we want to try separating some of those children from that *woman* they're following."

"I agree," Noam said. "Having help on this will be crucial, though with your most recent escapades back on Warine, I'd say you could probably take them all on your own," he joked.

"I can't," Nate said flatly. "If they're here on Laybor and have been killing people, they're going to be too strong to take out on our own. In case you forgot, the group I tackled was ranked in the low twenties. This group is going to be at least in the upper thirties and their leaders will probably be stronger."

If he was estimating correctly, Colette would be somewhere in the region of rank 46, perhaps 47. Killing people had its benefits or no one would do it.

"How will this other group from Warine help?" Freya asked.

"That's what we're here for," Nate said. "They also have Mallory and Carver with them and they're both exceptional fighters, so I wouldn't worry about them."

"You know, you still haven't told us how you know this Mallory woman," Freya said with a grin. "Care to enlighten us on this tale of intrigue and romance?"

"You know, sometimes I wonder about what's going on in your mind," Nate said. "Then I remember who you are and decide I'd be better off not knowing."

"You are a smart man, Nate," Freya said. "Best not to try peeking into the mind of a woman. It would only confuse you."

"Or in your case, scar me for life," Nate shot back.

"Wow, you are on fire today," Freya said. "I think I'm going to have to up my game."

"If you say so," Nate said, polishing off his water. "For now, I think we've got some errands to take care of and a day to fill. I won't have us sitting around and killing time waiting for Mallory to come."

"Oh, I know," Freya said. "We should all go look around and see if this city has a massage parlor and then…"

Nate rose from the table, not wanting to hear whatever hair-brained and likely inappropriate scheme the woman was cooking up.

47

"Here are your ingots, have a nice day."

Picking up the ingots went easier than Nate had expected, the woman behind the counter pulling them out and handing them over without fuss. He was glad her weird husband didn't come out to deliver them, as he didn't think he had the patience or braincells to spare.

"Thank you," Freya called as they left the shop.

"Well, that was easy," she said, looking at the ingots clutched in Nate's hand.

They had six in all, two of the ortium and four of the metal that the crazed borer had called vollter. While the ortium looked exactly as he remembered it – a blue-gray with striations of pockmarked tan – the vollter was like nothing he'd seen before. It was a bright silver, like polished steel, with the same hues of blue and purple when he turned it. It shone like a mirror, though when he tried seeing his reflection within, all he got was a blurred outline.

The metal felt dense and heavy, *far* heavier than ordinary steel had any right to be, and he had to wonder about its properties. The borer had called it 'supersteel' compressed by volcanic activity. Did this mean that this was a denser version of ordinary steel then? Because if it was, he was *very* curious about what its uses were.

So far, the best metal they'd come across – aside from the orantium – had been nickel ore. Iron was also rare, though not nearly as much as the former in the earlier planets. Regular steel would be extremely valuable in Warine – 50,000 points per ingot if he remembered correctly.

He was salivating at the mere thought of how much this might be worth.

They headed to the tanner next, where they picked up their new armor. The woman had made a single set for each of them and when Freya saw them, her eyes went wide.

"No *way*!" she exclaimed, reaching out and taking her set, running her fingers over the hide. "How is it doing that?"

"Those would be the properties of the fire fox," the borer said. "It'll turn off once the charge is out, but you can always power it back on."

The armor flickered with translucent red-orange flames, the fire licking across the exterior, and yet not burning it at all.

"So, which techniques and spells were retained?" Nate asked, as he took his set.

It was a hardened breastplate, tough leather pants and shoulder pauldrons. Half-sleeves stretched down from the shoulders, flaring at the elbow for better protection, before slimming down to the end of the wrist. A series of straps could be opened to bind the sleeves in place. No boots were included, but this was perfect as far as he was concerned.

"For the lady, it's the Flameshield," the borer said. "There's enough charge in there for around ten seconds."

Nate was surprised to hear that as he'd been unaware that any of the foxes had had the spell. It was good though, as Freya could use the extra protection.

"For you, it was the Flamespace technique," the borer continued. "And for him, it's the Flamecrunch. Yours has about ten seconds, his is a one-shot."

Nate thanked the woman and the three of them left.

"Are we going to change into this awesome armor?" Freya asked.

"Not yet," Nate replied. "I'd like the blacksmith to do some more work on them. This way, we'll have an even sturdier defense."

He knew that the armor likely wouldn't last them past the third planet, but having something last that long would be good. That was, if it wasn't irreparably damaged in a fight in the meantime.

"Morning youngsters, how can I help you?"

"Oh no, not another one," Freya muttered as they walked into the blacksmith's shop.

The borer here was gray-furred and strangely enough, he was the only one in the shop. Though calling it a 'shop' would have been a bit of a misnomer. It was more like a forge, with a single area around the door cleared of all clutter, so that people could walk into the building without smashing into an anvil.

"We need some weapons made," Nate said. "A two-handed, double-bladed ax. He can give you all the details."

"Oh? And what materials do you want to be usin'?"

"These," Nate said, setting the ortium ingots on the table.

"Very nice," the borer said, lifting them both.

He sniffed them – though not as creepily as the smelter – *licked* them – *that* was creepy – and even put them up to his ear.

"Yes, very nice," the borer repeated.

"We'd also like some thread worked into our armor," Nate said, placing their collective armor on the ground before him.

"I can do that," the man said with a nod.

"Two-thousand for the ax and five-hundred apiece for the armor."

"He's paying for the ax," Nate said, motioning to Noam, who seemed less than happy about footing such a *massive* bill. "And we'll each be paying for our own armor."

The borer nodded, removing a dirty-looking sphere from *somewhere* in a pile of junk and extending it to them. They each paid the cost, Nate once again bemoaning the loss. He *really* needed to get that upgrade.

"I can have this ready by closing time," the borer said. "Is there anything else I can help you with?"

"Yes, actually," Nate said, removing one of the Vollter ingots from his ring. "Can you tell me what you could do with this?"

The borer's eyes went wide as he took the ingot, the shock on his face clear to see.

"Oh…*Oooohhhh*," he said, his voice going deep, gravelly, and of course, creepy on the second 'oh.'

"I'm going outside," Freya said, turning and leaving quickly.

It seemed she wasn't going to be putting up with this for a second time.

The borer began *exploring* the metal, tapping it with one of his claws, sniffing and gnawing on it. Nate waited with crossed arms, sincerely hoping that the lifelong scarring was worth it, because this borer was creepy with a capital C.

Finally, after what felt like ages, the borer turned back to them, a distant, almost ecstatic look in his eyes.

"Sorry, I can't help you."

"What do you mean?" Nate asked, feeling a small flare of anger at the man's words.

"I mean that I don't have the skill or tools needed to work this metal," the borer said with a shrug, though he didn't hand the ingot back.

"Who would be able to work it then?" Nate asked. "And can you at least tell me what it *is* or what it can do?"

"No one on the entire planet can work on it," the borer said with a chuckle. "I'm the best smith there is and if I say I can't work on it, no one can. As for uses, use it for whatever you want. Weapons, armor, hell, you can even turn them into special *items* – that would be my preference – but not here."

Nate didn't want to know what items the borer was referring to from his tone when saying the word, so he moved on to the next question.

"But what exactly is it?" he asked. "I've never heard of vollter before."

"Almost no one has," the borer said. "They only form in volcanic areas with high temperatures and specific, mineral deposits. Meaning iron, limestone, shale, lithium and corrosium. It takes around five hundred years for it all to mix and compress. Pressures unobtainable by even our technology here on Laybor. It has roughly ten times the tensile strength of ordinary steel. It's really heavy once forged, so I doubt a scrawny kid like you could even wield a weapon made of it, let alone armor."

Nate pursed his lips. He'd managed to find a metal that couldn't be used until a later planet. That was interesting, as anything found on world was typically available for use.

"Do you know the approximate value of an ingot?" he asked.

"Here in Laybor, it's priceless," the smith said. "Though, seeing as no one could work on it, it's also worthless."

"What would *you* pay for it?" Nate asked.

Seeing as the smith had failed to release the ingot, he assumed the creepy borer would want to keep it.

"I could give you a hundred-and-fifty-thousand if you were willing to leave this beauty with me," the man said, lifting the block of metal and eyeing it lovingly.

Yes, lovingly, definitely not with anything else, Nate told himself.

"Are you sure we want to sell this to him?" Noam asked. "If it is so valuable, shouldn't we keep it for our own use?"

"I said it was useless," the borer said, seeming suddenly nervous. "But seeing as we're doing business, I can give you two-hundred thousand for it, but not a point more."

This was beyond Nate's wildest expectations. These were point values that shouldn't be thrown around until planets far down the line, when simple things cost thousands of points apiece.

"Again, I would caution you against selling," Noam said, looking between the borer and the metal."

"Don't think that'll work on me again, sonny," the borer said. "I wasn't born yesterday."

Seeing as Nate was still hesitating, the man jumped in with a higher bid of 225,000.

"That's it, I won't go any higher," he said, crossing his arms.

"How about all four for an even million," Nate said, removing three more blocks.

The borer just about fainted when he saw them. It was a good thing Freya wasn't in here right now, as they were being treated to an extremely disturbing sight that he would never forget.

"I don't have that much I'm afraid," the borer said, dragging himself to his feet. "Buying one'll just about clean me out. So, do we have a deal?"

Nate thought about it.

On the one hand, he could save all four for potential gain on a further planet, but on the other, they needed points now and they would still have three of the ingots remaining.

"You've got a deal," Nate said.

The borer shuddered again, then reached out to shake Nate's hand. Nate didn't take it, though he *did* take the points the borer offered – well, two-thirds of them, as Noam took his share.

Once their transaction was complete, they left the shop in a hurry, hearing some *very* disturbing noises following them out.

"We will never speak of what we saw in there, agreed?" Noam said.

"Agreed," Nate replied, knowing that this would haunt him for the rest of his life.

48

"Did the beaver guy banging the block of metal yet?" Freya asked when they emerged.

There was very clearly a double meaning to the question that evoked all sorts of imagery in Nate's mind.

"Let us just say that you were smart to leave when you did," Noam said with a shudder.

"That bad, huh?" Freya said, eyeing him with pity. "Guess I'm the only real smart one in this group. No one in their right mind would stay with a creep like that after the way he'd been acting."

"You were right," Nate said. "Now, do you want the seventy-five-thousand points I got you from selling one of those metal blocks?"

"That would be a strong *yes*," Freya said, appearing at his side so fast that she seemed to have developed the ability to teleport. "Also, I would like an explanation."

Nate explained how they'd sold one of the ingots to the borer. He didn't go into any details, though by the knowing look on Freya's face, she'd probably guessed.

"I can't believe it," she said, after Nate had transferred the points. "We finally found someone creepier than you, Nate."

"Oh, ha-ha," Nate said with an eyeroll.

"Okay, fine," Freya said. "You're still the bigger creep. Happy?"

Nate glared and Freya grinned.

"What's on the agenda for today?" Noam asked.

"Training," Nate said. "We're going to head out of the city and see what we can find. Once it gets dark, we'll go on another reconnaissance trip and see what that guild is up to."

"All of us?" Noam asked, surprised.

"Yes, all of us," Nate said. "We all need a good idea of what we're up against and Freya isn't good at sneaking around. This will be a good opportunity for her."

"That sounds like a good idea," Freya said. "Imagine all the peeping I can do."

Nate chose not to respond to that, heading down the road out of the city. That didn't seem to deter her, the woman continuing to chatter about seemingly nonsensical things until they found their first monster.

They fought nearly the entire day, taking only short breaks to recover. Challenging stronger monsters had them see more growth, Nate rising to rank 41, while Noam hit 38 and Freya got close to 40.

"You know, I'm really starting to feel the difference," Freya said, as they headed back into the city later that evening. "It was really slow at first, but I feel so strong now."

"Like you could knock a horse out with a single punch?" Nate teased.

He was in a far better mood than this morning. A good day of training and growth seemed to have that effect on him, though it was a bit demoralizing how much longer it took to grow while fighting monsters, even those who were close to their own ranks.

"Never going to let that one go, will you?" Freya said.

"Nope," Nate replied.

The three of them had an early dinner, went to pick up their weapons and armor, then headed out of the city once more, making their way down the road toward the area where Rose Sombre should be camped.

"I still can't get over this ax," Noam said, swinging the weapon in smooth arcs. "It feels so light, I'm half convinced I'm not even holding anything."

The ax blade shone with a dull blue-gray light, small pockmarks and holes pitting the metal. Despite its appearance, it was not brittle by any means. The pockmarks were a result of the pumice that had been worked into the orantium to make the ortium ingots. The handle was made of ortium as well, light enough to use instead of wood, as ordinary wood wouldn't really hold up to the pounding Noam was going to be dishing out with this weapon.

"Can you explain why we have to stay in our regular outfits?" Freya asked, looking down at herself. "I mean, I know I look hot and you want to keep staring, but shouldn't we be focusing on defense?"

"No," Nate said. "The fire fox armor might be powerful, but the fact that they're all carrying a charge, means that we'll be visible

312

for miles in all directions. Imagine trying to sneak around while wearing a portable bonfire."

"Good point," Freya said. "Though couldn't we just expend the charge?"

"We could," Nate said. "If you wanted to spend the next twenty minutes refilling it."

"It takes *that* long?" she exclaimed.

"The stronger the spell or technique, the more kanta it'll take to charge and power," Nate said with a shrug. "Besides, what we're wearing is fine. We're not planning on fighting."

"It always pays to be prepared though," Noam said, tossing the ax into the distance, then extending his hand.

The weapon came spinning back, slapping into his palm with a meaty *slap* – the man had been doing this for the last fifteen minutes. Nate didn't begrudge him, as he was testing the limitations of his augment and seeing what it could do.

"Yes, it's good to be prepared," Nate agreed. "But for right now, I think we're fine as we are."

There was no point in continuing this argument, so Noam stopped. Freya and Nate talked a bit, the woman trying to get more about Mallory out of him. Nate refused to be sucked into whatever she was trying to do, simply stating the facts. They'd worked together when they'd first come to Warine, and he'd dropped her and her children with someone he knew.

"Here it is," Noam said, gesturing to the side of the road.

The light was already fading from the sky and it would be fully dark soon. Nate wanted to arrive by the shelter before full dark, this way, they wouldn't need to pull a light source to be able to see.

It didn't take long for it to come into view, the small cabin perched between two small hills, just as Noam had said. They settled a small distance away, the group flattening themselves to their stomachs and watching. He could see movement from within as well as several people hanging around the entrance. He didn't recognize any of them until Colette walked outside and began gesturing the younger teens in.

His eyes narrowed as he saw her, the French woman's face pinched and hard. Her smile was easy, and her sparkling brown eyes and friendly demeanor lured all those she spoke to to her side.

"What can you see?" Nate asked in a lowered voice.

"I count forty-two," Freya said, her eyes swiveling back and forth, sweeping across the house. "I'm not good at telling ages, but more than half of them look young. A couple even look like they might just have entered high school."

Nate had been right. The youngest would only be around fifteen. This woman was sick in the head for leading these children to be murderers and cold-blooded killers.

Colette remained outside once the others went in, and a second girl exited.

"That's the one they reported to last night," Noam said in an undertone.

"She looks a bit like the older lady," Freya said. "A sister maybe?"

"Sounds right," Nate said, already knowing who this was.

Genevieve Bellecourt. She was Colette's younger sister. While Colette would be in her thirties, Genevieve would only be fifteen right now. She was the one who would be doubting her sister the most. Nate wanted to hear this conversation.

"I'm going to try getting closer," Nate said. "Keep a lookout and tell me if they look in this direction."

"Nate, *wait*," Freya hissed, but Nate was already moving.

He rose to a crouch, the uncertain light of the setting sun and gloom of the evening making him indistinct and hard to pin down. He slipped through the sparse cover, closing to within thirty yards of the sisters before he decided that he'd gotten close enough. He dropped to his stomach, moving forward using his elbows, knees, and hips.

Finally, when he'd closed to within fifteen yards, their voices became distinct enough for him to hear. He was behind a small boulder, protruding from another small rise, so he crept around, peering at the pair, who were apparently in the midst of an argument.

"...told you a hundred times," Genevieve was saying. "I don't like this Lettie, not one bit! We are *killing* people and we have to stop!"

"Oh, Ginny," Colette said, placing a hand on her shoulder. "When will you understand the reality of our situation? We are in a strange world, one filled with danger. The people here are not real, just strings of code that that man in the sky put here to try and fool us..."

314

"Oh, yeah?" Genevieve said, shoving her sister's arm off herself. "Then why do they *beg* for their lives? Why do they bleed, cry, and scream? Why do they soil themselves when the life leaves their bodies? Why do their eyes look so accusatory?"

"This is what I've been trying to tell you all along," Colette said. "They were put here to try and fool us. If we give even an inch, we will all end up dead."

"You can't really think that of everyone on Earth, we are the only ones who decided to come here," Genevieve said angrily.

Colette sighed and shook her head.

"I cannot convince you if you are unwilling to listen. Everyone else has fallen into line, so why do you continue to resist, even when we can reap the benefits together?"

"You're a murderer," Genevieve said, her cheeks flushing in anger. "How does that make you feel?"

Colette pursed her lips.

"Does this have something to do with Mother abandoning you?" she asked.

"*Don't* bring her into this. This is about you!"

"Calm, calm," Colette said, looking to the house behind her.

Clearly, she didn't want the others overhearing this conversation, which was likely why they were having it outside.

"Don't treat me like a child, Colette," Genevieve yelled. "I am not your puppet to order around as you will."

Colette's features darkened for a moment. It happened so quickly that in the uncertain light, Nate wasn't actually sure of what he saw.

"Do you trust me, Genevieve?" she asked, her voice suddenly sounding different.

"What?" the younger girl asked, clearly taken off guard by the sudden shift in topic.

"You yell and scream," Colette said. "Call me a murderer even, yet you stay. You must trust me, don't you?"

Genevieve hesitated, clearly torn between wanting to continue yelling and her own, personal feelings.

"Yes," she said, though she sounded hesitant.

"Good," Colette said. "Trust is very important between family. This is why I have to do what needs to be done. For the good of our family."

"I don't understand," Genevieve said. "Why do we have to go on to a new set of portals and start killing people again? It's not right!"

"That's not what I was talking about," Colette said, removing a small, metallic object from a ring on her right finger.

"What's that?" Genevieve asked, clearly never having seen the object before.

"Oh, this?" Colette said, holding it up higher.

Light from within the cabin reflected off its surface, revealing that the object in question was a pen. It was made of a shining silvery metal, but Nate could see tiny runes etched into its side.

No, he thought to himself, his eyes going wide. *This can't be...but it makes so much sense!*

"Yes, that," Genevieve said, looking annoyed. "I've never seen it before."

"This is my Magician's Tome," Colette said, twisting the metal with a light *click*. "It's called the Tome of the Mighty Pen. Not the most flattering, I know, but *quite* useful. Would you care for a demonstration?"

Genevieve was immediately on guard. Knowing some of the woman's background, Nate knew that no one had been sure about what she'd been able to do, and since her body had never been recovered, neither had her Magician's Tome. Now that he knew what it was, he understood the true depths to this woman's depravity.

"I think I'd like to go inside now," Genevieve said, taking a step back.

Her hand subconsciously rose halfway, before she stopped as though in a block of ice.

"W-why can't I move?" Genevieve asked, her eyes going wide as she struggled against invisible bonds.

"Oh, my poor, dear sister," Colette sighed, striding over to the younger girl. "This all could have been avoided if you'd just believed what I told you and did what I said. Instead, you had to go stirring up trouble and now, I have to take extreme measures. For what it's worth I am sorry it came to this, but alas, I must do what is necessary in these hard times."

"What are you doing?" Genevieve demanded, her voice rising in panic as she continued to struggle in vain.

"What I have to," Colette said, then raised the pen to Genevieve's forehead and began to write.

Silver ink traced across the girl's brow as she tried to move, but no matter how she struggled, she could not escape the trap that Colette had set for her. It took the woman just a few seconds to write the word, the silver ink shining bright for several seconds before vanishing, melding into Genevieve's forehead and disappearing from view.

"Genevieve," Colette said, her voice sounding unnaturally enhanced. "We're going to kill some more people to increase our strength. To do that, we will need to split our forces to maximize our potential. You will lead this second group, understood?"

"Yes, understood," Genevieve said.

She sounded completely normal, not at all like the brainwashed zombie one might expect when dealing with the Tome of the Mighty Pen. That was the scariest part of it all. *No one* would be able to tell.

"Good," Colette said her smile turning up to insane levels, warping her features and making her seem almost manic. "You may go inside now."

Genevieve tried to move, but once again, found herself unable to.

"I can't move," she said.

"Oh, I guess I haven't released you from your bonds," Colette said.

Her pen flashed as she slashed it through the air, and dozens of lines of silver appeared, wrapped around Genevieve's body, and constricting her like a fly caught in a spider's web. Then they shattered, allowing the girl's arms to drop to her sides, free of the trap her own sister had set for her.

Without a word, Genevieve turned and went inside, her mind now under her sister's control.

317

49

"What happened?" Freya asked, as Nate returned just a few minutes later. "I mean, I saw everything, but none of it made any sense."

"It's bad," Nate said grimly. "Much worse than I thought, but, also better, in a way."

"What do you mean?" Noam asked.

"She's a magician," Nate said. "But her Tome doesn't look like an ordinary book, nor is it even a weapon, like Freya's. It's an object."

"You mean that pen she was flourishing around?" Freya asked.

"Yes, the pen," Nate replied. "She has the Tome of the Mighty Pen and…"

"*Mighty Pen*?" Freya said, snorting out a laugh. "Sounds like something a five-year-old would pick."

"The name is deceptive, just like your Snipe Crack," Nate said.

"Hey, at least Snipe Crack sounds vaguely inappropriate," Freya said. "It suits me perfectly."

"Yes, I can agree with that," Noam said.

"We're getting off topic again," Nate said, finding that this was becoming a common occurrence. "The point is, she has the pen and that is her tome. What it can do is another matter entirely. The tome is limited to three and if used correctly, can be one of the most insidious tomes out there."

"Okay, now you're scaring me," Freya said. "What does it do?"

"That's just the thing," Nate said. "There are a variety of spells built into the pen, but the user actually gets to choose which they want. Colette's is at the second tier and it seems that she's chosen to go down a dark path. So far, the tier one spell Spider Snare is something we know she has. She can draw invisible lines in the air and snare people. The scariest part is that she can do it without you noticing. If she's holding the pen, she can use the spell.

"The other is one we really have to worry about. It's a spell called Subjugate and it does exactly what it sounds like. It subjugates people to her will."

"Wait, she can mind-control people?" Freya said, then. "Why didn't I pick that?"

"It's a good thing you didn't," Noam said. "I think the world is safer for it."

She stuck her tongue out at him, then turned back to Nate.

"Just imagine all the stuff you could make people do. Like making them dance their literal pants off, or do something mildly inappropriate in public, or walk around cracking witty jokes like I do all day, or…"

"Or making them murder people," Nate said, cutting in.

The smile vanished from Freya's lips almost immediately.

"She can do that?"

"There are limitations of course," Nate said. "She needs to gain her subject's trust before she can subjugate them to her will, but once she's got them, there's no going back."

"So, she's literally brainwashed a class full of teenagers into becoming her personal hit-squad," Noam said grimly. "That is messed up on more levels than I can count."

"What does this mean?" Freya asked.

"It means that they're all completely blameless in this," Nate said grimly. "And that there won't be any talking to them. If we try to approach them, they will attack and nothing we say or do will make them back down."

"How do we free them?" Noam asked.

"There are one of two ways that can happen," Nate said. "The first, is the person under her control surpassing her rank. If, for example, she's at rank ten and a minion rises to eleven, the control breaks. The second way is for her to voluntarily break control and free them herself."

"Is that it?" Freya asked.

"Yes," Nate said, his voice growing grim.

"I take it that you have a plan then," Noam said. "Because she likely knows of this weakness and assures that no one surpasses her in overall rank."

"I do," Nate said. "There won't be any going back once we commit though."

319

"I'm still lost here," Freya said. "Can someone please clue me in to whatever's happening?"

"Someone like that wouldn't willingly give up their power," Noam said. "So, the only way to do it would be to make her."

"Wait," Freya said, her confusion beginning to clear up. "You can't be talking about…"

"Torture," Nate replied, his voice hard. "Yes. We would need to capture her alive and force her to release everyone under her control."

"Oh," Freya said. "Well, that just took a dark turn. I'm okay with fighting an enemy, even killing them if it came to it, but torture? I just don't think I'd have that in me."

"No one is asking you to do anything," Nate said. "All we'd need to do is catch her. You can stay out of it from there."

"And what, let *you* do it?" Freya asked. "Do you have any idea what kind of psychological damage that can do to you?"

"You mean the kind that comes with dropping a city from the sky?" Nate replied, his voice soft.

Freya shook her head, not budging on the issue.

"There *has* to be another way," Freya said. "What about killing her?"

"That won't work," Nate said. "If killing her were the answer, I'd dive in with the two of you right now and take her by surprise, while she's not expecting it. If she dies, whatever orders those teenagers have will continue to be carried out, until they either run out of people to murder or are themselves killed. And, in case you're wondering, surpassing her rank at the time of death won't change anything. They will remain enthralled."

"Come on," Freya said, wracking her brain. "There *has* to be another way."

"Unless you can somehow convince her to voluntarily let them all go, this is a moot point," Nate said. "Now, it's getting late, and I would like to get at least *some* sleep before our backup arrives in the morning."

"That's it!" Freya said, as Nate went to move.

"What's it?" he asked.

"I honestly can't believe you didn't think of it," Freya said, grinning widely. "Though, I think it reflects your messed-up brain quite a bit if the first thing you thought of was torture."

320

"Get on with it," Nate said.

"You know, I feel like I'd like to bask in the moment for a bit longer. Me knowing something you don't. It's kind of refreshing."

"You done yet?"

"Yeah," Freya replied, though her grin didn't diminish. "The answer is so obvious, I feel like I should leave you hanging for *just* a bit-"

"Just spit it out already," Noam said. "We don't have all night."

"*Fine*," Freya said, rolling her eyes. "The two of you stick-in-the-muds would make a monk sworn to silence scream in frustration."

She ignored the strange looks the two of them gave her and carried on.

"What is the greatest weakness of someone who uses a weapon or object as their chosen path?" Freya asked, as though giving a lecture.

"That someone will take it away, depriving them of their ability to use their spells or techniques," Nate said. "Okay, I feel like a bit of an idiot for not thinking of this."

"I'll save *that* one for later," Freya said cheerily.

"Are you sure we can't just torture her?" Noam asked. "I imagine that stealing that pen will be extremely difficult."

"Not necessarily," Nate said, rubbing his chin. "It would take some doing, but we might, might be able to fool her into taking it out. We're just going to need the perfect bait."

"Wonderful," Freya said. "What kind of bait are we talking? Is it the worm kind or…it's me, isn't it," she said, looking between the two men. "Of course it's me."

"Hey, it's not my fault she preys on teenagers," Noam said with a shrug.

"Not mine either," Nate said. "You're the only one who fits the bill."

"Getting her to trust me won't be easy," Freya said. "What, do you expect me to just walk up to the front door, knock and ask her to show me her magical pen?"

"No," Nate said, grinning. "But I think I've got just the scenario in mind."

"I don't like this, Nate," Freya said, looking between him, Noam, and the monster the two of them had pinned. "I don't like this one bit."

"It'll only hurt for a little bit," Nate said. "Besides, you can heal yourself."

"You know, maybe you were onto something with that whole torture idea," Freya said. "She's a bad person. A little stabbing and maiming for the greater good wouldn't be too bad, right?"

"Hey, it was your idea to steal her pen," Nate said as the monster tried to buck from his grip.

"How do you know they won't kill me on sight for the kanta?" Freya tried.

"Call it a hunch," Nate said.

"You're going to risk my life on a hunch?"

"Yup," Nate said.

He and Noam released the monster, then leaped back, earning them a yelp from Freya, who drew her Magigun instinctively and shot. A Blazing Bullet glanced off the Terror Pig's hide, leaving a searing burn in its wake.

"You two are so dead!" Freya yelled right before the pig slammed into her legs, sending her flying.

She screamed as she hit the ground, her shins slashed wide and blood coating them.

"Way to make it look convincing," Nate cheered as he and Noam backed away.

"I'll murder your entire family!" Freya screamed, blasting the pig with her Magigun.

The monster closed once more, only to disappear with a *bang* as she used her Tele-bang spell.

"Good luck," Nate called, then joined Noam in watching Freya tangle with the pig.

"Are you sure this was a good idea?" Noam asked.

"Are you kidding?" Nate asked. "It's a terrible idea, but that's why it'll work. Probably."

"I'll roast you over a spit, you overgrown swine!" Freya screamed, flashes of light illuminating the darkness around her.

"She seems quite put out," Noam said. "I do not envy you if we come out of this alive."

322

"Yeah," Nate sighed. "She's probably going to want something from me and I'll be obligated to give it to her."

"I'm glad I am not you," Noam said.

"You and me both, buddy," Nate said as he watched activity coming from the cabin.

"Come on, keep it going," Nate muttered, as Freya's gun tore one of the monster's legs off, sending the pig toppling to the ground.

She needed to sell that she could fight, but someone from the group still needed to help her. Freya's next shot went wide as the boar staggered to its feet, and, with an enraged squeal, half-hobbled, half-ran to attack her.

The monster closed to within five feet of her, when a blur of movement came and a lance of pure crystal smashed into the pig, piercing it through the neck and pinning it to the ground. The monster struggled for a moment longer, the collapsed in a heap.

Nate watched as a group of six teens, led by Genevieve ran up to Freya, all looking between the girl and the pig.

"Are you okay?" Genevieve asked, sounding genuinely concerned.

"I'm fine," Freya said through gritted teeth. "Thanks to you."

"That looks pretty bad," Genevieve said, crouching to examine her legs. "We should get you inside. My sister is pretty good at dressing wounds and she'll want to talk with you. It's rare that we see strangers on the road, especially alone."

"*Not* bleeding out sounds very nice right about now," Freya said as she was helped to her feet.

She shot a glare in their direction as she was helped toward the cabin and only once she was inside did Nate rise.

"How did you know they wouldn't kill her?" Noam asked.

"Call it insider knowledge," Nate said.

"Can you elaborate?"

"Colette doesn't believe that the people in this world are fake, but she kills them anyway. Someone's bound to come after her, so how does she protect herself?"

"By taking in more strays," Noam said, nodding along. "Preferably those young enough to be impressionable, but old enough to fight."

"Exactly," Nate said. "Stay here and keep watch. I'll be back in the city. We'll meet back here in the morning."

"You will owe me for this," Noam said.

"I was completely fine with torture," Nate replied. "If this is the price you all want to pay for keeping my hands clean, that's on you."

"Can you do me a favor and at least bring breakfast?"

"Yeah," Nate said. "I can do that much. But nothing fancy."

"*You*, spend extra on anything?" Noam said. "I wouldn't even dream of asking."

50

Nate headed directly for the shop when he entered the city, plonking himself down behind the counter and removing his scroll.

"I'd like to upgrade this scroll to the next tier," Nate said.

The female gnark opened the scroll, peering at its contents.

"That'll be seventy-five thousand points," she said.

Nate placed his palm on the glass sphere and felt the points leave him. Had he held out for just a little longer, he'd have been able to upgrade his manual to the 3rd tier. He had been *very* tempted. But in the end, he'd decided that his survivability would depend more on how well he could recover from injuries right now, not how hard he could hit.

Had he not received the Magma Body technique, he might have had a harder time convincing himself of that.

The gnark nodded, then pulled the scroll to her side of the counter and removed a wooden seal. She stamped the scroll, then handed it back to Nate, who eagerly read the new line of scrawling text that flowed across the page. It took a moment for the knowledge to settle, but when it did, a wide grin stretched his features.

"Would you mind showing me a description?" Nate asked.

With a wave of her hand, the gnark made a translucent screen appear before Nate's eyes, showing the properties of the upgraded scroll.

Technique scroll: Cycle of Regeneration tier 4, 750,000 points to upgrade to tier 5.

Cycle of Regeneration: You may cultivate the energy around you to restore your body to full health with great speed. Passive regeneration of kanta is now 2.25X faster than before. Your body may naturally resist poisons and toxins on its own.

Just as he'd known it would, the cost to upgrade had increased massively, but to Nate, that didn't matter right now. He now had access to speed healing, which meant he could restore injuries within seconds to minutes, instead of hours. His kanta regeneration speed rising would be extremely helpful, and passive resistance to poison was a nice perk.

"Thank you," Nate said, tucking the scroll away in his ring.

"Can I help you with anything else?" the gnark asked.

"Yes, actually," Nate said, thinking of the strange happenings in the construction site shutdowns. "I've heard that there's been some trouble near the central area of the quadrant. Would you happen to have any idea what it might be?"

"I've only heard rumors," the gnark said with a shrug. "Some say it was a monster, others said it was aliens and others still, think they've just been cursed by Morgito the Mighty. Honestly speaking, who knows with these weirdoes?"

It seemed the gnark didn't have a very high opinion of the borers.

"Morgito the Mighty?" Nate asked, not having heard that name before.

"Oh, just some old borer myth," the gnark said. "It's not all that interesting."

"I'm interested," Nate said.

"And I don't care," she replied. "Either buy something or get out."

"Wow," Nate said. "Talk about rude."

"It's late and I hate the night shift," the gnark said. "I also hate it when people come bother me."

Nate decided to leave, making a mental note to ask a local about this Morgito the Mighty.

"Thanks for all your help," he said as he headed out of the shop, getting only an angry grunt in return.

Nate ignored the gnark's rude behavior and headed down the stairs, exiting the building and making for the inn where he'd be spending the night. He would have to be up early to meet with Mallory and Carver and explain the changing situation to them and it was already quite late. This seemed to be becoming a habit of his – staying up late, that was.

He was walking down the darkened streets, illuminated areas by lantern light breaking the areas of shadows, when he got the sense that someone was watching him. He was immediately alert, aware of every sound, scuffle and whisper, his ears straining for the slightest thing out of place.

He continued walking, not wanting to give away the fact that he was aware of his pursuer.

Nate didn't react when he heard the light scuff of a boot on the street, nor did he do anything when the rustle of cloth reached his ears. Someone *was* following him, though who, what, or why was still an unknown.

Nate turned a corner, his eyes flicking to the street behind him and caught the barest hint of movement as someone disappeared into a nearby alleyway. Curiosity made him stay his hand and continue walking, rather than turning to confront whoever it was. He wanted to give them some time to get closer before making his move.

He continued walking, catching the occasional flicker now as the figure flitted from alleyway to alleyway. He caught a glimpse of black-clad legs. A bare, slender arm. The flutter of a hood trailed in the breeze of her movement. It was a woman, of that Nate was sure.

Expanding his senses to their maximum, he continued to walk. He was nearing the inn, which meant he would need to confront her soon. The question was if she would make her move before then or try to keep tailing him.

Nate stopped once he reached the inn, turning towards the front door and placing his back directly to her – she'd flitted into an alley on the opposite side of the street. If there was any chance for her to make her move, *this* would be it.

The slightest scuff of a boot gave her away as she dashed from cover. In a single, smooth motion, Nate turned, a glittering sword appearing in his hand as he swung for the woman's neck. To his surprise, he missed, not because of the woman's skill, but because she'd stopped out of the blade's range.

Nate took the woman in at a glance and had to stop himself from reacting. Of all the places to meet, this was not where he'd been expecting to run into Hazel Wilson, the next team member he had on his recruitment list.

The woman's brown eyes were wide as she stared at the glittering point of the blade aimed right at her throat.

"Wait!" she said, throwing her arms up and waving them frantically. "I'm not here to cause trouble!"

She looked very different from how Nate remembered. The Hazel from Nate's past was a mass of scars and burn tissue, her face so disfigured by injury that it had been hard to tell she was a woman just by looking. Even when she spoke, her rasping voice – damaged by the same monster who'd injured her so – didn't give it away.

The details of how she'd been injured were a mystery, as Hazel had never really talked about it. All he'd known when they met for the first time on the 8th planet was that the injury had occurred on the 7th and that she'd barely made it out alive. It was unfortunate that she'd perished in the raid against one of the monsters guarding the only portals to the 12th planet, Destiny.

This version of Hazel had a pale complexion, a heart-shaped face, a small nose, plump lips, and a long curtain of black hair flowing down her back. She was shorter than him, only around five-foot-four, and her build was a good deal slenderer than Freya's.

If anything, she appeared less like the 22-year-old woman he knew her to be and more like someone who was perhaps fifteen at best. The splash of freckles running over the bridge of her nose and her large eyes helped sell the illusion even better. If that didn't do it, her voice – which was higher-pitched and youthful – would complete the image.

If only we'd had her for the plan instead of Freya, Nate silently groaned.

Hazel would have been a better fit for playing the part, not only due to her youthful appearance, but also because of her background as a stunt-double, gymnast, and actress. She was perfect for getting into hard-to-reach places because of all those traits and the specific Manual she'd chosen upon entering Warine.

"Why were you following me?" Nate asked, keeping his blade raised.

It was important to keep playing the part, even though he was cheering inside at having her basically fall into his lap.

"I wasn't stalking you or anything like that," she said, her accent giving away her North Carolina heritage immediately. "Honest to God, I wasn't!"

It wasn't a heavy Southern, but just enough for someone to take notice. The nervousness in her voice also made it stand out more.

"That doesn't answer the question," Nate said.

The woman was visibly sweating, that much was obvious by the beads of moisture on her face and how her clothes clung to her

328

body. The black pants, combat boots and sleeveless top were practical, though the hooded cloak she had draped over her shoulders wasn't really doing her any favors.

"Right, that's a good point," she said, letting out a small laugh. "I guess I should start by introducing myself."

She stuck out her hand, careful not to step any closer.

"Hazel Wilson," she said.

Nate looked between her outstretched hand and her face, then slowly lowered the blade. He didn't dismiss it, switching it to his left before cautiously taking it.

"Nate Chesterson," he said.

She had a surprisingly firm grip for such a slender girl, but he knew that would be her Path at work and her current ranking. He couldn't be sure exactly where she stood at the moment, but she was strong enough to have come here to Laybor, which meant she was over 30.

Nate released her hand and stepped back again, keeping his guard up while Hazel began talking.

"Sorry I was following you like that," she said, as she lowered her hand. "It's just that I saw you fighting, you know, outside that city on Warine and I thought that you were pretty strong and might be able to help me."

"Help you?" Nate asked.

"I know, I know!" she said, waving her arms again. "It's very presumptuous of me to just assume things like that, but I'm desperate. I know you have no idea who I am and the only point of reference you have for me is some creep who was following you, but like I said, I'm desperate."

Nate allowed his expression to soften and dismissed his Gilded Blade, though he remained on guard. It was so strange hearing this light and girlish voice coming from Hazel's lips, especially when he remembered that she'd once sounded like an aging bullfrog. But the way she carried herself was unmistakable. That and the list of techniques hovering over her head to Nate's Kanta Sight. This was her. He'd know it the second he'd laid eyes on her, despite all the differences.

"Is this your first day on Laybor?" he asked.

"How could you tell?"

"You're sweating like a pig," Nate answered.

She barked out a laugh, running her fingers through her sweaty hair and pushing it back from her face.

"I guess you've got a point there, though you look cool as a cucumber. Is there a secret to not being a sweaty mess?"

"Yes," Nate said. "A change of clothes. You can buy them in the shop up there."

He pointed to the building where the shop was located.

"Well, I really appreciate that info. I'll have to go get some ASAP then. I feel *so* gross."

"That cloak isn't doing you any favors," Nate replied.

"My cloak?" she asked, looking confused for a moment.

Then her eyes went wide in realization, and she smacked her forehead with an audible slap.

"I am such an idiot," she said, undoing the clasp at her neck, pulling the heavy garment from her shoulders, and stashing it in a ring on her index finger. "I'm such a klutz sometimes. My sister says I'd lose my glasses if they were on my face."

"Sister?" Nate asked, looking around, half expecting someone else to come out of the woodwork.

"Right," Hazel said, her joviality leaking out of her. "That's I was following you. Not to make the story too long, but my sister Becky got caught up with some bad people when we got here, and they dragged her along with them to Ashland. They're a guild who follows some psycho serial killer and this woman named Selena. Anyway, I've been trying to get her out, but every time I get close, someone chases me off. I know she wants to get out, but they won't let her leave. Say her power is too useful and that they'll never let her go."

Though Nate didn't outwardly show it, he was inwardly cheering once again. Rebecca Wilson was Hazel's sister? He would never have guessed that the tall redhead was related to Hazel in any way, shape, or form.

When coming back, Nate had made a list of people he knew where to find and get to join his group. He'd also made a list of people he hadn't known where to find, but really wanted in his team. Rebecca Wilson was at the very top of his list. Not only had she opposed Ashland at every turn – her exploits there were famous – but she'd also soloed a 3-star monster on the 5th planet. To say that was impressive was no exaggeration.

330

She had perished long before Hazel, dying before making it to the 6th. She'd actually been caught in the planetary explosion of Warine while trying to get people to safety. Hazel had never talked about her sister or even mentioned *having* one when they'd known each other, and Nate had to wonder why. Regardless, he had to help Hazel save her so he could recruit them.

"How do you know she doesn't want to stay with them?" Nate asked, still playing his part. "Especially since you haven't been able to see her."

He couldn't seem too eager, or she would become suspicious.

"I've snuck into the Ashland Guild more times than you can count," Hazel said, her cheeks growing flushed. "I've heard people talking."

"I thought you said they told you they weren't going to let her go?" Nate said.

"I tried a bunch of different things," Hazel said with a shrug. "When they found out who I was, they confronted me. I told them I wanted to see her, but they refused. When I tried to leave, they attacked me. So, I dealt with them and ran. I've been trying to find a way out for her ever since."

"That still doesn't explain it," Nate said.

"We're twins," Hazel said, sounding a bit desperate. "We have a special connection. I don't know how to explain it, but I just know. Please, you're really strong. I've seen it and I could really use your help."

This was news to Nate. Not only were they sisters, but twins? They must have been fraternal twins based on their wildly different appearances. Though, when Nate compared their actual features in his mind, they *did* share some similarities. Perhaps seeing them together would help.

"I'll get down on my knees and beg if that's what it takes!" She clasped her fingers together, apparently having taken his silence as hesitation.

"No need to do that," Nate said, as she began to lower herself. "I believe you, I just…I can't leave right now. I have friends who need my help."

"I can help," Hazel offered quickly. "I've tangled with Ashland plenty and killed my fair share of monsters too."

She scrabbled for a moment with her fingerless black gloves, then dragged her right one off, turning her hand so he could see the markings.

"I've made it all the way to thirty-one, and that was basically working alone."

"I don't know if that would make you a good team player though," Nate said, pursing his lips.

"I've been doing gymnastics nearly all my life and have been on a team for the last seven years," Hazel jumped in. "I know *plenty* about teamwork."

"Hmm," Nate said, pretending to waver. "Maybe. It would depend on what you could do though. The people we're after are dangerous and things are likely to become ugly."

"Well, seeing as I've already seen what you can do, I suppose telling you can't hurt," she said.

She took a deep breath, then tapped her ring, removing a white manual covered in intricate scrollwork and small patches of fur. She handed it over to Nate, showing a tremendous amount of trust and not even flinching when he took it from her hands.

"It's called the Path of the White Werewolf. I know it's a total cliché, but I was really into shifter novels and loved the paranormal, so when I saw it, I couldn't resist. It's only at the first tier, but I have three techniques. The first is called Wolf Paw, it changes my hands."

She held her hands up to demonstrate, her slender fingers turning into huge, shaggy white paws with blunted claws at the ends. It looked almost comical on her short body, like she was wearing massive gloves or something.

"The second is called Wolf Scream, but for your sake, I won't demonstrate that here. It's a sound-based attack that disorients my enemies. I've even seen eardrums bleed if I'm close enough. The third is my strongest. It's called Pack Attack. In a nutshell, I can summon a pack of wolves to tear my enemies apart. It's usually between three and four at the most right now, but I only used to be able to call two."

"That sounds more like a magician's spell than a technique," Nate said.

"It is and it isn't," she said. "I have more distance, but the pack is linked to me physically. If they take damage, so do I."

"That sounds like a pretty big weakness," Nate said, rubbing his chin. "But it makes sense that there's a tradeoff."

He extended his hand, returning the manual. If Hazel was relieved, she didn't show it.

"I guess since you've shown so much trust, I can return the favor," Nate said, after pretending to think.

He pulled his own Path Manual from his ring and was gratified by seeing Hazel's eyes go wide. Just like she had, he handed it over, knowing this would build trust. He explained what each of his techniques could do while she stared at the near-glowing Manual of Gilded Steel.

"That sounds amazing," she said after he finished with his explanation, handing the Manual back. "What about that lava thing you did though? Where you turned into some sort of raging molten stone thing?"

"That would be my Magma Body," Nate said, removing the tablet and handing it over for examination.

"Woah, this is much heavier than it looks," she said, hefting the chunk of stone. "I've never seen a technique on a tablet before. Where did you find it?"

"In a magma-filled cavern about two days from here," Nate said as she returned it to him. "Do you have any techniques aside from the ones your Path gave you?"

"No," Hazel said sheepishly. "I didn't really want to spend any points, as I wasn't sure if I'd need them later."

"Would you mind me asking how many you had?" Nate asked.

"A little over a 116,000," she said. "Why?"

Nate could have jumped for joy. Her Manual of the White Werewolf would need *far* less than that to be pushed to the 2nd tier, where she would gain access to two new techniques. Her manual, like his and Freya's, was from the limited list, though unlike his, hers was limited to 4. However, just like with Genevieve's Mighty Pen, there were a list of techniques that could be leaned and would greatly depend on the individual fighter to pull them out.

"Because you're leaving yourself with too many weaknesses when you could be cashing them in to make yourself stronger."

"I can *try*, but I just wouldn't know what to get, or where to even begin," she said sheepishly. "But does this mean that you'll help me?"

She sounded hopeful, her eyes shining. Even if she'd been a complete stranger, Nate would have had a *very* hard time saying no.

"I'm going to be meeting with some people in the morning. If you'd like, you can join us on our mission. If I see that you do well, I'll help you get your sister out of Ashland."

"Oh, thank you!" Hazel said, slamming into him and wrapping him up in a hug.

Seeming to realize what she'd done, Hazel quickly backed away, blushing furiously.

"Sorry about that, I'm a hugger. Happens when I get excited."

"Just meet me over by the portal in the morning," Nate said. "I'll be there early."

Hazel nodded vigorously, still blushing with embarrassment over the hug.

Nate wished her a good night, then headed into the inn, leaving the woman on the darkened streets of City 144G.

51

Nate woke early the next morning before the alarm call and got out of bed. He warmed up by doing his usual exercise, then cooled off in the bath. Once he was done, he donned his new armor, admiring the way it looked and felt. The flickering flames running over the exterior made it look really cool, and the metal woven in made it both light and far more durable.

Additionally, seeing as the fire foxes were adapted to Laybor, this armor would have the same effect as the clothes he'd been wearing until now. He had better protection, a built-in technique, and all with the same effects and comfort as what he'd been wearing until now.

Nate slipped from his room, making sure to stop in the common room for breakfast and grab Noam something to eat. Unlike him, the man would have slept on the ground last night, keeping watch over the cabin in case anything happened. Seeing as no one had come to bother him though, he had to assume that things had gone well or at least not horribly.

He left the inn shortly after, winding his way through the already-bustling streets of the city as he headed for the alleyway. On his way, he decided to stop by a small vendor's stall, where a few borers were chatting.

"Excuse me," Nate said, getting their attention.

"An *alien*!" one of them shouted, sounding shocked.

"Cool yourself, Thelonius," one of the others said. "They've been around the city for weeks."

"They *have*?" the beaver-man – Thelonius apparently – said.

"What can we do for you, alien man?" asked the other borer, ignoring his confused friend.

"I wanted to ask about a name that I heard someone mention," Nate said. "Morgito the Mighty?"

The silence that greeted his question was so palpable that Nate felt it as a physical force.

"What?" Nate asked, when none of them replied. "Did I say something wrong?"

"No," the borer said in a lowered voice. "It's just that saying the name is bad luck. You don't want ol' 'Gito's ghost coming after you."

The others were nodding along vehemently, all apparently agreeing with what he said.

"Ghost," Nate said flatly.

And here he'd been expecting something of substance.

"I know how it sounds," the borer said. "But trust me when I say that he's *very* real."

"Why would this man's ghost be bothering anyone?" Nate asked.

"Well, that would be on account of what was *done* to him," the borer said, still in a lowered voice. "Around two-hundred years ago, Gito was an overboss, overseeing the construction of the now-defunct quadrant-Q. Work was going quite well until he started running into some problems. Workers disappearing. People not meeting their quotas. Materials vanishing without a trace.

"He began to grow angry that the work wasn't being fulfilled, but there was no one to vent his anger *on*, because everyone who stayed was doing good work. One day, when a nearly finished building came crashing down, killing nearly ten full crews, he lost it and went stomping out into the wilderness to discover the cause.

"Gito was never seen again after that, and soon after, the project was abandoned and the survivors went home. But that's not the end of the story," the borer said, a small shudder running down his spine.

"Soon after returning home, the remaining workers of the abandoned project began disappearing. One by one, they vanished. Some right under their wives' noses. But soon enough, no one was safe, not even those who'd had nothing to do with it.

"Work slowed to a crawl, and we were the least productive we had been in centuries. So, the lead overbosses took drastic action, exiling all the remaining workers from quadrant-Q into the wilderness. None of them were seen again, but after that, the disappearances stopped.

"Many believe it was the ghost of ol' Gito, come back to take his revenge on those who never finished their work."

"And what would make people think that it's him who's responsible for all the disappearances and damaged construction in the center of this quadrant?" Nate asked.

"Because everything's the same as it was last time," the borer said. "The disappearances. The damaged goods, the work slowing to a crawl. Everyone knows it's him, only this time, we don't know what to do about it."

"Are you afraid he'll come here?" Nate asked.

The borers looked around in fear, telling him that yes, they *did* fear he would come for them.

"Just watch your back, alien," the borer said. "You never know when or where ol' Gito might decide to strike next."

Nate thanked them for their time, then headed toward the alley, his mind working furiously. This mystery was only becoming more and more interesting. By this point, he was itching to check it out, as it was unlike anything he'd heard of before.

"Good morning!" Hazel said enthusiastically when Nate entered the alleyway.

He was glad to see that she'd taken his advice and was now dressed in a similar outfit to Freya's, albeit a much smaller and slimmer version. Her hair was also tied back in two braids, assuring that none of it would get in her face during a fight. The hairstyle somehow made her look younger, which was a strange thing, considering that she was four years Freya's senior.

"Good morning," Nate said.

Though he kept his enthusiasm to a minimum, he *did* give her a smile.

"How long have you been waiting here?"

"Only half an hour," she said. "I wasn't sure exactly when you wanted to meet me, so I decided to come early, just in case."

"Have you had anything to eat?" He asked.

"No," she said, rubbing subconsciously at her stomach. "I was in such a rush that I completely forgot."

"Here," Nate said, removing a third breakfast he'd brought, just in case. "They won't be here for at least another fifteen minutes, so you've got time."

"Oh, you're my hero!" Hazel said, taking the proffered egg and cheese sandwich and digging in with obvious glee.

337

She tore through the sandwich in about five seconds flat, cramming huge mouthfuls with each bite and making happy noises all the while. When she finished, she picked at the crumbs still attached to the napkin.

"When was the last time you ate?" Nate asked, noting how quickly she'd eaten.

"Oh, not too long ago," she said. "Maybe a couple of days ago."

"A couple of days?" Nate asked. "Don't you have any rations?"

"I ran out while I was chasing Ashland and didn't want to lose track of them. I followed you here and didn't want to lose you either so I..."

"Didn't *eat*?" Nate asked.

She just shrugged, looking embarrassed. Her embarrassment vanished, replaced by another huge smile when Nate removed another sandwich – this one a hard cheese and tomato – and handed it over.

"You're a godsend," she said, biting into the sandwich with relish.

"Yeah, well, I can't have you going into a fight when you haven't eaten in *days*. You're also still growing, so not eating for that long has got to be rough."

"Still growing?" Hazel asked between bites.

"You're what, fifteen, sixteen at the most?" Nate said. "Don't tell me you've stopped growing already."

"I'm twenty-two," Hazel said flatly.

"No, you're not," Nate said, brushing her off.

"You think I'm lying to you?" Hazel asked, taking another bite of her sandwich.

"Hey, everyone at your age wants to pretend to be older," Nate said with a shrug. "I get that this is a dangerous world, but it's okay to tell the truth."

"I used to get that all the time back on Earth," Hazel said. "More often than not, I had to pull my ID out to prove it, and even then, people thought it was fake. Do you have *any idea* what a pain in the neck it is to look so young at my age?"

"You're serious," Nate said, noting the anger that had begun tinging her voice.

338

"*Yes*, I'm serious," Hazel sighed.

"Sorry," Nate replied. "I guess this is a sensitive subject."

"It's not your fault," Hazel said. "But I appreciate the apology all the same."

"So, what exactly did you do back on Earth? Aside from gymnastics, that is."

"I was a stunt double, believe it or not," she said after swallowing her mouthful of food. "Got cast for kids' movies for the most part, but I *did* start getting into acting before the whole world went to hell."

"Really, an actress?" Nate said. "Were you in anything I would know?"

Before Hazel could answer, the portal rippled and Mallory came stumbling through.

"Oh, I think I'm gonna be sick," she groaned, clutching at the wall for a moment.

Thankfully, she didn't throw up, overcoming the nausea a few seconds later and straightening to her full height.

"Hi, Nate," she said, giving him a wide smile.

"Hi, Mallory," Nate returned, as Carver stepped through behind her.

The man stumbled just like she did, the disorientation lasting just a few moments before he stood tall.

"It's *hot* here, isn't it?" Mallory said, tugging at her collar, then turned to Hazel.

"Is this Freya?" she asked. "She doesn't look anything like you described."

"I'm Hazel," Hazel said, extending a hand. "Nice to meet you."

"Oh, such a polite young lady," Mallory said, shaking her hand.

"Nate, why have you brought a child here?" Carver asked as several more men and woman came through behind him.

"She's actually twenty-two," Nate said, before Hazel could say anything. "And believe it or not, we met just last night."

Nate quickly explained the situation to everyone there, the group's overall demeanor turning grim as he spoke.

"That sounds like quite the mission we've got," Carver said.

"Yeah," Nate replied. "And the sooner we pull this off, the better. Freya's no actress, so there's a good chance she'll slip up before she gets a chance to see Colette's Pen, so we need to get there and see what the situation is."

"That sounds like a plan," Mallory said. "But, before we go anywhere, is there somewhere I can change? I feel like I'm swimming through the air here and I don't like it."

"You'll need new clothes for Laybor," Nate said. "I'll show you all to the shop where you can buy what you need. Then, we'll be heading out. Noam is waiting for us."

"Sounds like a plan," Mallory said, stretching her arms over her head. "Lead the way!"

52

"This whole time-difference thing is really messing with me," Mallory said as their group headed down the road.

Including Mallory and Carver, they had brought six fighters along for the mission, all of them appearing like hardened veterans and carrying themselves with the surety of those who'd fought for their lives on multiple occasions.

"Yeah, that seems to be the case with everyone who crosses over," Nate said. "Freya calls it portal lag."

"Portal lag, I like it," Mallory said, squinting up at the suns through the heavy haze. "It's still hard to believe that a world like this can exist. Two suns. Can you imagine?"

"Yeah, it definitely *is* strange," Nate agreed.

"Mallory, can I borrow you for a moment?" Carver asked, interrupting their conversation.

"I'll be right back," she said, then dropped back to speak with Carver and her group.

"She's got a thing for you," Hazel said.

She'd been walking to the side of the road, off on her own, but now that Mallory had moved, she came to join him.

"How can you tell?" Nate asked.

"I've got a pretty good knack for spotting things like that. Let's just say I didn't get a whole lot of dates back on Earth, so I can tell pretty quickly when someone's interested, and *she* clearly is."

"Well, isn't that nice to know?" Nate said with a sigh.

"She's pretty," Hazel said. "But something tells me you're not interested in the same way. Is it this Freya I keep hearing about? You got a thing for her?"

"That's not it," Nate said, being careful to keep his face as neutral as possible.

If Hazel had been able to pick up on Mallory's interest in him from a five-minute conversation, she would be able to read him like a book.

"It's this *world*," Nate said, gesturing around himself. "I feel like there's no time for things as frivolous as romance and relationships when we're constantly fighting for survival."

"Not to knock your choices or anything, but if the situations were reversed, I'd jump on it without a second thought. Life here *is* dangerous, but because it can literally end at any second, I'd want to live it to the fullest. Just my two cents though. So, how do you know her?"

Nate went into an abbreviated version of what had happened between the two of them, skimming over many of the more gruesome details, such as the battle with Mr. MC and his crew.

"Well, I can see why she'd have a thing for you after all that," Hazel said. "When a man shows that he can not only provide and protect you and your children, but also seems to genuinely *care*. Well, let's just say that you'd have to drag me away, kicking and screaming before I willingly gave up on someone like that."

"Hey, what are you two whispering about?" Mallory asked, catching back up.

"Oh, just talking about my miserable and non-existent dating life," Hazel sighed. "How about you, Mallory, you seeing anyone?"

"Well, I *was* married before the whole…well, you know," Mallory said. "But he decided to stay behind. So, no, I'm not seeing anyone right now."

Nate noticed the surreptitious look in his direction when she said that and had to fight to keep his expression neutral. He wanted to strangle Hazel for bringing this up, but two could play at that game.

"Well, Mallory, how about seeing if you can find someone for Hazel," Nate said. "From what I hear, she *really* wants a boyfriend, and her appearance really turns many people off."

"Could you really help me?" Hazel asked Mallory, sounding hopeful.

Well, that had backfired on him. It seemed Hazel was more than happy to have Mallory introduce her to someone.

"That would depend on what you're looking for," Mallory said. "For example…"

Nate allowed himself to fall back from the pair of women, thankful to have extricated himself from the situation.

"Want to tell me why you guys didn't bring that Damon guy along?" Nate asked, addressing Carver. "He seemed pretty strong."

342

"Damon might be strong," Carver said. "But he's unstable in battle, especially around Mallory. He has an unhealthy obsession with her, though I'm sure you already figured that out."

"Any reason you guys keep him around?" Nate asked.

"He's strong," Carver said. "And we're not going to throw someone out simply because they have a crush on Mallory."

"I wouldn't exactly call it a crush," Nate said.

"No matter his personal faults, Damon has never acted on his feelings, nor has he put anyone in danger," Carver said. "Until such a time as he does, we will continue to count on him for support and keep him within our city."

Nate nodded, though he wasn't sure he agreed with his sentiment. If someone posed a potential threat, you got rid of them, especially someone who seemed as unstable as Damon did.

"Now, I have a question for you," Carver said. "Why are you so intent on helping these captured children? Come to think of it, why did you help Mallory in the first place? She told me what you did for her, Jamey, and Lily. It seems exceedingly kind for someone so young."

"I like helping people where I can," Nate said with a shrug. "She came and asked me for help. How could I say no to that?"

"You must have another motive for wanting to help these children. None of them asked for your aid."

"They didn't," Nate agreed. "But that woman is using them to kill people. No one will want to leave Warine if they're scared of being killed the moment they step through a portal. If people don't advance, we'll never get back home."

"Ah, so that is your goal then? To return to Earth?" Carver said.

"Yes," Nate said. "I also have family who came here, but they were all over the world. These planets are large, but from what I can tell, they grow smaller as you progress. The sooner we make it to the farther planets, the sooner I'm hoping to find them."

"Hey, Nate!" Mallory called, turning, and walking backwards. "Why didn't you tell me we were traveling with a celebrity?"

"Celebrity?" Nate asked.

"Hazel Wilson!" she said, pointing to the woman next to her. "From the Little Dinosaur and Rumble-Tron!"

"What?" Nate asked.

"Right, I forgot that you weren't around kids much," Mallory said. "They were some of my favorites to watch with Jamey before coming here."

"I didn't play *that* big a role," Hazel said, blushing.

"Are you kidding me?" Mallory gushed. "Laser Girl was our favorite character! How did you…"

Nate tuned them out again as the pain continued talking, Mallory pelting the girl woman with questions about the movie and her acting career, which she did her best to answer, much to Mallory's excitement.

"It almost seems normal," Carver sighed.

"Yeah," Nate said. "Almost."

"Until you see a creepy-looking pig monster staring at you from the side of the road," Carver said, raising his guard. "We've got incoming!"

A rank-35 Stout Boar, came charging from the side of the road with a loud squeal, making straight for Hazel and Mallory, only to be caught in the woman's Snare spell. It let out a shriek as it staggered away, legs streaming blood.

"Move in!" Carver yelled, then dashed past them, drawing a curved saber and meat cleaver from his belt.

Carver's name, unironically, matched the path he'd chosen – the Path of the Carver. It specialized in hacking and slashing, hitting critical points and amputating limbs.

His cleaver glowed with silverly light as he used Cleave, swinging down at the pig's front shoulder. With a sickening *crunch*, the limb was severed, the monster flopping to one side, screaming even louder.

Hazel was on top of the monster a second later, her Wolf Paw cloaking both hands. Fingers interlaced, they came down on the pig's head with a loud *crack*, driving the monster's skull into the ground and sending a spray of blood across the road as it shattered like an overripe melon.

"Phew! Remind me not to get on your bad side," Mallory said, giving her a grin. "That was some technique."

"Collect the body," Carver said to his fighters as they caught up. "The meat will probably be good to eat."

344

"Almost normal," Nate repeated as Carver sheathed his weapons.

Their group continued on, making their way quickly to where Noam was camping out, but when they passed the halfway point, Nate was surprised to see the man appear on the road, speeding back on his scooter at a breakneck pace.

"Something's wrong," Nate said as the group slowed. "Otherwise, he wouldn't be coming back."

Sure enough, when Noam skidded to a stop next to them, he was breathing hard and sweating profusely. He must *really* have been moving to show such signs of exertion.

"What happened?" Nate asked.

"Freya's been found out," Noam said grimly. "They've confiscated her Magigun and have her tied up. They're also breaking camp and moving out. Colette is suspicious now."

"Update us as we go," Nate said, breaking into a jog, the rest of them following.

"It happened just thirty minutes ago," Noam said, keeping pace. "I heard shouting from inside and a few of Freya's spells went off. She ran out but was tackled by a couple of those mind-controlled kids. I don't know what gave her away, but after they took her weapon and tied her up, Colette came out.

"She ordered everyone to pack up and said they were moving south, away from the city."

"Did their group split?" Nate asked, feeling fear and guilt beginning to set in.

He shouldn't have sent her in there on her own. He should have gone with his original plan of taking the woman and torturing her until she let everyone go.

"No," Noam said. "They're sticking together. But Colette has her right next to her and she's surrounded herself with her brainwashed minions. She'll be on guard now too, so extracting Freya is going to be hard, especially if we don't want casualties."

"We need to get her out," Nate said, wracking his brain for any ideas.

This was as bad as it got. Every second she was with them, was another second in which they could kill her. She'd be able to create some space, but taking on some forty-odd fighters on her own and without her Magigun would be impossible.

345

"If you're open to it, I might have an idea," Hazel said, interrupting his thoughts.

"Let's hear it then," Nate said.

If anyone had something that would work, he would gladly listen. Freya's life was on the line and it was his fault, which meant that it was now his responsibility to get her out of it.

53

Freya could not believe she'd been so stupid. Things had been going perfectly fine until the point where she'd accidentally let it slip that she hadn't come to Laybor alone. She'd been sitting with Colette at the time, just talking idly.

The woman was so easy to talk to that she'd allowed herself to relax a bit *too* much. They'd been talking about going into the mines, where she'd punched a horse on a bet and when Colette had asked whom she'd made the bet with, Freya had said, without even thinking.

"Oh, just my friend Nate."

What had followed was immediate suspicion and more questioning, but when she saw she wasn't going to be able to talk her way out of it, she'd tried to run.

Colette then sicked her brainwashed hounds on her. Freya had managed to send a few of them away, but there were *far* too many and when they'd caught her, right outside the cabin, she'd wanted to scream in frustration.

She hadn't wanted to do this in the first place. She was a terrible liar, though in hindsight, she might have told Nate that before he'd pushed her into this situation. She was sure Noam had been watching and thought she'd seen him when she was being hogtied with her face pressed to the dirt.

"You know, the longer you remain silent, the worse for you it will be," Colette said, tugging hard on the rope around her neck.

Freya did *not* like being led around like a dog on a leash. She was seriously rethinking her ideas on torture.

"I don't understand why you keep refusing to speak with me," Colette said.

"Probably because you tied me up like an animal and are now treating me like some sort of criminal," Freya spat.

If there was one positive in this whole situation, it was that Colette wasn't sure why she was here, nor did she know how many friends Freya had. But someone who did things as awful as she did would be paranoid.

"I would be happy to remove the ropes if you would just talk," Colette said. "I am not the enemy here. The man in the sky is."

"You've sure got a funny way of showing it," Freya shot back.

"Come now, just speak!" Colette snapped, apparently tired of playing nice.

"You smell like a week-old turd left out to rot," Freya said.

"What?" the woman asked, blinking in confusion.

"You told me to speak. I spoke," Freya said. "You reek. Like, really badly. Have you heard of this new thing called bathing? I hear it's all the rage these days."

A ringing slap caught Freya across the side of her face. Her head rocked to one side, her neck jerking against the rope as stars danced in her vision. She tasted blood. Still, when she straightened, she gave the woman a bloody smile.

"For the life of me, I can't understand how any of your lackeys even follow you, what with how bad you smell."

Not a single one of the teens surrounding them had so much as blinked at her treatment. It was hardly a surprise, considering how this woman operated.

"They, unlike you, came from a *civilized* country," Colette snarled. "One where innate rudeness and pettiness isn't common."

"Really? So all French people are just the nicest in the whole world? Somehow, I find that hard to believe with all those angry chefs screaming in people's faces on those cooking shows all the time."

"You are a very strange girl," Colette said, narrowing her eyes.

She raised her hand to deliver another slap when someone called to her.

"Someone's coming," one of the girls said. "They're moving pretty fast."

"Get into formation," Colette ordered, glaring at Freya the entire time. "Who's coming?"

"How should I know?" Freya said. "You've been holding me prisoner all day."

"It's a girl," someone called. "She's running fast. Looks like there's a pack of monsters on her tail."

348

"How many?" Colette asked, looking suspiciously between Freya and the now-visible girl.

"Six," the boy replied. "Should we help her?"

"No," Colette said after a moment of thought. "Let them rip her to pieces."

"Wow, talk about cold," Freya said. "Did your mother drop you on your head as a baby, or were you always a sociopath?"

"Shut up!" Colette snapped, grabbing the side of her face. "Watch. Watch your friend be torn to bloody shreds!"

Freya watched, but the fifteen-year-old girl was *not* torn to shreds. When she saw the group wasn't going to be offering her any help, she turned and attacked the monsters, ripping them to pieces with fuzzy white paws covering her hands.

It was the most bizarre display Freya had ever seen, the girl dancing and twisting through the beasts, pulling feats of acrobatics that she'd never thought possible in avoiding them. By the time she'd killed more than half the pack, Colette had released her face and was watching in interest.

The girl quickly dispatched the remaining monsters, then whirled on the group angrily.

"What's the big idea?" she demanded, walking up to them and yelling. "I could have been killed and you all just stood there and did nothing!"

"Move," Colette commanded, and her brainwashed minions moved out of her way, leaving the space between them open. "I will not fall for this trick again girl," Colette said, dragging Freya with her. "We have already captured your friend. What makes you think we can't do the same to you?"

"Friend?" the girl asked, looking between Colette and Freya. "Lady, I've never seen her before in my life!"

Clearly, Colette could tell she wasn't lying, but that didn't stop her from rounding on Freya to demand answers.

"Who is she? Tell me!"

"Beats me," Freya said. "Never seen her before today."

"Grab her," Colette said to her mind-slaves.

Her pack of mindless minions moved to obey, seizing the girl by her arms.

"Oh, so first you leave me to fend for myself and then when I kill those monsters for you, you treat me like some sort of criminal?

Gosh, you people are *horrible*, you know that? When my dad's crew finds you, they *won't* be happy."

"What crew?" Colette asked suspiciously.

"I was traveling with my dad and some of his army buddies," the girl said with a shrug. "We got separated, but they're good at tracking, so they'll find us easily enough."

"And you expect me to be afraid of your daddy?" Colette sneered.

"I couldn't care less if you are or aren't," the girl said with a shrug. "But you'll pay if you so much as scratch me."

"Hey, do you think your dad can help me out too?" Freya asked, feeling hopeful.

"No one's going anywhere," Colette roared. "And if someone comes looking for a fight, we'll just turn them into more kanta."

"Whatever you say," the girl said with a grin. "Because it looks like my dad's found me."

There was a loud *bang* to the group's right and Colette spun in the direction the sound had come from. A loud shout followed, and a moment later, and several voices calling a name that Freya couldn't quite make out.

"Formation!" Colette ordered. "Everyone, forward positions!"

She backed away, dragging Freya along with her, looking nervous.

"Hey, lady," the girl said, and Colette whirled on her, glaring.

She froze, seeing her two mind-slaves lying on the ground, pinned there by a pair of insubstantial-looking white wolves. Before she could so much as react, the girl's fist cracked into her nose, her head whipping back and away from Freya.

In the same motion, she snagged Freya's rope, slashing it with a heavy-looking knife, freeing her.

"You little *brat*!" Colette snarled, not quite having lost her balance.

She clutched her nose, which was bleeding, but aside from that, she hadn't sustained much damage.

"I'll show you how to-" She abruptly cut off, as a glowing, white fist sank into her stomach, blasting the air from her lungs.

Colette folded over the fist, collapsing to the ground and heaving up her lunch.

"About time you showed up," Freya snapped, as the girl slashed the ropes from her wrist. "You know, I really hate playing the damsel in distress, but if you sweep me off my feet, I might just forgive you."

"Can you carry her?" Nate asked, turning to the younger girl and hooking a thumb over his shoulder.

"I can do that," the girl said. "But it'll be a bumpy ride."

"Good," Nate said, giving her a savage grin. "It'll teach her a lesson."

"Nate, what in the world is going on?" Freya asked, looking between him and the shorter girl.

"I'll explain later," Nate said, grabbing her arm and dragging her close.

"Oh, Nate, do we have time for this?" Freya breathed, fanning her face.

She knew they were in a dangerous spot as the distraction that Nate and the little girl had caused had only been temporary. Colette was wheezing and shouting to her brainwashed minions to come save her and they would be on top of them in just a few seconds.

Nate rolled his eyes, then grabbed her under her knees and lifted her in a princess carry.

"Oh, my shining knight," Freya said, placing her cheek to his chest. "I knew you'd come for me. Take me away to your castle, so that we may live happily ever after."

"You got her?" Nate shouted to the girl.

"Yup," the girl said, having seized Colette under her arms, locking her own to her sides.

This had Colette's back to the girl, shoulders pulled back at an awkward angle. Due to the height difference, Colette's feet were still touching the ground.

"Let's move," Nate said, exploding forward in w rush of motion.

The girl was able to keep up, her feet slapping the ground four times for every one of Nate's massive steps. She was quite sure he was using the technique built into his armor – which she noted he was wearing – as small jets of flame basted from his feet as he ran.

351

It was nice to be rescued in this way, Freya admitted to herself. Even if she hadn't much enjoyed being captured and slapped around. Still, she would be getting her revenge.

They were quickly pulling away from the group of pursuing youths and none of them dared cast any spells, for fear of hitting Colette. Their pace slowed a bit as Nate's armor stopped blazing, but they continued to outpace the group, running until they were nothing nut specs on the horizon.

"Seriously?" Freya said, when she saw where they were going. "Couldn't you have picked somewhere more romantic for our getaway?"

"Sorry, this was the best we could come up with on short notice," he said, stopping before the door and setting her down.

"Aww," Freya said, hanging onto him. "I enjoyed being swept off my feet like that."

"You're back!"

Freya turned, seeing a woman with long, curly hair, running from the open door of the cabin where she'd been held captive, Noam standing in the doorway behind her and looking relieved.

"So, Nate," she said, giving him a sly smile. "Care to introduce me to your pretty friend?"

"This is Mallory," Nate said, ignoring her barb. "Mallory, this is Freya."

"I'm so glad you're okay," Mallory said, grabbing her face and turning her jaw this way and that. "That bruise looks nasty. What did that witch do to you?"

"Nothing I won't be doing to her," Freya said, extricating herself from the handsy woman and cracking her knuckles. "You know what they say," she continued, looking at the still dazed Colette, lying on the ground and holding her gut. "Payback is a-"

54

The plan had been simple enough. Hazel would approach the group in the same way Freya had. They didn't think it would work twice, but once she dealt with the monsters, the group should be put off guard for a bit.

Hazel's job from there was to separate Freya and Colette from the rest of the group, using Carver and the six fighters they'd brought with them. Once they were separated, Nate, who'd be hiding nearby, would move, using his Whitefire Injection as soon as the opening was created.

They'd grab both Freya and Colette before the woman could react and then retreat.

One of Mallory's fighters was a Booster-type Magician, meaning that he'd been able to give them both a significant speed increase, which had allowed them to move as they did. He was now recovering within the cabin, as it had basically taken all his kanta to imbue them both for the ten minutes they needed the boost.

The plan couldn't have gone better if they'd tried, which was honestly a miracle. Hazel had improvised everything, pulling her part off flawlessly and convincing Colette she was in real and imminent danger.

"How much time do we have?" Mallory asked as she helped drag the kicking woman into the house.

"Ten minutes at most," Nate said, holding the woman's feet.

Freya and Hazel followed them in while Noam pulled some rope from his inventory.

They bound the woman to the table, Colette kicking and struggling all the while, hurling threats and promises of death.

"You've got a big mouth for a prisoner," Freya said, then clocked her in the jaw.

Her punch did a fair bit more damage than Hazel's, though in her defense, Hazel was only rank 32 – she'd gone up in the battle against the monsters – while Freya was at 40.

They tied her hands and feet and pulled the rope over her stomach which was burned and bleeding. It seemed Nate's punch had done a number on her.

"Okay," Noam said grimly. "If you can't stomach torture, you should leave."

No one left, the five of them remaining where they were.

Nate moved to the side of the table. "Let's see what we're working with here."

He seized the woman's hand then pulled the glove from her fingers, revealing a black 47 as well as a storage ring.

"No way," Nate said, staring at the ring. "You could *not* have been this stupid."

It was an ordinary storage ring. Nothing special about it whatsoever.

"Oh, my baby!" Freya cried when Nate handed her her Magigun.

She cradled it in her arms, muttering about how Mommy would never let it go again.

Ignoring her antics, Nate looked around the ring for a moment more then moved the gleaming pen, holding it up before Colette's face.

"That's mine," she snarled, trying to lunge for it, but found herself unable to move more than an inch.

"That it is," Nate said, tapping the pen against his palm – he knew they were short on time, and continuing to run wasn't really an option. "So, here's what you're going to do. You're going to let all those teenagers go."

"I don't know what you're talking about," Colette spat. "Everyone follows me of their own free will!"

"Sure, they do," Nate said dryly. "Just like Freya volunteered to tie herself up, right?"

"She was a spy," Colette snarled, turning her head to glare at Freya. "A filthy mongrel sent to sow discord within my group."

"Why would you think someone had sent her to spy on you?" Nate asked with a raised eyebrow. "Unless you were doing something amoral and were afraid of being caught."

Colette's lips peeled back, and she gave him a grim smile.

"I have nothing to say to you, *filth*!"

"Well, I'll just be keeping this then," Nate said, dropping her pen into his ring. "No more brainwashing for you."

"Go to hell!" she roared, thrashing against her bonds. "When I get out of here, I'm going to kill you all!"

"But that's just it," Nate said, his voice lowering to a menacing growl. "You're not getting out of here."

A gleaming dirk appeared in his grip, the tip of the blade tickling the woman's throat.

"Now, you can either make this easy on yourself, or we can do it the hard way. Your choice."

The woman spat in his face.

"Hard way it is then," Nate said, swiping a hand across his face.

He rose, looking around the room once again.

"I'll give you all one last warning. If you want to step out, now's your chance."

Once again, no one moved.

"I really don't want to do this," Nate said, moving around to Colette's side and seizing one of her hands. "Torture never was my specialty. Always preferred just killing things, but for you, I think I can make an exception."

"What are you doing?" Colette demanded, some of the anger leaking from her voice.

He raised her hand, dragging her index finger out and extending it straight, then pressed the tip of the dirk to the space between her finger and nail.

"Last chance," Nate said, staring the woman in the eye.

He could see the fear there, visible as the sweat on the woman's brow.

"Never!" she screamed. "I won't let some nobody force me to do anything!"

Nate's lips flattened, then he slowly slid the dirk home. Colette's scream was so loud that it caused everyone to flinch. Freya and Mallory both looked away, suddenly not so sure about being there. Hazel did not. She stared at the woman the entire time, even as Nate slid the dirk in farther. Blood welled at the point of the blade as he continued to slide it home.

"Stop! Stop! Please!" Colette screamed, tears welling in the corners of her eyes. "I'll let them go! I'll let them go!"

Nate paused, though he left the knife in place.

"I'll let them go," the woman panted, looking both terrified and in a great deal of pain.

Nate had to fight down the swell of pity that rose within him. It gave him no pleasure to inflict this kind of pain, especially when the person in question couldn't even fight back.

The door behind him slammed, and Nate turned to see Carver standing there. The man was sweating and breathing hard, clearly having run all this way.

"Please tell me you've got her," he said as he walked in. "They're right on our tail."

"Colette here was just about to let them go, isn't that right, Colette?" Nate said.

The woman nodded vehemently as the tears continued to run down her cheeks.

Nate dismissed the dirk, cutting off the flow of kanta. Blood began to pool under the nail, gathering in beads and dripping from her finger. Colette continued to sob, making him feel worse. He had to remind himself once again that this woman was a murderer, had killed dozens of people, if not more, and deserved nothing better than this.

"Get on with it," Nate growled, summoning another dirk. "That is, unless you want me to start again."

The woman's eyes went wide as saucers, and she quickly shook her head.

"I'm doing it! I'm doing it!" she yelled.

A wave of power washed over them, rippling into the distance, then another and another.

"I can see them!" one of Mallory's fighters – a woman by the name of Eve – said.

"Why are they still coming?" Carver demanded.

"She can only free them one at a time," Nate replied. "It's why I picked this spot in the first place. We needed somewhere defensible, and this was the best I could find given the circumstances."

The waves of magic continued as the group of teens drew closer. Even from here, Nate could see people dropping off, suddenly stopping their charge and looking confused. Only about half of them had been freed by the time they closed with the house. None of the Magicians fired on the structure – likely for the same reason they hadn't done so earlier – but the Cultivators closed

356

quickly, various techniques and powers running through their bodies as they attacked.

"Stunning blows only!" Mallory commanded, apparently having overcome her revulsion at the torture inflicted on the woman.

A tall boy rushed Carver, swinging a glowing fist at his temple. The man swayed to one side, then smashed him across the side of his head with the flat of his cleaver. The boy staggered away, only to be replaced by two more.

Now that they were close, Colette suddenly decided that she was strong again, stopping her spell to free them and screaming for her brainwashed minions to come save her. Nate drove another dirk into her thigh, eliciting another scream of pain from the woman.

"Stop one more time, and I'll take your eye next," Nate snarled.

The waves of magic started up almost immediately after that as Mallory's group began being pushed back toward the cabin.

"I'm going to join them," Noam said, stepping toward the door.

"Me too," Hazel said, moving to join him.

"This shouldn't take too much longer," Nate said.

Even as they spoke, several of the teens were stepping back, rubbing their heads and looking confused. There were still around twenty of them attacking though, including Genevieve, Colette's sister, but with everyone working together, Nate was hopeful they'd be able to hold the group back.

Already, two of Mallory's fighters had taken hits, one to the thigh and another to the side of his head. The latter had been laid out flat, while the former was still trying to fight. Having to only use non-lethal force would be difficult given the situation, but he was confident that Mallory and the others would be able to handle themselves.

Freya's spells continuously flashed, her Tele-bang driving many back and holding them long enough for Colette's spell to free them. Noam's Total Guardian technique was moving around the battlefield as well, blocking many of the advancing teens and keeping them at bay. Hazel dodged between attacks, smacking her attackers' legs and knees, dropping them like flies. There were more than a few broken bones, but as long as they remained alive, they could be healed.

Another of Mallory's fighters went down, and someone dragged them into the cabin, placing the unconscious woman on the ground near the door. Someone else limped in, dropping to the ground and clutching their bleeding leg.

The fight was happening too quickly, and even though Colette continued to free her prisoners, they still outnumbered them by more than two to one. Slowly, their group was pushed back until they were mere inches from the cabin door. Six more had been freed and several were down for the count. However, nine fighters remained, and they continued to push forward.

Freya cried out in pain as a gleaming spear struck her in the gut, blood welling at the point of impact as it was ripped free. In response, she blasted the woman in the face with her Blinding Buckshot, causing her to stagger away.

"I don't know how much longer we're gonna last!" Freya groaned as she staggered into the cabin, clutching her bleeding stomach.

She looked like she was going to be sick, but Nate knew that with her healing spell, she'd be fine, at least if they survived the next couple of minutes.

"Come on!" Mallory shouted. "We're nearly there!"

The woman would be the least effective of them all in this battle. Her Snare would be able to stop some of the attacking teens, but any of her other spells wouldn't work on people who were already ensnared by someone else. It was one of the weaknesses in her current pool of spells, one that Nate knew she'd be shoring up after this battle.

An explosion of toxin-covered needles drove into the legs of two more teens, dropping them with screams of pain. When last they'd met, the poison had done nothing more than cause a mild numbing. Now though, the teens remained on the ground for a full four seconds, completely paralyzed. Had Mallory wanted to kill them, she could have done so with impunity. Instead, she went about setting another trap.

Two more of Mallory's fighters staggered in, nursing injuries, but as the seconds crept by, things began to look better. Slowly, the fighters stopped getting up to return to battle as Colette's spell freed them of her control, and by the time only four of them were left, their group was able to keep them away long enough for the spell to run its course.

Genevieve staggered, clutching her head as the wave washed over her, the bonds on her mind vanishing in an instant. She swayed on her feet for a moment, then collapsed in a groaning heap.

"There!" Colette snarled. "They're all free!"

"We'll see about that," Nate said, then turned to the fighters who remained on their feet. "Let's gather everyone up. I want to make sure she's kept her word."

The first of those who'd been freed were already on their feet, many of them carrying a haunted look that Nate knew well. They would be remembering all they had done under Colette's control, and although they knew they hadn't been in control of their actions, the memories would haunt them.

In short order, everyone was gathered, the group of forty-odd teens shuffling slowly into place. No one wanted to look up or meet anyone's eyes. Some began crying, some began to scream, and others just *stood* there.

"Is everyone accounted for?" Carver asked.

He was bleeding from several cuts to his arms but was otherwise unharmed.

Genevieve slowly rose to her feet, looking between the group gathered behind her and the woman bound to the table in front of her. She looked afraid, repulsed, and, at the same time, worried.

"I know this is a lot to ask for," Mallory said, when Nate motioned to her behind her back. "But can you tell me if anyone here is missing?"

She spoke kindly, gently, with a compassion that the Mallory of Nate's time had never possessed.

Genevieve looked around, searching the faces of the gathered teens. Finally, she shook her head.

"Everyone's here," she said, her voice low and subdued.

Mallory gave Nate a thumbs up.

"Good," Nate said, his voice hard. "Get them out of here."

At his words, Genevieve turned in his direction, suddenly fearful.

"Wait...You're not going to hurt her, are you?"

"Help me, Genevieve!" Colette screamed, thrashing against her ropes. "They're going to torture and kill me! Help your sister! He-!"

Nate clamped a hand over her mouth, giving Mallory a meaningful look.

"Come on," Mallory said, pulling the girl away. "Let's get you somewhere safe where you can recover. You must have been through quite a lot."

"What are you going to do with her?" Genevieve demanded as the other teens gathered around Carver, the man speaking to them in soothing tones.

The remainder of Mallory's group was being tended to by one of their own – it seemed she'd brought someone who specialized in healing – and Carver led the uninjured away from the cabin.

"They're going to kill me, Ginny!" Colette yelled, managing to struggle free. "Please, stop them! Save me!"

Genevieve struggled in Mallory's grip as the woman dragged her away, looking to Nate and obviously not knowing what to do.

"Get her out of here," Nate told Noam, who'd just finished helping Freya recover from her gut wound.

Noam nodded, getting to his feet and helping Mallory drag the girl away, kicking and screaming all the while. The door slammed behind them, leaving Nate, Freya, and Colette as the room's only occupants.

The woman turned terrified eyes from the door to Nate, who still clutched a golden dirk in his grip.

"Please," she begged. "You don't have to kill me! You have my Tome; I can't do anything without it!"

"I think we both know that isn't true," Nate said. "You can learn plenty of magic without the aid of your Tome. Besides, you've killed far too many people for me to just let you go."

The begging continued, and Freya looked at him, the uncertainty of what they were doing clear in her eyes. It was one thing to kill someone in battle. It was quite another to murder someone who was begging for their lives when they were helpless like this.

"I'll give you anything you want!" the woman continued. "Do you want points? I'll give you everything I have!"

Nate was tempted, as he could only imagine how much the woman had amassed, but when he thought about the origin of those points, he decided he'd rather not.

"You've caused a great deal of pain and suffering," Nate said as the woman continued to sob. "This world will be better off without you in it."

"No wai-!"

Colette was cut off as Nate's dirk plunged through her chest, shattering ribs and piercing straight into her heart. The woman thrashed for a few moments longer, her brain not quite registering what had happened. Then the woman's eyes glazed over, and she went still.

A rush of kanta flooded into Nate as the woman expired, pushing him forward two entire ranks from 41 to 43. Killing someone that much higher in rank than you would do that, especially if they were human.

Freya looked at her own hand, tugging her glove off and examining the dark 41, standing out against her pale skin.

"I know what we did was right," she said, her voice somber. "But I still don't feel good about it."

"Yeah," Nate agreed. "Neither do I."

55

"What do you mean, *gone*?" Nate asked, looking between Carver and Mallory.

"Exactly what I said," Carver said, looking annoyed. "I turned my back on her for just a second and when I turned back, she wasn't there. We sent a party our to look for her, but I'm doubtful they're going to have any luck."

"It was like she vanished into thin air," Noam said, crossing his arms. "I have never seen anything like it."

"We can go look for her," Freya said.

"No," Nate sighed, shaking his head. "She'll be good at hiding. From what I got; she's got a spell that helps conceal her from prying eyes. If she doesn't want to be found, she won't be."

Nate and Freya had emerged from the cabin to find Mallory and Carver in a panic. Apparently, Genevieve had given them the slip and no matter how they looked; they couldn't find where she'd gone. Despite the fact that the landscape was flat and there were few true hiding places.

Carver let out a long sigh, looking into the distance with pity in his eyes.

"Wherever that girl is, I hope she comes to her senses soon. This world is *dangerous* at the best of times and downright *deadly* the rest."

"Tell me about it," Nate said, looking to the gathered group of teens standing a small way off.

The older ones in the group had come to themselves and were moving around, talking to the younger members in hushed tones.

"So, what are you going to do with them?" He asked.

"We're going to take them back with us," Carver said. "We have a couple of therapists who've joined us recently and after what that woman put them through, they're going to need someone to talk to."

"You won't be able to stay in Warine forever you know," Nate said. "That world is a ticking time bomb."

"We know," Carver said. "But they need somewhere stable to recover for the time being. Once everything is settled and everyone is strong enough to make the transition over to Laybor, we'll make our move."

"Don't wait too long," Nate warned, then, extended his hand. "Thank you," he said. "Without your help, there's no way we'd have been able to free them all of her control. Especially not without taking serious injuries or inflicting casualties."

"Thank *you* for coming to us," Carver said, shaking his hand. "I know there was some nasty business with that woman, but thanks to what you did, these kids have a chance at recovering and living a good life. Well, as good as life gets in this crazy world, we've found ourselves in."

Carver clapped him on the shoulder, then turned and went back to the group. In the distance, Nate could see Mallory's fighters returning. Even from here, he could tell that they were on their own.

"What about you Nate?" Mallory asked, looking over her shoulder. "Are you going to come back with us?"

"I'm afraid not," Nate said, shaking his head. "There's too much that needs to be done here."

Mallory sighed and gave him a sad smile.

"It seems like we have to keep saying goodbye."

"It won't be forever," Nate assured her. "I'm sure we'll be seeing each other again real soon."

Mallory wrapped her arms around him in a tight embrace, which Nate returned, ignoring Freya's presence, despite knowing she was going to be using this as soon as Mallory was gone.

"Take care of yourself Nate," Mallory said, pulling away from him. "I don't know if I can handle losing someone else."

She then leaned up and kissed him on the cheek again, though Nate noticed that she lingered *just* a bit longer this time as she did.

"I'll see you around Mallory," Nate said, as she stepped back, her cheeks colored pink. "Say hi to your kids for me."

She hesitated for a moment, as though she wanted to say something, then shook her head and turned to Freya, Noam, and Hazel.

"Watch his back. If anything happens to him, I'll come for you in your sleep...So, no pressure!"

With that, she walked away, humming softly to herself as she went to join Carver and the newly-freed teenagers.

"She's *scary*," Freya said with an exaggerated shiver.

"Tell me about it," Hazel said, watching Mallory go.

Nate didn't comment either way, though he had to wonder at the seriousness of her threat. *If* he were to die, *would* Mallory come after the others? If this were the old Mallory, he'd say yes, without a shadow of a doubt. But this new Mallory was different. More lighthearted and easygoing. She was nice and actually *cared* about people. Though, whether she would follow up on a threat like that or not, Nate would never know.

Either because she'd never have to fulfill it, or, because he'd be dead and have no way of knowing.

"So," Noam said, as he watched the group be shepherd away. "What now?"

"More importantly," Freya said, turning to Hazel. "Who exactly *are* you? I mean, thanks for saving my life and all, but I feel like I'm being left out."

"Hazel Wilson," Hazel said, sticking her hand out. "It's nice to meet you."

Freya shook the woman's hand, looking a bit put out by how friendly she was being.

"I met her in City One-Forty-Four G," Nate said. "She saw me defeat Ashland in Warine and followed me here. They've got her sister, and I told her that if she helped us, we'd help get her out."

"Ashland has your *sister*?" Freya asked.

"Yeah," Hazel said, her smile fading. "They've had her for well over two months now. I'm worried about what they're going to use her for."

"Use her?" Freya asked, looking between Nate and Hazel.

"It's a bit of a long story," Hazel said. "But here it is in a nutshell…"

Hazel explained what had happened, recounting the tale of her sister's involvement with the Ashland Guild and her attempts to get her out.

"Gosh, that sounds horrible," Freya said. "I can relate."

"What, to trying to get a sister out from under the clutches of an evil organization?" Hazel asked.

"Father," Freya said. "And yes."

364

"Oh…I'm sorry," Hazel said.

"Don't be," Freya replied. "As it turned out, he didn't need my help. Let's just hope for your sake that your sister isn't the same."

"She's not," Hazel said with certainty.

"The question still remains," Noam said. "What do we do now?"

That *was* a good question.

Nate had expected it to take *weeks* before Colette was taken down, but thanks to his friends, the operation had gone *far* faster and easier than he could have imagined. They didn't need to report their victory to Colin and his Guild for several weeks still, but going earlier would ensure that people started traveling through faster.

Additionally, it meant being able to set up security by the busier portals, to assure that no one would be waiting to kill them on the other side. There *were* still other Portal Reavers out there, despite their takedown of Rose Sombre. So, having someone to guard the portals would be of utmost importance.

On top of that, he had his promise to Hazel to fulfil and if her sister really was the same Rebecca Wilson he was thinking of, he *desperately* wanted her on his team. Keeping Hazel around was also something he *really* wanted, especially once she got the to second tier of her Path.

There was also the mystery of what was going on in the central area of Labor's G-quadrant and it was something that was nagging at the back of his mind.

"Alright," Nate said, finally coming to a decision. "Here's the plan. First, we head to the abandoned work sites and see what's going on over there. I have the distinct feeling that we're going to want to check it out. Once that's done, we'll head back to Warine and give Colin the good news. Once that's done, we'll go to Southside Eight, where we'll have a chat with my friend Dirk. With his help and the Ashland Guild divided, we should be able to put a stop to them on Warine, though Selena and her followers will undoubtedly escape, as they're already here on Laybor. Does that sound agreeable to everyone?"

"I have a question," Hazel said. "Why can't we go after my sister first? Who *knows* what they're doing to her while we're here."

"I understand that you're worried," Nate said. "But you need to do some training if we're going to stand a chance against Ashland. Right now, even with Dirk's help, it's going to be difficult to take a Guild that large. But if we have a team of powerful fighters – that being us – it might make all the difference."

"I wanted to go charging headlong when I knew where my father was being held," Freya said, patting the shorter girl on the shoulder. "Nate knows what he's doing, you can trust that much."

Hazel still hesitated, but slowly, she nodded, agreeing to his plan.

"So, where do we go from here?" Noam asked.

"We'll head back to City One-Forty-Four G for supplies and a shopping trip, then we'll make for the center of the quadrant. It'll take a few days to get there, so I'd like to make sure we move as quickly as we can."

Everyone was glad for the rest, so together, they all headed back to the city. They didn't run into Mallory's group, as they'd left some twenty minutes after they had, and they'd had to walk, thanks to Hazel's lack of a scooter.

They reached the city by early afternoon, where they resupplied, got something for lunch, then went to the shop to buy Hazel a scooter and hopefully convince her to upgrade her Manual.

56

"Are you *sure* this is a good idea?" Hazel asked, looking between the Manual clutched in her hands and the counter, where the gnark waited impatiently for her to hand it over.

"Either hand it over, or leave," the female gnark said. "I don't have all day here."

There wasn't a single other person in the shop and the gnark was going nowhere. Nate could have pointed that out, but he didn't really like the idea of having to even *talk* to this creature for any longer than he had to.

"If you won't take his advice, take mine," Freya said. "I'm *way* stronger with my second tier Tome and Noam over there's got his all the way up at the *third*!"

Noam nodded, watching the entire exchange impassively. He and Nate had gotten a chance to talk, and Nate had explained that Hazel would hopefully be becoming a member of their team, along with her sister, should they manage to rescue her.

"But it's so expensive," Hazel said. "What if I need the points for something else?"

"You won't even be spending *half* your points," Freya said. "It'll be worth it."

Hazel seemed to waver for a moment, even as the gnark continued tapping her fingers on the counter.

"Oh, okay," she said, shoving the Manual onto the counter and pressing her hand to the orb.

She looked like she wanted to jerk it away on reflex, so it was lucky that the points were taken almost as soon as she'd placed her hand upon the glassy surface.

"I hope this was worth it," Hazel said, staring forlornly at her hand.

She'd already had to spend 450 points on a Low-Kanta scooter and hadn't been happy about it, so spending a whopping 46,000 likely wasn't doing her any favors.

The gnark grumbled under her breath as she opened the manual, removed a stamp, and pressed it to the bottom of a page. Immediately, the manual shone, growing brighter, more detail flowing onto the cover and the patches of fur shimmering for a moment, before going still.

"Here," she said, shoving the manual back at Hazel. "Now, if that's everything. *Get out*."

Hazel quickly scrambled away from the chair, the venom in the gnark's voice clearly surprising her.

"You know, one of these days, someone not as patient as we will come in here," Nate said, as Hazel cracked the cover of her Manual. "When that day comes, I hope you remember this conversation."

The gnark spat at him, then turned her head and pretended they didn't exist, even going so far as to begin having a conversation with herself about how smelly and disgusting aliens were.

"Woah!" Hazel said, as light *literally* poured from the book, surrounding her in a halo of swirling white.

Nate felt her Core swell as her body was reinforced for a second time. Stronger muscle layered upon her thin frame, giving her greater strength, endurance, and speed. By the time she lowered her Manual, she felt significantly changed.

"Okay," she said, giving Nate a wide smile. "This was totally worth the point cost!"

"Don't keep us in suspense," Freya said excitedly. "What did you get!?"

"I only got two techniques this time," Hazel said. "But they both look pretty awesome. The first is called Sky Cry, this will boost the physical attributes of anyone in my group. The larger the group, the greater the boost. The second, and I can't believe I'm saying this, is called Werewolf: Stage One. It looks like I'll get a bit hairy, grow sharp claws and teeth and grow about six inches. I'll also have enhanced strength and reflexes while it's active, and I'll be more resistant to damage."

"I like that first one," Freya said. "Though the second also sounds pretty cool. I never imagined we'd get to see werewolves in this world."

"Are you a fan?" Hazel asked, surprised.

"Are you kidding me?" Freya exclaimed. "I *loved* Hunk Wolf. That show was the bomb!"

"Me too!" Hazel exclaimed. "Wasn't Corlio just the dreamiest?"

368

"He was alright," Freya said, giving Nate a sidelong look. "I liked Matt much more."

"Really?" Hazel asked. "He isn't a lot of people's favorites."

"He was shirtless in nearly every scene he was in," Freya said with a shrug. "What can I say? I've got a thing for boys who do that. Speaking of, aren't you a bit young to be watching shows like Hunk Wolf?"

"I'm twenty-two," Hazel said.

"No way," Freya said.

Nate sighed, then turned and left the shop, Noam following closely behind as the girls chatted.

"Look at the positive side," Noam said. "At least now Freya has someone else to bother."

The man did make a good point. Perhaps with Hazel around, Freya would forget all about teasing him now that there was someone else around to occupy her attention.

"Would you look at the size of that building, Nate?" Freya said, pointing into the distance. "You know what they say about people who build big buildings, right?"

"I'm assuming it's something along the lines of compensating for something," Nate deadpanned.

"Nate would never build a building that big," Freya said, turning to Hazel. "He's too busy being a sourpuss."

It had been four long days since they'd left City 144G and Nate's hopes of Freya leaving him alone had been dashed not half an hour after they left the city. It seemed that now that there was another girl in the group, she had someone to gossip with. Unfortunately for Nate, it seemed *he* was one of those topics. Much to his horror, Hazel had readily joined in the conversation, basically egging Freya on whenever they got onto the topic.

The shorter woman didn't have Freya's sick sense of humor, but she did enjoy talking. A *lot*. Which meant that the stretches of silence they used to get on their trips were now a thing of the past. If there was one thing Nate was grateful for, it was the fighting they'd been doing during their travels.

The death of Colette had bumped not only him and Freya up a few ranks but had pushed Noam up to 40 and Hazel up to 35. Their fights over the last few days had seen her rise to 38, their group

369

giving her the majority of the fighting to help her catch up. In the same time, Noam had grown to 41 and Freya to 42, while Nate had remained at 43.

He was feeling much more respectable now, despite knowing that the leaders were nearing 50 and the top fighters would already have passed it, he and his group were much closer to the top. If he had to guess, he'd say their small team probably ranked in the top 5% of humanity right now, which wasn't bad at all.

"You seem to call him that a lot," Hazel noted.

"Because he's no fun," Freya said. "He has no sense of humor and only ever grumbles at my genius wordplay and witty banter."

"That's because literally everything out of your mouth is in some way inappropriate," Nate shot back.

"Not *everything*," Freya said, giving him a sly grin.

"I rest my case," Nate said.

"I didn't even *say* anything inappropriate that time!" Freya said.

"No, but it was the *way* that you said it that matters," Nate replied. "Like you yourself once said, you can't turn it off. It's literally impossible."

"Is not," Freya said.

"Is so," Nate shot back.

"Is not!"

"Is so!"

"Is not!"

"Is so!"

"Is so!"

"I'm glad you agree," Nate said.

"Darn! Thought I had you there," Freya said.

"Are things always so lively in this group?" Hazel asked Noam, who'd remained mostly silent.

"No," Noam said, though a small grin touched his lips. "They're normally *much* worse. Freya's been on her best behavior since you joined."

"I'm always on my best behavior," Freya said. "An innocent and proper girl like me *has* to be. It's only right."

Hazel gave the woman a dubious look and Freya cracked a grin.

"Eh, being proper isn't all it's cracked up to be. I enjoy being loud and unapologetic instead. Life's more fun that way."

"I can agree with you there," Hazel said. "Do you remember the time Cartankus confessed his love to..."

Nate silently thanked the heavens that they were onto another topic, as he didn't think he could handle any more of Freya right now. She'd been pestering him for a dinner date for a while now, claiming he owed her after the whole fiasco with Colette. She'd bothered him so much about it that he'd eventually agreed, just to get her to stop. However, after he'd agreed, she'd started asking *when* and now that they were nearly in the final city before the abandoned sites began, he was planning on getting it out of the way.

They entered City 148G in the late afternoon, the group reluctantly deciding to stay in an inn, so that they could all gather more information before heading out into the wilderness the next day.

Noam and Hazel would be going in one group, while Nate and Freya would make up the other.

"Couldn't get enough of me, could you?" Freya teased once Noam and Hazel had left.

"I thought you'd want to go out on that dinner date you keep bothering me about," Nate said. "They both agreed to leave us alone, but if you don't want to..."

"If we're going to dinner, I need to change," Freya said, a wide grin stretching her face. "Come on Mister Sourpuss, follow me!"

Nate rolled his eyes but followed her all the same.

57

Nate stood outside Freya's room in the inn, tapping his foot impatiently. She'd dragged them back here, insisted he dress in something other than his armor, then vanished into her room. He was wearing his regular clothes, the ones designed to keep both the moisture and heat off himself. He doubted this was what Freya had meant, but he wasn't going to go spending points to buy something nicer.

This was a dinner he owed her, nothing more. If she wanted to call it a dinner date, she could, but he wasn't going to fall into whatever trap she was setting.

"Sorry I took so long," Freya said, as she opened the door to her room. "It took a while to do my hair."

All grumpiness at her lateness fled the second Nate laid eyes on her and his conviction from a moment ago that this wasn't a date was thrown out the window.

Freya was dressed in a sleeveless green top that flowed past her waist. A pair of cream-colored pants hugged her legs and she wore a pair of open-toed sandal-like shoes on her feet. Her fingers and toes had been painted green, as she wore a darker shade of the color around her eyes, making them stand out even more.

Her hair hung in long, golden waves down her back, framing her face and accentuating her cheekbones. Her lips were glossy and pink, and her cheeks had been dusted with something that Nate couldn't identify.

"That's okay," Nate said, hiding his surprise behind a calm façade. "I've never met a girl who can be ready as quickly as I can."

He was half-expecting some sort of crack from her, but she just smiled and did a turn.

"How do I look?" she asked.

"You look nice," Nate said.

"Just *nice*?"

"You look beautiful, as I'm sure you know," Nate said.

Once again, she surprised him by smiling instead of making some quip.

"Thank you," she said. "You look nice too, even if you decided not to wear a normal shirt."

"I wasn't going to waste points on something so pointless," Nate said.

"No, I guess you wouldn't," Freya said. "Now, are you going to offer me your arm, or am I going to have to take it myself?"

Nate extended his arm and Freya happily hooked her fingers into the crook of his elbow, the two of them heading out of the inn and down the road to the restaurant Nate had chosen.

"So," Freya said as they walked down the street, eliciting disapproving stares from *all* the borers there. "What made you finally decide to take me out?"

"You only asked me about a thousand times," Nate said. "How could I say no to that?"

"I can be a bit pushy sometimes, I know," Freya said, squeezing his arm. "I'm happy you decided to take me out. You can be quite stubborn."

"Look who's talking," Nate said, as they turned off the street and entered the restaurant.

"How can I...help you?" A borer waitress said as they entered, her friendly tone turning more guarded as she saw the two of them.

"A table for two please," Nate said.

He could see the borer visibly struggling not to say anything about the two of them physically touching in what they would see as an inappropriate manner. She managed to calm herself, forcing a pained smile onto her face.

"If you would follow me," she said, practically growling it out between her teeth.

She turned on her heel, grabbing a couple of menus and robotically walking towards the back of the eatery.

Freya laughed softly under her breath as the two of them followed. It sounded so genuine and unlike her usual barking laughter. It was strange, trying to compare the Freya he dealt with on a daily basis with this woman standing next to him.

The two of them were seated at a private table, shoved all the way into the back corner of the restaurant. Nate knew it had less to do with giving them privacy though and more to do with keeping the other customers from being assaulted by their inappropriate behavior.

"This place is so nice," Freya said, tucking a lock of hair behind one ear and raising the menu.

Nate noticed that she was wearing earrings, small emerald studs set in a yellow metal that he assumed to be gold. Just how much had she spent on these clothes and *when* had she even bought them?

"Yeah," Nate said, looking around. "It's supposedly the best place in the city."

"I can believe that," Freya said. "Never been to a place so nice in my entire life."

"Where was the nicest place you ever ate out?" Nate asked.

Freya got a far-away look in her eyes as they unfocused, a small smile playing at the corners of her lips.

"I had a friend back on Earth, Lucy. Her parents were pretty well-off, and I'd often stay by her when my father was away on extended trips. One time, he didn't come back when he'd promised. I was so upset that he'd extended his trip that her parents took us both to a place called Layna's Grapevine. It was one of the most fun experiences I'd ever had, though, I was only nine, so in retrospect, the place wasn't all that fancy.

"Still, we got to sit with napkins in our laps, and had waiters bring us a bread-bowl and some fancy-looking herb butter. I even got an entire steak to myself, even though I didn't come close to finishing it. It was a nice night."

"What happened? To your friend, I mean?"

"I don't know," Freya said sadly. "I saw her a couple of weeks before I ran off to America. Warned her to stay away from me. I think she knew something was wrong, because she kept trying to call, but I ignored all her calls. I kind of wish I'd have answered now though."

"Sorry I brought it up," Nate said, seeing her growing sad.

"No, don't be," she said, reaching across the table and taking his hand. "It's nice to talk about normal things. How about you? Did your family do anything interesting back on Earth?"

Nate chuckled at that, memories of his distant past flooding back in waves.

"We grew up in an area where people were constantly trying to outdo one another. Everyone constantly had to one-up each other. If the neighbor got a new car, you had to get a nicer one. If they got a new dog, you had to find a rarer and more desirable one. If someone threw a nice party, yours had to be nicer."

"That sounds both exhausting and expensive," Freya said with a small laugh.

"Oh, that doesn't even begin to cover the insanity of some of these people. This one time, my neighbors, the Jerkins, decided to rent an entire zoo and have it transported onto their lawn for their son's sixth birthday.

"Mind you, he only wanted a trip to the zoo for himself, but with his parents being who they were, there was no way they were going to do something so ordinary."

"They allowed the transportation of animals outside of zoos?" Freya asked, shocked.

"If you made a large enough donation, you could get anything in my neighborhood," Nate said with a laugh. "But, that's not the best part. They had some live demonstrations, and someone dragged Mrs. Jerkin up to hold some monkeys. Let's just say that the entire neighborhood found out that her supposedly real strawberry blond hair was just an elaborate wig, made up to cover up the fact that she was losing hair."

Freya snorted out a laugh at that, covering her mouth as people looked in their direction.

"Sorry," she said, still giggling. "I know it isn't something I should be laughing about. A girl in my school had a similar problem, but just picturing that lady in front of all those people..."

"Yeah," Nate said, still smiling. "She tired suing to have the monkey killed for embarrassing her. Claimed it had attacked her and was a menace to society. It backfired on her when it became state-wide news."

"How did she recover from something like that?" Freya asked.

"She didn't," Nate said. "The Jerkins sold their house and left. Never heard of them since."

"That *is* a funny story," Freya said, leaning froward a bit more. "Did it tell you about the time..."

The two of them chatted and laughed for the next couple of hours, pausing to place their orders and eat when the food arrived. Time seemed to fly by faster than Nate had realized and before long, the waitress was coming over to tell them the restaurant would be closing soon.

Still laughing, the two of them rose, Freya hooking her arm into his and leaving the dimly-lit room, exiting out into the damp air of the late evening.

The streets were already mostly deserted, lanterns coming on to illuminate the main road, upon which they had exited on to. The two of them lapsed into silence as they walked, making their way slowly back to the inn, where they both knew Hazel and Noam would be waiting.

Freya leaned her head against his shoulder, her long hair tickling his cheek. She let out a long sigh as the inn came into view, the two of them slowing even more as it did. Finally, they stopped, just a few short steps away from the front door.

It was dark out, the only light coming from the lanterns mounted to either side of the inn's door. Freya turned, her hands grasping Nate's, her thumbs moving in small circles over the sides of his hands.

"I had a really nice time tonight, Nate," she said. "The best I've had in a *long* time."

"Me too," Nate replied, thinking back to all the death and destruction he'd left behind.

This really *had* been a good night.

The two of them lapsed into silence again, neither really sure what to say next. Finally, Freya spoke, her voice containing a small hint of nervousness.

"You...wouldn't be interested in maybe doing this again sometime, would you?"

Nate wanted to say no. To put an end to whatever this was, right here and now. All the pain of his past, all the suffering he'd endured, the *mission* he had to save both his family and humanity coming to the forefront of his mind. But, the more he thought about it, the more they seemed like excuses, rather than valid reasons.

"Yes," Nate heard himself saying, even as he squeezed her hands a bit tighter. "I think I would like that very much."

Freya *beamed* at him then, a smile so wide that it lit up her entire face. She squeezed his hands in return, then released them, stepping back.

"I guess we should head to bed then."

"Yeah," Nate said. "It's gonna be a long day tomorrow."

Freya nodded, taking another step back.

"Well, good night then," she said.

"Good night," Nate replied.

She turned and headed for the door, then abruptly spun, walked quickly back, and kissed him on the cheek. It was just a peck, a small brush of her lips, but the area warmed as Freya quickly spun back, the back of her neck flushing red as she disappeared into the inn.

Nate reached up, touching his cheek where Freya had kissed him. On the one hand, he was happier than he'd been in a *long* time but on the other, he was silently asking himself what he'd gotten himself into.

Still, as he headed for his room, a smile broke out across his face, unbidden. Despite all that he told himself, he *had* enjoyed his time with Freya and was looking forward to the next opportunity when they might go out together.

58

"I'm going to *murder* that blasted wake-up bastard one of these days!" Freya snapped as they all met in the hallway the next morning.

And she's back, Nate thought, as the woman turned her eyes on him.

"You know, they're only doing their jobs," Nate said.

"Yeah, I bet you'd enjoy it wouldn't you," Freya said. "Banging down girls' doors at all hours of the night, hoping you could sneak a peek."

Nate sighed as she chuckled, though when Noam and Hazel weren't looking, her demeanor changed, and she gave him the same, warm smile she had last night. Her cheeks grew rosy, and she seemed suddenly shy, which was *strange* given the personality he'd come to know.

Had this been back on Earth, he might have wondered if this was some sort of serious mental condition, but here in the System of Twelve, this was her armor. Her way to keep unwanted emotions from being seen. She wasn't weak and that was the image of herself she was going to project to others.

"So, care to tell us what you found?" Nate asked, turning to Noam.

"It was actually Hazel who found the helpful information," Noam said. "All I got was a bunch of drivel about Morgito the Mighty and how he was going to eat all their children."

"Really?" Nate asked, turning to Hazel, who looked *very* tired.

"I'll be happy to tell you all about it, but over breakfast if you don't mind. It's too early in the morning to be awake, let alone having entire conversations."

"I'm with you there, sister," Freya said, throwing an arm around the smaller woman's shoulders. "Did I tell you about the time...?"

Nate walked with Noam to the inn's common room, where borers were already moving about, sipping their hot, green drinks, and speaking in hushed tones. There was definitely a feeling of apprehension in the air and those who were going out to work for the day did so with far more caution than Nate had seen with this race as a whole so far.

"So, how'd it go?" Noam asked, as the headed to the counter to grab their breakfast.

"It went pretty well," Nate said, covering a yawn. "Shockingly so."

"What did I tell you, eh?" Noam said, with a grin. "You just had to go for it."

"*It*," Nate said. "Was just dinner."

"If that's what you want to tell yourself, go right ahead," the man said, moving to get his food.

The four of them headed to the table, Freya apparently having gotten out all her frustrations about the borer who'd woken them up, as she didn't mention it once they'd sat down.

"So, what did you find?" Nate asked, as Hazel finished swallowing her second mouthful of eggs and toast.

She looked like she wanted to stay quiet, but sighed, as though resigning herself to their group's insane schedule.

"Noam and I split up after over an hour of searching, as we continued to run into the same story," Hazel said. "The people we talked to were all in either the market district or women in the housing areas. So, I decided to go look for someone who was older. Maybe lived near the walls. It took me nearly another hour before I found someone who had something interesting to say.

"This guy was a real old-timer. Looked like he'd seen his fair share o' days. His fur was all silver and his skin underneath was all wrinkled and everything. Anyway, I found him sitting outside on a rocker, staring out through the open gate, and muttering to himself. When I came over, he was nervous at first, cagey and unwilling to talk. But, I was patient and eventually, he opened up to me about what he thought was happening.

"He's convinced that the shutdowns have nothing to do with Morgito the Mighty. He claims he's seen it in the night, stalking around the perimeter of the wall."

"Seen what?" Freya asked, as Hazel paused to take a sip of water.

"He calls it the Phantom Wolf, claims it's the ghost of an ancient monster, the very same that caused the disappearances back in Morgito's days."

"How does he know it was a monster back then?" Freya asked.

"He claims his great-great-great-great grandfather was on the work site where it all happened," Hazel said, counting out the 'greats' on her fingers.

"That's an interesting claim," Nate said. "Didn't all the surviving members of that crew go missing?"

"Apparently not," Hazel said with a shrug. "He claims that a few people managed to escape by moving farther away from the abandoned quadrant."

"If that *is* the case, why has this monster returned?" Noam asked, puzzled.

"He claims it's come for him and all the survivors of that work site," Hazel said. "But after that his story starts getting a bit shaky. That was the best I could get out of him before he started muttering again about the Phantom Wolf."

"Have you heard at all about this Phantom Wolf?" Freya asked Nate.

"I can't say I have," Nate said, rubbing his chin.

"If you don't mind my asking, I've been noticing the two of you asking Nate a lot of questions," Hazel said, looking between the three of them. "Is there something I should know?"

Freya and Noam both turned to Nate. Clearly, they were waiting to see what he said. It would be a sign of how much he trusted this new member of their little group. Nate already did and he knew that once they saved her sister, Hazel would be more loyal still. The only known, would be Rebecca herself.

"Have you heard of augments?" Nate asked.

Hazel shook her head. So, Nate launched into the explanation, Freya helpfully chiming in to talk about her's and somehow getting Noam to promise a display of his own worked once they were outside.

"That's wild," Hazel said, shaking her head. "Talk about the odds."

"Odds?" Freya asked.

"Of me deciding to go after Nate when I saw him fighting Ashland. I guess I really lucked out, didn't I?"

"I wouldn't say you lucked out, so much as-"

"Anyway," Nate said, cutting Freya off before she could say anything else. "That's it in a nutshell. Though I have to admit that I've never heard of monsters having ghosts before. Then again, this could just be lore and superstition on the side of the borers. I would say we should be careful when we leave the city. Phantom or not, I've got a feeling we'll be in for a fight and I don't feel like being caught unaware."

Their group finished breakfast quickly, before heading out of the inn. They made a stop at a local tanner to sell their monster corpses and gained a small number of points that was split four ways. Once again, Nate bemoaned the loss of additional points now that the split was greater, but at the same time, knew that the larger group would be better, especially once they started hitting some of the later planets.

Hazel spent a few extra points for some armor and once she was done with her selection, their group headed out of the city and into the wilds.

As the day dragged on, Nate noticed the absence of borers. The first real sign of this was in the abandoned town they came across. It had only been half-built, but there were signs of destruction everywhere, from shattered and twisted buildings to cracked roads.

The most unnerving part of it all was that Nate felt as though he were being watched, and he wasn't the only one who felt that way.

"Anyone else get the feeling like something's breathing down the back of their neck?" Hazel asked, looking around nervously.

One and all, the group nodded, agreeing with her sentiment. They got out of the town as quickly as they could, using more kanta than was probably wise to keep their speed up. The day dragged on in the afternoon and then into early evening when the wreckage of City 153G came into view.

This was the first city they'd seen all day; the others having been towns and villages. It was truly a sight to behold. The soaring skeletons of abandoned buildings, the twisted metal, and stone. The chunks of masonry that had fallen to the ground.

"What in the *world* could have done this level of damage?" Freya wondered, as they passed a twisted metal beam that looked to have been shorn clean in two.

The beam was in the shape of an I-beam from back on Earth and made of bronze. The metal itself was over two inches thick and the entire length of the beam was right around 18 inches. For something to slice *that* cleanly, it would need an *immense* amount of cutting power and brute strength.

"Can you cut through a beam like this?" Freya asked, when they spotted another one.

"I honestly don't know," Nate said with a shrug.

"I wanna see you try," Freya said with a sly grin. "I'll be you a thousand points you can't."

"I don't think I wanna take that bet," Nate said.

Still, he tapped into his Gilded Blade, summoning a broadsword. He swung the weapon up and around, tapping his Steelshod as he did so and slammed the blade home against the I-beam. His blade collided with a ringing *clang*, against the flat side, shearing straight through the metal, and passing about a third of the way through the thick beam before its momentum was arrested.

"Well, I guess that answers that question," Freya said smugly. "You owe me a thousand points."

"I don't recall agreeing to that bet," Nate said, dismissing his sword in a puff of light.

"That was *impressive*," Hazel said, eyeing the cut in admiration. "I've never seen someone be able to cut solid metal so easily."

"It's thanks to the technique," Nate said with a shrug.

If he *really* put his full strength into it – meaning he tapped his Whitefire Injection – he had the feeling he might be able to cut all the way through in a single blow. Though, that was only theoretical as he wasn't actually going to try it. Cutting through six inches of solid metal in a single swing was quite impressive as far as he was concerned.

Their group continued picking their way through the city, even as the light faded from the sky, and work lanterns began flooding the area with iridescent orange, illuminating the area. It was almost eerie, as dark shadows were cast by the twisted buildings and the areas outside of the immediate light were dark as could be.

"This place gives me the creeps," Hazel said. "I think we should get out of here and find somewhere else to spend the night."

"I agree with you there," Freya said.

Nate agreed as well, and Noam was already moving for the skeleton city's exit. The group had only crossed about halfway through the ruined construction site, when a spine-chilling howl shattered the night air.

"By the bloody hells!" Freya exclaimed, jumping ten feet at the sound.

A similar exclamation came from Hazel.

"It's the Phantom Wolf!" She yelled, looking around wildly.

For someone who was such a fan of werewolves, she didn't seem to happy to have heard that howl.

"That did not sound natural," Noam said, drawing his ax.

"I agree," Nate said, looking around, trying to pierce the darkness beyond the massive work lanterns.

Another howl sounded, this one from off to their left this time, causing the group to whirl in that direction. A low snuffling growl came next, like the nose of a massive beast searching for food.

Subconsciously, their group pulled closer together, all four of them facing a different direction, searching for anything out of the ordinary.

"Do you see anything Freya?" Noam asked.

"No more than any of you," Freya said, her voice tense. "I might be able to see far, but I can't see in the dark. Especially not with these blinding lights all around us."

Another howl split the night and Hazel jumped again, her eyes flicking left and right, even as Nate felt the kanta coursing through her body. This was a type of enemy none of them had faced before. The type that stalked in the night, not revealing itself until it was ready to pounce. The anticipation was the worst thing.

Constantly on edge and expecting an attack at any moment, but not knowing what, from where, or *when* said attack would come. The snuffling came again, louder, and closer this time, as whatever was stalking them closed in.

The group was tense. Everyone had their weapons drawn and ready and Hazel already had a technique going, her Wolf Paw cloaking her hands.

"Anyone see anything?" Nate asked, even as another howl shattered the night.

It was a terrifying howl, one layered, one on top of the other, so that it sounded like several wolves crying at the same time. It was louder than the others had been as well. Closer and coming from behind Nate.

"Nothing," Noam said, his voice tense.

He stood directly to Nate's back and if he didn't see anything, Nate wasn't going to turn and take his eyes off the ground ahead. A shadow loomed, flickering in and out of view, just beyond the reach of the lanterns.

"I think I see something," Hazel said at the same time.

Of everyone in the group, she sounded the *most* scared, which was not unusual. Of them all, Nate suspected that she'd faced the least number of monsters and whatever this was, it was good at instilling fear within its enemies.

Another howl, followed by more snuffling followed, this time, from Freya's side. The snuffling continued, even as something scraped by one of the nearby buildings. This went on for nearly five minutes. Five, tense minutes of standing there, listening to howling, snuffling, and scraping as whatever was stalking them closed in.

Just when Nate didn't think their group would be able to take it anymore, he heard a gasp from Hazel. Whirling, Nate, Freya, and Noam were all witness to the same sight. Three massive shadows loomed up just beyond the lantern light, coming into view, even as their three shapes blurred into one.

A single look at the massive monster towering before them made Nate swear audibly.

"Nate," Freya said, sounding *very* scared. "This isn't...This isn't *it*, is it?"

"It is," Nate said grimly, staring into the nightmarish face of the Phantom Wolf.

Or, as it was properly known: the Nightmare Pack. The *only* monster Nate had specifically warned against facing on all of his drawings of the map they'd been passing around for weeks.

59

The wolf was *massive*, the tips of its ears topping eight feet in height. Its body was covered in matted, shaggy black fur, rippling muscle visible beneath. Black smoke clung to its hide, the natural mists of Laybor seeming to blend it with its surroundings, even when it stood right before them.

Massive paws padded the ground, moving almost silently. Claws, as long and sharp as knives, tore into the stone below, yet just like its paws, didn't make a sound, showing just *how sharp* they were.

The creature must have been some sixteen feet long, appearing like a miniature train cart than an actual monster. But, a single glance at the Nightmare Pack's face and you would be under no delusion of this being some form of locomotive.

The monster's muzzle was pulled back in a snarl, revealing massive canines and a row of jagged teeth. Its eyes were pinpricks of light in the darkness, one side of its face glowing a faint green, reflecting the color of its left. It was the right that was most terrifying though. The eye set into the monster's right eye socket glowed red, as did the two *other* eyes set right below, peeking out from within the fur and swiveling all over the place, as though having a mind of their own.

"I think I'm gonna be sick," Hazel whispered, staring at the monster, wide-eyed.

"What in the world is this thing?" Noam asked, as he moved to stand by her side.

The entire group fanned out as the wolf paused, its four, gleaming eyes taking them all in. Part of its body was still hidden in shadow, blending with the inky darkness at its rear. Framed by the twisted buildings all around, this monster *truly* looked like something out of someone's worst nightmare.

"It's called the Nightmare Pack," Nate said grimly, staring at the massive monster's shoulder, where a bright number 50 stood out in stark contrast to its inky fur.

A single, golden star hung beneath, marking this as a starred monster. It was only 1 star, but a star nonetheless and unlike with the Rattlegators, Nate knew this wasn't going to be an easy battle.

The wolf began to slowly circle the group, its eyes never leaving them, even as they turned in place, keeping their eyes locked on the titanic beast.

"Why is it called that?" Hazel asked.

"Because it can multiply," Nate said. "It's one of its techniques."

"So, it's a Cultivator-type then?" Freya asked.

"The marking is on the right shoulder," Nate said tersely. "So yes, it's a Cultivator-type."

His Kanta Sight showed him the monster's aura as a bright crimson, which was normal for this type of creature. It would only have basic intelligence, so things like hostility wouldn't rise past base hunger. It was only the later monsters whose auras would be turning even darker.

The creature's techniques floated out, hovering above its head, giving Nate all the information, he needed about it.

"Aside from the multiplication, it only has two other techniques," he continued. "The first is called Eye of the Storm. It's a dangerous technique with a dual effect. The first will imbue its attacks with the power of the entire *pack*, the second will cloak its body in shadow, making it harder to hit. The second technique is more dangerous still and the one that we'll have to be most careful of. It's called Assault and it's a much larger-scale version of the Pack technique it has. We'll be hit from all sides and…Get ready!" Nate yelled, stopping mid-sentence as the wolf raised its snout, unleashed an unearthly howl, then leaped at the smallest member of the group.

"Scatter!" Nate yelled, as the monster came flashing into the light.

Nate and Hazel dashed left, while Noam and Freya went in the opposite direction. Freya's Magigun flashed as he squeezed off a Poisonshot, the lance of purple striking the wolf in the ribs and vanishing. *Immediately*, the monster whirled on them, lunging with blinding speed, its massive teeth snapping at Freya who yelped and retreated.

Noam's body seemed to shimmer as a wave of fear blasted out from him, smashing into the Nightmare Pack at full strength. The wolf shivered, its body locking up for just an *instant*, even as the man *hurled* his ax right at it.

The gleaming metal whirled through the air, slamming into the wolf's shoulder, and lodging there. When Noam extended a hand, pulling it back, the injury the weapon had inflicted was so minor that none of them could see it.

Another Poisonshot smashed into the monster as it howled, breaking free of the Guardian's Dread, and making straight for Noam.

"Don't let it hit you!" Nate yelled, charging the monster, as Noam braced himself.

Too late, Noam tried to get out of the way, only for the wolf's paw to slam into him. There was a shriek of claws on metal as it scraped across the man's armor, then his raised ax, before Noam was sent *flying* into the wreckage of a nearby building, slamming into a twisted girder and hitting the ground with a *crunch*.

"Noam!" Freya yelled, half-turning to give chase.

"Stay on it!" Nate yelled, even as he closed with the wolf.

His backsword appeared in a flash, slashing at the monster's flank. His blade sliced through the thick fur, only to be halted an inch from the monster's actual flesh.

The wolf whirled on him, snapping at his face, but Nate was already retreating, while Hazel moved in to attack. The woman was shaking as she struck, her Wolf Paw lending her plenty of extra power as she smacked the monster in the ribs. The wolf actually staggered under the force of the attack, only to let out an annoyed howl as Nate's backsword slashed its hide again.

Two more shots came from Freya in the same instant, purple bolts lancing into its fur and disappearing as she poisoned the monster from within.

Noam was up, his hand pressed to his ribs and kanta flowing from him as he restored himself as best, he could.

"We need that boost!" Nate yelled, as the wolf whirled on him, snapping its teeth, eyes gleaming.

He staggered back, even as the monster lunged forward, paw slashing through the air. Nate's Gilded Skin appeared over his body in an instant, even as his Goldshield flashed at his side.

The wolf's paw *slammed* into the Goldshield, turning it into a mangled mess, even as its claws tore through the metal. The paw *was* stopped, but Nate was blasted off his feet under the force of the blow, the transferred kinetic energy of his shield sending him flying.

He hit the ground, tumbling a couple of times, thankful that he'd thought to use his Gilded Skin as the attack had come. Groaning, he dragged himself to his feet, seeing the wolf whirl on Hazel. It roared her in face, spittle spattering the small woman's cheeks as it showed its fearsome teeth.

Much to Nate's surprise, she roared back. It was a scream but layered with something darker and more insidious. A shiver ran down the wolf's spine as her Wolf Scream washed over it, incapacitating, and disorienting the massive monster.

"Now Hazel!" Nate yelled, even as a *fifth* Poisonshot hit the monster.

Hazel raised her head to the sky and unleashed another scream, though this one didn't instill fear. Sky Cry washed over their entire group, and a sense of implacable strength washed through Nate's body. It felt as though he'd just been given a slap to the face, been force-fed about fifty energy drinks and had been violently jolted with a live wire.

"Hit it while its disoriented!" Nate yelled, exploding forward with his Lightning Sloth boots to close the distance quickly.

He was at the monster's side in an instant, slashing and hacking with his backsword, shearing through the matted fur to reach its vulnerable hide. At the same time, Noam attacked with his ax, the blade biting deep into the fur with each swing, as clumps of black fell to the ground. Freya continued firing from afar, her Blazing Bullet punching into the monster's fur, sending small blazes across its dark hide as it burned away at the thick coating over the monster's body.

Hazel swung at the monster's face, her Wolf Paw slamming into its snout and driving it into the ground. Blood welled around the point of impact, but the *instant* the wolf hit the ground, its eyes blazed. It unleashed another howl, just as Nate's backsword cleared the last of the fur in its way and slashed into its dark hide.

The howl turned into a pained yelp as dark blood sprayed from the point of impact. Noam's ax cleaved into its hide just an instant later, and when he drew the ax back, a Blazing Bullet punched *directly* into the open wound.

Another ear-splitting howl echoed from the monster, even as its red eyes began glowing brighter.

"Incoming!" Nate warned, slashing again before leaping back.

A blurring paw smashed him in the ribs, crushing his armor and bones beneath. Lancing pain blasted through him, even as he was hurled off his feet. He didn't know how far he traveled before his momentum was arrested by a friendly building, that was nice enough to catch him with its sharpest bits.

The air was knocked from his lungs as metal smashed against metal and Nate's Gilded Skin vanished. He fell to the ground, coughing and hacking, as splinters of agony tore through his chest and back. Blood stained the front of his armor, the fox fur breastplate having stopped the claws, but having done little against the blunt force of the attack.

Nate looked up through blurry vision and saw the monster lunging at Freya, only for a massive monstrosity of kanta to appear before her. Noam's Total Guardian.

"Everyone back!" Noam yelled, his voice coming to Nate from a seemingly great distance.

Blood stopped leaking from his chest as his Cycle of Regeneration went to work, staunching the flow and beginning to knit his bones together.

Freya stepped back further – Hazel had already put some distance between herself and the monster – as Noam pulled a glowing bottle from his ring.

No, don't waste it, Nate wanted to yell, but it was too late.

The wolf howled, turning its attention on Noam, who grinned widely, then *hurled* the glowing bottle right into its face. The Ocean Breath's Bomb *exploded* in a tide of water, salty spray floating in the air as glowing, blue-green liquid rushed from the shattered vial.

It detonated with such force that the blast of wind from the backwash threatened to toss Nate off his feet once again. Glowing water lanced high into the air, as the expanding circle of water suddenly stopped, as though by an invisible barrier. The water roiled and spun, turning into a whirlpool with the wolf at its center, blades of water slashing deep into its hide.

The water began turning red, dark blood staining the glowing waters of the bomb before it ran its course in a *second*, massive explosion, tearing into the wolf and then vanishing in a spray of glowing mist.

Silence echoed through the night, the four of them watching as the wolf dropped to the ground, blood pooling around it from a myriad of cuts and slashes covering its body.

"Is...is it dead?" Hazel asked, her voice floating to Nate through the stillness.

"Not by a long shot!" Nate warned, feeling his ribs settling back into place and the pain starting to fade.

The wolf's body seemed to blur and a moment later, three stood where there had once been one. The new wolves looked different than the original. For one, one's eyes glowed green and the other's red. They only had two eyes, unlike the first wolf and were also a bit smaller in size – only around three-quarters of the original.

One appeared like a shaggy, feral beast, while the other was dressed in sleek armor that flowed over its hide in slim plates. Both had the markings on their shoulders of rank-50 1-Star monsters and both raised their noses, unleashing their howls into the night, as the original Nightmare rose to its feet, sodden and bleeding, but still very much alive.

60

The armored wolf lunged without warning, at Noam and Freya, both of whom were standing further back. Freya raised her Magigun, even as Noam's body was outlined in the crimson of his Brutal Guardian. Two flashes of light slammed into the wolf before it hit Noam, the man being driven back by the large monster, even as he raised his ax to fight back.

The shaggy wolf ran at Hazel, who abandoned her attempts at holding back and summoned her Pack Attack. Ethereal, white wolves shimmered into existence. There were five in all, light leaking off their fur in wisps. As one, they charged the monster as they were summoned, slamming into it from all sides.

The shaggy wolf tore into one and Hazel screamed as blood sprayed from her arm, coating the limb in crimson. The other four smashed into the monster though, tearing at its fur and hide, ripping chunks from its body.

The final wolf, the nightmare itself, came for Nate. Nate straightened, his ribs still twinging in pain. The edge had been taken off and his ribs had been stitched together. Now, there was just a bit of bruising and internal damage to deal with, but that would have to wait, as he was unable to heal and fight at the same time. The passive healing would only come once he maxed the technique out with a whopping 750,000 points.

Nate raised his hands as the monster bounded over to him, its body still glowing red. Nate let out a breath, summoned his Gilded Skin, then raised his hands. The wolf lunged, snapping at his shoulder and Nate used his Steelshod to throw himself to one side. He tucked his head, rolling over his shoulder and leaping back to his feet.

A Gilded Blade appeared in his hand as he swung back as he passed, the glowing backsword slashing a deep line in the monster's hide. Blood sprayed as the wolf howled, its tail whipping around to smash into him as the monster flew past.

Nate dropped to his stomach, the whistle of wind passing overhead tickling his hair. He leaped to his feet, spinning in place and using his Steelshod once again, leaping at the monster as it turned. Too close to use a blade, Nate *punched* the monster in the ribs. His Steelshod pistoned out at the point of impact and Nate heard a satisfying *crack* as his blow landed home.

The wolf staggered, nearly losing its balance and while it was teetering, Nate spun and dashed toward Hazel, who looked like she was having a *really* rough time. As the lowest-ranking member of the group, she was the most vulnerable. Already bleeding from half a dozen bite and claw marks, the short woman was having hard time keeping the shaggy monster off of her.

She'd already dismissed her pack and was now using her Wolf Paw, not wanting to tap her stronger technique for fear of draining too much kanta too quickly.

"Don't hold back!" Nate yelled, just as he smashed into the shaggy wolf from behind.

A broadsword cleaved into one of the monster's back legs, shearing to the bone. Nate knew that had Hazel not given them all a boost, his blow would have done far less damage. The wolf *howled* in pain spinning to attack.

One of its massive paws swiped at him and Nate blocked using his Goldshield. His feet slid back in the dirt, his feet leaving deep grooves in the ground. The blow had dented the shield, but unlike with the bigger wolf's attack, it had held this time.

Nate could feel the strain on his kanta beginning and knew that if the fight dragged out for too long, things were not going to go well for them. The wolf moved in on him, only for Hazel to tackle it from behind.

The woman had gone through a physical transformation in the two seconds since the wolf had attacked. She'd grown half a foot, nearly matching his own height now. Her muscles had grown larger, leaner, and more defined, even as her skin color had grown a few shades darker. Her arms were longer, fingers tipped with sharpened claws. White hair sprouted in small patches all along her arms and the sides of her face, which had taken on a more feral appearance.

Her face was sharper, more angled, her mouth larger and filled with jagged teeth. Her eyes glowed a bright, almost white-green, pupils slitted to points. Her hair had changed color, turning gray and shaggy and her nose had flattened somewhat as her jaw had elongated. All in all, she appeared to be absolutely *terrifying*.

The wolf howled in pain as Hazel smashed into it, her sharp nails tearing bloody furrows across its hindquarters. She latched onto its back as it tried to buck her, tearing and ripping with her fingers and teeth.

Nate spun as a loud snarl sounded, seeing the massive wolf coming for him again. It was noticeably slower now though, the glow gone from its body. Additionally, Nate could see purple froth gathering at the corners of its mouth. It seemed Freya's Poisonshots were finally taking effect.

Nate gathered himself once more, then leaped at the monster, summoning a backsword as he swung. The wolf met his sword with one its paws, knocking the blade aside in a shocking show of dexterity, and pinning it to the ground.

The wolf lunged, snapping at Nate's face, but he dismissed his blade and lunged back. Teeth scraped across his Gilded Skin, eliciting a horrible *shrieking* that left deep grooves in the metal. Nate slugged the wolf square in the snout in retaliation, knocking its head to the side.

He spun again, running back to Hazel, who was bleeding kanta like crazy. At this rate, he figured she'd be out in under a *minute*. The wolf's back had been all torn up, but it had finally shaken her free. It now stood on her, one massive paw pinning her back to the ground, while it lunged and snapped at her face. The problem was, each time the wolf got close, her claws would slice its sensitive nose, making it recoil.

Nate knew that wouldn't last forever though, so, taking the initiative once again, he lowered his shoulder and *smashed* into the monster's already-injured and bleeding back leg. It screamed as the bone snapped like a dry twig, white, jagged fragments tearing themselves from flesh as the monster – suddenly unbalanced – toppled to its side, freeing Hazel.

"Go for the throat!" Nate yelled, as the woman rolled back to her feet.

Nate turned, just in time to see the monster wolf already on top of him. A flash of light slammed into its side though and with a loud *bang*, the monster vanished, reappearing fifteen feet away.

"You're welcome!" Freya shouted, before turning back on her opponent.

She and Noam were looking *rough*, but so was the armored wolf. Noam's arms were both bleeding, one of his fingers looked to be broken and his face was covered in blood.

Freya was leaning heavily on one leg, her other looking to be either sprained or broken. Blood coated her stomach, but it seemed to be the wolf's not her own. The wolf was covered in large slashes, its body a series of open wounds and matted fur.

If there was a *single upside* about the summoned monsters, it was that neither of them could use the techniques of the main. All they had was the brutal strength and speed of a 50th rank 1-Star monster. Which was to say, a *lot*.

Nate let out a breath, turning to the lumbering wolf as it charged him again. Smoke trailed behind it as it did, and its body seemed to shimmer in and out of existence. They were divided, each fighting their own battles. If things continued on in this way, they would be worn down, their kanta depleted and their defeat, all but assured. He and Hazel were the least injured, in his case, due to his fast healing and in her's due to luck and skill in avoiding attacks.

She spun and leaped, turning into acrobatic feats that even *she* wouldn't have been able to do without the assistance of her enhanced body. As it was, it was leeching away at her kanta keeping them boosted in this way, which was the *only* way they were managing to keep up with the rank-50 monsters. The moment she faltered, they were all done for, unless he managed to tip the scales.

He could do that in one of two ways. The first would cost kanta, the second would cost his body. Yes, he had accelerated healing, but tearing his body apart and putting it back together multiple times would *not* be good for his long-term health.

Gritting his teeth, Nate made his choice. As the monster bounded in, his body began to glow as white light wisped off his skin. Heat suffused the air around him as he used Whitefire Injection. He had fifteen seconds. That was all the time he was going to give himself.

The world slowed as the wolf struck, biting at his shoulder. Nate allowed the strike to land, feeling powerful jaws clamp down and teeth pierce deep into his flesh.

In retaliation, he summoned a rapier, jamming it into the wolf's throat with all his strength. There was a loud *sizzle* as the superheated blade punched home, slicing through the monster's windpipe, and piercing through the back of its head. The wolf howled, releasing Nate's shoulder, smoke trailing from both its neck and mouth from where it had bitten him.

Not wasting a second, Nate closed, driving a fist into the side of its jaw. A loud *crack* echoed as the monster staggered to one side, its fur catching fire. It howled even louder as Nate's other fist drove into its nose, sending blood and viscera into the air.

The wolf dropped to its belly, whimpering as he summoned a broadsword, cleaving the weapon down on the back of its neck. Poison had greatly weakened the beast and now, Nate's blade sheared clean through the top of its neck and into its spine, severing it and causing total paralysis of the monster's entire body.

At least, that *would* have been the case if this *wasn't* the Nightmare Pack.

With an earth-shaking howl, the other two wolves turned away from their attackers, their bodies turning into outlines of light. One green, the other red. They streamed through the air, even as Nate drove his rapier through the monster's left eye, piercing into its brain.

The blade was shoved back as an explosion of force blasted him off his feet. Nate hit the ground, rolled several times, then leaped upright. His body *burned* as his countdown reached zero and he was forced to dismiss the technique, allowing his body to go back to normal.

"That thing was as good as dead!" Freya complained, as the body of the monster wolf rose once again, its spine reconnecting, wounds closing and fur regrowing.

"It won't be able to do that again," Nate said, narrowing his eyes at the fully-healed wolf.

All that work for nothing. It was enough to dishearten *any* group of fighters, even those who'd dealt with *many* monsters in their time. Seeing all your hard work being undone in a matter of seconds, while you yourself remained injured and weakened. It wasn't a fair fight, but, life in the System *wasn't fair*.

The wolf shook itself, then raised its nose to the sky and howled again, its multi-tonal voice sending chills down their collective spines.

"How's everyone doing!?" Nate yelled, as the wolf fixated on him.

"Down to my orb!" Freya yelled, raising her Magigun.

"About a quarter of my kanta is left," Noam said. "I've got a bit extra in the Tank, but not much."

"Down to a third," Hazel called, having dismissed her Werewolf form.

Her arms were still bleeding, as were wounds on her left thigh and foot, her cheek and collar.

"I'll be on my orb in under half a minute," Nate said.

It was unsurprising that he had held up best. For one, he was the highest-ranked here. Secondly, his passive recovery was the highest. Freya would be doing best right behind him, while Noam was doing the worst, due to his heavy usage of powerful techniques.

"Let's take this monster down!" Nate yelled, as the wolf leaped at him, its body trailing shadow.

Two of Freya's Blazing Bullets slammed into its left shoulder before it smashed into Nate. He'd tried avoiding it, but the shadows wrapping its form had thrown him off. Air exploded from his lungs as he hit the ground and the monster's sharpened teeth wrapped around his head.

Nate kicked up into the monster's belly, using his Steelshod, even as teeth punched through his Gilded Skin. He screamed in pain as the wolf was ripped away from him, leaving bloody furrows from his scalp all the way down to his neck.

He leaped to his feet, his head throbbing and blood pumping from the wounds. The wolf stayed on him though, preventing any chance at healing and Nate was forced on the defensive, even as the others continued to attack.

Despite her Augments, Freya couldn't seem to land a clean shot on the monster's weak points thanks to the shadows billowing around it. Noam's ax, similarly, continued missing the mark, while Hazel's Pack Attack bit ineffectually at the wolf's legs and hindquarters.

Nate used his Steelshod, trying to avoid yet another attack, only to catch a ringing blow across the side of his head. He spun, a backsword appearing in his hand and slashing at *something*. The wolf roared in pain and as he landed, Nate saw crimson on the golden blade.

It vanished in a puff of light and he rolled to one side, avoiding a stomping paw. Claws raked his back as he tried to rise,

396

slashing through a summoned Goldshield and his Gilded Skin. Pain like hot knives laid Nate's back open, the warm blood pooling beneath his torn armor.

He cursed, then spun around, throwing a backfist and – more by luck than anything else – managed to clip the wolf across the nose.

The nightmare staggered, howling in pain, and swiping at its nose, shadows dying down around it and giving the others the chance to attack. Freya's Magigun blazed, a Blinding Buckshot smashing into the monster's eyes. Blinded, the wolf staggered around, lunging, and snapping at nothing.

"I got this!" Noam yelled, then his body glowed.

A monstrosity of kanta flowed from him, taking shape in the form of the Maniacal Guardian. It slammed into the monster, driving into its ribs with earth-shaking force. The wolf was *blasted* off its feet as the crazed construct pounced on it, ripping away at its fur, and exposing skin. Blood and gore rained as claws shredded the monster's side, exposing muscle and bone.

This only lasted about five seconds though, before Noam swayed on his feet and the construct vanished. He clutched his ax, still looking pale and breathed out hard. He was out of kanta.

61

Even as the wolf rose to its feet, Freya placed four Blazing Bullet's directly into one of its eyes, the sizzling projectiles punching through the vulnerable area and blinding it. The monster swayed for a moment, smoke trailing from its burned-out eye socket, then it howled again, only this time, the howl was *far more* bone chilling.

A dark, crimson light began warping its body, an aura of menace radiating outward like a physical force. Hazel still attacked the monster, using her Wolf Paw to claw at its hind legs, shredding more fur and skin, but not managing quite as much as Noam.

"Everyone back!" Nate yelled, taking his own advice as the air around the wolf grew brighter.

Everyone moved, all subconsciously gathering together and facing the monster once more.

"I don't know how much longer I can keep going," Freya said.

She was pale and out of breath, still bleeding from several wounds that refused to close.

"I don't have much left either," Hazel said. "I can keep the boost going for maybe half a minute more before I'll have to let it go."

"I'm out of kanta, but I can still fight," Noam said, brandishing his ax.

Nate made a snap decision, even as he pulled kanta from the air to heal his sliced-up face and damaged shoulder.

"Freya, keep firing at weak spots until you're out. Noam, guard Hazel. Hazel, no more techniques. We need your boost to keep going. Without it, we're done."

He was glad that no one argued, as the danger was about to rise *significantly*. Three dozen copies of the Nightmare appeared around it. They were smaller, only around the size of the average Gray Wolf, but one and all, the glowed with the same, dark crimson light.

This was the true might of the Nightmare Pack. They were completely surrounded by the wolves, but Nate knew that focusing on them would be a mistake. Kill a smaller wolf and nothing happened to the others. The only way to succeed, was to take the leader out. It would be vulnerable now, as it was expending a *massive* amount of kanta keeping all these wolves here.

It would also have to concentrate, meaning that it would be slower to react.

"Brace yourselves," Nate said, then used his fire fox armor's technique.

The world around him blurred as he threw himself forward, burning through what was left of his kanta and starting on his orb. He reached the wolf in under two seconds, even as the others attacked the rest of the group.

Freya began firing at anything that came too close, Noam swinging his ax in wide, glittering arcs and Hazel dancing around to avoid taking any direct hits, even as he maintained the boost on the entire group.

Nate's backsword swept up and around, only to be met by one of the pack. The blade sheared straight through the monster, dissolving it to light instead of a spray of blood and guts. However, it had done its job and given others time to attack. Three of them leaped at him, two from either side and one from the front.

Nate gathered himself and *leaped*, relying on the speed of his armor and power of his Steelshod to clear the pouncing wolves. The larger wolf snapped at him as he came down, catching his leg in a crushing grip. It whipped its head, driving Nate *hard* into the ground and biting down with enough force to shatter both armor and bone. Blood sprayed, even as Nate triggered his failsafe. His Magma Body took hold in just a couple of seconds and even tough the pain didn't fade; the wolf *did* release him with a yelp of pain.

Nate's time was now limited as he rose, punching a burning fist into the wolf's hide. It tore through fur, burned flesh, and charred the wolf's shoulder, causing it to stagger. Several more of the pack threw themselves at him, but Nate spun, molten arms extending and burning through everything in his path.

He was *gushing* kanta though, his orb depleting fast enough that he'd be out in about twenty seconds it he kept this up.

Behind him, the others were in a desperate battle to keep the wolves at bay. Hazel was finally caught, only for Noam to slam his ax into the offending wolf. The move cost him, as a third pounced on his back, latching onto the back of his neck. A wave of red exploded from the man as he burned what he had left in his Cultivator's Gas Tank to fuel him. The wolf left bloody furrows as it was thrown off and a slash from Noam was enough to finish it.

Freya blasted anything that came within melee range with her Tele-bang spell, sending them further away and clearing room. She couldn't even focus on any damage-dealing, as there were too many.

One wolf latched onto her right arm as she swung around. There was a loud *crunch* and a scream as her arm was twisted back and she was dragged off her feet. Hazel was there in an instant, throwing a kick into the wolf's face. She was using her base strength, enhanced by her own Sky Cry and it was enough to free Freya.

"Come on!" Hazel yelled, dragging the sobbing woman to her feet. "Stay with me!"

"It hurts!" Nate heard her yell, even as she fired into another wolf's face.

Nate felt his anger rising as the Nightmare wolf threw more of its minions at him and his group. His arms swung again, blasting through the creatures as he lunged for the monster. Another punch drove into the wolf's snout, even as it bit down on his hand.

Pain flashed through his arm as it did, but Nate ignored it, throwing a second punch. It whipped around, the molten stone fist crashing into the side of its face and forcing it to release him.

"I've got ten seconds left!" Hazel yelled, even as another wolf leaped on her, clawing and ripping at her chest and belly as it bore her screaming to the ground.

Freya stepped in to help the time, kicking the wolf in the face and knocking it off. She then whirled, depressed the trigger of her Magigun and sent another wolf away. Then she swayed, dropping to one knee, looking to be on the verge of passing out.

She still had some kanta, but the shock and blood-loss were beginning to set in. Noam was beset on all sides, using his Augment and ax to keep the monsters at bay. He'd suffered *many* more injuries, his arms, legs, chest and stomach covered in scratches and teeth marks.

The Nightmare wolf lunged at Nate, snapping at his face, even as Nate slid back, driving his fists upward and into its throat.

The wolf roared in pain, but still managed to clamp its jaws onto his head and began squeezing down.

Fires bloomed in its throat as Nate's body burned it from within, but pain began mounting in his head from the pressure. He might be significantly resistant to damage in this state, but he wasn't immune. If the wolf's jaws squeezed much harder, his head would crack like an egg.

Splitting pain lanced through his brain as the monster bit harder and unable to use his fine motor skills, Nate was unable to get a grip inside the monster's mouth to try loosening its grip.

Instead, he did the only thing he could, slapping his molten hands to the monster's face and pooling his magma there, setting the wolf on fire, burning away its flesh, blood, and bone. This was a race. An effort of endurance. Who would crack first? Nate's skull, or the wolf's will.

Behind him, Nate could hear the battle going badly. There was another scream, though he couldn't be sure who it was, followed by a dull *thud*. More screaming followed, but the pain in Nate's head was too great to focus on that.

His kanta bled away, draining from the orb and into his technique. Smoke rose in billowing waves as he burned away the wolf's face, and mouth. Finally, when Nate thought the wolf was going to succeed in pushing through, the monster released him, staggering away with a howl of agony. One that was partially obscured by the molten stone clogging its throat.

Nate released the Magma Body technique with a groan, feeling a splitting headache. Face was covered in blood as he changed back, his breathing ragged. All around them, the wolves began to vanish, the Nightmare wolf before them unable to sustain the massive cost under the circumstances.

The wolf swayed in place, molten stone cooling all over its body. The monster was charged and burned beyond recognition, only its back half having survived the inferno Nate had unleashed upon it. Its bones were blackened and visible in many areas, Nate's technique having done some *serious* damage to this monstrosity.

Strength fled him then, as Hazel's technique died and Nate swayed on his feet, even as the wolf did. For several moments, silence reigned, then, the monster collapsed, its sides heaving. Its entire face was missing, blinded completely as crumbling stone revealed more of the damage.

It still wasn't dead though, which meant their battle wasn't over. Taking one agonizing step after the next, Nate approached the prone monster. His legs *burned* with every step and when he looked down, found them to be covered in bite marks and slashes. The other wolves must have been attacking him during his deadlock with the massive wolf. Due to the pain in his head, he hadn't even felt them land.

Nate stopped before the wolf, swaying as his head spun.

"Looks like we beat the Nightmare Pack," Nate rasped, giving the monster a bloody grin. "If only Noam could see me now."

Then he summoned a rapier and drove it through the monster's skull and into its brain. He left the blade buried there, even as the massive body thrashed. He only dismissed it, once the monster went still and the flood of kanta rushed into his Core, driving Nate up to rank 47 in a single go.

He turned, slowly, already reaching for the kanta in the air to soothe his aching body.

Noam was on his hands and knees, blood pooling all around him, even as he too pulled kanta from the air. Freya lay on her back, chest rising and falling fitfully, while Hazel just sat there, covered in blood, and staring dumbly at the back of her hand.

It dropped, revealing a dark 43 in place of the 38 it had been before the battle.

Nate staggered over to them, his body still aching as he left a blood trail in his wake. He dropped to his knees before Hazel, grabbing her face in his hands.

"Are you okay?" He asked, making sure the woman focused on him.

"I feel like…I'm losing a lot of blood," Hazel said.

She was pale, her breathing erratic and her entire body was trembling. Nate looked to Noam, who was in much worse shape, but already working on recovering on his own. Freya, similarly, was pale and breathing shallowly. But, he could sense the steady inflow of kanta into her body. If they could both keep going, they would survive this.

"I'm going to need you to drink this," Nate said, pulling the spare Healing Draft he'd purchased after the last disaster.

"O…okay," Hazel said, taking the bottle in shaky hands.

She raised it to her lips, still trembling and managed to get most of it down her throat. The woman let out a groan of relief, lowering the bottle to the ground as her wounds began closing themselves up, the pain fleeing her body.

"I…feel lightheaded," she said, looking confused, then pitched over in an unconscious heap.

62

It was nearing evening on the day following the battle when Hazel finally woke from her slumber.

"I feel like I've got the worst hangover of my life," she groaned, clutching her head.

"Welcome back to the world of the living," Nate said, handing her a bottle of water.

She took it with a grunt of thanks, took a swig and then squinted around. The body of the wolf lay some distance away, in several pieces. Noam and Freya both lay on their backs, the bodies covered in blood. Their eyes were closed, but they were both breathing easily. Additionally, most of their wounds were no longer there, and the blood coating them had already long dried.

"What happened?" She asked, taking another swig of the bottle.

"We won," Nate said, giving her a warm smile.

He looked to be perfectly fine, that was, aside from the tattered armor hanging from his body. Looking down at herself, she felt her cheeks grow warm at how much skin was showing.

"Well, that's embarrassing," she said, looking back to Nate.

"I've set up the tent," he said, pointing to a small hollow in one of the half-constructed buildings. "You can go change there."

"I think I'll do that," she said, getting to her feet and marveling at how good she felt. "What was that you gave me to heal me up like that?" She asked.

"That was a Healing Draft. A very *expensive* Draft at that," Nate said.

Hazel winced after hearing that.

"H-how expensive?" She asked, afraid to hear the answer.

If Nate had used it to save her life, she wasn't going to complain, but the cost would still hurt. A *lot*.

"Expensive," Nate said.

"Let me rephrase then," Hazel said. "How much is this gonna cost me?"

"Nothing," Nate said.

Her eyebrows shot up, a feeling of absolute shock running through her. He *wasn't* going to demand she pay him back for using such an expensive item on her, even though it had saved her life?

"Nothing?" Hazel repeated, not sure if she'd heard correctly.

"Well, I won't ask you to pay me back, if that's what you're worried about," Nate said with a smile. "It's only thanks to you that we won, so I kind of owe you."

"Yeah, but everyone else fought too," Hazel said, looking at the other two.

"I won't charge you anything," Nate repeated. "But I've got a couple of conditions."

"Okay," Hazel said cautiously. "What conditions do you have?"

"When we reach the next settlement, you're going to purchase a healing technique from the shop there," Nate said. "You're then going to upgrade it until I'm happy with it."

"A...healing technique...For myself," Hazel said, unsure if she was hearing this right.

"That's right," Nate said. "I won't have you dying on me because you're not equipped to handle a real monster fight."

"Okay," Hazel said slowly. "What's the second condition?"

"Don't tell Freya I gave it to you for free," Nate said with a grin. "I've had to use one to save her twice now and she's had to pay me back both times."

"Not that I'm complaining about not having to pay, but why are you being so nice to me?" Hazel asked.

"Because you're a nice person, Hazel," Nate said with a shrug. "Everyone likes you and you can handle yourself in a fight. Also, I'd like you to stick around once we help your sister. You fit in well here."

Hazel felt her cheeks go a bit warm at the compliments – she wasn't really used to getting many, especially not from men – and she looked away, trying to hide her embarrassment.

"Thanks," she mumbled. "I think I'm gonna go change now."

With that said, she made a beeline for the tent, letting out a sigh of relief once she was away from Nate's appraising gaze. He was definitely honest about how he felt that much was for sure, and his open admission of wanting her to stay was kind of nice. It felt good to be wanted, and, she had to admit that she'd been enjoying her time with this group as well.

Sure, Freya was a bit rambunctious and Noam a bit surly, but overall, these were a good group of people. They'd also shown that they were capable of doing terrible things if the need arose, which was good, as before things were over, they were going to have to confront Ashland and more blood would be spilled.

She let out another shaky breath as she stripped out of her torn clothes, wishing there was a shower nearby so she could wash all the blood out of her hair and scrub herself clean. As it was, literally *everything* she'd worn had been ruined, meaning that she would have to toss an entire outfit.

Silently bemoaning the loss of points, Hazel changed into her spare outfit. She took the time to undo her braids, combing her fingers through her hair to get the bigger knots out. She then pulled an old brush from her storage ring and began cleaning her hair as best she could.

It took her nearly twenty minutes of vigorous brushing to get all the dried blood and tangles out, and even then, her hair needed work. Still, as she ran her fingers through it one last time, she found that it was smooth enough and free of any knots.

She left her hair to flow freely as she exited the tent, finding Nate over by the massive body of the wolf, making one chunk after the next, disappear. Her stomach grumbled as she approached, letting her know just how hungry she was.

"You wouldn't happen to have any food on you, would you?"

"I do," Nate said. "But *this*, you're going to have to pay me back for."

She sighed, but nodded, extending a hand, and waiting for the food.

"Guess it's too much to expect that my lovely charm will get me everything for free," she said, as Nate gave her a sandwich wrapped in brown paper.

"You could probably get plenty if you tried," Nate said with a shrug. "It's just a matter of finding the right person."

"Yeah, like I'll ever find anyone in this monster-infested hell-hole," she said, biting into the sandwich.

She let out a groan of pleasure as the mix of flavors hit her tongue. There was some sort of sweet and spicy meat inside, accompanied by a crunchy, lettuce-like vegetable and something similar to tomatoes. The bread had a hard crust, but a soft and fluffy interior. It was like no one on Earth had *truly* known how to make a sandwich.

"Not everything here is bad," Nate said, as he pulled the last chunk of the wolf into his ring.

"Yeah, I can agree with that," Hazel said, thinking he was talking about the food.

"I mean, just take a look around," Nate said, letting out a long breath. "You don't get views like this back home."

Hazel just shrugged at that. The landscape didn't really hold much appeal for her. Sure, it was different, the suns shining one behind the other. The haze of the day and the way the light shimmered about them. Some of it was pretty, but it was mostly just *hot* and *damp*.

Speaking of...

"I don't feel nearly as hot as I did yesterday," she said. "Is it cooler today?"

"No," Nate said with a smile. "Hotter, actually. You've just jumped five ranks in a single go. That's going to bring some noticeable bonuses along with it."

"Oh *yeah*!" She said, turning her hand over and staring at the dark 43 now occupying the back of her hand.

It felt strange to see, but now that Nate mentioned it she *did* feel a good deal stronger. Looking to her bare arms, she could also begin to see some real definition and she *knew* she'd definitely bulked up some in the last few days spent with Nate and his group.

Looking at Nate, she could see some real differences. For some reason, he'd kept the tattered armor, though why, she didn't know. She could see clearly-defined abdominals through a rend in his breastplate, as well as clear lines along his arms when he moved them. If someone had asked her back on Earth what Nate did for a living, she'd probably have guessed he was some form of fitness instructor.

"Something on your mind?" Nate asked, snapping her from her thoughts.

"Oh, nothing," she said, giving him a smile and taking another bite of her sandwich.

Gosh, he could be intimidating sometimes, what with that physique and almost-overbearing manner. He was a pretty good-looking guy too. She could see why so many girls were interested in him, though someone else had caught her eye. Not that she would ever have the guts to make a move, or even *say* anything for that matter.

"So, what do we do now?" She asked.

"We wait for those two to recover," Nate said. "Noam should be done first. Probably sometime tonight. Freya will hopefully be done by tomorrow morning. Once everyone's up, we can head back to the last city, give them the good news and get a bit of rest. Once we're recovered, we'll head back to where we started, go give our friends back on Warine the good news and after that..."

"We'll go rescue my sister?" She asked, feeling a small twinge of hope.

"Yeah," Nate said, his expression serious. "We'll get your sister out and hopefully destroy Ashland's presence in Warine for good."

Hazel nodded, taking another bite of her sandwich – it really was *good*. It was hard to be angry or moody when eating such good food. Besides, she was confident her sister was still alive, even if she wasn't enjoying herself. Before, she'd only really been confident in Nate's fighting abilities, but after that battle with that terrifying monster wolf, she knew that they could *all* hold their own.

Noam was a complete monster with those techniques of his and if not for Freya's fast shooting and absolutely *insane* aim, she'd have been dead ten times over.

"I'm honestly just glad we made it out of there alive," she said, looking around at the wreckage of the battlefield.

"So am I," Nate said gravely. "That opponent was unexpected, but thanks to everyone, we managed to pull through."

There were several moments of silence following that statement, as Hazel thought of what would have happened had they failed. Then, she gave herself a shake, forced a smile onto her face and turned to Nate.

"So, it looks like we've got some time to kill. Got any ideas?"

"Training," Nate said.

"Oh, come on, you need to cut loose every once-in-a-while," she said with a laugh.

Nate was too serious for someone his age. He needed to lighten up.

"How about we play a game instead," she suggested.

"Game?" Nate asked, seeming confused by the mere *word*.

She stifled yet another laugh. She could see why Freya enjoyed teasing him so much. It really was *too* easy.

"Yes, a game," Hazel said, feeling the last of her dark mood fading.

Who knew, maybe staying with them once she freed her sister wouldn't be too bad after all. She could use friends like these watching her back, though that would all depend on whether Becky wanted to stay with them or not.

She banished all thoughts from her mind for the time being though as she began to explain the rules, laughing every time Nate asked a question. Like, 'but what rules are there?' and so on.

He was a good sport though and played for a whole thirty minutes before going off to train. She watched him as he moved around, throwing punches, kicks and switching between stances.

As she watched, she thought that she might be able to understand Nate's sentiment about this world. Though, in her case, she thought that the friends she was making here far exceeded anything she could have managed back on Earth. Without all the constant distractions in the way and the need for survival outweighing all, she could take pleasure in the small things, rather than constantly searching for the next.

Hazel sighed as she watched the twin suns descending beyond the horizon, feeling relaxed, despite her surroundings.

This was the first time she'd felt this way, since stepping through the portal on that fateful day, which by now, felt so very long ago.

63

"Well, now that everyone's up and healthy, I think we're ready to head back," Nate said to the tired-looking group.

It was the following evening. Noam had recovered faster than anticipated, while Freya had taken a bit longer, waking only by mid-afternoon and demanding to be fed.

Now that everyone had recovered from the battle, Nate was itching to leave. He hadn't liked staying here the past couple of nights and he wanted to keep the momentum going. The battle had been terrifying and had nearly resulted in *all* of their deaths, but in the end, they'd pulled through and grown tremendously from it.

While he was at the 47th rank, Frey and Noam both were at 46. Right now, the weakest in their group was still Hazel, but she herself was now at rank 43. As far as *teams* went, they'd jumped from the top 5% to the top 1% in a single battle. Sure, they weren't all quite with the frontrunners, but they *were* close. Nate himself was *right* at the tail end at his current rank.

If he could hit 48 by tomorrow, he would be squarely in the ranks of the most powerful humans currently alive. Yes, he would still be behind the monsters of humanity, but not for too much longer.

"I think we should stay the night," Freya yawned, rubbing at her eyes. "We're *exhausted* and this place is much safer than anywhere out there."

"We'd be wasting travel time," Nate said. "Also, we're all filthy from the fight. I know you want to wash off as much as any of us."

"You do have a point," Freya said, chewing on a fingernail. "Alright fine, but we stop before dark and dinner's on you."

"I can agree to that," Noam said.

"Ditto," chimed Hazel, happy to take advantage of any and all free food.

"Fine," Nate said. "But we're going to have to push. No taking it easy."

"You heard the Drill Sergeant soldiers," Freya said, shooting to her feet and giving a terrible salute. "Wouldn't wanna disappoint Sergeant Grumpy Pants."

"So, I've become a Sergeant now?" Nate said. "What did I do to earn this promotion? Also, I don't think you're qualified to be handing those out."

"I'm your queen," Freya said. "I can do as I like."

Nate pulled the glove from his right hand and rotated it, so that she could see.

"Oh, pish posh," she said, waving a hand. "Only a temporary setback. I'll be the strongest again before long. Also, you think there's a chance we can find any horses around here?"

"Come on you bloodthirsty animal-hater," Nate said, pulling his scooter from his ring. "If you want your free dinner, we're leaving now."

A threat to her dinner was apparently enough to get Freya to move, the entire group being on the road within just a couple of minutes, speeding back toward City 148G.

They stopped to camp for the night, though they didn't run into any monsters. Setting out early the next morning, they made good time to the city, entering by around noon. Once there, they all headed straight for the inn, where they booked rooms and went to wash off.

It felt *so* good to wash the grime and blood from his body, scrubbing himself clean before dressing in an ordinary set of clothes. He would need to take his armor to an armorer to have it repaired, as would Freya and Noam. Both liked their armor, the built-in techniques having saved them during the battle.

"I feel fresh as a daisy," Freya said, emerging into the hallway, just a minute after Nate, then, seeing that no one else was, there, gave him a warm smile. "How are you feeling? You're not still injured at all, are you?"

Her worry for him was touching.

"I'm doing okay," Nate said. "How about you?"

"My back's still a bit sore," she said. "My shoulders too. But I think I'll be fine in just a few more days."

She'd moved closer to him as they'd been speaking and was now standing right in front of him. Slowly, she reached out, grasping his hands in her's and looking up to meet his eyes.

"I was really worried you know," she said in a subdued voice. "That we were all going to die in that fight and that we'd never get a chance to go out again."

"So was I," Nate said. "But we're still here and we will be going out again."

Freya gave him a beaming smile. She opened her mouth to say something, but one of the doors rattled and she quickly stepped away, her mask slipping back into place as Noam exited his room.

"You actually finished before me?" He said, looking at Freya in astonishment.

"What? Girls can shower quickly when they have to," she said with a shrug, then, turned to Nate with a sly smile. "You were just picturing me in the shower, weren't you?"

"You caught me," Nate deadpanned, raising his hands. "Alert the authorities."

"I always knew you were a perv," Freya said.

"Who's a perv?" Hazel asked, stepping into the hallway, running a brush through her damp hair.

"We're going to sell the wolf parts if anyone wants to come get their share," Nate said, turning abruptly and walking away.

He was *not* going to get sucked into this again. Throwing a look over his shoulder, he saw Freya's smirk still in place. That was fine by him though. Now that he knew her true feelings, he could let her tease him all she wanted, provided she didn't go too far. Sure, it was a bit messed up that she had to keep acting in this way, but everyone needed their armor in this insane world they were living in, and this was her's.

"It was a miracle that we made it out of that fight in one piece," Noam said, catching up with him as they left the inn.

Freya and Hazel trailed behind, chatting about makeup or something along those lines. Whatever it was, Nate was happy to leave them to it.

"I know," Nate said darkly, thinking about how close they'd all come to dying.

"We need to be better prepared in the future," Noam said. "If I hadn't had that bomb, we might all have died."

"If you'd actually *asked* me how to *properly use* the bomb, instead of just throwing it at the monster, it would have done more damage," Nate replied.

He wasn't going to mention it, due to the nature of what they'd all gone through, but, if Noam was going to start throwing blame around, he was going to defend himself.

"It was a bomb," Noam said. "How else was I supposed to use it?"

"By pulling the cork and placing it in its target location," Nate said. "Then charging it with kanta to the explosion would be more forceful. Because you just *threw* it, it wasn't nearly as damaging as it could have been."

Noam looked like he'd been punched in the gut.

"I...had no idea," he said, looking ashamed.

"It's not your fault you didn't know," Nate said. "Just like it isn't mine that we walked into that ambush. None of us could have known what kind of monster we'd be running into."

"But weren't you giving warnings about that *specific* monster, telling people to stay away?" Noam replied.

"I *was*," Nate said. "But the monster wasn't supposed to be here. It was supposed to be in a completely different *quadrant*."

"So, how did it end up here?" Noam asked.

"There could be any number of reasons," Nate said, thinking. "For one, we're here really early and what we might not have considered is that this monster might like to wander through quadrants instead of remaining stagnant. If I had to guess, that would be it."

"That sounds like normal, animal behavior though," Noam said. "Especially for a predator that large."

"No," Nate said. "It's not."

His mind had been working furiously, ever since the fight, to try making sense of it. *Why* had the Nightmare Pack been in the G-quadrant when it *should* have been in quadrant C, over three hundred miles from their current location? This monster was *not* supposed to wander, but, then again, perhaps the changes that were occurring here were affecting monster behavioral patterns as well?

Nate sighed inwardly, dismissing the thought. This was not a road he wanted to go down.

"Regardless," Noam said. "We still nearly all died and because we don't have proper coordination and assigned roles."

"Adding a new member to the mix just threw us off a bit, that's all," Nate said. "Besides, in a fight like this, assigned roles

413

would have done us very little good. There's a reason why I advised people to stay away from this monster and that's because it fights on a level higher than any One-Star monster should."

"What do you mean by that?" Noam asked.

"I mean that it was able to completely divide our team, throwing more numbers at us than we had, and therefore, tipping the scales in its favor. A proper-sized team for that fight would have been eight to ten fighters, not *four*."

"The Froster Drake we fought separated us," Noam said.

"But it was still only a single opponent," Nate replied. "This monster was basically three opponents in one. A very *dangerous* way to go into a fight against a starred monster is to think that you can match it one-on-one. Every 1-star monster is worth at minimum four fighters and ideally five. We went into a ten-person raid with less than half those numbers. It would have been like facing a rank 22 Froster Drake with just the two of us."

Noam pursed his lips at that as he allowed the information Nate had just given him, to sink in. It was good that he was thinking about it, as this battle had been extremely close. So close that it made him uncomfortable to think of what could have happened if anything was just the slightest bit off.

If a single one of them had made a wrong move, it all could have ended in disaster.

"How can we avoid running into situations like that in the future?" Noam finally asked.

"For one, we go in better prepared," Nate said. "For another, we add more members to our team. I want to turn our group into a Guild once we get to the third planet, one that can lead the way and pave a smoother path through the System of Twelve."

What he left unsaid was that he was hoping to run into his brother Wilbur there and join up with him. That, and try and find out what had happened to his parents. He was still unsure if they'd come through or not, but for his sanity's sake, he was sincerely hoping they had. He didn't know what he'd tell Wil if his parents died, and he'd had the knowledge to save them.

He also knew that he'd had to explain to his brother – and his brother's friends – how he had prior knowledge to what had happened. Unfortunately, he wouldn't be able to use the same excuse that he had for everyone else, as he'd warned Wil *before* the portals

414

had shown up. He just hoped that history would remain true and that he and Wilbur would meet up again once they all reached Raven.

"Looks like we're here," Nate said, stopping outside of a tanner's shop. "Let's go in and see if we can't get a good price of a half-charred and burned monster corpse."

64

"How can I help you?"

The borer behind the counter of this particular tannery was dressed – for lack of a better term – in something racy and Freya noticed right away.

"Why're you dressed like that?" She blurted out almost as soon as she entered.

"What? There something wrong with my outfit?" The female borer asked, giving Freya a *look*.

"Well, it's just that your kind are normally so…"

"So, *what?*" The borer asked.

"Ah hell! You're all so prudish and stuck up, like someone rammed a rod up your collective backsides."

The borer stared at her for a moment, then began to laugh. It was one of the strangest sights Nate had ever seen. A beaver-lady in a *way*-too-tight – and small – shirt laughing away at the idea that her entire race were a bunch of stuck-up prudes.

"Ah well, you got us there," the beaver-lady said, wiping tears from her eyes. "Yeah, they're all a bunch of sissies, the lot of them. Not me though. I'm *normal*."

She was anything *but* normal. But, every race had their rebels and it seemed like this tanner was one of them.

"Well, good," Freya said, clearly unsure of what to say either. "So…they don't have anything to say about…*that?*" She asked, waving her hand and gesturing to the borer's outfit.

"Oh, they had *plenty* to say," she replied with a wicked grin. "Though it's mostly the ladies, coming in here and demanding I change my ways, due to their men always coming to visit. It's not my fault they can't get enough of me. If their *wives* did more for them, they wouldn't need to keep visiting Thelma the Throaty."

"Throaty?" Hazel asked, sounding afraid to hear the answer.

"Oh yeah, they call me that because I'm very vocal and outspoken against the restrictions my race places on women," Thelma said, drawing herself up straight. "For some reason though, they seem to think that I'm a heathen and that my presence here is causing all the disappearances."

"Speaking of disappearances," Nate said. "We found your culprit."

With that said, he started unloading all the wolf pieces on the counter, the woman's eyes going wider and wider as he did so.

"By Yolanda's snaggled tooth!" The woman exclaimed, once Nate had removed all the pieces. "It's the freaking *Phantom Wolf* that old coot is always going on about! I can't believe he was right!"

"You mean the old guy living down by the wall?" Hazel asked.

"Yeah, that's the one," Thelma said, coming out from behind the counter.

Nate had to avert his gaze in order not to be sick, as he caught a flash of something very short and very pale.

"Now *that*, is an outfit," Freya said, clearly doing her best to hide her grin.

Nate declined to reply.

"So, what can you give us for it?" He asked.

"For the monster itself, I'd probably only give you around eighty-thousand," Thelma said, circling the corpse. "It would have been worth much more if it was in even *decent* condition, but it's covered in so many burns and chunks of stone that there won't really be much to salvage.

But, seeing as you brought me the body, and thus the pleasure of rubbing it in everyone's faces that it wasn't my fault, I can give you a hundred-and-fifty."

"The entire backside is nearly intact," Nate argued.

"It is, but the real value is all burned away," Thelma said, turning to him.

Nate stared resolutely at the floor. He had enough disturbing imagery for several lifetimes. He didn't need to add to the pot.

"Real value?" He asked.

He'd never fought this monster in the previous timeline, only heard about how dangerous it was. So, he was unsure of what parts – aside from the pelt – were of value. Though, he'd been expecting a *lot* more than what she was offering.

"The head," Thelma sighed. "The head alone would be worth half-a-million. Someone would want to mount it. To display that they were a 'mighty hunter' and taken this monster down. Of course, everyone would *know* that they hadn't, but would pretend he did, just to stroke their ego."

"I bet she does plenty of stroking," Freya muttered under her breath.

Hazel snorted out a laugh at that.

"So, we lost out on a half-million payday because Nate burned the head to a crisp," Noam said.

"Hey, I'm still offering you a hundred-fifty," Thelma said. "Besides, this thing looks like a real *beast*. I'm shocked your group even managed to *survive* an encounter, let alone kill it."

"It was an extremely *dangerous* mission," Nate said, deciding it was time to try haggling. "We nearly *all died*. A hundred-fifty would only net each of us around thirty-seven-thousand. That's hardly even worth all the pain and suffering we had to go through. Not to mention the fact that you now get to rub it in everyone's faces..."

He paused, pretending to think.

"I think two-fifty is more reasonable, don't you?"

"For that much, you can take the stupid thing," Thelma said with a shrug. "It's worth eighty. Everything else I'm giving is out of my own pocket-"

"There's no way those tiny shorts can fit pockets," Freya muttered.

Hazel laughed again, though she was clearly trying to contain herself.

"But," Thelma continued, not having heart Freya's comment. "I understand it was hard. So, I can offer you one-sixty, but I really can't go any higher..."

After nearly fifteen minutes of haggling, Nate got her to come up to 200,000 even, which meant 50,000 each for everyone who'd participated.

"Come again!" Thelma called, waving to them, the front of her shirt moving *disturbingly*, as she did.

"Wow," Freya said as they exited the shop. "Thank you, Thelma."

"Why are you thanking that disturbing woman?" Noam asked, confused. "Is it for the extra points?"

"Obviously not," Freya said, placing her hands on her hips. "It's for all the new material she's provided me with. I mean,

Thelma the Throaty? Because she *speaks her mind?* Come on, you *know* there's another reason why they'd call her that."

"Come on," Nate said, letting out a sigh. "We're headed for the shop."

"Ooo! Yes! More makeup and nail polish here I come!" Freya cheered, pumping her fist.

"No," Nate said. "If I'm doing my math correctly, you have exactly enough points to upgrade your tome, and that is what you're going to spend your points on."

"Okay, *Dad*, if you say so," Freya said, sticking her tongue out at him.

Nate just sighed, their group trudging through the streets until they reached a shop.

"Woah, customers!" exclaimed the gnark sitting at the closest counter.

"Lucky us!" a second chimed, all but shooting out of his chair.

"Cus-tum-ers!" cheered a third, making disturbing motions as he did things to the counter before him.

"Let's go to that one," Nate said, pointing to the closest one.

"But there are so many of you," the third called. "You can't *all* be going to Garm. He's a new guy, so I'm not sure he can handle it. *Me*, on the other hand. I have *experience.*"

"I think I'm gonna be sick," Freya said, as the creepy gnark waggled his eyebrows.

"Why is it that this gnark makes you sick, while Thelma gave you 'material?'" Nate asked, as she sat at the counter.

"Thelma was funny, *this* guy is creepy. There's a difference."

"What can I help you with?" Garm asked, all but vibrating in his seat.

"I want to upgrade my baby," Freya said, placing her Magigun on the counter.

"Okay," The gnark said, looking down at something out of their line of sight. "That'll 168,000 points. Wow, that's a *lot.*"

"Yes," Freya sighed, placing her hand on the orb. "It is."

Every point Freya had, vanished in an instant, going to fuel the advancement of her Tome.

"Thank you very much," the gnark said, removing a glowing stamp from beneath the counter.

He pulled Freya's Magigun closer, then pressed it to one of the five, still-dark circles on the grip of the weapon. There was a flare of light and then, a new symbol appeared on the Magigun's stock.

"Your Tome has been upgraded," the gnark said cheerily.

Freya took the weapon reverently, watching as new lines of filigree traced themselves over the stock and barrel, the grip became more comfortable, as carvings appeared, swirls and twists forming even as she held it.

Nate felt her core swell as she gripped the weapon, her eyes unfocusing and a wide grip touching her lips.

"I just learned *three* new spells!" She exclaimed, all but vibrating with glee. "Today's my lucky day!"

"Well," Nate said, mimicking Freya's words from every time someone had had an upgrade. "Don't keep us in suspense."

"You can't steal people's lines Nate," Freya said, swiveling in her chair. "It's very uncool."

"Yeah Nate," Noam said, hiding a smile. "*So* uncool."

"Glad you agree with me," Freya said, nodding her head. "But *fine*, if you want to know *so* badly, I'll tell you."

She paused, as though waiting for something, but when no one humored her, she rolled her eyes and went on.

"The first spell is called Blam!, like, with the explanation point and everything. It's really weird but, it looks pretty awesome. It has less range, but it hits a wide number of targets with buckshot. It's supposed to pack a *serious* punch, though from what I'm getting, it won't have much piercing power. Not that it'll matter if it breaks bones.

The second is called Burning Bullet. It's basically a projectile made of molten metal. Supposedly, it has much more stopping power than Blazing Bullet, but I'll want to test it first. The third is the most exciting. It's called Freezepop-"

"Freezepop," Nate said. "Like the frozen and sugary treat given to children."

"Yeah, yeah, the name is weird," Freya said, waving him off. "But the effects sound pretty awesome. It freezes a target in place, then pops them. Literally exactly how it sounds."

"It *pops* them?" Hazel asked, sounding horrified.

"Does this work on every target you hit?" Noam asked, sounding interested.

"Well, it *does* have limitations," Freya admitted. "Like, if they're strong, it'll only pop an arm or leg, or if they're really strong, maybe just a finger? Again, I'd have to test it."

"How long do the freeze effects last?" Nate asked.

"Again, that would depend on the target and how strong they are," Freya said.

"That sound unreliable," Nate replied with a frown. "Not knowing how well your own spells work is more of a liability than anything else."

"Cool your jets mister worrypants," Freya said, waving him off. "We'll do some tests. I'm sure the spell works relative to rank, so I should be able to figure this out pretty easily."

"Worry pants?" Hazel asked.

"You seem to use the word 'pants' in just about every name you call me," Nate said.

"I could call you worry*skirt* if it would make you feel better," Freya volunteered.

"Or, and here's an idea, you can just call me Nate."

"Oh, but what fun would that be?" Freya asked with a sly grin. "This is so much better."

"How would you like it if I started calling you miss perv-girl? Or better yet, miss..." Nate trailed off, unable to think of anything else.

Freya raised a hand to her ear, as though waiting to hear what he had to say, but when Nate could come up with nothing else, her grin only grew wider.

"How about you leave the witty banter to the professionals. Wouldn't want you to get hurt after all."

Nate grumbled under his breath, even as Hazel took Freya's place by the counter.

"So, what can I help you with?" The gnark asked, looking puzzled by their argument.

"I'm looking for something I can use to heal myself," Hazel said.

"We have Healing Drafts," the gnark replied.

"How much are they?"

421

"Well, there are drafts of varying quality, but the cheapest will run you eight-thousand points."

Hazel's jaw just about dropped to the ground, and she whirled on Nate, her eyes wide. Nate kept his features schooled as he spoke.

"She's looking for a technique, not a draft. Preferably something that works well for shifter-type Manuals."

"Shifter, you say," the gnark said, tapping his fingers against the counter. "I don't know if I have anything for that."

"Can we see the Limited list?" Hazel asked.

"Oh, you don't want that old thing," the gnark said, waving her off. "Nothing but junk there. Why don't we try and get you some Healing Drafts instead. They work within *seconds*."

"I want the Limited list," Hazel said again.

"You really don't," the gnark insisted. "Healing Drafts are the way to go, trust me."

Hazel insisted for a third time and the gnark finally cracked.

"Okay, *fine*," he grumbled pulling it up.

"Now, do you have anything for shifter-types?" She asked.

"We do actually," the gnark said.

Nate watched the list fly by as he moved through the more common ones until it stopped by a specific technique.

Regenerate 48/50 - 41,000

"This looks promising," Hazel said.

"We'll pass on that one," Nate said, after reading over the description.

"Why?" Hazel asked. "It's exactly what you wanted me to get."

"It's expensive," Nate replied. "And also, not exclusive to shifter-types. Trust me when I say that you'll get *far* more for your points if you get something exclusive."

"Alright, let's see what else you've got."

Only once Hazel gave the okay, did the gnark move on. Just because Nate said she shouldn't pick it, didn't mean the man behind the counter would listen. Only the person actually *paying* got to make that choice.

They stopped on a couple more, and each time, Nate told her to pass it up.

"You know we don't have all day," Freya said, as Nate passed the fifth option they'd been shown.

"Keep your pants on," Nate said. "We have patience with everyone. You got your turn, now *wait*."

"Ooo, so *demanding*," Freya said, fanning her face. "I *like* it."

"How about this?" The gnark asked, stopping by yet another technique. "If this doesn't work, then I only have one more to show you."

Moonbeam 0/2 - 33,500

"That's the one," Nate said, staring at the technique.

He was honestly shocked it hadn't all been taken yet. He was honestly hoping to find the Shift Reset technique, one used to restore shifter-type fighters while in their shifted forms. It would greatly speed up the healing process by burning kanta but would work quite effectively by drawing on the strength of the shifted form to make the process fast and painless.

But *this*. This was *so much* better!

"Can you pull up the description?" Hazel asked.

"Of course," the gnark said.

The description flashed in the air before Hazel, though Nate was able to read it quite easily from where he stood.

Moonbeam: Suffuse your shifted form with the light of the moon. Restores injuries, strengthens the shifted form's attack power, and increases kanta regeneration for a short period.

"Okay," Hazel said. "I agree. This is definitely the technique for me."

"Great," the gnark said, gesturing to the sphere.

She paid the needed point cost, then took the proffered scroll from the gnark, opening it and staring at the parchment. For a moment, nothing happened, then a shiver ran through her and she closed her eyes, a small smile stretching her lips.

"Should I be buying the upgrade?" She asked, turning to Nate.

"How much is it?" He asked.

She repeated the question and the gnark told them.

"Wow," Hazel said with a low whistle. "That is *much* more than I was expecting."

Hazel's Moonbeam would cost a whopping 45,000 points to bump to tier 2. There were a total of 5. For reference, Nate's Cycle of Regeneration only cost him 2,500 to get to the 2nd tier. Then again, he didn't have a technique *this* good or specifically tailored to his chosen path, but there *was* reason for that.

He planned on amassing a wide array of useful techniques and skills, and boxing himself in wasn't going to be a good idea. Additionally, the Cycle of Regeneration was a *good* technique and one that he was *happy* to have.

"I think you should be good for now," Nate said.

"That'll be all then," Hazel said, rising from the chair.

"Can I help anyone else?" The gnark asked.

"Yes, actually," Nate said, taking a seat himself. "I would like an upgrade for this."

He set the Kanta Orb on the counter, knowing it was going to cost him *everything* he'd gained from the battle with the Nightmare Pack.

65

"Was it *really* worth it?" Freya asked, kicking her foot to keep pace with him.

It was the following morning, their group having set out early on their trip back to their starting point at Village 212D, from which they would return to Warine.

"Was what worth it?" Nate asked, having no idea what she was on about.

"I mean spending fifty-thousand points on that upgrade when you were so close to what you needed to upgrade your manual?"

"Firstly," Nate said. "I was over twenty-five thousand points away from that goal. And secondly, yes, it was definitely worth the cost."

He could now charge the Kanta Orb with far more power. It would match his own up to the 75th rank, instead of the 30th, where it had been stuck beforehand. Sure, it would cost him 100,000 to bump it to the next tier, but right now, he had plenty of room to grow and the additional kanta would, without a doubt, be life-saving.

"If you say so," Freya said, seeming worried.

"Something on your mind?"

She was silent for a few moments, gathering her thoughts.

"It's just that we keep getting involved in fights with other people. You'd think that everyone could just get along. Band together to fight the monsters and get us all back home."

"You would think that, wouldn't you?" Nate said. "Unfortunately, not everyone will see it that way. Especially criminals. They like it here. A world where you can gain godlike power and might. Where there's no law and order. No prisons to be locked up in. They're free to act as they like with no legal repercussions.

"Sure, they might run afoul of someone else and end up dead, but that's just the risk of living that kind of life."

"Don't you ever get sick of it? All the killing?"

"Every day," Nate sighed, thinking back to his previous life.

There had been so much death. So much needless violence and destruction, and for what? So someone could snatch just a little more power. It made him want to find all of the dark guilds and personally wipe them out to a man, so that humanity would have a better chance. So that his family would have a better chance.

"You don't like the idea of going after Ashland," Nate said, when Freya remained silent.

"I was there with you," she replied. "I heard that woman speak and saw the look in that man's eyes. I know they're bad people, but this feels too much like…"

"Like what we did to save your father," Nate said softly.

Freya's lips pulled tight, her eyes growing moist.

"Yeah," she said, swiping at them, refusing to allow tears to fall. "I just don't know if I can go through something like that again. Seeing that sort of thing…I don't think I'm ever going to forget it."

"Well, you can rest assured that whatever happens, we're going in there to stop someone who will hurt a lot of people," Nate replied. "And if we get even a whiff that something's off, we'll leave. Does that sound good?"

Freya nodded, though her mood didn't seem to have improved much. Still, it was the best they could do given the circumstances and Nate would just have to leave it at that.

They traveled quickly over the next few days, covering the distance back a good deal faster than when they'd been coming this way. Their increased ranks meant greater stamina and speed, and with more kanta to pour into their scooters, they were able to cover bigger distances each day.

Fights were also much faster, and after Freya's first demonstration, the group was quite impressed with her new techniques. Well, at least the single one she'd showed them anyway. Every time they came across a monster, she used her Freezepop, watching in fascination as the monster's entire body locked up, then burst like an overripe fruit.

Of course, this didn't always work, and they'd discovered that any monster 20 ranks below her own, would pop. Any monster within 10 ranks would lose a limb. Any monster within 10 above her own rank, would only lose a small digit, like a toe or piece of their ear or something.

The time they remained frozen was also affected. At 20 below her own and more, they remained locked in place for a full 10 seconds. Within 10 ranks, they were only locked up for 6 and within 10 above, they stayed locked for 3.

They had no reference for anything stronger, as no monsters more than 10 ranks above her own made an appearance, which was a good thing.

Though they didn't spend much time fighting, they still all benefitted from the 4-day journey back to Village 212D. Nate jumped a rank to 48. Noam jumped one as well, moving up to 47. Freya jumped 2 ranks, tying Nate – she hadn't shut up about it since. Hazel had the largest jump, going from 43 to 46, as they'd once again given her the majority of the kills.

However, now that she'd basically caught up – if at the tail end of the group – they could rely on a more balanced style of fighting.

"Oh, you're back."

Nate turned, seeing Bobbonius, the borer who'd first started this entire thing for him, approaching from his cart. It was the end of the day, and he was probably just returning from work.

"Yup," Nate said. "We're back."

"You coming back to the mines tomorrow?" he asked, sounding hopeful.

"Why do you ask?"

"Well, you see, we've lost a few workers and our productivity has gone down. The overboss isn't happy."

"Still the same old, ruthless and sociopathic borers I see," Freya said.

"Socio…what?" the borer asked, clearly confused by the word.

"It's a word we use for someone who feels no guilt or remorse for harm caused to others," Freya said. "Or at least, I'm pretty sure that's what it means."

"Of course I feel guilt!" Bobbonius said, vehemently. "Because of our lack of proper workers, we're way behind schedule! Do you have any idea the kinds of delays that will cause!?"

"I have a question," Freya said. "Why are you all constantly building things?"

"Because that's what we do," Bobbonius said, like it was the stupidest question in the world.

"Well *now* it all makes sense," Freya exclaimed, throwing her arms up in the air. "It's what you do."

"Well," Bobbonius sniffed, drawing himself up a bit taller. "I wouldn't expect a *woman* to know anything about the importance of construction. Your kind belongs at home, tending to the household chores and the children. Now, why don't you leave the talking to the me-"

Bobbonius' head rocked to the side as Freya slugged him across the jaw, his work helmet flying off and spittle, and blood, flying from his lips. The man spun around in a full circle, before hitting the ground like a sack of bricks.

His fingers twitched as he lay there, his eyes rolled up into his head and drool beginning to leak from his gaping mouth.

The beaver-man had been knocked out cold.

"How's that feel, ya little git?" Freya yelled, pumping her fist in the air. "How about you go tell your mine buddied about how a little *girl* knocked you on your furry butt!"

All around them, borers were staring at the violent display. There was clearly some shock but that only lasted until Bobbonius began to stir, a low groan escaping from his lips.

"Bobbonius was knocked out by a *girl*," someone shouted.

Laughter erupted all around them as the male borers crowded around the poor bastard as he came to.

"Bobbonius, how does it feel to be such a wimp?" One of them asked, wiping tears from his eyes.

"Look at her," another said, pointing to Freya. "She can't be more than two-hundred pounds soaking wet! What a joke you are Bobbonius!"

"Two-hundred pounds!?" Freya exclaimed, going red in the face.

Nate and Noam had to physically restrain her from going after the borer who'd said that, dragging her away from the gathering crowd of jeering and laughing male borers.

"These people are *messed up*," Hazel said, looking back at the crowd.

"Tell me about it," Freya muttered as she pulled herself loose. "Two-hundred pounds! I've never even weighed *close* to that in my entire *life*. Not even *close*!"

"How much *do* you weigh?" Nate asked, hiding a grin.

428

"Oh, don't you start with that," Freya warned, whirling on him. "There are some things that are off-limits, and *this* is one of them."

The deadly serious look in her eye told Nate it was probably a good idea to back off.

"Hey, look on the bright side," he said.

"What?"

"You finally knocked someone out cold in a single punch."

Freya paused at that, looking between her still clenched fist and the fleeing form of Bobbonius as he ran from the jeering crowd.

They stood there, watching him trying to get into his house, only for a female borer to appear at the door, throw a bag in his face and slam it. The laughter redoubled then, as Bobbonius scrambled to gather his things, trailing items as he ran towards the inn.

"Did...Did Freya just ruin that man's life?" Hazel asked, sounding shocked.

"That she did," Nate said, watching the man disappear inside the inn.

"Well good," Freya sniffed. "Serves him right for what he said."

"He insulted you, so you ruined his life," Noam deadpanned. "And you think *he's* the sociopath?"

"Hey," Freya said with a shrug. "All I did was punch him. It's not my fault their entire race is so messed up."

"Come on," Nate said, not wanting to stick around here any longer. "It'll be morning on Warine, and we have a meeting with Colin and his Guild. The sooner we get this over with, the sooner we can head for Southside Eight and Hazel's sister."

"Yeah, yeah," Freya said. "We're going."

Still, despite what she said, she continued to face backward, watching the gathering crowd around the inn growing. A wide – and somewhat evil – grin plastered across her face.

66

"Are you *sure*?" Colin asked for what had to be the tenth time in as many minutes.

"Look, pal, you can either believe us, or not. We didn't have the corpse to drag back with us, if that's what you wanted," Freya snapped, making the man jump.

It had taken them several hours to track the man down once they'd returned to Warine and seeing as the times between worlds were messed up, everyone was a bit on edge. They were tired, as they still hadn't gotten any sleep and knew they wouldn't, until nighttime fell here.

Just as Nate had suspected, Colin and his Guild had fled Southseer Seven as soon as Ashland had started making their moves. In fact, he wouldn't be shocked if no one remained. This place was the most likely he'd have come to, which was why he'd been so confident Colin would be here, rather than any of the other dozen cities nearby.

Colin had begun expressing doubt from the moment they'd found him and given him the good news, which was annoying, given that there really wasn't any way they could. Even if they'd dragged Colette's body back here, there was no proving that she'd been the one to do it.

"Well, your *tone* doesn't exactly make me what to trust you," Colin said, bristling.

"Look," Nate sighed. "It's been a *very* long day. Your culprit is gone and her guild has been dismantled. We've been going back and forth through the portals without any problems. If you want, you can go check for yourselves. I'll even go through personally if you're still too afraid to do so yourself."

Colin flushed a bit at the insinuated insult, but Fiona, thankfully, had maintained a cooler head.

"What do you want us to do with this information?" she asked.

"Do what you like with it," Nate said with a shrug. "Though I do have to warn you that just because we dealt with one threat, doesn't mean there aren't more. If you want my suggestion, why doesn't your guild work on providing safe passage between planets. You claim to care about them, so why not make it your mission?"

Colin opened his mouth to snap, but Fiona once again intervened.

"That actually sounds like a pretty good idea, doesn't it everyone?"

The remaining members of the MacDaddy Guild voiced their agreement, though several seemed nervous about the prospect of going through.

"The area on the other side of the portal is safe," Nate sighed. "Like I said, we can take you through ourselves."

"That sounds like a fair exchange," Fiona said, before Colin could say anything.

"Great," Nate replied. "So long as your group is all above rank twenty-eight, you should be good to go through. Though I will warn you that anyone below rank thirty will be damaged by the suns on Warine."

Luckily for the MacDaddy Guild, it seemed they'd actually been working hard.

Colin and Fiona were both at the 37th rank, while the rest of their Guild were hanging in the low 30s. Had they been on Laybor, they would have been much stronger, but Nate kept his mouth shut in that regard.

They all followed him out of the city and to the portal, where Nate stepped through first, then returned for the all-clear. Colin's guild followed, emerging in the darkness of night, outside of Village 212D.

Nate told them where they were, the general location and all the basic information their group had discovered about Laybor, its inhabitants, climate, and monsters that he could. He made sure he didn't speak for too long, before heading back to the portal.

Before he left, Fiona approached him, clutching a small bottle of Scotch.

"Thank you for all your help," she said, handing it over. "We brought a few bottles over from Glasgow when we came here. We have a couple left, but I wanted to give you something for all your trouble. You didn't have to help, but you did. So, thank you again."

"We didn't do it for you," Nate said, though he *did* accept the bottle – it was a 25-year Douglas Maine, and he wasn't going to pass it up.

A bottle like this had gone for right around two grand back on Earth and the system had nothing like it. It had been decades since he'd had a proper drink like this and though he wasn't showing it, he was ecstatic.

"I know you didn't," Fiona said sheepishly. "In fact, I'm sure you went through no small amount of trouble. Still, you don't see how great a weight has been lifted from Colin's shoulders. He was carrying all those deaths with him, you know. If there's ever anything we can do to help, you just let me know."

She extended her hand and after a moment's hesitation, Nate shook it. The woman seemed sincere enough, so he wasn't going to hold a grudge. Against *her* anyway.

"Ooh," Freya said when he stepped back through the portal. "Where in the world did you get *that*?"

"It's a present from Fiona," Nate said. "And, if you're nice to me, I might even *share* some later tonight."

Freya looked like she wanted to say something, but sealed her mouth shut tight. Nate hid a grin. Perhaps there *was* a way he could get her off his back.

"So, you're back," said Dirk, or Colonel Eagert as Nate knew him presently.

He and the rest of the team stood in the small office, gathered before the older man and his two advisors. Dirk's operation had grown in the last few weeks, going from some thirty people to over seventy soldiers of varying ranks.

Some were even veterans who'd moved on from their military lives once serving their tours, but had been drawn back here by both the stability and safety it would mean for them, and their families.

"Yes, we're back," Nate said, placing his hands flat on the table. "How is the fight against Ashland going? I ran into a few of their fighters near Eastfringe Six. Seems to me like they're trying for an expansion."

Dirk didn't give anything away, though both Ash and Thomas were looking grim.

432

"Ashland has been troublesome as of late," Dirk admitted. "Though I see no reason as to why we should be telling you this or involving any of you in military ops."

"This isn't Earth, Colonel," Nate said. "This is an alien planet, filled with people who can do impossible things. If Ashland isn't stopped, who knows what kind of damage they can inflict? We need to stop them and *now*."

"We don't have the manpower," Dirk said flatly. "I won't risk my men on a suicide mission."

"What if we had someone on the inside?" Nate asked. "Someone who knew the ins and outs of how Ashland operates and how best to combat them?"

"Son, have you even *seen* what those crazies have done to the city they're currently occupying?" Dirk asked. "It's a fortress. No one gets in or out without their head honchos knowing, so I see no way any of *you* can get in."

"I was a solider once," Noam finally said, stepping forward. "Israeli Special Forces."

"You were IDF?" Dirk asked, eyeing him appraisingly.

"Fourteen years," Noam replied.

"May I ask what unit?"

"You may," Noam said. "But I will not tell you."

"Fair enough," Dirk said, leaning back in his chair. "So, what do you make of all this solider?"

"I know you don't know Nate, but I do," Noam said, his voice calm and even. "And I have seen him pull off successful operations that would have made my old squad jealous."

"Give me an example," Dirk said. "A *good* one."

"We raided the compound of a Russian Mob Boss by the name of Gregory Pavlov. It was a rescue and assassination op, but things didn't go as anticipated. The target turned out to be part of the gang, so we had to improvise. We found the target and injured him, but he ran and lured us into a trap. It was a dangerous monster, a One-Star creature who could breath freezing flames.

"We killed the monster and then were ambushed once again by Pavlov. We took him down and scattered his group. As far as I know, the Rusband no longer exists."

"That sounds more like a horrible mess than a clean operation," the colonel said, placing his hands on the table.

"Yes, it was messy," Noam said. "But with what we had and zero casualties, I'd say we came out alright in the end."

"How many men were there?" Dirk asked, interested.

"He had over forty in his gang at the time," Noam said. "They were lured away from the city Pavlov had taken and that was when we made out move."

"How many of you were there?" Dirk asked.

"Just me, Nate and Freya over there," he said.

Freya gave a small wave.

"Your story seems a bit wild and unbelievable," Dirk said after a few moments of thought.

"If you need further proof, here it is," Noam said.

He pulled the glove from his right hand, bearing it so that the others in the room could see.

"*Forty-Seven?*" Dirk exclaimed, showing real shock for the first time.

His rank had been on clear display since they'd walked in here. The man was at 39, quite strong for Warine, given how hard it was to grow past the 30th rank over here. Lieutenant Colonel Williams was only 35 and Captain Shelby was one higher, at 36.

"I am not even the highest-ranked among us," Noam said, slipping his glove back on.

Dirk looked to the other three, all of whom removed their gloves. Nate and Freya's 48 were a bit more impressive than Hazel's 46, but *all* were impressive, nonetheless.

"Okay, you've got my attention," Dirk said, interlacing his fingers. "Talk."

Their meeting with the Colonel took nearly four hours, Nate outlining his plan for their assault on Ashland. Dirk stopped them partway through and brought several others in as well to listen and give their opinions.

In the end, the man agreed to most of Nate's plan, though he did have a few changes he wanted to make based on the numbers they were going up against and unknowns, like Ashland's elites.

"If this works, we'll rid the world of a massive threat," Nate said, near the end of their meeting.

"Son, if this works, it'll be a miracle," Dirk said, a hint of a smile touching his lips. "But it'll be one hell of a ride."

67

Nate, Noam, Freya, and Hazel all moved silently, approaching the eastern wall of Southseer Seven. Several miles behind, Dirk and his soldiers moved, the Colonel having split them into several squads, each headed up by one of his most trusted officers.

They'd already begun fanning out, doing a perimeter sweep to make sure they didn't run into any traps ahead of the invasion.

It wasn't quite dark out, as Warine never truly was, but it *was* noticeably darker than the last time their entire group had been here. The stars were falling and Warine would soon be going along with them.

According to Dirk's intelligence, Ashland currently had over 200 members gathered in the city. With Nate's small group, they had a total of 72 fighters on this mission, which meant they were outnumbered by more than two-to-one. Sure, Dirk's men were all trained soldiers, but in this world, one never knew if that would be enough, especially when someone with the right set of spells could wreck an entire squad.

Nate pressed his back to the wall, breath steaming in the air before him.

"Do you have any idea where they might be keeping her right now?" He asked in a lowered tone, as Noam and Hazel joined him.

"Probably somewhere near the manor," Hazel said, watching the top of the wall.

Members of the Ashland Guild were patrolling, though by this time of night, Nate *knew* they had to be tired, so, he was confident they could deal with them quite easily.

Freya, who'd remained a bit back, was flat on the ground, stomach to the dirt and Magigun at her side. Nate waved to her, motioning that they were in position. Freya waved back, then raised her weapon.

Nate heard the scuff of boots going past, then saw the flash from Freya's Magigun as he fired. There was a rush of air as the Burning Bullet distorted the wind around itself before it vanished over the wall.

There was a muffled cry, followed by a *thump*, as a body hit the wall. Nate waited, watching Freya sighting down her Magigun again, as two people came running at the sound. Two more flashes of light, and they both dropped without so much as a sound.

Burning Bullet, as Freya had discovered, had a much longer range than her Blazing Bullet, in addition to its other effects. Of course, it was a costly spell, one that Freya couldn't use too many times in a row, but one that was very effective for the time being.

There was one advantage that Freya had over the army snipers that Dirk had with him, in that Freya's spells didn't all make a lot of noise. Burning Bullet, for instance, made almost *none*. His soldiers' modified guns however, *would* make noise. Noise that would attract attention, especially out here, where there were few sounds to deaden the shots.

"Up we go," Noam said, backing away from the wall and pulling a rope with an attached grapple from his ring.

A few swings and the man landed the anchor on top of the wall. It only took him a single try. He gave it a couple of experimental tugs, then stepped aside, allowing Hazel to move up first.

"Thanks," she said, snagging the rope and beginning to climb.

The woman practically flew up the side of the wall, moving with such grace and speed that Nate felt a bit jealous. Her form was excellent as well.

Noam went next, moving evenly and efficiently. He'd had the training to do so, but seeing as he wasn't an acrobat like Hazel, it didn't look quite as smooth. Nate went next, relying on brute strength to drag himself to the top, pulling himself hand-over-hand.

It wasn't graceful, but it got the job done. He took the longest of the three, reaching the top of the wall and looking around, getting their bearings.

They had two jobs to do. The first was to locate Rebecca and get all the information out of her they could. Once they'd done that, their second job was open to gates along three of the walls to allow Dirk's soldiers entry into the city and give them the info they'd collected. With that done, they'd hopefully be able to find Simon and take him out of the picture.

Dirk had been monitoring the city over the past few weeks and was confident that the man himself was currently within the walls. They just had to know *where*.

Freya came scrambling over the wall, landing in a heap on the ground behind the parapets and breathing hard.

"I always hated climbing," she panted.

"Good shooting," Nate said, eyeing the bodies of the three Ashlanders.

All had been nailed through the centers of their skulls, dark burn holes visible as well as the gleam of cooled metal. Now that they'd made it over, Noam secured the rope with a slipknot, allowing the group to drop down to the other side, where he was able to pull his rope back with him.

The bodies were stashed in a nearby dumpster, pieces of garbage and other debris heaped over them so they wouldn't be found. The missing guards would be noticed, but seeing as there would be no bodies, the assumption would be that they'd all just gotten lazy and gone to bed.

"Follow me," Hazel said, then began moving quickly through the darkened streets of the city, her footfalls all but silent.

Nate and the others followed, crouching low to avoid being seen.

"Wait," Hazel said, stopping suddenly as they reached a corner. "Someone's coming."

Nate looked around quickly. There was nowhere to hide.

He pulled his combat knife and tossed it to Noam, who caught it deftly. The man then moved to the other side of the street and waited, even as Nate mirrored his pose.

Two women came around the corner, both dressed in Ashland robes and looking bored out of their minds. It took them a moment to realize that there were people standing there, but before either of them could scream, Nate and Noam moved.

Nate's hand clamped over one's mouth, a dirk appearing in a flash as he drove it into her temple. The woman let out a half-scream, muffled by Nate's hand, then slumped in his grip as her body went limp.

Noam killed his target in much the same way, though he jammed her up against the wall, driving the knife into the center of her forehead. The light *crunch* of shattering bone was the loudest sound they made.

Nate dragged gloves off the woman's hands, finding that his target had been at the 24th rank. It was no wonder his attack had gone through so easily. It felt like there'd been zero resistance at all. Noam did the same, finding that his was at the 20th.

"What do we do with the bodies?" Hazel asked, looking around nervously.

"We take them with us," Nate said, sliding the corpse over his back. "Until we find somewhere to hide them."

"This is *so* messed up," Freya said, shaking her head.

Noam slung his victim over his back as well, staining his clothes with her blood. Nate knew the same was likely happening to his outfit, but he didn't care. It was on loan from Dirk, so it was no skin off his back. Besides, these combat uniforms were built to take a beating, so a little blood wouldn't hurt.

Hazel led them through a twisting maze of buildings, their group depositing their load into yet another dumpster and covering it up. Several times, they were forced to stop as pairs of guards moved through the streets, but these they managed to avoid, having taken care to make sure that hiding spots were close at hand.

"There," Hazel said, crouching behind a stack of barrels and pointing out across the main street. "That's where they were keeping her the last time I was in here."

"How do you know she's still there?" Nate asked.

"I don't," Hazel said. "But it's the best we're got."

"We could always nab someone and make them tell us," Freya said.

"That would be too noisy," Nate said. "We're trying to stay under the radar."

"We've already murdered five people," Freya said. "If you call that flying under the radar, then I'd hate to see what you consider going in with your guns blazing."

"Look, we can either hang around here all night debating on it, or we can just *go*. What's the worst that can happen?" Hazel said.

She was nervous and eager to get this over with. Nate could understand that. She was closer to her sister than she had been in weeks and hope was a powerful motivator. As was fear.

"Lead the way," Nate said, keeping an eye on the main road.

As far as he could see, no patrols were nearby, which meant they were clear to cross without being seen.

Hazel nodded, then moved swiftly across the road, her feet sliding smoothly across the ground, once again, showing how good she was at sneaking around. The rest followed, crossing to the low-set iron gate surrounding the large house.

"Do we go in through the front?" Hazel asked.

"No," Nate said, scanning the building. "We go in through the basement. There's less likely to be anyone down there, and if she's really being kept prisoner, that would be a good place to start."

The basement wasn't hard to find, a pair of circular hatches mounted on either side of the manor, showing the way in.

"Locked," Hazel said, tugging on the handle.

That was unsurprising.

"What'll make less noise?" Nate asked. "Breaking the door, or smashing a window?"

"Window," Noam said. "If you do it right."

They moved to the side of the door, where a narrow window lay, low to the ground.

"Only one of us is small enough to slip in through there," Nate said, eyeing the slim pane of glass.

"I'll go in and open the door for you," Hazel said.

"Are you sure you want to go in alone?" Nate asked. "It might be easy to move from one entrance to another on the outside, but inside will be a whole different story."

"I can do it," Hazel said confidently.

"If you're sure," Nate said, motioning for Noam to get on with it.

The man wrapped the hilt of Nate's knife with a strip of cloth, then popped the window. The tinkle of glass was far quieter than Nate had been expecting, even as Noam cleared away the frame, giving Hazel her way in.

"Wish me luck," the smaller woman said, dropping to her belly and sliding backward into the house.

"Don't let any baddies sneak up on you," Freya said, just before the woman vanished into the darkness beyond.

68

Several tense moments passed as they waited for Hazel to appear. At one point, Nate was convinced that someone had been waiting there in ambush. That was, until the handle on the hatch spun and the door opened, revealing Hazel's grinning face.

"Told you I could do it," she said.

"You know," Freya said, as they slipped into the dark and musty basement. "I was half expecting something to go horribly wrong."

"Please don't say that," Nate said, feeling a surge of panic at her words.

"Right, I know you're superstitious and all," Freya said, waving off his concern.

Still, she didn't say anything else, as they began moving through the basement. The floor was made of dirt, the walls covered in dust, though no cobwebs – no spiders lived on Warine – which was a good thing. Spiderwebs were disgusting and Nate had had *way* too many bad encounters with spiders on later planets to be relaxed in their presence.

The first few rooms they checked were abandoned. Pitch black and filled with random bits of junk. However, as the moved closer to the staircase on the far side of the basement, Nate began to hear some noise.

"You hear that?" he asked, stopping the group halfway down the hall.

Everyone was silent as they listened, Freya finally nodding.

"A swishing sound, right?"

Nate nodded.

"No idea what it is though," she said.

"Could be nothing, but it could also be something," Nate said.

Despite the noise coming from the far side of the hall, they checked each and every room. Some had stashes of food, which Freya gladly raided. Others had even more junk, while one contained a collection of rusty-looking swords and spears, as well as several bodies in various states of decay.

"Oh," Freya groaned, pinching her nose and closing the door quickly. "That was horrible."

"Did you see any people in there?" Hazel asked worriedly when Freya told them what she'd found.

"Looked like winges to me," Freya said. "No human body would look like *that*."

The closer they moved to the far room, the more they could hear, and soon enough, it became obvious that someone was in there.

"Everyone ready?" Nate asked, pressing his back to the doorframe.

The group nodded. Freya held her gun, Noam, his borrowed combat knife and Hazel had her Wolf Paw already going.

Nate held his hand up, counting down from three, then spun, smashing into the door and shattering the latch with almost no effort.

He took the entire room in, in an instant, spotting three people sitting by a table, guarding a makeshift cell set in the corner of the room.

"What the-?" one of them said, half getting up, before Freya's Burning Bullet blasted through his skull.

The second extended a hand, obviously intending to cast a spell, only for Nate's rapier to skewer him through the eye. He spun, already having dismissing the blade and slashed a curved saber across the side of the third's neck.

The man gurgled, dropping to the ground and a flash from Freya's Magigun finished him off.

Only once he was sure everyone was dead did Nate look to the corner of the room, where a woman was huddled, clearly terrified, against the far side of the small cot placed within.

"Becky!" Hazel yelled, pushing past Freya and dashing into the room.

"H-Hazel," Rebecca said, sounding more shocked than anything else. "What are you doing here?"

Rebecca had the same accent as Hazel, though her voice was deeper and richer, sounding more her age than the almost-childlike Hazel.

"Getting you out, obviously," Hazel said.

She jammed both hands between the bars and with a *heave*, *bent* them open enough for Rebecca to climb out. She had her Wolf Paw active, but seeing such a display of brute strength was enough to remind Nate of one of the many reasons why he wanted her on his team in the first place.

"Wait," Freya said, as Hazel wrapped her much taller sister in a crushing hug. "She's your twin sister?"

"Uh, yeah," Rebecca said, still seeming to be a bit out of it.

"But you look *nothing alike!*" Freya exclaimed.

That much wasn't strictly true. Nate could tell that much just by looking at the pair standing side by side. There were similarities in their facial features. The shape of their eyes, bone structure and even the way their hair grew. They were siblings alright, though they were about as different in built as Nate was from his future self.

Rebecca stood at a tall, five-foot-ten, with long, wavy red hair. Her complexion was lighter than Hazel's and she had more freckles splashed across her nose and cheeks. Her eyes were a light blue and quite striking. As far as build, well, she was basically every modern man's ideal woman. A figure that curved, filling her outfit quite nicely and with a muscle tone that spoke of her years of track and field.

"Yeah, we get that a lot," Hazel said. "Genetics, am I right?"

"Much as we would love to stick around and chat, we should probably get going," Noam said, looking back over his shoulder.

"He's right," Nate said. "That fight definitely made some noise. Someone was bound to hear."

"Come on," Hazel said, seizing her sister's hand. "We're getting you out of here."

Nate paused, looking to the woman. It was the moment of truth. Would she turn on them? He got his answer when Rebecca's eyes began growing watery and she nodded several times.

"I can't believe this is happening," she said, following Hazel. "You really came for me."

"Hey, we've gotta watch each other's backs, right?" Hazel said, flashing her a smile.

Rebecca nodded as Hazel led her past, Nate catching a glimpse of the back of the woman's left hand. She was a magician at the 29th rank. It seemed that whatever work Ashland had been making her do, it hadn't hurt overall strength. Though, if they believed they could still keep her in check, even at her current rank, it meant that there was someone – or several someones – here that she was afraid of.

Noam took the lead position as they moved out of the room, Hazel and her sister going next, with him and Freya bringing up the rear.

"Can you believe this?" Freya exclaimed in a hushed whisper. "Those two are *twins*."

"I've seen stranger things," Nate said with a shrug.

"Well, so have I, but still," Freya said, shaking her head. "Unbelievable. Could you imagine if I had a short and chubby twin with dark hair?"

"Weirdly enough, I could," Nate said. "But I feel like you're selling Hazel a bit short there."

"Short," Freya said with a snort. "Sorry, didn't mean that," she said, almost as soon as the words had left her mouth. "Force of habit."

"We're going to have to work on that," Nate said as they headed for the exit of the basement.

He fell silent as Noam slipped from the house, followed by the twins. Nate exited onto the same darkened street yet for some reason, there seemed to be a distinct aura of menace hanging around the place.

The group crowded close, Hazel speaking quickly and in a hushed tone.

"Simon is in a small cottage on the western edge of the city. He sleeps there in case anyone decides to attack. The leaders of Ashland will all be in the manor and surrounding houses. There are twelve in all."

"How strong are they?" Nate asked, his eyes swiveling around the streets.

The longer they stayed here, the greater the chance of discovery, but they were going to be splitting up and tackling each of the gates, to maximize their efficiency. So, it was important that everyone have the same information.

"The strongest is his current vice-commander, Paula," Rebecca said, her voice sounding steadier now that she'd had time to acclimate to the idea that she was actually getting out. "She's at rank forty-one. The others will be between thirty-four and her rank."

"What about Simon?" Nate asked.

Rebecca shook her head.

It seemed she didn't know, which was to be expected.

"You said that Simon likes to sleep in that cottage when he's *here*," Noam said. "How often is he away?"

That was good. Nate hadn't even thought to ask that question.

"He's only here a few days a week," Rebecca said. "Though he's been here for the past four days now. He's been pretty angry, spouting off about something that happened in the east."

"Could he have been going to Laybor for training?" Noam asked, turning to Nate.

"It's entirely possible," Nate said, looking around once more. They'd wasted enough time.

"Do you all remember the plan?" Nate asked.

"What plan?" Rebecca asked, when everyone nodded.

"We're headed for the closest gate," Hazel said. "Once we're there, we'll open it for the soldiers waiting there for us. I'll get you out of the city and somewhere safe, then I'll be coming back to help."

"Hazel, you can't," Rebecca said, perhaps a bit too loudly. "These people are too strong!"

Hazel ripped the glove from her right hand and brandished it before her sister's nose.

"Don't worry about me, Becky. I'm strong too."

Rebecca's eyes widened once again as Hazel slid the glove back over her right hand.

"The meeting point's the manor," Nate said, tuning to Noam and Freya. "If anything goes wrong, and I mean horribly wrong, you run. Understood?"

"Yes, sir, captain sir," Freya said, giving him a salute.

"We'll be careful," Noam said.

"Then I'll hope to see you all soon," Nate replied.

He took one last look around at their small group, then turned and began jogging towards the north gate, the one furthest from their current location.

He heard the others moving off as well, the light scuffing of boots and their breathing as they picked up their pace. Within a few seconds, everyone was out of sight and Nate was all alone.

Nate hadn't liked the initial suggestion that they all split up, but after listening to Dirk's reasoning had eventually agreed. He didn't like it, but it made the most sense. When they were going in

444

for the rescue, they needed the larger group in case of any larger-scale fights. But to open a gate, one that might not even be guarded, would be much simpler for a single person or team of two.

It had been decided that Nate would go on his own. Hazel had insisted she go with her sister, which left Noam and Freya as the third team, the one tackling the eastern gate. That had been another addition to the plan, for the attack to come from all directions *but* the south, as Simon might be aware of the Warband Guild's presence outside their walls.

Nate slipped from cover to cover as he ran through the city streets, ducking behind carts and other stalls as he wound his way through the market district. There were fewer guards here, only a couple of patrols, both of which he was able to avoid.

The night air steamed before his lips as he continued running, keeping an even pace as he wound his way through the city. It was eerie, knowing what was about to happen. That the silence would soon be shattered by the sound of gunfire and blazing spells.

He'd been expecting something to go wrong already. For someone to have made the discovery of Rebecca's disappearance or notice the missing guards and go investigate. There was also the chance for someone to have heard the noise they'd made when breaking the glass to get into the manor, yet none of that had seemed to raise the alarm.

"You hear that?"

Nate skidded to a halt, pressing his back to a wall as a voice floated to him from down the street. Looking around, he once again found the area devoid of cover. That was unfortunate.

"I didn't hear anything," another voice said. "You're imagining things."

"That's what everyone in horror movies say, right before the killer turns them into the next victim," the first replied.

"You watched *way* too many horror movies then," the first said in exasperation.

That wasn't good. One of the guards was alert and searching for danger, which meant there would be no sneaking up on them.

"I'm going to check it out," the first voice said, footsteps echoing closer.

They were coming his way.

445

Letting out breath, Nate gathered himself, then pounced. He cleared a solid eight feet unassisted, snagging an outcropping piece of stone on house closest to him. The stone was slippery, as the side of the building was smooth, so he was force to use only his hand to drag himself up, which was not easy.

He made it, getting his feet lodged into the stone and leaping again, catching a circular window and hauling himself inside.

Two people were in the room, a man and a woman, and both of them were in a state of undress.

"What the hell?" the man exclaimed as Nate came tumbling in through the open window.

Well, that's not good, Nate thought, even as he dashed across the room towards the pair.

The woman let out a scream, throwing her hand out towards him and unleashed a spell. Nate dodged around it, the streaking sphere of fire blasting past him, right out the open window and exploding.

"I told you I heard something!" The guard's voice echoed up through the window, even as Nate reached the pair.

His backsword appeared as he swung down, decapitating the man in a single stroke, showering the woman in his blood. She didn't have long to scream, as Nate's sword continued on through his neck, shearing halfway into her own.

Another Fireblast, aimed at his head, exploded through the window frame as the woman's hand fell away, sending the fiery projectile out into the night and attracting yet *more* attention.

Of all the rotten luck!

Net cursed himself for not just running at the guards or turning back the other way. This had seemed like the smartest idea at the time. No one was supposed to be up, and from his vantage below the open window, the room had appeared to be dark. It was only after he'd hauled himself in, that he'd seen the small lantern, placed on the nightstand on the other side of the bed.

"Raise the alarm!" the first guard shouted.

Nate swore, then dashed from the room and exploded out into the hallway, even as a loud *boom* echoed behind him.

Everyone else in the building must have been asleep, the couple he'd just murdered having been the exception, as he made it back to the ground floor without running into anybody.

Nate emerged onto the street, seeing a second flare and then a third, rising into the sky, as the other guard patrols carried the message along. It would only be a matter of minutes before the entire *city* was awake. There was no more time of subtlety.

He exploded into a full-out sprint, tearing through the remaining streets as he ran for the gates.

A pair of guards suddenly ran from a nearby alleyway and Nate collided with them both, the guards screaming in surprise as they were all hurled from their feet before Nate gored one through the eye with a glowing dirk.

The other guard threw a hand up, eyes wide in terror as he unleashed a glowing, green ball of fire, right before Nate crushed his skull.

He was back on his feet in an instant, the dead guards' kanta flowing into him as he made for the gate. That green flare had been different. A signal most likely, which meant that Ashlanders would be coming to his location. He just hoped that the others had managed to avoid detection, unlike him.

He swore again.

Thankfully, he managed to reach the barred smaller gate without running into any more opposition, only to find it guarded by yet another pair of guards. They were alert and watching the streets for any signs of an intruder.

"Kill him!" the female Ashlander screamed as Nate barreled towards them.

The man lifted his hand, unleashing a javelin of flaming kanta. Nate's Gilded Skin appeared and he allowed the projectile to slam into him. He barely even slowed down as the spell was blasted apart, too weak to penetrate his armor.

"I said *kill him*!" the woman screamed, as the man unleashed two more spells before Nate reached him.

A blur of his backsword sheared the man's hand off at the wrist and while he was screaming, a dirk took him through the eye. Nate wasn't even paying attention to him though, as the woman threw a haymaker right at his jaw, flames gathering around her fist. Nate's hand snapped up, deflecting the blow to one side, and driving a straight punch into the woman's nose.

There was a horrendous *crunch* as his steel-clad fist was coated in blood, the woman's head whipping back to violently that it slammed into the door behind her. Even before she began sliding to the ground, blood pouring down her face, a dagger took her through the eye.

More kanta rushed into Nate as he shoved the bodies aside, grabbing the heavy beam and lifting it out of place.

The door swung open on silent hinges, to reveal Captain Shelby flanked by three squads of seven men each.

"I was getting worried for a moment that you'd been caught," Thomas said, as Nate dragged the gate open.

"Ran into some trouble," Nate said, stepping aside.

Shelby looked to the dead guards lying on the ground in pools of spreading blood.

"I can see that," the man said, as his soldiers streamed in around him, rifles raised in combat-ready positions.

"All clear, sir," one of them said after a preliminary sweep of the street.

"Where are we going?" Shelby asked.

"There's a cottage on the western edge of the city," Nate said. "That's Simon's most likely location. The commanders will all be in the manor and surrounding houses. There are twelve of them ranging from thirty-four to forty-one. Simon's current strength is unknown."

Nate had already briefed Dirk – in secret – as to what Simon's abilities were. So, there was no need to repeat himself now that the mission was in full swing.

"Then Simon will have to be handled by Lieutenant Colonel Williams and her team," Shelby said, turning to his men. "We're moving to the manor. Shoot anyone not wearing our colors."

This was another reason they'd all been dressed in army fatigues. With matching colors, it would be easy to tell friend from foe, especially with the night-vision enhancements many of the group were sporting. All would have been purchased at the shop, as technology had stopped working the moment the Mystery arrived, but all would be pretty close to the real thing.

"Are you coming with us?" Shelby asked.

"I'll show you the way," Nate said, his voice growing hard. "After that, I'm going after Dalefield."

That psychopathic serial killer had done enough damage for several lifetimes. His reign ended tonight.

69

Though Nate had seen it many times before, he never tired of watching the military precision of an active unit in combat. The soldiers moved through the darkened streets quickly and efficiently. Just as Thomas ordered, anything that moved was shot, bolts of blue energy firing from the modified guns and blasting into any Ashlanders who made an appearance.

Of course, some engagements were easier than others and more than once, their group was forced to take cover, when larger groups of Ashland magicians came streaming into the narrower streets, blasting the fire spells without a care.

Buildings began burning, smoke rising into the sky and soon enough, night-vision wasn't needed.

Nate coughed as he inhaled a lungful of smoke, but pushed through, kicking the Ashland man in the chest. There was a loud *crunch* as he was hurled off his feet, smashing through a burning support. He was buried in debris as soon as he broke said support, kanta flowing into Nate as he turned to attack the next in his path.

A glowing beam winged the woman's shoulder as she threw herself at him, knocking her to one side with a scream as blood sprayed. Those modified rifles packed a *serious* punch, but it was important for Nate to remember that they didn't have an infinite amount of ammo. Once the ones handling them ran out of kanta, their rifles would be as useless as ordinary sticks.

Nate's backsword sliced through the air, cutting partway through the woman's neck as she fell. Her kanta too flowed into him as she dropped to the burning ground, blood pouring from the gaping wound.

"Clear!" He heard someone shout.

"Move! Move!" Thomas yelled, and his platoon of soldiers jumped to follow his orders.

They all burst from the alley, coughing, and hacking as thick smoke clogged the narrow streets behind them. The entire row of buildings had been set ablaze in that last exchange and Nate was glad to be back in the fresh hair of the main street.

He took a moment to gather himself, seeing fires burning all over the city. Smoke rose in billowing clouds, blotting out the stars. He could hear distant gunfire and see flashes of light as fireballs rose into the sky.

"That way!" Nate yelled, pointing to the series of houses surrounding the larger manor.

People were already beginning to stream from within. They were *very* outnumbered, so instead of rushing in, Shelby began barking orders.

"Give us some cover!" He roared. "Snipers, pick your targets and fire at will!"

"Good luck Captain," Nate said, clapping him on the shoulder, then dashed to one side, into a line of brush and trees, as blasts of blue and orange began flying between the two sides.

He moved quickly, avoiding the groups of Ashlanders who looked panicked and half-asleep, all running to the fight. This was going to be a bloodbath, but as long as Simon ended up dead and their leaders along with him, the Ashland Guild on Warine would be done.

Nate was forced into another confrontation as he approached the back of the manor, a man dressed in elaborate robes emerging along with three others from within the manor.

The man reacted without a second's hesitation, raising a hand, and sending a sheet of fire blasting across the intervening space between them. Nate began to run, leaping into the air and spinning to avoid the line of flames. His body failed him as he landed, his muscles unused to the smooth movements of his past. He landed hard, twisted his ankle, and hit the ground.

"Get him!" The man barked and all three of his followers pounced on Nate.

The first stabbed down with a blazing knife and Nate rolled to his left to avoid it. The knife slammed into the ground, even as Nate drove a dagger into the man's gut. He screamed, but didn't immediately die. His body was pinned and even as Nate struggled to free himself, a blast of scorching fire caught him square in the face.

His head slammed into the ground, ringing and heating up as the blazing flames washed over him. A heavy club streaked down at him as the flames cleared and a Goldshield appeared over him. He was driven partway into the ground by the tremendous force the

450

weapon generated, his vision flashing red and black. The club bounced back, but the man was strong enough to keep it under control.

The man on top of him continued to scream, even as Nate *finally* managed to get him off, grabbing him and rolled hard, pinning the man beneath him.

The club came down again, smashing into the stone road. A wash of flames hit him again, cooking the man beneath him and forcing Nate to swivel his shield around. His ankle throbbed as he got his legs beneath him, but instead of rising, he used his Steelshod, hurling himself forward and tackling the club-wielder around the ankles.

The man went down with a cry of alarm, the club flying from his fingers as the air exploded from his lungs. Fire blasted into Nate again, but he ignored it, allowing it to hit his shield and deflect back.

He scrambled up the man's body, taking powerful kicks to the face and chest. His head was throbbing, but he pushed on, ignoring the pain. A blazing fist flew at him as he reached high enough and instead of trying to move, Nate dropped to his stomach, driving his clenched fist down into the man's neck. A gleaming blade appeared right before impact, piercing through the man's throat and into the road beneath him.

The man's body bucked as he gurgled. Nate twisted the knife, then dismissed it, rolling aside as another torrent of flame washed over him.

Kanta slammed into his core – far more than the other's he'd killed tonight – as he got to his feet. Two were down, one had run and the magician still faced him, throwing lances of flame at him.

"I take it you're one of the commanders," Nate said, keeping his shield in place. "That guy I just killed was one as well, wasn't he."

"Die! Die! Die!" The man screeched, continuing to hurl fire at him.

The trees all around them were ablaze, the bodies of the dead Ashlanders burning. Smoke curled up into the air. People were running around as screams echoed through the city.

Nate ran at the magician, backsword appearing for an instant as he swung. The back backpedaled, a shield of iridescent flame appearing as he did. Nate's first strike was blocked, but his follow-up punch, clad in his Steelshod, shattered the barrier.

The man tried to throw a punch and Nate kicked him between his legs. He howled as he doubled over, presenting Nate with a perfect target.

Nate's broadsword sheared the man's head from his shoulders, leaving it to spin away into the darkness. He'd definitely felt some resistance when he'd struck and when the man fell, his kanta rushing into Nate, he was pushed over the edge to rank 49.

He crouched to examine the man's hands, finding that he'd been at the 39th rank. It was no wonder he'd given Nate so much trouble. His skin beneath his armor was blistered and red, his ankle *throbbed* as did his head, but he'd managed to stay alive without taking any horrible injuries.

He began healing himself, even as he began moving towards the manor, that was, until he saw the blazing figure rising into the sky. The Hellfire Archdemon himself.

It seemed Simon had finally made an appearance. Worse, Nate could see that the man's Inferno Demon technique was active. It was both a shifter technique *and* a longer-range attack at the same time. Much like Nate's own Magma Body, this form's flames were a part of Simon, meaning that he could control and manipulate them at will.

Nate spun on his heel and began running in that direction as quickly as he could. The others would have to manage without him, because if Simon was already on the move, it meant things were about to turn ugly.

His ankle's throbbing lessened as he ran, kanta flowing into him in healing waves. His passive regeneration worked to restore what he'd lost, even as he dashed through an empty street and out into a second courtyard.

Blasts of blue light flashed through the choking smoke that greeted him, screams of agony, shouts of anger and the death throes of those who were lying on the ground, all echoed throughout the area.

A man wearing Ashland robes came running out of the smoke, his body on fire and screaming all the while. Nate slashed his throat open, ending the man's misery, then dove in headfirst. He held his breath as he ran, using his Steelshod to speed his movements.

The smoke made it nearly impossible to see, so when he slammed into the corner of a building, scraping his shoulder, Nate cried out involuntarily.

Two Ashlanders came running out of the smoke, both wielding flaming weapons. One held a sword and the other an ax.

Not having time or space to summon a blade, Nate ducked the sword swipe, then punched the man in the face with his Steelshod. The piston-like effect crushed the man's skull, sending blood and bits of whatever was inside, to paint the man behind him.

The man with the ax turned and ran, screaming for mercy. He didn't make it two steps before a beam of blue caught him in the temple, blasting through his skull. A soldier wearing fatigues came running out of the smoke. He was wearing a cloth over his face and goggles over his eyes.

"What are you doing here!?" The man demanded. "Lieutenant Colonel Williams is under heavy fire."

"Which way!?" Nate asked, trying to stop himself from coughing.

The solider pointed, then spun, dropping to one knee, and raising his rifle. Even as Nate ran, he heard a thud and saw the soldier's body slumped against the side of the building. He couldn't see what had killed the man, due to the smoke, but he silently cursed whoever had done it.

Nate burst from the heavy smoke, eyes streaming and coughing his lungs out. His body had filtered most of it away, but there was only so much it could do against *that* much smoke inhalation.

Now that he was clear of the buildings, he could see Simon much more clearly. The man's hands, formed into claws, were whipping down from above, tearing into buildings and setting everything around him on fire. From below, blasts of blue tore into his body, but they had little effect. Flickers of fire flew as they struck, but his body reformed almost instantly, as though nothing had happened.

Crimson flames made up the man's form, blazing eyes, a crazed smile and curling horns being the only features that were obvious. Those and the clawed hands and feet that continued to tear into the soldiers on the ground.

Nate burst into the open courtyard, feeling his heart stop when he saw both Hazel and Rebecca there. Hazel couldn't reach Simon up in the sky, but Rebecca could and she *was* trying. Not that it was doing her any good.

He'd heard about Rebecca's Tome of Spun Glass, but had never really seen it in action, though by the two spells she continually used, it was obvious that she didn't have anything else at her disposal. The first came in the from of a condensed line of swirling sand particles that seemed to buzz as they flew through the air.

Nate had the feeling that it would likely have the same effects as a sander running at high speeds. A very *painful* burn, followed by stripping flesh. In a concentrated form like that, it could probably punch through something pretty quickly. Not that it seemed to be doing anything to Simon.

Her second spell came in the form of dozens of shards of iridescent glass. They rose in the air around her, almost as though she'd lifted them with her mind, then flew at the man in a hailstorm of death. The blazing heat around Simon's body melted the glass before it could touch him.

Soldiers were all crouched behind barriers, firing up at the man, while he struck back in waves. Flames were spreading all across the buildings to their right and slowly traveling to encircle them on all sides. Several Ashlanders were on the ground as well, engaging with the soldiers. Several on both sides already lay dead, though the Ashland dead outnumbered those of the soldiers nearly three-to-one.

Rebecca was screaming something as Nate charged in.

"You can't hold me anymore you bastard!"

Sand blasted from her hands, finally getting the demon's attention.

"Who needs you anyway?" Simon said, his voice echoing eerily, sounding through the crackling flames.

Then he raised both hands and aimed his inferno at Rebecca. Nate saw everything happen in slow motion. Rebecca still attacking, Simon's flames kindling and blasting downward, Hazel leaping in front of her sister in her shifted form.

She was going to be burned. There was no way she'd be able to stand up to that level of heat. Almost without thinking, Nate

454

tapped his fire fox armor, flashing between the two of them. There was no way to get them both out of the way, so this was the best he could do.

"Nate!?" Hazel exclaimed, eyes going wide, the instant before the inferno slammed into Nate's Goldshield, engulfing them all.

70

Superheated air burned at Nate's lungs as the inferno blasted around them. The Goldshield was tough, but it had its limits. Flames washed around them, deflected by the shield and preventing both Hazel and Rebecca from being engulfed.

"Don't move!" Nate yelled as his feet slid back under the tremendous force of the conflagration.

The air burned, his Gilded Skin heating up in an instant and beginning to burn him. Nate gritted his teeth, then used his Steelshod to dig himself in deeper. His Goldshield began to melt under the extreme heat but he didn't move. The burning grew worse, scorching his skin and sinking deep into his bones. He felt like he was being cooked from the outside in and suddenly knew what a steak must feel like when it hit the grill.

"Nate, you can't keep this up!" Hazel yelled.

His entire body was glowing cherry red, steam and heat rising off him, but he refused to dismiss his Gilded Skin, as it was the only thing keeping him standing.

The Goldshield pushed back some of the fire, but it couldn't last forever. Nate reinforced it with more kanta, pouring it into the shield to keep its structural integrity.

"You need to move!" Hazel screamed, sounding almost beside herself. "You can't die protecting us!"

"That's what friends do," Nate yelled, keeping his shield in place. "We protect one another. No one dies today. Do you hear me? No one!"

With a roar, Nate summoned a second Goldshield, despite the massive cost, then swiveled it front of the first and angled it upward. Flames blasted into the sky, then abruptly cut off. He dropped to his knees, dismissing his Gilded Skin, and feeling the agony abate somewhat. He began healing himself immediately as he looked up, seeing the blazing figure in the sky.

"Nate!" Hazel yelled, reaching out but not daring to touch him.

"Are you okay?" Rebecca asked, sounding horrified and shocked.

She hadn't said anything while Nate was tanking that hit, which was good, Hazel had been distracting enough. But now that the blaze had halted, she'd snapped out of it.

"You dare stand in my way?" Simon asked, ignoring the fire coming at him. "No one stands in my way. You will all burn!"

"Get back!" Nate snapped, leaping to his feet, and triggering his Magma Body.

He wouldn't have been able to use it in defense of those two without cooking them alive, but now that the flames had stopped, he was free to use it as he saw fit.

"I can still-" Rebecca cut off as Hazel grabbed her around the waist, lifted her off the ground and ran.

Even as she did, a loud howl echoed, flooding Nate's body with strength. Her Sky Cry.

The road beneath Nate began to bubble, even as the pain of his burns receded. He knew this was only temporary, but if he didn't feel the heat, it could only help.

"What in the *world*?" Simon exclaimed before a blazing fist of molten stone crashed into his chest.

Unlike with all the other attacks so far, Nate's struck home, smashing into the flying demon and knocking him from the sky.

"Give us some room!" Nate shouted.

"You heard the man," Lieutenant Colonel Williams yelled. "Move! Move! Get out of the line of fire!"

Soldiers moved back into the *not* burning block of houses and buildings, as Simon slowly got to his feet, flames melting the stone around him as well.

"Interesting," Simon said, rising. "You can hit me."

A second blow crashed into the side of his head, rocking the man in place. Nate drove himself forward, moving slowly, even as he whipped his arms around smashing into the man from all sides.

Simon roared in pain as Nate's fist crashed into him again, sending a spray of blood into the air. His form flickered for a moment, switching between human and demon, before turning back. Simon returned fire, hands punching out and smashing into him as well.

The man's flames burned hot enough to damage Nate and he knew it. The Goldshield appeared again as Nate switched to his Kanta Orb, his own having just run dry. Flames poured around him, as Nate angled the shield up. His arm whipped out in a sweep, catching the man across the hip, and sending him careening into one of the nearby houses. He crashed through it with a roar, beams and debris collapsing on top of him.

Nate dismissed the shield, waiting. The house exploded as the demon came flying out, blazing fires melting the road behind him. He was closing to melee, seeing as he couldn't land a clean hit at range. That was good. Nate was stronger at melee as well.

"Die!" Simon screamed, throwing a punch at Nate's face.

Nate threw an arm up to block, then blasted a fist into his stomach. Simon doubled over, blood spraying from his mouth, then slashed at Nate with claws. They raked across his stomach, burning pain radiating from the points of impact.

In retaliation, Nate slapped a hand to the side of the man's face, then began covering it with molten stone.

"Aaagghhh!" Simon roared, blazing hotter as he raised the temperature once more.

A wave of flames radiated outward, blasting Nate back. His hands flew in the opposite direction though, smashing into the man's chest. Nate hit the ground in a puddle, then reformed, coughing, and sputtering at the damage to his body.

That wave of heat had seared him to the *bone*.

Taking damage in this form was different than damage to a flesh and blood body. Any pain affected him on a sort-of spiritual level. Meaning that because he was made up of kanta at the moment, every strike was felt far more *deeply*.

His kanta was burning out fast, but Simon's shouldn't be able to last much longer with how much he was burning through. Nate's Kanta Sight showed Simon to be at rank 47, just a few lower than his own 49. It meant he'd likely been training in Laybor, as he'd suspected.

Simon moved in once again, his flames blazing hot enough to leave a molten trail of slag in his wake. Nate braced himself as they clashed again. Four more times the two of them collided, inflicting burning damage to the other. However, when Simon moved back for the fifth attack, he faltered.

The man dropped to the ground, flames flickering around his body as he panted. The man was nearly out of kanta, just as Nate had suspected.

That didn't seem to stop him. With a roar, he leaped back to his feet, blazing even hotter as he charged Nate. Punches flew, claws raking across his chest and face, as Nate returned fire, his own molten fists causing massive burns along the man's face, chest, and torso.

Nate was heaving for air by now, his Kanta Orb over halfway empty and Simon showing no signs of stopping. The man was taking plenty of hits, and when Nate caught him with a stunning right across the jaw followed by a powerful blow to the stomach, the man was blasted away.

Simon hit the ground in a heap, chest heaving. Slowly, he clawed his way to his feet, flames flickering around his body as he did. Teeth were bared as the man tried to push through, but the flames continued to die down, signaling that this technique was at its end.

"Fine," Simon shouted, blood and spittle flying from his burning lips. "We'll deal with this another way!"

The flames vanished, leaving the man standing, unprotected. He was still breathing hard, blood coating his lips and chest. Sweat plastered his hair to his forehead but despite all of that, his eyes still burned with that same manic light.

Blazing claws appeared over his hands as the man laughed, extending them out wide in an invitation.

"Come at me as a real man, if you da-!"

The man didn't even get to finish his sentence as dozens of blue bolts tore from the nearby alleyway, ripping his body to bloody shreds. The man's body rocked in the air, his arms, head, and torso jerking as the soldiers opened fire.

It continued for several seconds, then stopped at a cried command from Williams. Simon Dalefield hung in the air for a few moments longer, then toppled to the ground, dead.

A rush of kanta flowed into Nate, even as he dismissed his Magma Body. He gasped as he dropped to his hands and knees, his entire body trembling with the agony he currently felt.

"Confirm the kill!" he heard someone shout.

His vision fuzzed for a moment, blood leaking from his lips and dribbling to the ground below. Kanta was rushing into him as he used his technique, trying to recover from the horrendous damage to his body and core. That had been a very near thing.

"Confirmed! The target is dead".

A ragged cheer rang up from his surroundings, and Nate felt a strong hand on his shoulder.

"Are you okay?" Hazel's worried voice asked, sounding from behind.

"I will be," Nate rasped, even as he felt another small amount of kanta flood into him, pushing him to the 50th rank.

He forced himself to look up, and through bleary eyes, he could see the soldiers routing the remaining Ashlanders within the area. They were running now, having seen their leader put down like a dog. Simon had expected to fight Nate on his own and had completely forgotten about the armed soldiers surrounding him.

The instant he'd been vulnerable, he was a dead man. Rank 46 or not, a weakened body and core meant that he hadn't been able to resist at all.

"Come on," Hazel said. "We need to get you out of here."

"That sounds nice," Nate said, feeling himself being hauled to his feet.

He was leaning heavily on the short woman, kanta still working to soothe his wounds. He might be able to heal himself quickly, but with such extensive injuries, it wasn't going to be a two-minute thing. Injuries of this level would probably take him between eight and ten minutes, in which time, he'd be vulnerable.

Another set of hands, these a bit more delicate, grabbed his other arm, dragging it over a taller shoulder, so he was half hunched onto Hazel.

"We'll get you out of here," Rebecca said. "Don't you worry about a thing."

"That sounds nice," Nate muttered, then slumped forward, his mind going blank as his body began the process of repairing the massive damage that had been done to him.

One thing ran through Nate's mind as he was dragged from the burning city. Against all odds, they had accomplished their mission. The psychopathic serial killer was dead. Ashland – at least on Warine – was no more.

They had won.

Epilogue

Wilbur Chesterson let out a shaky breath, his hand trembling and covered in blood. He was on his knees, next to a prone Hana, the girl's chest rising and falling rapidly. Blood covered her stomach, where the 1-Star dog-like monster they'd just killed had mauled her.

The side of his head was caked in blood and his leg refused to support his weight. Not that it really mattered right now. Hana was running out of time.

He pursed his lips, looking up to the sky, the twin suns blazing their heat down upon him.

Why had they come here?

They should have ignored the map. They *should* have remained in Warine, where things were safer.

"How's she doing?"

Wil looked up, seeing Jess coming over, carrying a small bucket of steaming water.

"I'm fine," Hana coughed, her voice sounding ragged.

"She's still alive," Wil said, squeezing her hand. "We all are. That's what matters."

Jess dropped to her knees next to the shorter woman, pulling a soaking rag from within. Her long brown hair was matted to her face by blood and gore, her bare arms streaked up to the elbow. Of them all, Jess had suffered the least amount of damage, which was why she'd been tasked to run for water.

Dan had taken some heavy hits, but he was the most resilient of them all. He'd taken off in the direction of the nearest Village, nearly an hour away. It was their only hope of saving Hana's life right now.

"Here, let me help you with that," Wil said, taking one of the rags and wrapping it around Hana's mangled left leg.

She was losing too much blood. They'd wrapped a tourniquet around the limb, but it was still bleeding, as none of them had known how to do it properly.

Hana groaned as he did so, biting her lip and trying to concentrate on her breathing.

"There we go," Jess said, binding her stomach tight. "Nice and warm."

Blood soaked through the rags immediately, staining the tan-colored cloth crimson.

"I...don't know if I'm going to make it," Hana gasped as Wil dabbed at her forehead.

"Don't even *think* like that," Wil said, his voice cracking. "We're *all* going to live; do you hear me!?"

"Dan will be back any minute now," Jess said soothingly, though she shot him a worried look.

The truth was, neither of them were sure. There were no healers in their party, though if Hana survived this, Wil knew he'd be springing for one, despite the cost.

"I still can't believe we killed that thing," Hana said with a bloody smile. "At least the bastard died before I will."

The massive body of the creature was a bloody mess of broken bones and pulped flesh. One of its legs had been torn off and half its face was missing, but it had been a *rough* fight and one that none of them had seen coming.

They'd been exploring a series of caverns on the outskirts of Village 16A, having been told about a potential treasure there by one of the locals. They'd found what they'd come looking for, as well as the monster, which had ambushed them, leaving no path of escape.

"C-can I have a jacket?" Hana asked, her teeth beginning to chatter. "I feel so c-cold."

Her lips were beginning to turn blue, despite the blazing heat of the day. Wil could feel his panic and desperation rising as the woman's eyes began to flicker.

"Come on Hana, you need to stay awake," Wil said, squeezing her hand.

"So...tired," Hana said, her voice slurring.

Jess slapped her across the face, the sound sharp in the stillness of the day. Hana's eyes flashed open momentarily and she looked confused, then they began to droop again.

Her breathing began to slow, even as Wil and Jess continued to urge her to stay awake and *alive*.

Despite all their efforts though, Hana's eyes began to close, her breathing growing shallower and the blood seeping from her body more slowly.

"No, no, no, no, *no!*" Wil yelled, grabbing her by her shoulders and shaking her hard. "Come on Hana! Wake up! You can't quit on us now!"

"Wil," Jess said, placing a hand over his own.

Her voice was soft and her eyes watered.

"She's gone."

"No! She can't be gone! She can't-!"

Wil cut off as Dan came sprinting around the small overhand. His legs were streaked red, his chest heaving and he looked about ready to pass out.

"Made...it," he gasped.

"It's too late," Jess said, tears beginning to well in the corners of her eyes. "She's...she's *gone!*"

Dan dropped to his knees next to her, still heaving.

"She's not dead!" Wil insisted. "She can still be saved!"

"Wil, she has no pulse!" Jess snapped. "She's *gone!*"

"Help me with her," Dan heaved.

Wil grabbed Hana's head, pulling her lips apart and tilting her chin back. Dan pulled a bottle of shining, red liquid from his ring, dragging the cork out with his teeth, then placed the mouth of the flask to Hana's mouth.

"You're wasting it!" Jess yelled. "Stop!"

The liquid poured down Hana's throat, pooling in her mouth as it left the bottle. Wil watched with bated breath. Hana had only been gone for a few seconds, so maybe...

He let out a shaky laugh as the wounds all across her body began to rapidly close, blood retreating back into her skin. Her complexion changed in a matter of seconds, giving off a healthy glow. Her fingers twitched, her back arching off the ground and her eyes flashing open.

She dropped back, then twitched again, back arching once more. When she dropped this time, her chest began to rise and fall. Again, her body went rigid and then, Hana let out a loud gasp. When she landed, her body lay still, her eyes flicking all around, confusion clearly written on her face as she took in her surroundings.

"I...I died," she said, sounding like she didn't believe her own words.

"Thank the heavens for this Healing Draft," Dan said.

He was crying, laughing, and still gasping for breath at the same time.

"How?" Jess asked, though she too was grinning from ear to ear. "I've never seen a Healing Draft that could do *that*!"

"It was the third-most expensive one they had," Dan replied, even as Wil wrapped Hana in a tight hug, his entire body shaking.

"Only the *third*-most?" Jess asked.

"It was the most expensive one I could afford," Dan said. "It all but cleaned me out."

Now *that* sobered everyone up. Dan had had just over 100,000 points, which meant the Draft had been *expensive* indeed.

"The gnark said that short of losing her head, this would be able to restore Hana back to full health, even if she'd been dead for as long as thirty minutes."

"*Seriously*!?" Hana exclaimed. "They have Healing Drafts *that* powerful!?"

"Well, he *did* ask me about your rank before I bought it," Dan said. "I told him you were at forty-two when I left. Apparently, the higher your rank, the more time you have."

"Do we know the maximum?" Wil asked.

"Afraid not," Dan replied. "I was in too much of a hurry."

"Well, thank you," Hana said, giving Dan a beaming smile. "You saved my life. *Literally*."

"Hey," Dan said, giving her an easy smile. "I'm just returning the favor. If not for you, we'd *all* be dead right now."

That much was true, and they all knew it. Hana had dealt some *serious* damage to the monster. Not only that, but the hit she'd taken had given them the chance to finish it off, and, had she *not* taken that hit, *Wil* would have taken it instead. Without Hana's tough skin, the monster would have torn through him like wet paper.

It was why he decided to share something with the group. Something he'd been keeping to himself for fear of what it might mean.

"There's something I need to tell you all," Wil said fidgeting.

Sensing the seriousness in his voice, they all quieted, giving him their full attention.

"It's something that's been bugging me for a while. Something that I didn't want to talk about. But, seeing as Hana very nearly *died* and Dan basically lost all his points, I don't think I can keep this to myself anymore."

"What is it?" Hana asked, reaching out to take his hand.

Her fingers were warm and strong. They gave him the comfort and reassurance he needed to forge on ahead.

"This map we got," Wil said, pulling the folded-up piece of parchment from his ring. "I'm pretty sure I know who made it."

Now *that* got everyone's attention.

"I didn't want to believe it at first, because how would it even be possible for him to *know* so much. But, the longer I studied it, the more I couldn't deny what I was seeing."

Wil looked up, meeting the collective gazes of their small group.

"My brother, Nate, drew this map. I'm *sure* of it."

Silence greeted his declaration, that was, until Dan spoke up.

"You said he knew about what was going to happen before it did, right? That he called to warn you?"

"It's why we're all here," Wil said.

"Now there's a mystery I'd love to solve," Jess muttered, looking between Wil and the map.

"You're...not mad?" Wil asked, surprised by his friends' reactions.

"Why should we be mad?" Hana asked. "You're not your brother. And besides, that map *helped* us. It's our own faults for walking into this death trap unprepared."

"You guys are being *way* too nice about this," Wil said, though he was grinning.

"Tell you what," Dan said. "You treat us all to dinner and we'll call it even."

"You've got yourself a deal!" Wil replied.

There were still their own injuries to deal with, but with Hana's help, Wil was able to hobble along okay. Their team left the cave system just a few minutes later, carrying the pieces of the monster in their rings.

They all seemed to be in a good mood, and why shouldn't they be. Hana had been bought back from the dead and they were all going to live to see another day.

Despite that, Wil couldn't help thinking of his brother. Every time he thought he'd figured something out, the mystery deepened.

Wherever you are Nate, I hope you're alive, Wil thought as he hobbled along with his friends. *Because you have a lot to answer for.*

***

Nate sat on the outskirts of the burning city, watching as the last remaining dregs of Ashland fled into the night, pursued by blasts of blue light. He'd fully recovered from his battle with Simon and was working on restoring his kanta. That battle had been costly, but in the end, they'd succeeded in their mission.

Hazel sat next to him, she and Rebecca talking in lowered voices. Both of them had benefitted from the battle against Simon, though Rebecca had taken a *much* larger jump in rank than Hazel's 1-rank increase to 47. Rebecca had jumped from 29 all the way to 37, a massive 8-rank increase from that *one* battle.

"You're all still alive!"

Nate looked up, seeing Freya and Noam running over to them. Both of their faces were streaked with soot and blood, their clothes burned in places, but both looked mostly uninjured. There were some cuts and bruises, but everyone seemed to have made it out okay.

"Glad to see the two of you are alright," Nate said, giving them a tired smile.

Freya dropped to her knees and wrapped him in a tight hug, whispering into his ear so that no-one else could hear.

"I was really worried about you. I'm glad you're safe Nate."

Her lips brushed the side of his face as she pulled away, the motion natural. To the outside world, it wouldn't look like anything out of the ordinary, but to Nate, the meaning was clear. He gave her a warm smile, just before Noam moved in.

"That was one hell of a battle," the man said, clapping him on the shoulder. "We definitely took some casualties, but as far as I can tell, most of Dirk's men made it out alive."

"I guess we'll find out more once they finish with whatever they're doing," Nate said.

The entire city was burning by now and Nate knew that come morning, all that would be left, was city of ashes, filled with the dead.

"I jumped two ranks in that battle," Noam said. "Freya did better than me though, she jumped three."

"Did you now?" Nate asked, surprised.

"Yup," Freya said, grinning from ear to ear. "I tangled with a few of their bosses on my own. They never saw me coming. So, how many did you get?"

Nate debated lying, but in the end, told her the truth.

"The Queen is back baby!" Freya cheered, pumping her arms in the air.

At rank 51, she was once again the highest in the group.

"The queen?" Rebecca asked, sounding very confused.

"It's a long story," Freya said. "Anyway, I don't think any of us got properly introduced. I'm Freya," she said, sticking her hand out.

Rebecca took it hesitantly and shook it.

"Noam," Noam said, though he remained where he was.

"And you already know Nate," Freya said, clapping him on the back. "Welcome to our merry little group of misfits. We aren't much, but as the queen, I can promise we'll be great someday!"

Rebecca looked at Hazel in confusion.

"I told you they'd be happy to have you along," Hazel said with a warm smile.

"But...None of you know me and I'm so much weaker than all of you."

"We know Hazel," Nate said. "And if you're her sister, you're welcome with us too. Ranking doesn't matter either. Hazel was just over rank thirty when she joined us. We caught her up quickly enough. We can do the same for you."

"I...I don't know what to say," Rebecca said, beginning to tear up.

It had been a *long* night for her. She was likely wrung out and needed to sleep.

"You can thank us later," Freya said, still grinning. "For now, you can leave the chattering to us."

She pointed to where a group of soldiers were approaching, headed up by Dirk. The man looked like the grizzled veteran he was, his fatigues littered with burns, his face bloody and scarred and his eyes blazing.

Sighing, Nate dragged himself to his feet, knowing it would be rude to face the Colonel on his behind, no matter how tired he was.

"Colonel," Nate said, inclining his head.

"Do you know how many soldiers I lost today?" Dirk asked. He didn't sound angry, which was good.

"No," Nate said.

"Twelve," Dirk said. "I lost twelve of my men in total. Twenty-nine more were badly injured but will live. Not a single one of us escaped some form of injury, light or otherwise."

The man went silent, and Nate looked to the soldiers behind him. Near the city, he could see Williams and Shelby working on transportation for the wounded, as well as taking care of the bodies of the dead.

"I want to thank you," Dirk said.

Nate swiveled his eyes back to the man. He looked sincere.

"I'd have thought you'd want to punch me in the face," Nate said.

"Losing men is tough," Dirk said. "As their commanding officer, those lives are *mine* to bear and mine alone. What you did in there though, saved the lives of Lieutenant Commander Williams's entire platoon. We went in on a mission against overwhelming odds and *won*. Ashland wasn't wiped out to a man, but they *were* defeated, and their leaders killed. You have my respect, Mister Chesterson."

The man stuck his hand out and Nate shook it.

"I hope to meet you back in Southside Eight sometime," Dirk said, already turning.

He paused for a moment, then turned back, reaching into one of the many pockets on his shirt.

"I've already looked this over, but I think you might find it of interest. Best of luck to you."

The man turned then, his soldiers following him back towards the burning city.

"What have you got there?" Freya asked, as Nate unfolded the piece of parchment, reading it quickly.

I don't recognize the man you've described, nor have I seen him at any point in my visions. All I know is that he does not belong

468

here. He is out of place. Perhaps he is like me, a seer, and knows of things beyond the eyes of normal men. Regardless, he is to be killed on sight. He is very dangerous.

Watch out for Blood Swarm. They are dangerous and will be gaining steam soon. Send more members as soon as you can. We have already secured a city and are working on a second. Rose Sombre has been dealt with, though I don't know by whom.

*Keep in touch and **do not** burn another city to the ground while I am away.*

~Selena

Nate lowered the parchment, feeling it snatch from his hand by Freya, who immediately began reading it aloud for the others. Nate's mind, however, was somewhere else, spinning wildly as he put all the pieces together.

Selena knew too much about the events that were coming, and no one had known the name of Rose Sombre but him, at least not yet. This led him to one conclusion, one that sent chills creeping down his spine.

Selena Maylard was from the future as well, though from what *time* he did not know.

"We need to find her," Nate heard himself saying, even as he stared out at the burning city. "We need to find and kill her before she can do anything else…"

"Don't worry," Freya said, patting him on the shoulder. "We'll get her soon enough."

But Nate wasn't listening, his mind still churning with the knowledge that there was another person here from his previous timeline. Or was that even the case? If he'd come back, could Selena have come from a *different* time? And, if there were two of them, were there *more*?

Things had just gotten a *lot more* dangerous and complicated. If there were others like Selena, then he needed to be *extremely* careful. He didn't know their motivations, or reasons for doing what they might.

They were going to have to be *a lot* more careful from now on. Nate more than anyone. If there were others here from the future, they'd likely figure out what he had: that whichever one of them survived the longest, would decide the course of this timeline's future.

For the sake of everyone he cared about, Nate *knew* that it *had* to be him. No matter the cost. No matter the sacrifice. No matter *how many of them* he would have to kill.

***

Water trickled back into the steaming pond as the woman washed her face, feeling the sting of the scratches she'd received during her battle. She looked up sharply, as a shadow fell across her, reaching for the weapon she had stashed within her shirt.

"There's no need for that," a voice said.

It was male, the accent sounding to be of Irish origin, though the man's tone was off somehow.

The woman rose to her full height, stepping out of the line of the sun and bringing the two figures standing on the opposite side of the pool into focus.

One of them was indeed a man, one with wild hair and a look of utter insanity in deep, sunken eyes. His frame was emaciated, the tips of his fingers curling inward into hooked claws. His mouth was stretched into an impossibly-wide grin as he took a step forward, his bare foot splashing into the water without him seeming to notice.

The other was a woman, one who looked to be built like freaking *tank*. She was massive, athletic to the point of absolute insanity. Her bare arms were muscled in the way of competitive bodybuilders and yet somehow, it seemed to suit her just fine, despite the fact that she looked like she could snap a horse's neck with her bare hands.

Her face was smooth and unmarred, though her eyes were mismatched. One appeared normal, while the other was a bright, vivid blue, so deep and mesmerizing that it seemed to want to draw her in.

"Are you sure she's the one we're looking for?" The woman asked, crossing her arms over her chest.

She had a Russian accent, her voice demanding of the smaller man.

"Oh yes. Yes, yes, yes, yes, yes," the man said, stepping into the pool and approaching her.

"Stay back!" The woman warned, pulling her weapon from her shirt, and brandishing it before her.

The Russian woman laughed, though the man stopped where he was, his deep-set eyes flicking between her and the weapon.

"That's quite the Tome you've got there," he said. "So, mind telling me how you did it?"

"Did *what*!?" She demanded, remaining on the defensive.

If it came to a fight, she was confident she could deal with the skinny man, though that monster of a woman on the other hand, not so much.

"Escaped the clutches of death," the man said. "Obviously."

"I don't know what you're talking about," she said, feeling a small worm of fear working its way into her gut.

"Oh come, come, there's no need to lie to us," the man said, still grinning. "We're all friends here, aren't we Anastasia?"

"We are not friends," Anastasia said. "We have a mutual enemy. That is it."

"Ah, but what are friends if not those who all share in a mutual goal?" The man said.

"Your twisted logic will not work on me, crazy man," Anastasia said. "Now, tell me lady, why are you hiding behind that mask?"

The woman felt her heart rate quicken. How had she seen through her disguise?

"She needs to keep up appearances, I'm sure," the man said, turning back to her. "But, how rude of me not to introduce myself. My name is Sean and I'm forming a little Guild."

"Guild?" The woman asked, unsure of where this was going.

"Yes, Guild," the man said, beginning to pace in the water. "You see, my beloved daughter *Freya*, took someone very special from me. I want to kill her, but she has powerful friends and I'm afraid we can't do it ourselves. So, a Guild is the only natural way to go about it."

The woman shivered at the intensity with which the man seemed to speak. He seemed perfectly calm, until he spoke the name of his daughter, at which point his voice had deepened to a gravelly tone, before returning to normal. He was clearly insane. It would be best if she ran and hoped they couldn't catch up with her.

"Now, I know what you're thinking," Sean said, stopping in the water. "But, I know that my daughter is traveling with someone who killed someone very dear to you as well. A man by the name of Nate, I believe."

The woman froze, a deep-seated rage igniting within her chest when she heard that name.

"Ah, there it is," Sean said, his smile growing even wider. "So, have I piqued your interest?"

The woman nodded, slowly lowering her weapon as she looked at these two in a new light. The man might be crazy, but he seemed to be functioning alright, and as she'd already noted, the woman looked to be able to snap trees in half by bumping into them. Perhaps they *were* the ones who could help her get what she wanted.

"So then, how about an introduction?" Sean asked. "I would love to see what you *really* look like under that getup. I don't have an eye that can pierce illusions like Anastasia over there."

The woman hesitated for a moment longer, then allowed her disguise to drop.

"Ah," Sean said, his eyes widening. "Now I see. How *very* sneaky of you. So, introductions?"

"My name," the woman said. "Is Colette Bellecourt."

"And the mask?"

"My sister, Genevieve," Colette said, feeling anger boiling up in her chest once again. "She died in my place. A spell I had placed on her, to swap our positions and appearances, if one of our lives were in danger."

"Except, *you* were never supposed to be the one in danger, now were you," Sean said, his eyes going wider.

"No," Colette said, clenching her teeth. "If it wasn't for those accursed *women* and that *Nate*, Genevieve would still be alive!"

"How did you manage the deception?" Anastasia asked. "Your ranking must have been much higher. Surely, they would have noticed?"

Colette raised her left hand, showing a dark 31 where the 47 had once been.

"There's a cost to the spell," Colette said. "Ironic, isn't it? That my extra ranks were transferred to Genevieve, only for them to benefit those *filthy dogs* instead!"

"A complete deception then," Sean said, seeming delighted. "But what about that Pen of yours. Surely, they'd have noticed?"

"I have *both*," Colette said. "No one buys a second Manual or Tome because they're useless. I did, so that I could have a decoy, just in case."

She reached into her shirt and removed an amulet, one with a blood-red stone set at its center.

"No one thinks to check for something they've already found."

"Clever girl," Sean said, practically hopping up and down in place. "Fooled them with the decoy ring and pen, while you slipped away. Clever, clever, *clever*!"

"How did you get the ring on your sister's finger though?" Anastasia asked, clearly trying to find any loopholes in her story.

"That's just the irony, isn't it," Colette said with a dark laugh. "I had just charmed her and had her hang on to the spare for me in case we needed to switch places. I had the feeling that something was off, so I left it with her, so that *someone* might make use of the extra Tome. Someone who was unaffiliated with another path…"

She'd had someone in mind. Someone in Genevieve's group, but it had all fallen apart when that *girl*, Freya – which she now realized these two were after – had ruined *everything*.

"Ah, I see," Sean said. "Yes, yes, I think you will serve us quite well."

"I *serve* no one," Colette said, standing up straight.

"Yes, yes, just a figure of speech," Sean said, waving her off. "So, what do you say? Care to join our little crusade?"

Colette hesitated for a moment longer, looking between the pair. There was no way she could do this all on her own, which meant a team was her best chance of revenge. She'd need to charm some more people, but that would take time. The others had been much easier, as they'd known her. She would have to do it this time, with complete strangers.

"Fine," Colette said. "I'll join your little group. Just what *are* you calling yourselves anyway?"

Anastasia rolled her eyes at that, though Sean seemed delighted by the question.

"Oh, it's a lovely name. One that suits our little band of revenge killers quite well. We are, Death to *Freya*!" The man roared.

Colette looked to Anastasia, who shook her head.

"That is not the name we agreed upon," the woman said. "I like the name we chose yesterday. It's much better."

"Fine, fine," Sean said, waving his hand. "That works too."

Colette looked to Anastasia with a raised eyebrow. The woman, let out another sigh, then turned and began walking away, Sean hopping out of the water and following. Not really sure what else to do, Colette followed after, though she maintained a healthy distance from them both. One could never be too careful.

As they walked, she could hear Seam muttering to himself, his voice carrying back to her on the light breeze.

"Yes," the man said, twiddling his fingers in a most-disturbing manner. "The name Blood Swarm will suit our Guild quite well indeed."

Afterword

What's up, Super-People? I hope you enjoyed End of the World, Book 2! Thanks to you, my amazing fans, this book was over 150K words due to your ratings and reviews on book 1!

So, let's keep it going! If you want book 3 to be just as long, make sure to leave a review or rating. If we get over 1,000, I'll make sure to make it just as long! If we can get it over 1,500, I'll bump the total count up to 175K!

There's so much story still to tell, so I'm looking forward to writing book 3.

I hope you all have a super day, and I'll see you back for the next one!

If you love GameLit or LitRPG as much as I do, you should check out these amazing pages. You can keep up with your favorite genre of books, all while being part of an awesome community.

GameLitSociety
Spoiled Rotten Readers
LitRPG Books

You can check out my website for all news on current and upcoming releases, blog posts, artwork on characters, and other exclusive content. You can also contact me directly through the site if you have any questions.

We're also taking **submissions** for **new manuscripts**, so, if you're an aspiring author and would like to be one of the first to be published by my very own publishing company, click the link, and contact me through my website!

Or send an email to: Aaron@aaronosterauthor.com

AaronOsterAuthor.com

Follow me on Amazon to be notified of all releases as they come out.

Author Page

You can support me on Patreon if you want some exclusive previews, benefits, and access to a full beta read of the books before they release. You can also follow me on my various social media accounts, as that is where I do giveaways and the like.

Patreon: Rise to Omniscience
Instagram: Aaron Oster
Facebook: Aaron Ostreicher
Facebook Fan Group: Aaron Oster's Supermage Army

A special thanks go out to my beta readers: DJ & Optimistpryme

Coming Next

We Hunt Monsters 6 (August 2023)

Series by Aaron Oster

Complete

The Rules
Somerset: Book One
Pendrackon: Book Two
Grempire: Book Three

Buryoku

Power: Book 1
Light: Book 2
Water: Book 3
Wind: Book 4
Fire: Book 5

Earth: Book 6
Darkness: Book 7
Weakness: Book 8
Spirit: Book 9
beast: Book 10
Ghost: Book 11
Archfiend: Book 12

You can also pick up the series as a box set on Kindle or Audio!

Ongoing

We Hunt Monsters

Book 1
Book 2
Book 3
Book 4
Book 5
Book 6 (August 2023)

End of the World

Book 1
Book 2
Book 3 TBA

Rise to Omniscience

Arc One
Supermage: Book One
Starbreak: Book Two
Skyflare: Book Three
Solarspire: Book Four
Stormforge: Book Five

Arc Two
Silverspear: Book Six

Sandqueen: Book Seven
Sunscorch: Book Eight
Serpentlord: Book Nine
Soulstream: Book Ten

Arc Three
Book Eleven coming final quarter of 2023.

You can also pick up books 1-5 and 6-10 as a box set.
Audio box sets are now available as well.

Land of the Elementals

Rampage: Book One
Emerald: Book Two
Origin: Book Three
Reign: Book Four
Book 5 (Series Finale) TBA

Shattered Kingdoms

Age of Ancients: Book One
Time of Titans: Book Two
Book 3 (Series Finale) TBA

All dates are only an estimate and are subject to change. Please
check my social media for any and all updates.

Made in the USA
Middletown, DE
27 September 2023

39489562R00265